HOW 'TWAS

SHORT STORIES
AND SMALL TRAVELS

BY

STEPHEN REYNOLDS

' *That's how 'tis, I tell thee, an' thee casn't make it no 'tis-er !* '
DEVON SAYING.

MACMILLAN AND CO., LIMITED
ST. MARTIN'S STREET. LONDON
1912

COPYRIGHT

TO

JOSEPH AND JESSIE CONRAD

NOTE

THE Author acknowledges with thanks the hospitality of the following periodicals, some of which, however, are now extinct :—*Albany Review*, *Blackwood's Magazine*, *Daily News*, *English Review*, *Fortnightly Review*, *New Age*, *Open Window*, *Pall Mall Gazette*, *Pall Mall Magazine*, *Speaker*, *Throne and Country*, *T.P.'s Magazine*, *T.P.'s Christmas Weekly*, *Tribune*, *Weekly Critical Review*, *Week's Survey*, *Westminster Gazette*.

CONTENTS

I.—PEOPLE

II.—KIDS AND CATS

III.—SMALL TRAVELS

I

PEOPLE

BENJIE AND THE BOGEY MAN

I

THE change of weather foretold by Benjamin Prowse came, just as he had predicted, during the night with the turn of tide. First a little billow rolled in from the sou'south-east ; then the wind dropped out to that quarter. The sea began to make. A misty cloud hid the setting moon, filled the sky, and cloaked the tops of the cliffs in vapour.

At peep of day Benjie's nephew crept round the foot of West Cliff towards Western Bay. So long as his feet scrunched companionably on the narrow strip of shingle between the cliff and Broken Rocks he continued talking to himself. "'Tis full o'it," he complained, glancing at the cloud and mist. "Benjie won't never stay down along there—just when he'd better to for once. Who'd ha' thought thic fellow'd ha' turned up here this time o' day? Never see'd the like o'it ! "

Arrived at the bay, Bill Prowse sat down and waited silently, peering along to the westward, and at intervals looking above his head to make sure that the soft red cliff was not falling out upon him.

It was one of those very grey dawns, when there seems to be plenty of light long before any distant object can be made out distinctly. The white calm of the evening before, when Benjie had put to sea, was replaced by several broken lines of surf flowing in across the flat sand, fading westward into the loom of Steep Head, and filling the whole bay with a re-echoed plaintive rattle. Gulls, looking nearly twice their size, stalked about in the shallow water after sand-eels.

By and by a boat became visible suddenly, just outside the broken water. Prawn-nets were piled up high on the stern. One man was sheaving—standing up with bent back and rowing forwards—whilst the other man pulled in the ordinary manner, seated face astern.

"That's ol' Benjie, right enough," observed Bill Prowse.

He got up, walked to the water's edge, and, putting his hands funnel-wise to his mouth, shouted as if he did not want to be overheard. "Bogey man! Bogey man to beach! 'Spector! Bide here a bit."

The rowing ceased. A word like "What?" came from the boat.

"Bogey man! Fishery 'Spector!"

The next words from the boat sounded like, "Be the capstan fixed?"

"Bogey man!" answered Bill.

But voices failed to carry across the noise of

the surf, and the boat could approach no nearer. Benjie had to turn it quickly in order to meet a broken wave bows on. He began rowing again with short, irritable strokes, and finally steered the boat outwards to clear Broken Rocks.

Bill Prowse's shouting died away helplessly : "Bogey man ! Bogey-ey-ey. . . ."

And still the boat held on its course for Salterport beach.

Bill followed hurriedly alongshore. "This here's what comes," he grumbled, "of Benjie blowing his hooter to the likes o' Vivian Maddicke. 'Don't care,' he says, 'for no inspector what ever lived.' But 'tis best never to say nort to gentry —always was an' always will be."

II

Two or three fishermen, and one other man slightly apart, stood waiting at the foot of the beach. Benjie ran the boat ashore, high on the crest of a wave ; then jumped into the wash and lifted out half-a-dozen prawn-nets with their lines and cork buoys. "That'll lighten her," he said. "Now haul ! "

His round sailor's cap was perched on one side of his head ; his torn jumper was askew ; sea-water ran in streams from his patched greenish-blue trousers, which also were askew ; and his wrinkled face, within its fringe of grey beard, was noticeably haggard after the night's toil. With his arms spread wide over the hoops of the nets and his head bent down by their weight, he almost

bumped into the stranger.   Whereupon he pulled
up short.   Screwing himself still farther sideways,
he quizzed the man ; mocked him silently with
deeply crowsfooted blue eyes, at once both childlike and shrewd.

"Who be *you* then ?" he inquired, placing
his prawn-nets very deliberately on the shingle.
"Who be you ? 'Tisn't often the likes o' you
starch-collar sort o' people comes down for to
help lend a hand."

The fishermen drew nearer.

"N'eet any o' our own sort nuther," flashed
Benjie, "so early as this in the day."

The stranger, a man in a peak-cap and a
dark blue overcoat of indifferent fit, cleared his
throat.

"'Tis the bogey man, Benjie—the 'Spector ! "
put in Bill Prowse breathlessly.

"I knows that," said Benjie with scorn.   "I
know'd 'en all right.   How long is it since you've
a-favoured us wi' a visit, sir ?   Eh ? "

"Let me see your crabs and lobsters," demanded the bogey man.

" Hold hard, Mister 'Spector.   Us been shrimping—prawning you calls it—prawning wi' the
boat-nets—an' the prawns I catches I never shows
to nobody.   I an't got no lobster pots.   They
was washed ashore an' broken up last October
gales, an' I can't afford to replace 'em."

"But you catch lobsters in your prawn-
nets. . . ."

"For sure us do."

"Well, I want to see them."

" There they be then."

Benjie pointed towards the boat and made as if to lift up his nets.

" Show them to me," said the Inspector, taking a measure from his pocket.

" You *be* the 'Spector, ben' 'ee ? "

" No nonsense, now," replied the Inspector irritably. " It's my duty to inspect the catches in this fishery district."

" Very well, then ; inspect away. If 'tis your duty, you can't help o'it. You'm paid for the same. But 'tisn't my duty for to help 'ee. I bain't paid for thic. There's the boat."

Benjie scratched his whiskers : " And lookse here, Mister 'Spector. These here's me prawns what I've a-laboured for this night. Be so kind as to look."

He took a small canvas bag from the bow or the boat, walked into the sea, and shook out its contents. The few prawns that stuck in it by their spines he picked out and threw into the water after the rest. " There ! " he said amiably. " Nort but prawns there. You see'd that. But you didn't see how many Benjamin have a-catched, an' you never won't ; n'eet they there starch-collar jokers nuther—gen'lemen they calls them-selves—what goes downshore disturbing o'it an' catching a man's living for sport, so they says. *Sport !* Poaching, *I* calls it. 'Twas some o' they set 'ee on to me 'cause I won't tell 'em what I catches, nor where I shoots my nets. Iss, 'twas ! *I* knows. There's the boat. You can b—y well 'spect the rest o' what I've a-catched. I be going in house for me dinner an' a couple o' hours' sleep. An't had a bite since yesterday noon nor any sleep this three nights. I on'y hope your *duty* won't never bring 'ee to keeping a roof over your head wi' shrimping—an' measuring the crabs and lobsters what you catches wi' an inch-rule in the dark."

Leaving the boat and the nets where they were, Benjie shouldered some drift-wood and strode up the beach.

"I shouted to 'ee t'other side o' rocks," Bill Prowse protested.

Benjie stopped and turned, his bearing and appearance that of an ancient prophet. "Hell about your shouting ! Let 'en 'spect, *I* say. I'll get in out o'it."

He did.

The other fishermen stood with their hands in their pockets on top of the sea-wall, while the bogey man routed about in the boat. Under-sized lobsters had been thrown for'ard, among some old cordage and bottles of tea ; crabs were scuttling all over and under the bottom-boards and stern-sheets. Most of them were wildsters, but the bogey man did find half-a-dozen or so of tamesters. Doubtful specimens he measured carefully. When he had finished, he put the undersized shellfish into one of Benjie's sacks.

"An' the sack alone's wuth half a pint," Bill Prowse remarked in the bogey man's hearing. "Ol' Benjie's so honest an' harmless a man as ever put to sea, for all he has his say out when he's a-minded. He've a-worked too hard all his life for to deserve a turn-out like this here, I reckon. I tried to warn 'en, but Benjie won't never hear. . . ."

"What be talking 'bout. You can swim, can't 'ee ? Could ha' done that—could ha' swimmed out to 'en."

"*You* didn't try to warn 'en 't all, did 'ee ? An' then you blames me. . . ."

"What's the fine ? Ten pound ?"

"Benjie 'll never pay thic out o' his profits. He'll hae to sell up his fishing-boat an' nets— aye, an' then go short after that. P'raps they won't make 'en pay, fust time an' all. If the likes o' they, what makes such laws, know'd what the likes o' us has to contend with. . . . But there ! they don't know, nor never won't, n'eet care. Benjie 'll tell 'em off, you see. . . ."

"G'out ! Let's haul up the boat for 'en. What's the use o' Benjie blowing his hooter ?"

III

Benjie was all but late for court. He had gone west downshore to pick up some driftwood for firing, and an unexpected easterly breeze gave him a pull home against wind and chop such as few men would have attempted. No time was left him to change his clothes.

Vivian Maddicke was on the bench. He always is. He takes his duties as a gentleman and a magistrate almost as seriously as he takes himself. That is to say, he does try, at considerable personal inconvenience, to administer justice—to hold the balance between an efficient and respectful police force and an unruly lower class. He spends, indeed, not a little of his abundant leisure in pointing out to the poor the advantages of hard work, and in impressing upon them his own view of right and wrong. Hence it is, possibly, that his subscriptions and charities and justice hardly bring him a fair return in popularity.

When Benjie entered the court in his ragged discoloured longshore rig, a faint expression of disgust passed over Vivian Maddicke's pale but otherwise healthy face. He ordered two windows to be opened. " Let us have some fresh air," he said. " Never mind the draught."

Benjie, though he appeared to be examining the nail-heads in the floor, was all the time looking up at the bench from beneath his shaggy eyebrows. He understood the slur very well. Still fingering nervously his old round cap, he turned a pair of candid eyes full on Vivian Maddicke, and Vivian Maddicke, who had been gazing benevolently round the court-room, turned his face to the papers on his desk.

The case proceeded. There was no legal defence : Benjie had not purchased legal advice. " When I tells 'em how us be situated. . . . " he had said. But he was too much on his guard to give any useful evidence, even on his own behalf. The undersized crabs and lobsters were produced —it is wonderful how they fall off in appearance when they have died otherwise than in boiling water. Vivian Maddicke took the opportunity of remarking, " I thought we should require some fresh air."

The Clerk to the Sea Fisheries Committee—a spruce young lawyer in a hurry—did not wish to press the case too hard. They would be satisfied with a fine sufficient to show that the regulations of the Sea Fisheries Committee must not be trifled with. The costs of inspection and of prosecution were heavy. He would respectfully suggest to his worship. . . .

But his worship was not to be hustled among his own people, as he regarded them, by an outside lawyer. He sat back in his chair, crossed his legs in the magisterial manner, and dug his quill into his desk. When the lawyer had quite finished, he began.

In fining Benjie one pound, including costs, he remarked that it was not a large sum (murmurs of disapproval from fishermen at the back of the court), and that fishery inspectors were not to be trifled with or defied. Furthermore, he impressed upon Benjie in the most kindly manner possible that little lobsters grow into big ones.

"Iss, sir," said Benjie, "but the little ones be better eating if people only know'd it, same as mackerel."

With a passing reference to the depletion of the North Sea fisheries, the magistrate stated it as a fact, that if the fish were not in the sea they could not be caught out of it.

"For sure, sir!" Benjie assented. Under cover of being ready and willing to learn, he was edging in his remarks skilfully; for it was by no means the first time he had tackled the gentry who think they can teach fishermen their trade.

With every show of respect, moreover, he was capturing the laugh in court.

Fishery Committees, Vivian Maddicke continued patiently, were created to protect the fisheries. Their regulations were framed in the interests of the fishermen themselves, so that there might be more fish caught.

"Don't you believe that, sir," burst forth Benjie with intense conviction. "Do *you* think the likes o' they makes rules and regylations so that the likes o' us can catch more fish? 'Tisn't likely! They bain't afeard o' us not catching fish. What they'm afeard o' is that *they* won't hae no fish to eat, or won't hae 'em so cheap. Us! I've a-know'd the time when I could go down along an' catch a pound's-wuth o' lobsters in half-a-dozen rounds wi' the boat-nets; but I can't do it now. An' why for? Not 'cause *us* have a-catched 'em. That's just what us an't done. An' nuther you, sir, n'eet they there Fishery Boards, nor eet me, that have know'd this coast for sixty years, can tell where they'm gone to. Don't you believe they makes their regylations for the good o' us. I can tell 'ee better. How have 'em bettered fishing? That's what I wants to know."

The magistrate's clerk had risen during Benjie's passionate harangue. Vivian Maddicke motioned him down. Benjie, by force of his sincerity and in virtue of his long hard experience, held the court.

"I did not, you understand, frame the regulations," Maddicke explained. "My duty is to see they are enforced."

"Iss! Duty! That's what thic Inspector said down to beach. . . ."

"One pound," Vivian Maddicke repeated with dignity. "And you can have a fortnight to pay in."

Rising from the bench, he added, "If you care to talk to me out of court about the conditions of your work, I shall be pleased to hear ; and perhaps, if there is any special hardship, I can do something in the matter."

"Hardship! Hardship, do 'er say?" Addressing every one around, gesticulating, trembling with speech, Benjie was hustled from the court-room by those whose duty it is to do such jobs.

He did not go home as he was told to do ; he waited outside the magistrate's entrance (other fishermen waited too at a discreet distance), and when Vivian Maddicke appeared, picking bits of fluff from the front of his coat, Benjie stood resolutely before him.

"You said as you'd like to know, sir ; an' you ought to know how we'm situated ; an' I be going to tell 'ee. You ought to know the nature o' it, sir ; you ought to know what us got to contend with, afore you fines a man more'n he can pay wi'out selling up some o' the gear what he's got to earn his living with."

"But you've a fortnight to pay in."

"An' I thank you, sir, for that. An' I tell 'ee what. . . . I know'd your father ; a proper gen'leman he was ; he used to go fishing 'long wi' me afore you was born. You come down 'long wi' me one night an' see what 'tis like for yourself. Then you'll know. Duty ain't never no excuse for not knowing. You can row, can't 'ee ! "

" I used to go in for rowing ; and if you'll send up and let me know when you're going, I *will* come."

" That's spoken proper, sir, like your ol' man hisself. 'Tisn't everybody I'd take 'long with me ; but you come, just for one night. That'll teach 'ee more 'n any amount o' chackle. I'll send up for 'ee right 'nuff. Why ! I mind when . . ."

Maddicke said " Good morning " with the air of a man who has an appointment to keep.

" Good morning, an' thank you, sir," returned Benjie.

To the other fishermen, who joined him for the walk back to the beach, all he would say was : " You bide a bit an' see. The likes o' they sort thinks they bain't ignorant, an' us be."

IV

Benjie had luck. One afternoon the next week he hauled his boat down the beach, piled his prawn-nets beside it, then waited, instead of telling his fisherman mate to get ready.

" What be biding for ? " asked Bill Prowse. " You bain't going to take *he* t'night, be 'ee ? "

" Iss, I be. Why for not ? Nice calm night, ain't it. 'Er can't very well be sea-sick."

Bill Prowse jerked his head to seaward.

The sun had begun to sink behind the dark

mass of Steep Head. The water, a dead calm,
was nevertheless not white calm, as it should have
been, for to the south'ard and overhead the piled-
up sky was black and heavy. It overshadowed
the sea ; seemed to be pressing down upon the
water. And there was a feeling of unrest in the
still air.

"Looks thundery, don' it ?" Bill observed.
"'Twas just such another day as this us had thic
waterspout. Don't like the looks o'it. You'll
get he catched in a storm o' rain, an' wind too,
p'raps."

"What if I do ? 'Twon't hurt 'en. An't
never hurted me. Send your Polly up to tell 'en
I be shoving off in an hour an' should be glad o'
his company if he's minded to come. Tell 'en
'twill be perty cold come midnight."

Vivian Maddicke, clothed as if for a shooting
expedition in the Arctic regions, was down to the
minute. "You might have given me a longer
warning," he remarked with make-believe jollity.

"Ah !" said Benjie, "so might, if you was
going for a drive on land, like you'm used to.
But when you'm depending on the sea you never
knows from hour to hour what you'm going to
be about."

Very polite as host, but as skipper of his own
craft not to be played with, he put the bow-oar
into Maddicke's hand. With the fleet of sixteen
nets and their buoys piled up on the stern seats,
they rowed away westward over Broken Rocks,
along the shore, into the wet golden haze of
sunset. Whether or no Maddicke found his sea

oar and the beamy boat heavier than he had expected, they did not arrive underneath Steep Head till its outlines were blurred in the twilight, till its redness was become black, and it seemed nothing but a vast overhanging shadow tenanted by mewing but hardly visible seagulls.

"Now," commanded Benjie, "you row wi' both paddles, please, while I baits the nets, an' then us'll shoot 'em across Conger Pool just the other side o' the Head. Keep her like that. You'll get wet if you splashes. You don't need for to strain yourself."

From one of his catty sacks Benjie took out a mass of putrid fishmonger's offal—fish heads and plaice from which the meat had been filleted—which he cut up and fitted into the cross-strings of the nets. The smell made Maddicke shudder ; he turned his head this way and that, but there was no escaping the stink—the various sorts of stink. It took the strength out of him as the smell of dead things will do.

"An' now," directed Benjie with a quiet chuckle of satisfaction, "you paddle along slow across Conger Pool, while I shoots the nets."

Taking up the hoops from a tangle of corks and lines, trying the baits again to make sure, he cast the nets into the water about three boats' lengths apart, and threw the buoys and lines after them. Maddicke was glad to see them go. He heard Benjie talking all the time, but his brain did not gather very well the sense of what the old man was saying. He sweated at the oars, and yet he was cold. Steep Head loomed above them.

The sound of the swell, breaking, rattling, swishing among the rocks, had in it a sullen wildness not noticeable during full daylight.

"An' now," said Benjie, when he had shot the sixteenth net and had taken its bearings, "you can hae a bit o' supper. Us got a night's work afore us.—No ? Won't 'ee hae nort ? Well, I never don't nuther when I be shrimping, 'cept a mouthful o' cold tay. The bread and butter I brings I gen'rally gives to the birds or else carries it home to breakfast. There ! Did 'ee hear thic cliff rooze out to the west'ard ? 'Twill all be into the sea one day, Steep Head an' all. Aye ! '*tis* an ironbound shop, this here, but the sea has it sooner or later, specially after rain."

"There hasn't been much rain lately ?"

"No. But there's been frostises, an' that's every bit so bad. Now us'll haul up an' see what's there. Perty night for shrimping, this, if it don't come on dirty. Can 'ee see the end buoy ? You can't ? There 'tis ! Now row t'ards it—easy now !"

Benjie's directions came fast and peremptory while, with the help of the tiller, he grabbed the lines and hauled the nets up through the water, at first gently, then as swiftly as possible. "Pull your outside oar—pull inside—inside, not outside —back outside—back both. You'm on the line —steady—steady there ! Pull outside—both— easy. Easy, easy now ! I can't haul 'em up straight while you be pulling. Wants some learning, don't it, this here job ? Now row easy up to the next buoy while I shoots this out again.

c

Can't 'ee see it ? *I* can. There 'tis, thic little
black mark in the water just outside the shadow
o' the cliff."

Feeling around the inside of the net, shaking
it, holding it up dripping to what light there was,
Benjie caught the lobsters and threw them for'ard
in the boat, chased the wild crabs with his hands
and threw them aft, and placed the prawns carefully in a basket beside him. Then he shot the
net, and the volley of directions began all over
again—all over again for each net. Maddicke
was confused by them. He was still more confused, and irritated also, by his own mistakes.
He breathed hard with vexation. At the end of
the fourth round, the sixty-fourth haul, he was
plainly flagging. He was " proper mazed."

"You be jumping the water wi' your oars.
You'll catch one o' they there t'other sort o' crabs
an' crack your skull if you bain't careful," Benjie
warned him with perceptible satisfaction. " Better
to take a rest, an' while I counts the prawns, you
measure the lobsters like they says us ought to.
Here's a foot-rule I got. The lobsters be under
your feet an' for'ard. If you can't see, better to
strike a match. We'm out o' everybody's sight
hereabout."

Maddicke felt for a lobster in the dark, and
after several gingerly attempts — and several
amiable warnings from Benjie to mind its claws
—he succeeded in holding it. He found also the
nine-inch mark on the rule ; but while he was
trying to spread the lobster out flat on a thwart
and to feel where the tip of its beak was, according

to regulations, the thing nipped him suddenly
and savagely.

"Ough !" he cried like a child. "Ough—
ah-h-h ! "

"What's the matter there ? Can't 'ee do it ? "
he heard from the shadow of Benjie, aft.

"It's bitten me—it's biting me—*now* ! "

"Squeeze his eyes, then he'll leave go. Lord !
They bites me every night, but I don't take no
heed o'it."

Maddicke tore at the lobster. His other hand
was nipped—in the fleshy part of the thumb. He
broke off one claw, and still the other held fast.
He stood up and dashed his hand about. He
trod on lobsters and crabs. The boat seemed
alive with them. The squashy cracking of their
shells, partly heard and partly felt. . . . He
breathed hard with excitement and with something
not far short of horror.

"Aye !" remarked Benjie coolly, breaking the
nipper from his hand, "a boat in the dark ain't
no fit place for measuring lobsters. You've a-
spoiled thic. He won't fetch sixpence now.
Fine cock-lobster too, what didn't never need
no measuring."

Maddicke, having done the wrong thing, tried
to put it right. He fumbled in his pocket and
held out a shilling to Benjie.

"What's that for ? "

"Well, I've spoilt a lobster that didn't need
measuring at all, you say. . . ."

"You just put thic whatever 'tis back into
your pocket, please. The likes o' us an't got the

money for to pay for what us spoils. 'Twasn't
your fault. You didn't know. But there! You
wasn't brought up to it like us be. A bit upset,
be 'ee? I could feel 'ee shaking. You hae a rest
while I goes ashore an' looks in one or two lobster-
holes I knows for. You stay in the boat. 'Tis
nearly low tide an' her won't hurt for an hour or
so where I'll leave 'ee : 'tis a little natural harbour
like. If you got time, you can measure the rest
o'em an' chuck the undersized ones overboard,
when you'm feeling better. My senses, ain't
it dark ! "

Maddicke saw Benjie jump out of the boat
with a skim-net in his hand, glimpsed him hopping from the nearest rock to the next one, then
saw nothing except the black darkness ; but he
heard an uncanny chuckle which might equally
have come from a man or from a half-awakened
sea-bird. Unstrung already by the cold, by
hunger, by the unusual toil, by the blind savagery
of the lobster, by Benjie's relentless volleys of
directions, and above all by his own failures to
carry them out, he heard with an oppressive sense
of something terrible impending that mutterings
of thunder to the southward were being answered
by rumblings overland. Everything else was for
the moment hushed. A flash of lightning revealed
Steep Head, its pinnacles and the patches of bush
and bracken upon its upper slopes, and showed
up brightly the tumbled rocks around the boat
and the blackness of the hollows between them.
Rain splashed down. Maddicke shrank into his
coat.

Presently, with a flash that made the blood prick in his veins, and crashes that hit like blows, the storm broke right overhead. Flash followed flash ; crash followed crash, and echoed against the cliff. There was no rest from blinding light and overwhelming noise. The solid earth was in an uproar. Steep Head, it seemed, was toppling over, was tumbling down upon him.

He tried to reassure himself, then suddenly gave way. In obedience to a blind impulse of flight, he scrambled out of the boat into water that was knee-deep. He gained the rocks, slipped on some seaweed, bruising himself, and fell headlong into a pool. Jumping up quickly, he felt around him. Rocks were everywhere—wherever he felt, wherever he tried to go. By the light of the flashes they looked like squat live things, extending on every side, endlessly. The boat was what he wanted again most of all ; that at least seemed to be partly human, to be company for him. But the boat he had lost. He did not even know in which direction it lay. Another flash lit it up only a couple of paces from where he was standing. He lunged out and clutched it, as if it would have slipped away from him. It was a refuge, though the rain ran down his back as he sat on the wet stern-seat. "Benjamin ! Benjamin Prowse !" he called. "Benjie ! Come back ! "

Had he looked the right way during a flash he would have seen Benjie's face, screwed up with laughter and mockery, peering at him round a rock close by.

There was no escaping the cruel brightness of the storm; no escaping the continuous tumult of thunder. Flashes there were that sounded like the crackling of dry twigs; others like the flicking of whips. The thunder, reverberating in the darkness, was a relief from the lightning. Sometimes Maddicke caught sight of the grotesque shapes of the shellfish: crabs standing up on their hinder legs, bubbling at the mouth, and looking at him with their stalk-like eyes; lobsters —black, shining, and fantastic—brandishing their claws. He crouched down on his seat, away from the madness of the sky. He tried to lift up his feet, away from the malice of the wild crabs. The noise they made, scuttling around the boat, teased the silences between the peals of thunder. He covered up his face and ears. He ceased struggling to escape. A shapeless fear, a formless misery that was almost a relief, took possession of him. He was done.

At last Benjie stepped carelessly into the boat, as if he were boarding a railway train. Maddicke grabbed his wet trousers. "Let's get home!" he gasped. "I can't stand this."

"Why, what's the matter?" asked Benjie coolly. "You be flittering like a sail that's up in the wind's eye. *We'm* going home right 'nuff. There'll be wind along after this. My senses, what a storm! Did 'ee hear it? But I've a-see'd worse, aye! an' down hereunder too."

Maddicke stayed still; did nothing to help put the boat to rights. He was helpless. Benjie took hold of him, laid him gently in the bow of

the boat, covered him up, head and all, with
sacking, took both oars, and rowed homewards.

Underneath the sacking that smelt of cats,
Maddicke dozed off, with the regular rocking
sound of the oars in his ears.   When that stopped
he awoke and looked out dully.   The storm had
drifted away to the eastward.   It was bright starlight above.   The boat was just outside Salterport.
To see the sheltering town, with its gaslights so
close at hand, was like waking from a nightmare
to find the morning sun shining into the room.
Maddicke, safe at home, was another man.   His
confidence returned, and at the same time he felt
ashamed—so ashamed that he did not think of
helping to haul up the boat.

While Benjie was saying, "An' now you know
what the likes o' us got to contend with," he
poked stiff, damp fingers into one of his pockets.
"If you will send up to-morrow," he said with
returning dignity, "I will give you the sovereign
to pay your fine. . . ."

Benjie flared up.   "If *you* thinks I be 'bliged
to call on the likes o' you for the pound to pay
me fine wi', you'm much mistaken.   I be only
too glad you knows the nature o'it.   Now you
can tell 'em what *you* thinks.   Tell 'em all o'it,
not only what's suiting to 'ee.   *I* don't want no
pound for teaching o'ee.   Be your gold for to pay
me for me silence on what I've a-see'd this night
when I peeped at 'ee there in the boat to Conger
Pool ?   Didn' know I was looking, did 'ee ?
A perty sight for any one as calls hisself a man !

Pity they fishery people, what you does your duty to, couldn' ha' see'd it ! "

Maddicke, with a miserable gesture, turned towards the sea-wall lights to go up the beach ; and, on catching sight of his woebegone face, Benjie added in a kindlier tone : " Lookse here, sir, you an't got no call proper for to be ashamed o' fearing the storm. There's many a man born an' bred to fishing what's mortal afeard o' a thunderstorm to sea, an' 'tis worse down under they cliffs ; an' nobody what an't been there wouldn't think what 'twas like ; for 'tis a great an' terrible thing, look you, an' man be nort in the midst o'it. Lord's sakes, an't I felt like it when I been down there by meself ! Will 'ee hae a lobster or two to carry home ? You'm very welcome.—Well, then, good night to you, sir, an' thank you. Only don't you deceive yourself that I be going to send up to 'ee for money to pay for what *you* didn't know. That ain't Benjamin. Good night ! "

Benjie went so far as to pat Maddicke on the shoulder.

The sovereign was sent down right enough next morning, together with a note which nobody has ever seen ; and Benjie did accept it. As to the bogey man—Benjie congratulates his own self that the bogey man has seldom been seen on the beach since.

JASPAR BRAUND'S BOAT

I

JASPAR BRAUND did not row in last year's regatta. He is not likely to row this year. Probably he will never row in any race again. "And a good job, too ! " he says, with the flaming up of a long-standing bitterness. And then he sometimes adds, more in triumph than with an old man's resignation : "I an't got no need for to row any more. I've a-won my race for good."

All the year round, now, the *Bubble* lies high and dry on the beach just below his house. For lobster-potting and prawning, and for working his pollack-nets, he uses a little punt he has had built ; but he still keeps the *Bubble* in such good order that she would look like a new boat if certain parts of her stem and stern did not look even newer. Every second year he scrapes her outside and in, and every spring he gives her a couple of coats of best yacht varnish. For that purpose he wears his reading spectacles, which cause him to peer rather closely into his job, and nearly always, when he is working the varnish well underneath the boat's ribs, his longish white beard brushes against it. "Summer's coming," is the word that travels across the beach. "Summer's coming, sure 'nuff. Ol' Jaspar's varnishing his beard !"

At those who stand around, watching and chaffing him, Jaspar flashes back sharp, but not very disagreeable answers. He has mellowed lately. Not so very long ago he was an awkward man to fall foul of, especially after he had had a pint or two. Strangest of all, when he catches anybody measuring the *Bubble*, instead of flying into a rage, he merely defies them to build another like her. It used to be one of the adventures of the place to measure the *Bubble*, in order to find out, if possible, why she was so speedy. Hard words, and even blows, were the result if Jasper happened to come along. On one occasion he spent a night in the lock-up for knocking down a member of the Corinthian Sailing Club, then picking him up again like a baby, and throwing him into the sea. Jaspar at the time was almost twice the other man's age.

All that is over now. The *Bubble* is pointed out to people as she lies on the beach, shapely enough in midship outline, but curiously stumpy about the stern and bows. "That's Jaspar Braund's boat ; that there's the *Bubble*. Bought her to Plymouth, he did, an' rowed her up therefrom in a day, which is fifty-six or seven miles, and he was turned fifty hisself. No doubt he worked the tides—trust ol' Jaspar for that—but 'tis a terrible long distance for to dig out with one pair of arms. And after that her won him every pair-oar race for ten years following, till nobody didn't

care for to turn out against him. W'er 'twas the
boat won the races, or w'er 'twas Jaspar, nobody
can't say.   Anyhow, they won 'em together, an' thic
boat was like a wife to ol' Jaspar—a wife wi' a
hellish jealous husband. *Bubble* he called her,
and a bubble her is on the water.   I don't suppose
there's other boat like her up an' down the coast
—not all along South Devon.   And they can't
copy her—none of 'em can't—not exactly, though
they've a-tried hard enough.   Ah ! a perty little
boat her was, afore he spoilt her for to win his
last race. . . . What ?   An't 'ee heard tell about
thic turn-out ?   Why, 'twas like this here. . . ."
    But, as a matter of fact, the yarn that is told
across beach is not complete.   In the affairs of
old Devon coast towns there are many wheels
within wheels, and men are so given to secrecy,
that they keep hidden, simply for the sake of
doing so, what every one might hear without
harm.   In consequence, of course, everything
becomes known in the end, for everything is
worth knowing ; but the wheels within wheels
unroll themselves rather slowly ; in Jaspar's case
the more slowly, first because the common story
seemed to furnish a full explanation of the affair,
and, secondly, because a fuller explanation could
only come from him.   What everybody knows,
he himself overhead by accident, just in time.

II

    One evening, about a week before the regatta,
Jaspar strolled into the public bar of the Beach

Hotel, and called for a pint of beer. He had
been moping about for some days, had spent a
great deal of his time on the sea-wall, looking out
to sea, and had hardly been troubling whether he
did anything or not. The landlady, who hears
everybody's business discussed, mostly by some
one else, tried to cheer him up.

"Well, Jaspar," she said, "you'll be winning
your prize again next week, I suppose?"

Jaspar took a drink, put down his pint cup
exactly into its own ring of overflow on the table,
and said nothing.

"There's a regatta committee meeting upstairs
now," the landlady went on, jerking her head
backwards in that direction. "They're late out
with the prize-list, aren't they, Jaspar? I suppose
'twill be the same as usual."

Jaspar shifted in his seat. "I don't trouble
me head about it," he growled. "I've finished
wi' it. And 'bout time. Not but what I bain't
so fit as ever I was—Braunds be, till they packs
up. I reckon the *Bubble* and me could show a
stern to the likes o' they any day. But I an't got
no heart for it, Missis, an' that's the truth. An't
got no heart for nort!"

"Jaspar, for shame!" laughed the landlady
with a more than professional cheeriness, and
possibly a spice of mischief. "You'm like a
young man crossed in love, you are. You ought
to know better at your age.—Here they are,
coming down from the meeting. I can hear the
chairs moving back. I must get some more
glasses washed up."

The old man jammed himself into the corner of his seat till he did really look old—old in body, as well as grey. "Crossed in love!" he mumbled to himself, after the fashion of those who are much alone at sea. "At my age. . . . P'raps I be, Missis. An' p'raps I bain't."

Most of the committee passed straight through the private bar, on the other side, and out into the street. Three remained, to judge by the drinks they called for—namely, a special Scotch and soda, a glass of Burton, and a pint of cider. One voice spoke in the tones of those whom fishermen call "they there haw-haw articles." The second spoke a bastard local English. The third voice kept on falling into the broad dialect of the beach. Now that the meeting was over, they were very full of what ought to be done in order to improve the regatta.

Although the partition between the private and public bars at the Beach Hotel rises right up to the ceiling, and divides the counter as well, it does not extend into the space behind the counter. Jaspar, sitting in his corner, could hear every word that was said on the other side, and soon the landlady was walking up and down nervously, unable to warn either Jaspar or the committee-men without everybody hearing it. And, knowing Jaspar, she feared a row in her house.

For very soon the subject of the pair-oar race was brought up.

"D'you think that'll take all right?" asked the second voice, "putting the limit for the pair-oar boats at fourteen feet? Twelve to fourteen, isn't it?"

"What I always say is this," answered the first voice. "If you want to make a race popular and get a good entry, you must arrange it so that the majority *can* enter. Years ago there used to be more fifteen-foot boats on the beach; but now, since they have gone in for thirteen- or fourteen-foot punts, there are hardly any but sailing boats over that length. And by putting the limit at fourteen feet you make the conditions equal for the greatest number. At least, that is my opinion."

"Certainly," remarked the third voice, "there isn't so many fifteen-foot rowing boats as there was back along. We've a-found out our mistake. They'm no good for a beach like ours; 'cause if you got to haul a fifteen-foot rowing boat up an' down the beach, why you may just so well hae a sailing boat, an' done wi' it. 'Tis nigh the same weight ashore, an' the sail 'll do the work afloat, 'less 'tis a flat calm. 'Sides, a beamy little thirteen-foot punt 'll carry so much, an' earn 'ee just so much money, as a narrow fifteen-foot gig."

"Of course. And you're the fisherman member of the committee; *you* ought to know. But they are all so confoundedly conservative here, except when they are wanted to vote straight. Drink up, William. Have something else. You'll have another, won't you, Mr. Kerswell?"

"No . . . ."

"No, you have one 'long wi' me, sir."

"No, no, thanks. I'm late for dinner already. Let me leave one with you."

Jaspar heard the louder rap of empty glasses

upon the counter ; then heard the haw-haw article say " Good-night," and go out.   Mr. Kerswell was the first to speak.

" I should have thought," he said, " that if a man wanted to handicap himself in a race by rowing a bigger boat, there wasn't no objection. Won't a fourteen-foot limit put Jaspar Braund out of the running with his racer ? "

" Course 'twill, an' serve 'en right, too.   Mean ol' scrawler !   But that wasn't his real reasons what he gave—him that's just gone out.   *He* don't care about no entry, 'cept to stop ol' Jaspar entering.   Ah ! he've never forgiven ol' Jaspar, nor never won't, for chucking of him into the water when he was trying to measure the *Bubble* after dark for to get another built like her.   And he wouldn't never have got the *Bubble's* equal copy, after that ; so Jaspar might just so well have bided quiet.   Boats is like people, I tell 'ee ; it takes all sorts to make a world, and no two o'em's alike.   But that's what was in *his* mind, right 'nuff, when he proposed fourteen foot —to get to win'ard of ol' Jaspar."

" But I thought it was *you* mentioned it first at the meeting, Mr. Barton. . . ."

" Certainly I did—for to get it over.   I know'd 'twas going to be brought up.   'Tis a bit hard on Jaspar, but there 'tis ; he've a-had his day or ought to have, and I don't care who hears me say it."

Jaspar heard him plainly.   The landlady had been making signs and grimaces to him, but he motioned to her to keep quiet, and as he seemed 'to be taking the conversation very well, she did so. Mr. Kerswell went on :

"What's that they're saying about old Braund and Tom Sandover's maid ?"

"G'out !" said William Barton. "Silly ol' fool ! Ought to know better at his time of life ; so did the maid ; walking out wi' her grandfather up along dark lanes. Her's plenty old 'nuff for to know what's what. Pretty nigh thirty, her is. But Tommy Sandover hisself has put his foot down on that. My sister, what lives to the back of the gentleman's house, where her's in service, and used to see 'em, her's see'd ol' Jaspar hanging round, but her says her an't see'd 'em together this week or so. The maid don't come out. 'Tisn't no use for to talk ; Jasper's getting on ; he's sixty if he's a day ; and if he don't know it, he'll have to be teached. He've a-brought it on hisself. But he's going to be teached now, you see. He won't win thic race not in another boat ; and certain sure he won't get thic maid. . . ."

There was a noise of heavy boots on the other side. "You're a liar !" shouted Jaspar Braund in a voice very thick and hasty. "You're a liar, Bill Barton ! You always was. Who backed out of the lifeboat thic time, saying 'twas doctor's orders ?"

The boots clattered again. Instinctively Bill Barton shaped himself to fight, and Mr. Kerswell drank up hastily. But Jaspar did not come round to the private bar. He went away.

Next morning, by breakfast time, the *Bubble* was gone from her berth on the beach. It was

reported that Jaspar had taken her through his
house and up behind, into his linhay ; furthermore, that he had had a shindy with Bill Barton,
and that Bill Barton had threatened to put his
boot through the *Bubble*. "Ol' Jaspar," they
said, "would so soon have a boot through hisself ! " It was also said that Jaspar, enraged by
the fourteen-foot limit, had broken up the *Bubble*
for firewood, and this second rumour was traced
back to a chance remark of Jaspar's own.

III

Regatta day broke very calm and fine. Cats-
paws, driven out to sea by a light land wind, were
just enough to keep the water in a ripple and give
it life. So quiet was the breaking of little waves
against the shingle that the sound of them seemed
dreamlike and far-distant. When the sun lifted
itself over the eastern cliff, driving away a lurry
of mist to the south'ard, it lighted the ripples
with colour ; pearl-grey and milky pink, and
flashes of red and orange, all twinkling into one
another, till the sea, for a few moments at break
of day, was one vast jewel. Then the sun caught
the cliffs to the westward, so suddenly lighting
them up that they seemed to advance against the
sea. And in the midst of it all, looking black and
very small in size, lay one little boat at moorings.
Later on, several arguments took place along
the sea-wall about that boat. Men who can tell
every craft on the beach a mile off disagreed.
Those who saw her broadside-on declared that

D

'twas not the *Bubble*, for its stem and stern were singularly upright, whereas the *Bubble's* had raked outwards, fore and aft, and her over-all measurement, as every one knew, was much greater than the length of her keel. Those, on the contrary, who saw the little boat swing round, endways-on, were equally certain that it *was* Jaspar's *Bubble*. By and by, a fleet of racing dinghies, coming up from the westward astern of a steam tug, and fishing-boats arriving from other ports, drew men's attention away from the moored boat.

The dinghies, with their silken sails, made sport of the light airs. The fishing boats, with their great dipping lugsails, formed a splendid spectacle on the water, but they could hardly get along, and had to be called off after their first round. Last of all, and late, was the pair-oar race.

"Didn't I tell thee so?" was said on all sides when Jaspar, stripped to his short-sleeved, low-necked sailor's flannel, rowed out to the moored boat, boarded her, and pulled himself, with long, easy strokes, to the starting-buoy. "What on earth's the use of he turning out?" said some.

"Jaspar'll beat 'em all, you see," said others ; and such, when it came to the point, was local pride in the old man and his boat and his oarsmanship, that they cheered him off, shouting his name, and caring little whether his boat was qualified or not. The race was the thing to be won, not the prize.

Three buoys marked out the triangular course of a mile or so. At the first buoy Jaspar was leading. At the second buoy he had increased his lead far beyond what was necessary. Then, doubling down and putting his back into it, he rowed right away from the rest. "Ol' fool!" said the wiseacres, "doing more than he's any need to." But the biggest cheer of the day welcomed him home.

A motor boat sped out and hailed him. He changed his course, and landed opposite the committee's tent.

"You'm over length?" some one shouted just as his boat touched the beach.

"Be I?" he answered, crawling out. "Here, give us a hand to haul her up a bit, will 'ee, please?"

Jaspar himself did not touch the boat. The veins in his neck were working, and by the twitch of his grizzled face he seemed to be in pain.

"Is that the *Bubble* you've got there?" demanded the regatta secretary.

"For sure 'tis—or 'twas," replied Jaspar. "You can measure her if you'm minded."

"She's over length. We know that already. You're disqualified."

"Measure! Measure!" said Jaspar. He spoke with a threatening quietness.

They did measure her. She was under length by an inch.

"Why, what have you done to her?" they asked eagerly. "'Tis the *Bubble* right enough. You've cut her down. You've spoilt your boat, Jaspar."

"I knows it," said Jaspar. "I've a-spoilt me

boat. I've a-cut down the *Bubble*—the *Bubble* as used to be. You thought you was going to get to win'ard o' us, an', blast you, I've a-won!"

His voice rose. In a wailing shout, as if he might break into tears, he flung his curses at everybody near, raising his hands and shaking his fists. He made as if to put his own boot through the *Bubble*, and then stooped down and smoothed her varnish.

And suddenly, again, he stopped. He had caught sight of a face among the crowd that was gathered round. Almost running up the beach he gripped a young woman by the arm.

"Come on!" he said. "I've a-won, and you knows what you told me."

"Oh, I didn't say it, Jaspar!"

"Come on!" he repeated, "an' let's get away from the hellers. Come on, 'long wi' me, to sea, out o'it!"

Half enticing, half compelling, he put her aboard the *Bubble*, and shoved off; and, with lame, short strokes of his oars, he rowed away to the westward.

The spectators gathered together in twos and threes. "That's Tommy Sandover's maid he's took away. Where's Tommy? If Tommy know'd this. . . . 'Fore all thic crowd o' people. . . ."

But the *Bubble* was beyond hail. She kept on her course, westward under the cliffs; and though she was watched by many far-sighted eyes, first the shadow of the cliffs and then darkness spread over the sea and hid her.

IV

That was the *Bubble's* last trip. Ever since then she has lain on the beach. Barely a month after the regatta, Jaspar took Tommy Sandover's maid home to his house ; and it was quite recently, when I happened to ask him why he never used the *Bubble*, that the rest of the story came out.

"I never uses her," he said, "'cause I can't bring myself to it. I an't got no pride in her, not to go to sea in, now her's cut down. It didn't change her water-line, nor yet her speed in smooth water, but it did spoil the shape o' her, and there 'tis. Her's the *Bubble*, sure 'nuff, and yet her isn't ; and *I* remembers what the *Bubble* was. I an't got no heart for to use her."

"Why ever did you spoil her," I asked, "simply to win a race ?"

"'Twasn't that," he replied quickly. "And 'twasn't on account of Bill Barton. Him 'twas that started the fourteen-foot limit, because several of 'em agreed across beach to share and share alike with the prizes, whether they won or not, and I wouldn't fall in with it. 'Course I wouldn't ! The prize was mine by rights, and always had been. So they put he up to tricking me out o' it.

"Do 'ee think I'd ha' spoilt the *Bubble* for that ? Not me ! You see, 'twas like this really :

"After my first wife died, I did get lone-lier an' lonelier, till I thought I was going fair mazed wi' it ; and I took to talking to my ol' woman that is (only her isn't old) for the sake of

passing the time ; an' 'fore I know'd where I was,
I was a-courting of her.   An' her was kind-like
to me, although her people tried to stop it all they
know'd how.   Made me feel young again, it did.

"Then her people persuaded of her that I was
too old for to marry—gone past it—me that felt
so young an' strong as ever I was!   And her
wouldn't come out to me, till one night I catched
her going to post wi' her missis's letters, and then
her told me.   Crying her was, too.

"So I says to her : 'Annie,' I says, 'have any
of they there young men winned the pair-oar race
this nine years.'

"And her was bound for to answer, 'No.'

" ' Well,' I says, 'will 'ee believe I'm fit for to
marry 'ee if I wins thic race this year again ?'

"And her didn't answer, which I took for
'Yes' ; though, mind you, I was got so mazed
wi' it all that I didn't believe I *could* win it.   That
is, I wasn't feeling sure, and I was in two minds
whether or not to drop all o'it.

" 'Twas that same evening I heard what they
was saying in to the Beach Hotel.   You must
know what I felt like when I heard 'em, same as
you knows how it turned out.

"If it hadn't ha' been for all o'it, if it hadn't
ha' been for my wife that is, I'd never ha' cut
down the *Bubble*—never, so long as I lived.   My
God, I'd never have hurt thic little boat !   A
perty little boat her was to me.

"But they said I was grow'd too old for to
marry.   They said Jaspar was done for.   And
they persuaded *her*.

" How's that ? " he went on, going over to the
Bubble and lifting a small child out of her, where
children in the old time were never allowed to
play. "How's that ? Do 'ee think her's like
me ? Her's mine—Daddy's Nannie, bain't 'ee,
smutty-face—twenty year younger than the young-
est of my first family what's scattered all about
the world, and maybe dead ; and I tell thee
Braunds bain't never done for till they'm dead !
And I reckon I've a-proved it, too."

"You'll win that race again yet," I said, half
in joke, because the old man was so terribly
serious.

He took my hand and placed it inside his coat
against his shoulder.

"Do 'ee feel thic hollow ? 'Twill never go
away, the doctor says, not at my age. I busted a
cord there thic day —a sinew, they calls it, broke—
and 'twill never join up. I can paddle about, you
know, but I shan't never race no more. I've
a-won my race for good.

"The missis'll tell 'ee 'tis true. Her's so
proud as can be o'it—'cause 'twas done on account
of her, no doubt. A sight prouder, her is, I do
believe, o' me an' me Jacob's hollow than her is
o' thic there kid. But *I* bain't, 'cause Nannie's
my prize, what I've a-winned."

Jaspar smiled to himself, as men do when
they've won their race.

TO SAVE LIFE

"HE's in the town, I tell 'ee."

"G'out! What be talking 'bout?"

"Why the lifeboat 'spector, for sure; an' he's in the town, I tell thee. Dickey Whimple see'd 'en up to station last night."

"Maybe 'er is in the town," said another, an older fisherman, "but it don't follow 'er 'll send the lifeboat out a day like this yer. 'Tisn't fit. My senses! bain't it cold. I told 'ee us'd hae it when us did."

The little knot of men—fishermen unable to go to sea, old fishermen and shivering beach-combers—attracted as usual to the lifeboat-house by rumours that the inspector was around, talked and argued in a lee corner behind the west wall of the squat red-painted building whose tall doors face the Channel. Continually the group broke up and formed again, because first one man, then another, peeped out to the south'ard or stamped across the road to warm his feet. For two days and nights a south-easterly gale, with savage snow-squalls in it, had been blowing upon the coast. More and more the measured thump of a great ground-swell had, except at low tide, drowned the noise of breaking water, the rattle of shingle, and the hollow booming of the wind ; for when a ground-swell grows heavy enough to shake the beach, then the ear awaits each wave and listens for little else.   During brief bursts of sunshine the sea outside looked almost calm, so uniformly churned-up was its discoloured surface. When squalls darkened water and sky, blobs of foam blew overhead across the road, mixed with snowflakes, and almost as white.   Both swirled even into the corner where the fishermen and beach-combers stopped talking only to light their pipes.

"Tisn't as if we fellers don't want the money, 'cause us do," declared a lifeboatman.

"Aye ! an' the helpers wants their couple o' shillings, too."

"If 'tis wuth a couple o' shillings," said the lifeboatman, "for you chaps as stays ashore an' only hauls on ropes, 'tis wuth ten pound for to go out there this day.   Not that I can't do wi' the six shillings they gives 'ee.   I an't earned a pound this month."

"'Tisn't fit !" the old fisherman repeated. "Better to go short than to go out there, practising, the likes o' this weather.   Practising, they calls it !   Practising short cuts to t'other place. 'Tisn't a case o' saving life ; that's another thing. Would 'em like to go out theirselves, what sends 'ee an' calls 'ee brave fellows, an' puts 'ee in the paper.   Not they ! — Here 'er is though, sure 'nuff !"

The inspector, the coxswain, the local secretary, and the chairman of the lifeboat committee were even then making their way along the sea-wall against the wind. They opened the doors of the lifeboat-house. Already the men were beginning to run up.

"Well, coxswain ?" the inspector asked.

"'Tis like this, sir," said the coxswain, in his slow way; "if us can get off through the surf, we'm there for better or for worse; but 'tis a middling gert lop—so big as I've a-see'd this twenty year—an' I can't say about getting ashore safely or wi'out damaging the boat. . . ."

"You'd go out to a wreck, wouldn't you ?" the chairman interrupted brusquely.

"Why, yes ; o' course, sir."

"Well, then, inspector, there is no reason why they shouldn't go out now."

"And there ain't no reason why they should ! " growled a man among the crowd.

The rocket was fired. The town, hitherto so small-looking and quiet beside the furious sea, sprang to life. Men hurried to the lifeboat-house from all directions. In spite of the storm and the driving, blinding spray, the townsfolk and some visitors gathered on the sea-wall, where they could get a good view ; children flocked out of lanes and the women stood at the tops of them, holding their skirts down with one hand and sheltering their eyes with the other. The coxswain distributed helpers' tickets to the men he required, and the lifeboat, standing high and proudly on her carriage, was hauled as far as the middle of the road. There she stopped, helpless on land by herself.

"Come, lads!" the coxswain shouted to his men.

But the lifeboatmen, instead of lending a hand with the ropes, collected together on one side, shouting to each other with much gesticulation in order to be heard above the storm. Between the prolonged thuds of the ground-swell certain angry phrases detached themselves from the hubbub.

"'Tisn't fit!"

"Oh, I be willing enough. . . ."

"There's reason in all things."

"The likes o' they. . . ."

"Ought to be 'All together, boys!'"

Finally, one man stood forward and refused to go. Perhaps because he is well known to be a rough-weather fisherman—Old Hell-About-It, he is called—three others followed his example.

"Turn them out of the boat and call for volunteers," said the chairman.

Not a fisherman was willing to replace them. A visitor and two townsmen did volunteer, but the coxswain, after looking them up and down, said shortly: "I bain't going to put to sea 'long wi' they."

"Call a committee meeting—at once!" snapped the chairman, losing his temper. "Are the fishermen here afraid of the sea?"

"Liar!" and "Go theeself!" and "Thee's take care not to go!" reached his ear as he left the lifeboat-house with the inspector and the secretary to attend the meeting.

Another snow-squall blew up and the spectators scuttled away into shelter, until the lifeboat was left alone in the road, still high on her carriage, still spirited in outline and proud in her white, red and blue paint, facing the sea, ready to take her buffeting, but buffeted now only by wind and snowflakes and blown spume ; and the men who should have been in her, stood on the lee side of her, cursing.

Though the committee meeting was private, what passed at it soon leaked out. The lifeboat, the chairman said, had done no work for a long time. Because, explained the secretary, there had been fewer wrecks, owing to the decrease in sailing-ships. " She is called," retorted the chairman, " the fishermen's plaything ! " On that account, the committee agreed, subscriptions were falling off. That was the point ; but the inspector's question, whether the lifeboat ought not to be removed, was heartily negatived, for a lifeboat is held to be a profitable attraction to a seaside town. The chairman spoke of mutiny, and wanted to throw out of the boat the whole of the old crew, until the secretary advised him that a new crew might be difficult to obtain. In view of the falling subscriptions, however, the lifeboat had, if possible, to go to sea. It was resolved to use one more effort to bring the men to their senses ; a compromising soul offered to make their pay up to half a sovereign each ; and the meeting broke up.

Down by the lifeboat, beachcombers and loafers, afraid for their shillings, taunted the lifeboatmen with being afraid of the sea, and threw out such other slurs as they dared. Visitors, coming out of shelter after the snow-squall, asked questions and remarked that they thought lifeboats could put to sea in any weather. Useless to explain to them the difficulties of getting off from, and landing on, a lee shore. The crew did not want to explain. They put their heads together, cowering like a herd of bulls yapped at by terriers, and kept to themselves.

"Well, men," said the inspector, returning to the lifeboat-house, "are you going to do your duty?"

"They are all looking at you," added the chairman, with a glance at the row of people in great-coats, mackintoshes, and gloves along the sea-wall.

"Hell about it!" burst out the man whose nickname that was. "Let 'em look. That's the use o'em—looking on. I'll go—an' it's me last time!" He made a move towards the ropes; the rest followed.

"Haul away, boys!" the coxswain shouted.

"We will make your money up to ten shillings," said the compromising soul.

Old Hell-About-It turned round on him. "You keep your b—y money an' take it with you when you dies. Do 'ee value our lives at four shillings more than six? Us don't, n'eet our wives an' chil'ern. A life for a life, us reckons, an' you says a life for ten bob. Come on, chaps! Haul away, an' let's get to sea, out o'it."

Steadily, very steadily, the lifeboat on her carriage was lowered down the beach, until she was poised over the topwash of the surf like a

huge sea-bird springing for flight. Hot words
ran up and down the strings of men on the tackle.
The hawser, which runs from a mast beside the
lifeboat-house out to sea, was slacked, so that the
crew could catch hold in order to haul their boat
out bows-on against the waves. Cork-jacketed,
they climbed in over the gunwale. The bowman
took his place up for'ard ; the coxswain braced
himself to the yoke-lines of his rudder.

Unwilling work, the launch was badly judged.
The boat touched ground, and while the crew
were hauling her off-shore on the hawser, a
still greater wave rose up outside, curled over
cavernously, and broke aboard. Still they hauled
off ; but when the lifeboat shook herself free, it
was seen that the bowman had disappeared. And
on the oars being put out one short, it was
rapidly noised along the sea-wall that another
man must have been injured. The spectators,
being thrilled uncomfortably, now said that the
boat ought never to have been launched.

She kept on her course, at one time lifted high,
a small thing among the crested seas ; at another
time hidden behind a wave. Her stumpy masts
went up ; then her bits of sails. The crowd's
indrawing of breath, every time she disappeared,
was like a groan. Fishermen pointed excitedly at
her, keeping their arms held out, each time they
saw her sheet let fly.

Nevertheless, she beat to windward, sailed
home free, and made a lucky landing among
waves that, had she sheered, would have stove her
in against the beach.

When two bodies were lowered from her and carried up the beach, the old fisherman who had been talking in the lee of the lifeboat-house lifted his voice above the shouting and the din :

"Poor fellows ! " he cried, in a wild, moaning voice. "All for nort ! Two lives lost an' not a life out there to save ! "

They were not dead, however. The bowman was badly bashed and the other man had some limbs broken. They were taken away to the hospital ; and on going to hang up their cork jackets, the remainder of the lifeboatmen, with the exception of the coxswain, who was near his pension age, resigned in a body.

" 'Tain't wuth it ! " they said.

The lifeboat was without a crew.

As if to mock human squabbles, the south-easterly gale blew itself out that evening. The sea calmed down. Boats and gear were got out on the beach ready for the herrings. Then the wind veered, and soon it blew a living gale from the sou'west.

Just before dawn, people in their beds heard the whirring hiss of an ascending rocket. Was it, they wondered before it broke, for the lifeboat or a fire ?

It was for the lifeboat.

Daylight, grey and stormy, revealed, some miles to windward, a coasting schooner in distress, drifting inevitably, with the wind in that quarter, upon the lee shore. A cross-sea was running, steeper and more broken than that of the recent south-easter. " Better to let her run ashore under the cliffs," was the advice of several, "and take them off with the rocket apparatus."

But the lifeboat's men, who belonged to her no longer, would have none of it. "Aye!" they said, "an' let 'em get knocked abroad under they cliffs an' be drowned to a man. Come on! Launch the lifeboat, an' if us fails to take 'em off then you can but try the rocket apparatus afterwards. Come on, coxswain! Haul her out. Thee ca'st hae a volunteer crew this time, skipper, o' men as *bain't* afeard o' the sea."

After that, chaff and work went together.

Leaving their boats and gear for old men, women, and children to drag away from the rising tide, the lifeboatmen put to sea. Cheers sent them off, and, after several hours, much more than cheers welcomed them back. Their long heavy fight to get to the schooner and to take off her crew was fully reported in the newspapers of the day. They saw themselves described as heroes, and though they were not displeased, the remarks they made were bitter.

The same men are still in the lifeboat, except the coxswain (retired) and the broken-limbed man who died of hospital pneumonia, and had a lifeboat funeral to console his wife and children and to add to the attractions of the town. The crew spoke their mind plainly for once when the inspector returned after the wreck and the committee had them before it to pay them. While the chairman was opening the proceedings with a speech about the possibility of overlooking offences due to ignorance, Old Hell-About-It interrupted, addressing himself to the inspector alone : " You'm a seaman, sir—they there ignorant coons bain't— an' you ought to know how us be situated. What's the good o' thiccy chairman blowing his hooter ? The likes o' they don't know what us got to con- tend with, an' if you tells 'em they won't believe 'ee. *I* be willing to join the lifeboat again if *you* askis me. We'm always ready to save life an' us don't want nort for thic ; us never knows when we'm going to be wrecked ourselves in our own little craft ; but us bain't going to risk our lives, what's got wives an' chil'ern depending on us, for to make a spectacle for they to look at, not for six shillings. . . ."

     " Aye ! aye ! "

     " N'eet for ten ! "

ANOTHER PRODIGAL

" KISS me, then."

The Man, evidently a labourer tramping to find work, spoke so to a rough-coated black and tan dog of the lurcher type, that was walking beside him. As they went on down the rough, long hill to Salterport, the dog appeared more graceful, more intelligent, altogether less animal, than his master. Yet the Man also had the picturesque quality of a living being in harmony with its surroundings. The mud on his trousers seemed hardly out of place. His corduroy garments, split here and there, had become earthy in colour ; his discoloured scarf was riding up his throat ; his shirt for want of buttons gaped open over a hairy chest ; and, as visible property, he carried an old greenish-black jacket slung over his shoulder, and some smaller things tied up in a red handkerchief spangled with what once upon a time were white stars. He reminded one of those sculptured figures which scarcely emerge from the rough-hewn marble ; only in his case the marble was like the soil of the fields round about.

Except to pick blackberries from the high tangled hedge, his clumsy tramp was uninterrupted. When he stopped the dog would go on a few yards and stop too. In the way the dog looked round and waited there was something very forbearing, strangely significant.

At a turn in the road they were able to see below them the narrow green valley, made hazy by the creeping smoke from Salterport village, the cornfields and pastures of the heather-capped hills, and the rippled waters of the English Channel. Little white houses were dotted among the trees near the sea. The sun shone on a window as if a star was resting on earth. A dog's barking and a slight murmur uprose.

The Man walked on, merely turning his face towards the village. He ceased, however, his frequent calls to the dog. What he thought, if he did think, there is no telling. Neither sadness, nor joy, nor any other emotion was reflected on his face. The hills were more expressive. But as he lumbered down the last part of the hill, his pace was so much faster that his hob-nails rattled on the flints.

About two hours afterwards, a small group of fishermen stood where the Shore Road merges into the beach.

"Here's a Weary Willie, an' no mistake," said one.

The Man, his dog beside him, was lurching out of a public bar the other side of the road. He made, in as straight a line as possible, for the little group. One or two moved off, but not out of hearing.

He stumbled up to a tall, bearded fisherman and poked him in the chest.

"Yer. D'jou know I?"

"Can't say as I do."

He went on to a second, whom he likewise poked familiarly in the chest.

"Yer. D'jou know I?"

"No. *I* don'."

The second fisherman had flinched and moved back distrustfully. Therefore the Man returned to the first.

Among the fishermen—his loose, torn, dirty yellow corduroys by the side of their muscular forms clad in tight jerseys and navy-blue—he looked a poor figure. But some change had come over his face. Perhaps the drink, which has its use not only in baring the inner man to the world and in showing sepulchres unwhited, but, sometimes, in resuscitating for an hour the finer thoughts of a man, so long and so far trampled beneath as to be usually forgotten—perhaps the drink had done that same treacherous service for him. His skin was no less thick, his beard no less scrubby; but now his eyes, deeply crows-footed, shone fervently, as if they had never been dull and lifeless, mere instruments for seeing the way, as if they had been used to look afar, not merely beneath his feet. Like a man who had never sold but little less than the whole of himself for bread, he glanced around, free-eyed. Drunk —repossessed by a hope, maybe of his boyhood, he looked more of a man than when he was sober.

Again he poked the tall fisherman in the chest, and asked with a tone of cajolery in his voice:
"Yer, you knows I now, don' 'ee?"

"No."

"You 'member Mrs. Fricker?"

"Yes."

"What used to sell winkles on the beach an' mend nets?"

"Yes."

"Well.   She never cheated nobody, did she!"

"No."

"Well.   She was my mother."

"Oh."

"Yer.   D'jou know I now?"

"Yes, I knows 'ee."

"Well, will 'ee sell I yer fish?"

"H'm. . . ."

"Look yer.   You 'member my mother?"

"I've a-told 'ee."

"She was straight, wasn' 'er?   She never did nobody, did 'er?"

"No, her didn'."

"I be her son.   Will 'ee sell I yer fish, what you catches?"

"Us knows who to sell 'em to now—when we got any."

"You won't?"

"No."

"Yer"—each time he said *yer* he accompanied it with a dig in the fisherman's chest—"yer! You 'member my mother, Mrs. Fricker, as was?"

"Yes, yes."

"An' you won't sell I yer fish?"

"No. Us won't."

He turned unsteadily to the dog, put his jacket on the ground and said : " Lay down ! " At once the dog laid his head and forepaws on the jacket. His master and he watched one another.

"Is that right, what he says ? " a bystander inquired of the fishermen.

" Oh, yes. That be right enough. I recognised 'en so soon as he said who he was."

" The dog seems obedient. Is it his own, do you think ? I saw him go to a butcher's in the village and buy it a pound of beefsteak—good meat. He cut it up with his jack-knife and threw it to the dog."

" Did 'ee ? Beefsteak, aye ! "

Once more the tall fisherman was poked in the chest.

" Yer. You knows I now, don' 'ee ? "

" Yes, I know."

" An' you knowed my mother ? "

" Yes."

" Well. Will 'ee sell I yer fish ? "

" No ! " shouted the fisherman.

" Yer won't sell I yer fish ? "

" No," said the fisherman quite gently.

The man waited a moment, hesitating. Then he called the dog from his jacket : " Yer. Come yer, then ! "

The dog drew near him. He dropped his bundle, which some one picked up and handed him, together with the jacket, as if it were time for him to take the hint, and move on.

"Kiss me, then," he said to the dog, which thereupon jumped up and licked his face.

"Yer," he asked again, "you knows I ?"

"Us knows 'ee."

"Well, will 'ee buy my dog ?"

"But us don' want 'en."

"'Er ain't no good, an't got no blood in 'en, no pedeegree ; but 'ee's so good a dog as ever you see'd. Will 'ee buy 'en ? Now !"

"No."

He stopped speaking and looked up the road which runs out of Salterport. He could hardly stand without stepping forward and backward and sideways. For the last time he poked the fisherman in the chest.

"Yer. You *did* know I, didn' 'ee ?"

"Yes, yes, *I* knowed 'ee."

He shouldered his bundle. "Yer, come on !' he called to the dog.

He stumbled up the hill to the westward. The dog ran alongside licking his hand. In a few moments they were both gone out of sight.

"What could us do wi' a dog ?" asked a fisherman.

Nobody replied, and they all remained silent, looking out to sea.

It seemed that they felt a little guilty of something or other.

THE MISSIONER

I

IT was far too hot to do much. Salterport beach looked sleepier, more peaceful, and more contented than usual. On that account, Jabez Jones, a strange lay-missioner, was the more noticeable as he zigzagged across the Front distributing yellow handbills.

For some days the weather-wise had been saying that such a summer was bound to break up with a heavy gale. The trees, a little shrivelled and over-coloured by too much sunshine, dropped now and again a leaf, and rustled as if they were gathering an invisible garment round them. Everything—the sea even—seemed to be pausing and holding its breath. Men stood among their boats as if fixed there. Now they talked in spurts, and now they watched the sails which were planted, as if for ever, on the leaden horizon. The beaching and shoving off of boats looked curiously mechanical in the shimmering light ; it was like a beautifully devised illusion of some far-distant place where great silences swallow up the noise and fuss of mankind. Life seemed all undercurrent, with scarcely a swirl in it.

There appeared to be no good reason why the Salterport fishermen, or even consumptive visitors, should occupy themselves any more than usual with the state of their souls. Yet this fussy little man, from some unrestful city, almost compelled them to receive his yellow sheets of paper. Young men read them, and laughed loudly at their own jokes. Girls took them gladly : they were something fresh. Some visitors graciously acquiesced in Mr. Jones's desire that they should take one. Fishermen, lounging about ashore, after a night's mackerel drifting, gave, as politely requested, their opinion of the weather, were presented with handbills, and swore genially over them. Small children, even, had one for their illiterate little selves, and one to take home to father and mother. Most people smiled at Jabez Jones : he was the sort of man one does smile at. Respectability clothed him hotly. In his all-black clothing, which seemed to be stifling the pink and sandy him, he looked as if he had come from a cooler, murkier climate, or like a bird that wanted to moult and couldn't. Stares received him, but he livened up the beach.

Just before dinner-time he stopped a red-cheeked fair-haired little girl, who was walking down the sunny side of Fore Street with a confidence born of finding it ever the same, and offered her two handbills.

"Now, my little dear, will you have one of these for yourself, and take one home to father and mother ? What is your name, my dear ?"

"Git 'ome an' die, or I'll 'at thee head off ! "

answered the small child, who resented her way
being stopped.

" Do you like sweeties ? " asked Jabez.

She looked very stolidly at him.   Then she
inquired abruptly, with the disconcerting insight
of childhood : " Who be you, man ?   What do
'ee want ? "

" Keep this for yourself, my dear, and take the
other one home to father and mother.   Will you ?
And here's a sweet for you.   There's a good
little girl ! "

She neither said that she would nor that she
wouldn't.   She trotted home to dinner, and Jabez
Jones did the same.

II

" Wants me dinner, Mam ! " cried Polly
Forder, running into a house where, for want of
dwellings handy to the beach, three generations
of Forders still lived under one roof.   Dinner
was just dished up.   Silas Forder, Polly's grandfather, was spread out at one end of the table,
and his best catch, as he called her, now crippled
with rheumatism, was propped up in a high-
backed chair at the other end.   At the sides sat
two of Silas's seven sons (the five others were
away at sea) and the wife of the elder.   Polly's
chair was near her mother's.   The food was
roughly spread, but plentiful.

Conversation would have been freer without
Silas.   He was holding forth on motor-boats,
speaking as he always did when innovations were

in question. " I don't believe in 'em at all. They
costis more. Do 'em catch more fish after the
rate ? 'Tis because 'tis less trouble. They'm
afeard of trouble nowadays, that's what 'tis.
Why, I've a-took fifteen hours rowing in from
the offing, whiting catching ! What's the good
of they there motors, I say, if you bain't no better
off in the end, come sharing-up time ?"

Silas held to his youth in more senses than
one. Though his stubby grey beard and his
thick white hair made him appear venerable, he
still had the upstanding figure of his young days.
But for his greyness, his staider gait and his
weather - wrinkled brown face, he might have
passed for a sturdy man at his bodily best. His
opinions, which were those of his youth—chiefly
negative and concerned with what he didn't believe
in — must have hardened with his bones and
muscles. In his obstinacy there was a touch
of grandeur, as well as of childishness.

And as the father must have been, so now was
the elder of the two sons—a man in every respect
fixed and settled in life.

Jim Forder, the younger son, was the dubious
member of the family. Dark, tall, stooping and
raw-boned, he nevertheless gave the impression
that he had yet to grow in some way. He looked
anywhere, at sea or on land, a little awkward and
out of place, and by some means or other he
managed to spoil the general effect of nearly
everything he did. It was as if some relentless
devil alternately whipped him up and reined him
in. As a boy, his dreams and restlessness had

been a nuisance ; he had been mad to go to sea and had not gone ; he had refused to fight a man one day and had provoked a fight with him the next week ; he had sought heaven and feared hell in two or three religious sects ; and, worst of all, he had fallen headlong in love with several girls, yet still was unmarried. It was all remembered against him. And because, when it was necessary to face danger, he had a habit of gaping for a moment, he was regarded scarcely as a coward—he had proved himself not that—but as a bit soft-like, a mazed-headed article. He constantly annoyed his father because he stuck so firmly to his own opinions, which, as any one could find out by baiting him, swayed and tore like seaweed in a storm.

At the same time, he was liked by all, and all enjoyed fooling him. They even went so far as to feel it easy and natural to admit his goodness of nature. " Jim's often kinder'n *I* should be," his father would say. " But 'er's that curious sometimes. . . . There ! I never could make 'en out. Wants a steady-going sort o' maid, wi' a bit of devil in her, for to take 'en in hand—that's what our Jim wants. But 'er don't stick to the maidens no more than 'er sticks to ort else."

On Polly's arrival with the handbills, both Jim and the old man looked up. " What's got there, Polly ? " demanded Silas.

" Let's look," said Jim, half rising in his place.

" Bring 'em here, Polly," commanded the old man.

Polly obeyed. Jim sat down, and then, on

seeing that there were two handbills, he got up again and took one. Silas read his aloud, holding it at arm's length, and as he went on his anger seemed to be rising, much as Polly's had done with Jabez Jones.

" *Thursday, July the eighteenth*—that's to-day, isn't it ? *At seven p.m., Mister Jabez Jones of Bristol will conduct a meeting*—who's Mr. Jabez Jones of Bristol ? Bristol be big enough for forty Jabez Joneses—*will conduct a meeting on Salterport Beach.*—Us don't want 'en on the beach, bringing all they mischevious chil'ern 'bout by the boats. There won't be a thole-pin nor a footing-stick left ! —*The Word*—what's 'er mean by *the Word*, now ?"

" *His* word, I 'spect," remarked Dick, the elder of the two sons.

" The gospel," put in Jim.   " That's what they call the gospel—the Word."

" Why don' 'en call it that straight out, then ?" growled the old man.   " 'Tisn't proper. Swearing is words, isn't it ?"

Jim flushed and turned to his dinner. His father continued reading.

" *The Word will be preached.   Music.   Hymns. A hearty welcome to all.*

" Umph !   That's it. People as wants summut always says you'm welcome.   *I* shan't be, that I do know. Us don't want none o' they folk to Salterport. Why don' 'em go to church if they wants to go anywhere ? Mr. Jabez Jones ain't wanted hereabout. You see if he don't have to go away again like they there peer-rots [pierrots] last summer !"

"Why for?" asked Jim.

"Because us don't want 'en here. That's why for. The religious peer-rots is worse'n t'other ones, by far. You mind how James Amber's sister went mad? Her wasn't moon-struck. 'Twere worse'n that—religious madness—the sort as never gets no better. I've a-see'd plenty o'it in my time, too, from some of they reg'lar places wi' their hell preachments. This here Mr. Jabez Jones—us got plenty to do wi'out the likes o' he."

"He'll do for Jim," said the elder brother with a teasing laugh.

"Hold thee row!" said Jim uneasily. Such stray hints led often to fierce baitings.

"Hark at 'en!" Dick continued. "*He'll* go, but he's like as if he's got a girl and don't want to walk arm-in-arm 'cept outside the village. Eh, Jim?"

Silas's patience was at an end. "I'd a sight sooner see 'en running after a girl. 'Tis only natural then for to cuddle in a corner. But this here preacher. . . . Look here, Jim; see thee doesn't get mixing up wi' it. Thee mayst go off wi' the Cowfield Chapel folk, but I won't have any one of mine fooling round wi' beach-preachers and such-like; so I tell thee plain. I won't have it in my house, and if you do, you'll shift herefrom, an' pretty quick! Thee's got plenty to do wi'out that, wi' the fish not coming into the bay like they used to do, an' the boat rended in twenty places an' rotten-old. Go'n dry the nets. They'll want barking soon. Only, mind what I says, now. . . ."

Silas when roused was best left to himself. This Jabez Jones he did not trust. He could not get rid of him, and, on account of his own son, he could not ignore him. After Jim had gone out to turn the nets, which were already spread on the beach, it was almost mournfully that Silas said to his daughter-in-law : " I'll be bound he'll go, he's that contrary ! "

III

At seven o'clock, punctually, that evening, Jabez Jones was ready on the beach. About seven o'clock, also, the fishermen began to shove their big boats down to the sea, to hoist their white and brown sails, and to set out for the night's mackerel-drifting. Therefore, although many people were on the Front, they all gazed steadfastly to sea. No one joined in the missioner's weak opening hymn. No one was interested enough to jeer. Small children stood by, looking up into his face. Bigger children stopped a solitary young woman's first whisper of song by bawling out : " Bide quiet, will 'ee, an' let the gen'leman sing." Jabez announced another meeting for the next night at the same time. All, he said, would be welcome.

The following morning brought wind and rain. Jabez, however, was none the less active. He distributed more handbills, posted them up in conspicuous places, and obtained promises of help from a man who had been in the Salvation Army, and one or two others. His failure, moreover,

had raised a laugh, so that many thought it would
be a fine thing to go and see him fail again.
Though the stiff breeze had veered, there was a
heavy swell on, and the sky looked too wild for
mackerel-drifting. A small crowd awaited Jabez
Jones. Jim Forder was not far off, and Silas
himself was within sight, glancing back.

Jabez tripped down the beach, opened out his
portable harmonium, and began to press hymn-
papers into spectators' hands. "The hymns we
shall sing, the hymns we shall sing," he murmured
to each one with a hiss on the s. Then he stood
upright and surveyed his congregation.

The evening was very beautiful—so beautiful
that the earth seemed unearthly. Sea and sky
were beginning to grow pearly. Largish waves,
coming in slantwise, broke on the shore and
continued breaking far along to the eastward.
Each thud and rattle, travelling ceaselessly, died
away in the distance with a sound like the lament
of many spirits, fled from earth and murmuring
an eternal complaint over the restless sea. At
one moment the atmosphere was charged with
their muffled torment, at the next moment imbued
with peace.

In the midst of this scene, Jabez fingered his
wheezy harmonium, and with a worn voice began
to sing by himself :

> "Art thou weary, art thou languid,
> Art thou sore distressed ? . . ."

Slowly he laboured through the seven verses.
His new-found recruits joined in. They sang

more or less together, more or less in tune.
Music. . . . There was no music. But it did
not so strike those who were standing on the
beach ; for hymns, very badly sung, have a
plaintive effect that is mostly lacking in good
sacred music. One by one the listeners seemed
to be overcome by a feeling that they *were* weary
and languid, that they did yearn for rest ; and
before the singing was ended, the Salvation Army
man, some women and girls, and two or three
young men, including Jim Forder, were all uttering,
and in some degree satisfying, their hazy desire
for rest—singing in a wail which baffled faintly
against the noise of the surf, but overcame murder-
ously the lament of the spirits over the sea.

Jabez proceeded to offer up a very long prayer.
The Salvation Army man spoke on the text
" Whoso convinceth me of sin," inviting any of
those present, whose consciences convinced them
of sin, to step forward and testify. Another
hymn followed, and another.

The hymning appealed particularly to Jim,
who, being spiritually a tenderfoot, and ill at ease
in any path, old or new, had sought fresh roads
all the days of his life. He shared the feelings of
those around, but what for them was walking idly,
for him was running the race. As always, when
he was thinking or feeling intensely, he gaped ;
and, unconsciously also, he gradually edged forward
into the centre part of the circle. He was, so to
speak, an idealist without ideals. He stood self-
convicted, not of sins, but of sin. An extraordinary longing—akin to that which causes

F

primitive peoples to worship collectively and to
share their mental troubles—was compelling him
to take all men into his confidence. With hesitation, he stepped still farther forward to testify.
"Dear bretheren . . ." he began. "Dear bretheren
. . ." The new strangeness of the familiar faces,
packed together on the beach, diverted his attention for a moment. He lost grip of what he had
wanted to say. The very desire to testify was
slipping away from him.

After more hesitation, he raised his head,
lowered it, and continued lamely : "When I
came here to-night and heard the message. . . ."

Some one laughed and he stopped again. He
wanted to rebuke the laugher, yet felt that some
sort of acknowledgment was due to Jabez Jones.

A choice was not needed. A strong hand
clutched his arm, and he heard in his father's
angriest voice : "What be you fooling here for ?
I thought I told thee I wouldn't hae it. Damn
it all ! come 'long wi' me, an' us'll settle this. I
bain't so old but I can master you, my lad, an'
that you knows. Come 'long, now ! "

Jim allowed himself to be led from the meeting,
whilst Jabez, who was not without experience of
such awkward moments, called for the hymn,
"Onward ! Christian soldiers."

Lustily they sang now.

Partly because the old man felt he had gone
too far, and partly because he was growing dumb
with anger at having been led into making a show
of himself, he said nothing to Jim all the way
home. But he continued to grasp his arm as if it

had been a heavy oar in a head wind, and the sound of the hymn, borne bodily on the breeze, gave Jim the impression that the whole meeting was turned to watch them, and was singing at him. "And we'll settle this," was still repeating itself in his mind, when, on nearing their door, Silas said abruptly and as if the matter had been already sufficiently discussed : "Now then, you'm not going to do that again, or I'll see 'ee somewhere else."

Jim's answer was to step off in the direction of the meeting.

"Jim!" shouted the old man. "Where's going to ?"

"Where I come'd from."

"I won't have 'ee back 'long with me!"

Jim stood still, and Silas, who by no means wanted a permanent quarrel with one of his boat's crew, changed his tactics. "What do 'ee want to go off there for ?" he asked. "I told 'ee I won't hae it, an' I won't!"

The reply startled him. "What do *you* want, interfering wi' a man's religion ?"

"*I* don't want to interfere wi' no man's religion. But going off to a place like that beats me fair, it do. Never used to be like it. There ain't no good in it."

"There *is* good in it," Jim burst out, "else I shouldn't go, should I ? If 'tisn't nothing to you for to feel Someone's a-watching over you when you'm out to sea, 'tis summut to me. 'Tis ter'ble 'nuff to be drownded—wi'out black sins on your soul."

Religious dispute was beyond Silas. Still determined to have it out with his son, he once more changed his attack.

"Why doesn' learn to swim then?"

It was astute of the old man. Jim had never learnt to swim ; he was one of those who sink like a stone. As an answer to his father's question he began resolutely to walk towards the Shore Road.

"You take heed," shouted Silas. "I won't have 'ee here *and* at thic there beach preaching. So I tell 'ee straight, once an' for all!"

IV

Jim did not go back to the meeting ; he shrank from the laughter and questions, the jokes and slurs, he would have had to face. Instead, he walked westwards along the Front, till he came to the spot where Silas's drifter was hauled up beneath the sea-wall. There, out of habit, he stopped. "I won't stand it! I'll clear out! I'll get away off to the sea!" he exclaimed to himself. He thought with revengeful satisfaction how difficult the old man would find it to get another good hand—a proper fishing chap—for his drifter. And at the same time, without thinking, he jumped down to the beach, and began gathering up the foot of the spread nets, preparatory to heaping them upon hand-barrows for the night. Nevertheless, he fully meant to clear out, although he hardly knew in what way.

Three girls came walking along the Front and

stopped on the wall above him. One of them—
Annie Stowe by name—had been a sweetheart of
Jim's.

In a flash, his question solved itself. Annie
Stowe would do. He had always liked her. He
would clear out. He would marry Annie Stowe
and live in a house of his own, even if it were a
mile on land. "Evening, Annie!" he called up
brightly.

"Good-evening, Jim," she replied, tuning her
voice to something between offended dignity and
a giggle. "Where have 'ee been keeping yourself? Us an't see'd nort of 'ee this long time."

The two other girls sheered off.

"Will 'ee come up 'long for a walk over
Kalecliff, Annie?"

"My senses, Mr. Forder, how suddent, like,
you be!"

"Bide a minute, then, till I've gathered up
this here net. Tide's coming in. . . ."

Annie Stowe was less silly than she sounded.
Jim Forder, the only unmarried young fisherman,
was well known to have a nice little bit put
by—enough to buy a boat and nets of his
own.

At the top of the Kalecliff they sat down in
the long grass that grows on the edge, where the
scents of land and water mingle. High up over
the darkening sea the sound of the surf was weak-
ened to a heaving silence; the noise of the beach
was but a far-away murmur, purified in the sweet
clear air. Jim and Annie Stowe took up their
courting just where they had left it off, a year or

more before. In the darkness they sat with their arms around each other, not speaking very much. On parting, at the house where she worked, Jim asked her to tell him her next night out, and she told him definitely. It was as good as a promise to walk out with him. And his own mind was made up. His father would never give way. Neither would he. For the moment, at all events, he was well pleased with himself.

Next morning at breakfast his brother quizzed him until he was driven to ask : "What be laughing at, then ? "

" Our new beach-preacher, I 'spect."

" I shan't stand it any longer, I tell 'ee ! I'm going to get married and clear out of here."

" Who's that to ? Which o'em is it, I means ? "

" Anyhow, we'm going to keep company—me and Annie Stowe."

" What's that ? " asked Silas, who had been indulging in an old man's table-reverie.

" He's going to marry Annie Stowe and cast off," laughed Dick.

But nothing could have been more likely to make Silas drop the quarrel of the previous evening. " That's better," he said. " Nice handy sort of girl, she ! Her'll keep 'ee away from they there meetings. Her'll want all of her man, I'll warrant. Women is used to their fellows being in public-houses, but they bain't used to 'em being off to meetings."

" I shall go to what meetings I like."

" Will 'ee ! Us'll see. In married life you've

a-got to do what's best to be done, an' that you'll find."

The old man was very cock-sure. Jim himself felt doubtful. It was a point to clear up before-hand.

V

In the evening, the three Forders stood lean-ing over the side of their drifter. After another breezy morning the wind had veered, but not much, and the sea was still running as high as is good for an open boat, however large and sea-worthy. "Pity us an't got a harbour, so's us could use bigger boats," Jim was saying.

"If we'm going, 'tis time for to get ready," said Dick. "What about it, Jim?"

"Don't look very fit, do it?"

"There's mackerel out there," said Silas, "and 'tis just the night for to make a haul. I thought I see'd 'em playing up in the bay this a'ternoon, but couldn't be sure wi' this here lop on."

"That don't say we'm going to get 'em. Most often us don't when they plays up. Besides," added Jim, "'tis Sunday to-morrow, and there won't be no trains if us do."

"Dost want to go to a meeting, then?" said Dick. "Easy git a cart to Exeter if we has a haul. What's say? Be 'ee going?"

Jim still hesitated. He had been examining a bad rend in the bilge. All three knew that the boat was half rotten; Jim had noticed that the rend was opening farther and spreading.

"I'll go meself, if thee doesn't!" exclaimed the old man.

"Who's to prevent a fellow going, if he's minded? *I* didn't say I wouldn't go."

"Come on!" urged Dick. "Haul her down a bit and fill up the ballast-bags. Us can but come home again if 'tisn't fit."

They pushed the boat down over the pebbles, and in a short time shoved off.

Exactly how the accident happened is even now a matter for argument in a place where the accidents of fifty years ago are still recollected and argued over. According to the best account, they shot their nets about a couple of miles out and west, and rode to them for the best part of an hour. Then, as the wind was backing and freshening, they hauled in for only a few dozen mackerel, and up-sailed for home. It was already nearly dark; they had been so late in starting. About a quarter of a mile from shore, with the wind still backing and the sea making, they gybed over the big dipping lugsail. The backstay parted, the heavy mast broke out and came down, the knees of the forethwart gave way, and the boat opened out like an old box. Jim, his brother and the nets were all capsized together into the water. The net rose again near Jim like an evil sea monster, curling about in the waves. He became entangled in it; managed to grasp one of its cork buoys; and at last had time to realise what had happened. To his brother, who was swimming towards him, he shouted hoarsely :

"Go'n get in for a boat. Nobody won't see us here. I've got holt of a buoy. Tide's right. Go on!" And Dick, a strong swimmer, made for land.

Jim was alone, between the swishing water and the darkness. He waited so anxiously, peered so keenly for the boat, when waves lifted him up, that his eyes felt as if they were projecting out of his head, on stalks. They smarted with the salt water till he could keep them neither properly open nor shut. But for being mixed up with the net-buoys he would have sunk.

When the boat arrived, with Dick in it, they found him so blue from the cold, and so exhausted, that they had to lift him aboard and afterwards carry him home. He was beyond answering questions. Silas, more upset than he cared to show, took him upstairs in his arms, gave him brandy, tended him while he was sick, and put him to bed.

For two or three hours Jim remained in a state between waking and sleeping. He mumbled to himself and called out loud from time to time. It seemed as if he was mixing up in his mind the accident and his quarrel with his father. Silas refused to go to bed. "'Tis summut to think about," he said to his daughter-in-law, "that I might ha' losted both they there boys—and all the rest o'em to sea. Take care thy Polly don't go down so near the water, like her do."

Towards morning, however, Jim slept, and did not awaken till Silas came into his room long after daylight. "How do 'ee feel now?" inquired the old man.

"Better. . . . All right. . . ."

"Better'n thee didst, I'll warrant."

"What's the time? Time to get up, is it?"

"You bide there a bit, and I'll bring 'ee up a cup o' tay. What's think about when thee wast hanging on to thic there buoy?"

"Don' know," said Jim. "Wondered how long the boat 'd be, I s'pose. Couldn't help thinking they was a hell of a long time."

"Ah! best thing, I tell 'ee, for to do is to learn to swim like Dick—came in like a steamer, they said, what saw him land—a sight better'n they there meetings. . . . Bide still, now, an' I'll bring 'ee up the tay."

Annie Stowe was downstairs. "Milkman told me he was drownded," she began. "Postman said he wasn't. Is he all right, Mr. Forder? I couldn't but look round and see. People tells up such tales, don' 'em?"

"Jim's all right," replied Silas, "only he's staying up to bed a bit. Here!" he went on, as if a thought had suddenly struck him, "I said as I'd take 'em up a cup o' tay. Do you run up wi' it. I bain't so fond o' stairs. . . ."

"Oh, Mr. Forder!"

"Git along with 'ee! You bain't bashful, be 'ee? You can't see sick people unless you sees 'em in bed. 'Tisn't as if he was all right. . . . Here thee a't; here's his tay."

First of all, Annie Stowe gave Jim his tea in a quite good sick-room manner. Then, with the empty cup in her hand, she stood beside the bed, scarcely knowing what to do or say.

"Be 'ee glad you'm back?" she asked. "What do it seem like to be back again after you'm nearly drownded like you was?"

"'Tis like . . ." said Jim as if he were collecting his thoughts. He put out his hand and pressed her down into the chair at the head of the bed. "'Tis like as if you was woke up, as if you was got proper to heaven, for to be back out o'it an' to find 'tis all the same home here—all o'it just the same!—You'm in the same mind, bain't 'ee, Annie?"

"Same mind as what?"

Jim pulled her head down to him. He didn't seem very weak. . . .

Meanwhile, downstairs, Jabez Jones had knocked at the cottage door to inquire. "Is the poor fellow getting on all right?" he asked Silas. "You don't mind me coming to ask? Can I see him?"

"Hush!" replied Silas impressively. "'Twouldn't do for to wake 'en out o' his sleep afore he wakes natural-like."

"No, certainly not," agreed the missioner.

"So I'll wish you good-morning," concluded Silas; and on getting back to the kitchen he remarked almost gaily to his daughter-in-law: "There's lies an' lies, I reckon; an' I 'llow there's things as a maiden 'll cure quicker an' better'n any parson. I knows it. I've a-proved it."

And apparently he was not far wrong. In the evening Jabez Jones held a fairly successful meeting on the beach, but Jim walked over the Kalecliff with Annie Stowe.

HIS MAJESTY'S MEDAL

I

THE medals were first heard of during a very slack time. With an easterly breeze and a blue sky the sea was at its liveliest and brightest. Swift white-topped waves flashed in the sunlight, as if the waters were flinging themselves up for warmth, and in so venturing were turned to shining snow that melted as quickly. But the racing surf would have swamped or capsized any boat that tried to shove off against it. Nothing at all was doing across beach. Fishermen left their boats and gathered into groups, chatting, joking, recalling old times. Beachcombers hung about near them, on the off-chance of being asked to drink a fore-noon at the "Capstan Bar." When Mr. Elliot—Customs Officer, Registrar, and what not, of the neighbouring harbour-port of Bitcombe—came along the sea-wall on his periodical visit of inspec-tion, it took him half an hour to stroll half-way across, so many men were willing to have a yarn with him.

"Yes," he agreed, "I can see this sort of weather's no good for you men, without a harbour.

Fine sailing breeze outside. . . . Why don't you get them to build you a little harbour ? "

" Harbour—aye ! Nobody ain't going to do nort for the likes o' us. They leaves we to rub along best way us can. Good job we'm used to it."

" It's worth trying for," said the Customs Officer. And then he added very casually, " Is William John Wintle anywhere about ? "

" Bill Wintle ? Why, there he is, down by his boat. Bill ! Bill ! Casn' hear ? Billy Wintle ! You'm wanted."

" All right. Never mind. . . ."

The Customs Officer picked his way down to Bill.

" Not much doing, Mr. Wintle ? " he began.

" Nort 't all."

" You can't get out after them ? . . ."

" I'd get out a'ter 'em if they was there, an' take me chance w'er I got capsized or not. But the mackerel bain't come into the bay. They don't, nowadays, not like I've a-see'd 'em."

" Let me see," remarked the Customs Officer in a disinterested tone, but eyeing his man. " You are William John Wintle, aren't you ! Weren't you in the Royal Naval Reserve for twenty-six years ? "

" Twenty-seven years I was in it, all but a month. You ought to know that, Mr. Elliot, seeing I came down to your office less'n a year ago an' took my discharge an' my fifty-pound gratuity—'stead o' four bob a week after I was sixty, which I mightn't never live to see. I joined early, being a big youngster, bigger'n I be now,

after the rate; put my age on to join, I did;
though I an't never told 'ee thic before. I was
in it 'fore I was married, an' I was married an'
had Harry 'fore I was twenty. Aye! twenty-six
years an' 'leven months, I done; sixteen years a
first-class trained man; an' I come'd down to
Bitcombe to do my drills twenty-four years wi'out
missing once, till Bitcombe battery was shut down.
An' now, time my fifty pounds is gone, which
won't be long, I shan't hae nothing to show for
it all—all the best years o' me life."

"Don't you be too certain," said the Customs
Officer.

"I bain't never certain 'bout nort—'cept what
I knows."

"His Majesty the King," said Mr. Elliot
grandiloquently, "is giving long-service medals
to men of the Royal Naval Reserve who have
completed fifteen years' training with good conduct reports throughout."

"Oh! When did that come out? I an't
heard nort. Long-service medals. . . . Well, I
reckon they ought to give 'em to us same as to
the Navy, what's thrown out slurs at us often
'nuff, for all we could beat 'em at shooting. We
was ready to die for our country, an' they bain't
ready for to do no more. Be 'em?"

"I thought, Mr. Wintle," said Mr. Elliot
(they were treating each other with great respect),
"I thought you were entitled, and Henry Waycott and James Short; so I've brought up three
forms of application with me. Where can you
sign yours?"

"Come in house, sir; come in house."

Bill led the way as if he were hurrying out to sea. "Where's the ink, Missis? Us got some, an't us? Look sharp! I got to 'pply for a medal."

Dinner was waiting on the kitchen table: Bill Wintle's sort are always either early or late for meals. It was shoved aside. Very carefully, with watery ink and one side of the pen-nib, he signed his name in the shaky letters of a man excited and unused to writing. His children swarmed round. "What is it, dad? Tell us. What is it? Dad! dad!"

"Git out the light! The King's going to give me a medal. . . . What's think o' thee ol' dad!"

"A metal! A metal! I'll wear 'en for 'ee, Sundays.—Gie us a penny, dad."

The paper was folded. The Customs Officer was directed to several other Royal Naval Reservists. Bill Wintle got up from his dinner to show his boys a drill now obsolete in the Navy.

For the next few days you could spot the Naval Reservists. In blue guernseys, in patches, in corduroys, and in starch-collar suits, they forgathered as in the old battery days, and talked— talked their way, as often as not, into the "Capstan Bar." Bill Wintle had day-dreams over his meals. "I was thinking about thic medal," he would wake up and say. "His Majesty the King's medal. . . . I wonder w'er *he's* got ort to do wi' it."

His Majesty. . . . It seemed as if the King

was brought nearer ; as if we were living, so to
speak, in the purlieus of the Court ; or, better, as
if we had our harbour, and the Royal Yacht in it.

II

For a couple of months nothing more was
heard. The medals hung in men's thoughts like
doubtful light at sea. Mr. Elliot on his next
visit said that the applications had been duly sent
in ; that a man's having taken his discharge some
years ago made no difference, provided—and so
forth. Age-yellowed parchment papers and dis-
charges of the old Preventive Men, who existed
before the Coastguards, were brought to light.
They were no good. "An' t'other's bain't no
good nuther, seems so. Why an't us heard
nort ?"

It was in vain to point out that Government
offices work slowly, and that it takes time to strike
medals with the men's names upon them.

"Ah !" said Bill Wintle, after a tiring night
at sea. "Ah ! they kicked up a buzz about they
there medals for some purpose o' their own—to
find 'ee out, where you lives to, p'raps, or what
your conduct was ; an' now they bain't going to
trouble no more about it. That's how they serves
'ee, I tell 'ee ; always was, an' always 'twill be."

But a day came when the Customs Officer was
able to say that a batch of medals had arrived
for Bitcombe men, but none, as yet, for ours.
"They're to be presented by the Commander
himself in full uniform, with as much ceremony

G

as possible—those are the Admiralty's instructions."

" Then the King ain't going to pin 'em on, that's certain sure. . . ."

We read an account of it in the newspaper. Medals were presented, too, at Fowey, at Falmouth, at Bideford, at Appledore, at Plymouth. " It may be," said some of us, without much believing it, " that they are going in alphabetical order. Appledore, Bideford, Fowey, Falmouth—all at the beginning of the alphabet."

" Then how about Plymouth ? They got 'em there."

Old Tommy Yabsey, who has had three sons in the Navy, and is quickly jealous on its behalf, wanted to know why, for God's sake, the Royal Naval Reservists should have medals, unless they did something. " You were paid, wasn't 'ee ? " he asked. " And you drew your retainers, didn't 'ee ? "

" Well, us did our drills, didn' us ? "

" You never fought. You was never aboard a battleship ! "

" We was trained men, most o'us, ready to be called up if us was wanted ; an' that's more'n you ever was. *Us* could ha' fought 'long wi' the best o'em."

" Now, just you tell I this," said Tommy, bobbing his head. " If you'm so much use as you says you be, why for did 'em do away with Bitcombe battery ?—Didn' want 'ee ! No use for 'ee ! "

His age protected him. "Us don' know for sure yet," was the mild answer, " w'er us be going to get any medals or no. P'raps us bain't, an' I'm sure I don't much care."

Anticipation, in fact, was growing stale. When the Customs Officer announced that the medals had really come, and that Bill Wintle, Harry Waycott, and Tipsey Short were to go down to Bitcombe by an early train, and walk straight to the Customs Office, Bill asked in confirmation of his misgivings : " I s'pose there ain't nort attached to 'em—no gratuity like ?"

And when the Customs Officer was gone along, he burst forth : "Then what the hell's the good o'em ! They bain't money. An' thee casn't pawn 'em. Better to have give'd us a watch. Thee cou'st ha' told the time wi' thic out to sea. But these here medals. . . . I reckon 'tis a thing got up for pleasing them as is fools enough to be pleased wi' 'em. The likes o'us does the fighting, an' they gives us toys. Why couldn' 'em send the medals up to us, 'stead o' wanting us to go to Bitcombe for 'em ? 'Tis half a day's work lost : I s'pose they sort don't take no heed o' thic. I don' know w'er I shall trouble to go down for mine or not."

On the morning itself he started for the station, fresh-shaven, though it was not his day, and in his best clothes, but with a jersey, the fisherman's uniform, underneath ; and his last words were : " I reckon they might ha' paid a chap's expenses. 'Tis money spent, what you've had to dig out for hard 'nuff. Thee casn't go down to Bitcombe

wi'out meeting an old friend or two, an' thee
casn't see 'em wi'out asking o'em to hae a drink ;
an' five shillings don't go far when you gets in wi'
a lot o' chaps on an occasion like.　I shall be back
by the mid-day train.　I bain't going to stay down
there an' make a fuddle o'it.　'Tain't wuth it ! "

But his step was springy, and in his bearing
there was as much of the drilled man as the labour
of fishing had left to him.

III

" Where's Bill ?　Is 'er home eet ?　What
train's 'er coming by ? "

" The mid-day train, he said, for certain."

" Ah ! you won't see nort o' he till t'night,
if thee dost then.　He's out for to make a day
o'it, Bill is ! "

Towards the end of the afternoon, however,
a small blue figure wandered to the Front, aim-
lessly, as if the light of the sea was rather dazzling.
It was Bill right enough ; but shrunken and bent,
so that his coat flapped on him.　His eyes were
bright and a little staring.　His face, poked out
from his shoulders, was become in an hour or two
pinched, wizened.　In the morning a drilled man
had started.　In the afternoon there came back
a man past it.　It was as if the silver medal hanging on his jersey had marked off suddenly the
end of youth and the beginning of age.　" Done
for now ! " it seemed to say, with a grim waggle.

" I been home a couple of hours—I didn't
come straight down from station," he was explain-

ing. "Got in up-street 'long wi' ol' Tommy
Yabsey an' one or two more o'em. *Their* blasted
chawl! Wanted to know why *us* was entitled to
medals. . . . As if us hadn't done nort for 'em!
I'd ha' slatted 'en, I'd ha' slatted 'en through the
window if 'twasn't for him being old! That's
how they ol' men gets at 'ee, I tell 'ee, an' takes
the youth out o'ee, 'cause they'm jealous o'it;
an' thee casn't do nort. . . ."

"Never mind, Bill; you've done your service,
and they haven't. . . ."

"They don't know nort about it, what 'tis
like; they an't done nort theirselves, an' they
throws out their slurs at them as have. I got
summut to wear on me chest now for to show
I been through it."

"Did the Commander pin them on?"

"Commander—no! *'Twas* a hole-an'-corner
turn-out. Us only went to a room in the Customs
Office, an' a chap what wasn't no better than the
likes o' ourselves pinned 'em on an' chattered 's if
we was kids. Miz-mazed affair, I call it. Why
couldn' 'em ha' bringed they medals up here an'
give'd 'em away where anybody could see? Let
Tommy Yabsey an' they sort know what we *was*
entitled to. See us hae it, too, proper like.

"Come over an' hae a drink," he continued.
"Come on! Won' 'ee? What's say? Had
'nuff? *I* an't had 'nuff. 'Twasn't wuth a fuddle,
this day's turn-out.—Well, if thee wousn't hae it.
. . . I an't got but a penny left. I was going to
chalk a drink up for 'ee, what I an't never done in
me life before. . . ."

A child came out and took his hand. "Dad, dad! Mother says tea's ready."

"Tay! Who wants tay? All right. I'm coming. P'raps a cup o' tay'll do me good."

He fingered the medal on his chest. "I an't been in to show *her* eet."

In house, a wise old woman who was present said : "Ah! ah! ah! Can see where they been to! Don't thee say nort. Let 'en sleep. That's best. I reckon they'm very good boys for to come home so early. Blow'd if *I* would! Be 'ee turned teetotal, William John?"

" 'Twarn't wuth it," said Bill, already nodding over his tea.

During the evening a knot of men waited outside, opposite Bill's house, like a troop of cats at a mouse-hole. Some may have thought drinks round were due ; others, being teetotalers, can have wanted only to satisfy their curiosity. But they had to wait, and to go away unsatisfied. Bill was asleep, curled up in the arm-chair, just as his children curl up in it when they are tired and ready for bed. On his face was a young peacefulness like theirs ; on his chest the medal of long service done.

And there he slept, breathing slowly, so that the medal flashed in a ray of sunlight as it rose and fell, till he had to be awakened because it was time to go mackerel-drifting. Full of complaints, dazed and stiff, he was rowed off to the drifter at her anchorage. Having clambered aboard, he felt in all his pockets. "Where's his Majesty's medal!" he said, with half a laugh. "Must ha' lef' it in house, I s'pose. I meant to bring he out an' look at 'en from time to time."

Sail was set—the big white dipping lug. Bird-like on the darkening water, the drifter beat out to sea against a short southerly chop. Night closed down. Nets must have been quickly shot, for soon the drifters' riding lights began to twinkle through the thick darkness over the water.

The great day was over ; Bill Wintle was safe at sea. Out there, I knew, lying in the open boat and full of pain, he was trying hard to sleep. And I knew, too, the cruel strain it would be, hauling in a fleet of nets against the southerly chop—haul, haul, haul, three-quarters of a mile of head-rope and net, letting slip a fathom and dragging it in again, picking out the meshed-up fish, for three or four hours, cold and sweating at once. That, and the twenty-seven years' service done, and the sleeping face in the chair, and the under-lying, the childlike, the almost absurd innocence of it all—those were the things that mattered, that could not be gainsaid.

AN UNOFFICIAL DIVORCE

"The parson hisself has been at my poor missis to-day. Somebody's been chattering to him, seems so."

Tom Gillard spoke sorrowfully and turned his face away to seaward. With his huge mottled hands gripping the oars as if they had grown there, but hardly a movement of his long lean body, the rowing muscles of which tightened and slackened visibly beneath his jersey, he continued paddling along ; for had the boat stopped way the pollack lines that we were trailing would have sunk to the bottom, and our rubber worm-baits would have hooked themselves into the oar-weed on the dark rocks below. In the growing dusk, the red cliffs, about half a mile to the inside of us, changed shade by shade to black. Smoothed in outline by the twilight, all their jaggedness gone, they appeared to be gradually sinking into the sea. We could hear the lazy surf swishing among the boulders along-shore ; and from time to time gulls flew off their nests, screeching wildly, and towered into the setting sunlight above, then glided in narrowing circles back to their cliff ledges. The spaciousness of the wild dim sea swallowed up every noise.

Sound did but intensify the silence ; and in that
silence Tom's serious voice—the measured re-
pressed voice of a man who has an interior pain,
whether physical or mental, and is afraid to dis-
turb it by breathing deeply—seemed to spread out
from him and to be filling all the vast empty air
with indefinable trouble.

I had asked him, "How is your wife?" and
he had replied unawares: "My wife or my
missis, which d'you mean?"

The Mrs. Gillard, I said, whom I had so often
seen sewing in the doorway of his cottage. She
could neither walk much nor stand for long, that I
knew ; and her patient contented face, with its
expression of timidity when she looked up to pass
the time of day, had always struck me.

"Why, sir," Tom explained with an intimate
bitter laugh. "That ain't my wife. I wish her
was. That's my missis."

"What on earth d'you mean?"

"Well. . . ."

At that point he had made the remark about
the clergyman. After rowing awhile with his head
turned away, he fixed his eyes on me as a child
might—curiously deep-set eyes he has, sleepy yet
sleepless—and said :

"Well, you : you'm sure to hear something
sooner or later. 'Tis a mazed turn-out, and if I
don't tell you how it came to be what 'tis, you'll
be thinking there's a lot of harm in me, which
there isn't. They always says, 'There ain't no
harm in Tom Gillard.' I've heard 'em myself;
though, mind you, I've done harm in my time when

I've been roused to it, and I've been roused to it sure enough. You knows me ; you've been to sea with me all times and weathers. . . .

" 'Twas like this : when my brother, Harry, and me lived 'long with Father in the little cottage where Harry lives now, opposite mine, we was after two maidens, both of 'em then so nice girls as could be, and one of 'em a clipper to look at. That was Mary, my girl, and she was nice with it too, not like some o' they smart girls. The other one, Emily—Harry's maid—she was't so much to look at ; her had bad teeth, so that her whistled sometimes in speaking ; but she was a masterpiece at cooking, and gentry would come begging of her to go up to their houses and cook for 'em when they had something special on. Both the maidens had a habit of coming down to Father's house evening times, and Emily, her'd cook up something for supper, saying she didn't see why *we* shouldn't have supper parties so well as likes o' gentry. Not that Father'd ever eat her dishes. He'd prefer what he'd been used to, and I should the same now ; but, you see, we was courting then and everything was what we thought 'twas. Those days, Father used to have a couple of big, old-fashioned armchairs, more like settles they was, one on each side of the fireplace. There we'd sit, Mary in the chair 'long with me, and Emily on Harry's lap, and we'd sing songs and be so jolly as you like. Harry, he used to make jokes and play round, specially when he'd had a pint or so of cider or a drop of summut short (only he didn't drink that in front of Father), and he'd say things

about when he should be married to Emily, what
he'd do, till we'd split our sides laughing, and
Father'd chuckle and cough, and let his pipe drop
out of his mouth and smash on the stones, and
then wish we was all o' us married out the way.
Half-past nine, Father'd say 'twas time for everybody, what wasn't to sea, to be abed. (Harry and
me was working lobster-pots at the time and
didn't go to sea by night.)   We'd turn outdoors.
Harry and Emily, they'd go into one dark lew
corner of the lane, and me and Mary into t'other ;
and there we'd stand, very close together, till 'twas
time for the maidens to be getting home—aye !
and more than time very often.   Kiss-kiss Lane
they calls it to this day, and 'twas only our goings-
on, I reckon, what give'd it that name. "

Tom's face softened and brightened at the
recollection.   He rowed faster—too fast for pollack.

"You an't got a maid yet, have 'ee ? " he went
on.   "You'll know what I'm talking 'bout some
day, unless you acts like gentry and don't closen
to 'em afore you marries. Come to it, though,
my brother Harry didn't marry Emily and Mary
didn't marry me. She married Harry. "

"She didn't throw you up for Harry, did she ? "
I asked, comparing the two brothers : Harry who
still bears himself like a drilled man, somewhat
gone to pieces, whereas Tom has always been fit ;
and, though his powerful shoulders make him, like
most fishermen, appear to stoop, he has the sea's
strength, an entirely natural vigour, plain all over
him.

" She didn't throw me up," he said, " and yet in a manner of speaking she did. A lady what come'd down from London, thinking she'd look nice in a drawing-room, I s'pose, handing cups round, took her away there. She'd have looked better 'long with me. I was a smart young chap then ; didn't wear none of these patches and polished my boots every morning, whether I'd been to sea or not. I tried to persuade Mary from it, but 'twas high wages offered her and a nice enough lady, and Mary didn't want to get married till she had something saved up for to make her home all shipshape like. We quarrelled over it, I don't deny. ' Mary,' I tells her, ' if you goes up there you'm so good as losted to me.'

" ' Tim,' her says, ' if I can't bring nothing to thee, I wouldn't find thee.'

" Her's told me since that 'twas her pride in me made her say it, but I didn't take it that way then. I wouldn't wish her ' Good-bye,' and they told me afterwards that her cried bitter when her didn't see me first starting off, and couldn't find me up to station neither.

" About that time Harry took and joined the Navy, saying there wasn't no prospect for a man hereabout ; and them two quarrelled worse'n us did. ' I bain't going to share my man with no Queen,' her said. ' The Queen can hae 'en and keep 'en.' Her made a proper scene, seeing of 'en off, called him all the names in creation, and had to be brought back in a cab. And when Harry came home on leave in his uniform—that's

what makes it up wi' most maidens—her told
him he could go back to his Queen or go to hell,
didn't matter which to her; and he did go—to
both, poor fellow!

"So Emily and me was left at home together.
I don't say her set her cap at me, though they did
tell of it and to my face.   Father was getting very
shaky—he'd a-worked hard in his time, the Ol'
Man had.   Emily used to come down to our
house and cook 'en up tasty slops and suchlike.
He had to eat they 'cause he couldn't stomach no
other.   Then we'd sit together watching him off
to sleep on account of his wandering in his mind
and thinking the boat was runned ashore or nets
was losted or 'twas time to take a reef in the sail.
He'd seen some turn-outs to sea, the Ol' Man
had.   Then, when we was sitting there by the
light of the lamp outside Father's window. . . .
Lord! what is it to slip your arm round a
maiden's waist?   'Tis only natural when you'm
up for it.   We was young things, in the pride of
our blood.   And Father, he was fond of her too,
and said he'd like one of his sons to be married
afore he packed up.   We fixed it together, me
forgetting Mary and her forgetting Harry—for
which we all had to do our punishment afterwards,
I reckon.   Young people an't got long memories,
and all the same they have; only it sinks down
under so that they forgets for a time, and then,
one day, summut or other turns up and it all
comes back to 'em, splashing on the top like a
school of mackerel.

"Proper fine wedding 'twas, and when we was

come home and unlocked the door of the cottage I'd took, opposite Father's, and lighted up, I thought to myself there never wasn't nothing like getting married ; for all Father's brother, what had come down in his boat to the wedding from up along, had been saying as we were putting to sea wi' too much sail up, and talked about new boats leaking. Always did croak, Uncle Henry Gillard.

"Mind you, I don't say 'twas altogether Emily's fault. Soon after we was married, I losted all my lobster-pots in the same gale what washed down Outer Gull Rock, and I had to go mate to another man mackerel and herring drifting. Emily, then, was that lonely and anxious when I was to sea by night. . . . And Father, he wasn't satisfied with me being in another house, and he got somebody to write and tell Harry that if he'd come home again Father'd buy 'en out of the Service, which isn't often a good thing for a chap once he's there. Us didn't know the Ol' Man had the money ; but he had, seems so, put away upstairs. Mostly you'll find the Navy is either the making or the ruin of a young man ; and 'twas the ruin of Harry. If he'd stayed at home and married Emily hisself . . . I could have waited for Mary. He was one of them jolly happy-go-lucky sort o' fellows what goes on the spree, and breaks their leave if they'm minded to, and answers back their officers for the sake of talking, not meaning any harm. Consequence was—though there wasn't a smarter man in his ship, I've heard say—he was always in trouble if he wasn't right in chokey, and he got disrated, and that took the heart out o'en for getting on in the Service.   He was glad 'nuff to come out.

" Soon afterwards Mary come home from London so pale as if her'd been wished [bewitched], and they two reg'lar flew to each other, Harry telling everybody : ' Exchange ain't no robbery.   Blast thic b—y Tom ! '   For he wasn't pleased, and he didn't want her, not in his heart.   The night they was married, Mary took 'en home drunk to Father's house where they was to live ; which wasn't nothing strange, for if you can't have a bust when you'm married, when can 'ee ?   But with them 'twas a foresight of what was to come.

" All the while, things had been going wrong 'long with us over the way, and as I've a-told 'ee, 'twasn't altogether Emily's fault.   Two herring seasons and the mackerel between 'em was all a total failure, and we was on our hoppers.   That took the heart out of Emily : her'd always worked among plenty in gentry's houses.   I carried her in all the money I could pick up, which wasn't much, and with the weariness of it her let things go all to pieces.   Her'd scarcely do her washing, and her didn't trouble to cook ; sent out for something when her could.   ' Why, Emily,' I'd say, ' what's become of the money I've a-brought thee in ? '

" ' Gone towards the rent,' her'd say, and I didn't know no other then.

" ' But,' I says, thinking to give her some

encouragement, ' I thought you was cook enough to do ort wi' nort.'

" ' Cook ! ' her slats back at me. ' *Cook !* Do 'ee think I married you for to be a cook ? I married you for to get away out o'it.'

" I didn't say no more. But I found where what I did bring in was going to. Her was drinking of it. Her used to go round to the pub a dozen times of an evening, when I was out to sea, after three-pen'orth of heartsease, her'd call it. And her didn't have no child neither. . . .

" Aye ! I tell thee—you there—'tis a terrible thing to get home from sea in the night or the chill of the morning, when you an't catched nort, wet through, perished with cold, and tired out with hauling in the nets ; and to find your house all up and down ; no fire, and nothing to eat, let alone ready, and no dry clothes to put on ; nothing at all to a man's comfort ; and your wife snoring, red in the face or else so pale as death, flinged on the bed if her's got so far. Tires a man out. Tires him out, it do, body and soul. I wasn't fit for to go to sea, and they know'd it, too, all across beach. I'd go to sleep standing. I couldn't see to mend the nets, which was my job. The meshes o'em mazed me.

" For all that, I didn't hit her, nor knock her about, not then. Pity I hadn't, p'raps. I turned religious for a time, thinking to bring her into better ways ; but when I mentioned anything religious to her, her'd curse me till her was out of breath, and her'd say : ' Where is thic God o'

thine? Where is He? You've a-found 'En, hast?
Bain't He God enough for to find me wi'out help
from the likes o' you? Has He put fish into thy
fleet o' nets? Five dozen, seven dozen, half a
hundred! Thee hasn't catched a thousand to
once all this year. You don't go where they be
to is my belief; 'fraid of having to row in if the
wind drops. Lazy! Thy God! He've a-laid
a curse on 'ee an' you'm a-creeping up to 'En.
Why dostn't bring 'En along instead o' chattering
'bout 'En? He won't come. Thee't under a
curse, thee a't!'

"Her wouldn't have spoken like that if her
hadn't been half seas over.

"'Twas no good, not religion; I *was* like
under a curse; and I tries buying in the bread
and things myself, without giving her the money
to spend. One night when we was driven in early
from sea by dirty weather, afore us could shoot
out nets, I buys two loaves, not having had a
mouthful to eat since breakfast, and takes 'em in
house and lays 'em on the table. There wasn't
no lamp, only a candle-end. Her hadn't got the
oil I gave her money for.

"At sight of they loaves her flared up.
'Do 'ee think you'm going to trick me by
laying out your money yourself,' her screamed.
'Take your loaves. Take 'em! Eat 'em outside!'

"And with the same, her takes 'em up and
chucks 'em at the window.

"Thinking to save the window, I catches hold
of her.

H

"'Murder, murder, murder!' her screeches. 'Murder! Murder!' like a poll-parrot.

"'Shut up!' I says. 'Shut thee maw!' And when I feels her struggling under me. . . ."

Tom had taken in his oars, regardless of the pollack lines. "When I feels her struggling under my hands," he went on, gripping at the air, "summut rose up in me and I could have killed her there where us scrawled. I swore. I cursed. I hit. I bit my tongue, I did; and then, suddenly, something came into me—fear o' myself, 'twas like—and I flings her to t'other end of the kitchen; when who should walk in but Father, that hadn't been off his bed for months. All of a shake, he was, and not dressed neither.

"'You so well as they!' he said. ''Tis bad enough over our way. They think I don't know it, but I do. And you'm worse. You—you—you—you—you. . . .' he bubbles, like, and then goes off into a mumble, twistis up, and falls. 'Twas a stroke! I took 'en back and put 'en to bed, and he never rose therefrom till he was carried out on his last cruise.

"Emily, her was like a beat dog, that night, showing the whites of her eyes. Her'd always looked up to Father, her had, through it all. I told her her'd so good as killed the Ol' Man, thinking 'twould prove a warning to her. And it did frighten her—frightened her further into it. Her didn't care for nothing no longer. Her said her didn't.

"After the Ol' Man was put down under,

things got worse over opposite. Harry'd got
work up on land—twenty-two shillings a week,
which is enough for a man like he wi' no chil'ern,
and Mary, too, knowing how to lay it out to
advantage. But he'd took to going out all
evenings, and by'm-bye they told him at the
pubs they didn't want him there, because direc'ly
he'd got a drop in him—didn't take much—he'd
start fighting, and he'd come home like it. Bit
of a sunstroke 'twas, while he was in the Navy, is
my belief.

"Our two cottages was 'xactly opposite, like
they be now, and Mary, as her've told me since,
used to leave the blind up when her was there
alone so that I could see in and be company, like,
for her. But when Harry did come home like it,
her'd know what was coming, and her'd try to get
to the window for to draw the blind down, him
trying to prevent her. I've a-heard 'en hit her
after 'twas down—softy thumps—you knows the
sound. 'Let 'em all see what sort of wife you
be to a man,' he'd say. 'Let Tom there see.
Staring wi' your gert saucer-eyes an' saying nort,
blast you!' And then, as I say, he'd hit. What
could I do? They was man and wife; and Mary,
her never complained nor cried out. I was never
free from wondering what was going on behind
thic dirty yellow blind; I'd hear what wasn't to
be heard, like a man do when his ears be on the
stretch.

"One night her did cry out—a little sort of
scream, squeezed out o' her, like. All the life o'
me seemed to stop. Froze me towards Emily

more'n towards Harry—turned me right against
her—'cause I knowed 'twas her started things
going wrong. I'd be took all of a shiver if her
even touched me, accidental like. Distance gives
enchantment, they do say, but when I was away
from her—even to sea, where you thinks kindly
of them you've left behind, if ever you do—when
I was away from her I hated her more than when
I was by. And that's the turning-point, I reckon,
between love and hate, come you'm like that.
Not that I didn't pity her, too, when I see'd what
her was sinked to.

"Her began selling the furniture till going
into my house was like going to sea in a boat
what's rotted on the beach and all its gear been
stolen. If her didn't get money that way, her
lyed abed, and didn't trouble even to get food for
herself, let 'lone me. There her'd stay until the
evening, and if I tried to get her out of it . . .
Lord! you should have see'd. 'Twasn't what
her said: 'twas how her looked, lying there,
poking her head out o' the sheets.

"At last, being mazed with it all, I did the
wicked thing I did do. Just afore Christmas, us
had a good catch of herrings which fetched a good
price. Out of that money, I bought a dozen
bottles of brandy, and I took 'em in house to her,
saying: 'Here's a Christmas present for 'ee,
Emily. I thought I'd get 'ee something as
maybe you'd enjoy.'

"P'raps 'twas my tone of voice; p'raps 'twas
casting out that slur about enjoying of it. I
didn't ought to have said it, not if I wanted to

carry the job through proper; I ought to have
said they was for my medicine, or I was to keep
'em for somebody.   Then her'd have tackled 'em
right enough.   As 'twas:

"'What is it?' her asked.

"''Tis brandy,' says I, 'for a Christmas present
for 'ee.'

"'What be you giving me a present for?'

"'To please 'ee, 'cause 'tis Christmas.'

"'You lie!   You lie!' her said quite quiet,
and as might be out of breath. 'You've a-tried
to murder me, and now you think to make me
kill myself, or else to have me put away.   That's
it.   D'you think I can't see your move?'

"And then her began to carry on and screech.
Her took up the bottles in her hand and one by
one her bashed 'em on the floor.   The tenth or
'leventh, I can't be sure which, hit the candle
over, what was standing in a patch of grease on
the corner of the table.   And time I lighted a
match, there her was—there her was, scrawling on
the floor, wi' her feet sticking out of her skirts,
licking of it up.   The smell o'it fetched her.   I
didn't try to stop her.   I was like paralysed.
That night I carried her up to her bed.   I was
gentle with her, awful gentle. . . .

"Howsbe-ever, it all come'd to a head suddently and very soon.   After he was turned out
of the pubs—policeman gave 'en the tip not to
force his way in—Harry used to have his whack
sitting at home.   He wouldn't go to the jug and
bottle counter hisself; his pride wouldn't let 'en
to.   Mary wouldn't go neither, and do what he

would he couldn't force her. So he used to get
Emily to fetch it for him, and then they'd sit
together drinking of it—Mary looking on and
them casting out slurs at her.

"One night I was watching across from my
house, like I used to, and I see'd Emily go in
house with a quart in one of Father's old jugs,
what was worth some money, a gen'leman said
once. Then I see'd Mary try to take it from her.
'Twas upset and broke, Father's jug. A scuffle
there was. I heard Mary cry out—hurted—and
I couldn't see her standing up no more.

"With that, I rushes across, burstis open the
door ; and there was Mary laying across the floor
in a faint, them jeering at her. Right in front of
'em—seeing me, they'd stumbled together into
one of Father's big armchairs—right in front of
'em, I kneeled down in a terror and took Mary up
into my arms. And I kissed her again, after all
those years.

"But I misdoubt they saw that. 'Twasn't
their first quart, and they was dazed. 'Twas
some time I must have been reviving her, and time
I had, they was falled asleep, gone stupid like.

"'Come with me into my house, Mary,' I
says. ' 'Tisn't fit for 'ee here if they wakes up.
Come 'long with me,' not intending to do more
than look after her for the time.

"With the same, I takes her into my house
and 'cause 'twasn't fit for to take nobody into, I
half carries her up into my room, what I used to
look after myself and lock up when I went out.
'Twas the only fitty room in the house. I laid

her on my bed—her ankle was hurted, though disease didn't set in till afterwards—and her burst out sobbing more than ever her'd cried with Harry. Her sobbed and sobbed, and I did try to comfort her.

"And it all come'd on me clear while I was sitting there a-stroking her hand, like so, and her was sobbing herself out. 'Twasn't the drink; that only followed; and, mind you, I've see'd far worse misery than ours, only not so showy, wi'out any drink at all. The misery ain't in what shows. The fault was further back than that. 'Twas me and Harry having our wrong maidens. That's where the fault was. Aye! I see'd it plain. . . .

"'Mary,' I says, without reckoning on consequences, nor how us would manage, nor what should happen. 'Mary,' I says, 'will 'ee stay 'long with me?'

"'Tim!' her cries. 'Timmy, boy!' And her clinged to me; clinged to me, her did; buried her face in me jersey. . . .

"Oh, I tell you, 'twas so natural like, her coming to me—so natural as that a breeze should come and ruffle the water. We'd a-courted, you see, and kept company years before. 'Twas only like going back, like coming ashore from sea. 'Twas only joining the two ends of a parted hawser.

"I wasn't ashamed of Mary coming with me, no more than you might be for falling asleep or waking up. Don't 'ee think that. Why for should I be? But next morning I'd got to face Emily and my brother Harry, and I didn't know what to do, whether to lie to 'em or not. Only walking across the lane, I thought of a hundred things as might happen, and just what I didn't dare think of did happen. For there they was, still asleep in Father's armchair with their arms around each other and their faces bent down touching. Emily stirred first.

"'He's come for to murder me,' her screams. 'He've a-tried to do it, and now he will. Harry! Harry! Keep me from 'en!' her cries.

"'Be 'ee coming out o' this?' I asks, more for the sake of saying something than ort else.

"'Harry, Harry!' her goes on crying, shrinking back. Her was genuine afraid, if ever I've see'd her.

"'What about Mary?' I asks.

"'Thee's took her away and thee ca'st keep her, Tom,' my brother Harry says. 'I don't want her staring at me no more wi' her eyes. I won't hae her. This here's my girl. Always was. Thee hasn't made much o' her, thee hasn't. . . .'

"Which was true enough.

"Appears they'd come to some agreement together in the night. We didn't; not Harry and me; us simply followed on. When I got back in house, Mary was getting me a bit of breakfast as if her'd always been there, only 'twouldn't have been like 'twas if her had. So us went on as we was; and that's how 'tis my missis isn't my wife. Her's my brother Harry's wife. And his missis is my wife that was."

"What are they doing?" I inquired. "Do they get on all right?"

"They rubs along," Tom replied. "They'm better than they was. You'll generally find, when drunkards comes together, either they urges each other on, or else they holds each other back, knowing the ways of it. *They* wouldn't change. They said so the night my Mary went across when they all thought Emily was dying with her first. That's when they made it up.

"Aye! 'tis a nice little home I got now, and when I gets in from sea there's dry sticks by the fire, and tea in the pot, and cups put ready on the table; and Mary, her always wakes up for to ask me what we've a-catched. Oftentimes out to sea I says, 'Let's haul the nets aboard and get in out o'it,' when before I should have asked my mate, if he'd a-proposed it, whether we was fishing or on a pleasure trip. Hours I've a-kept 'en out there 'cause I wouldn't go home; and now 'tis all the t'other way about.

"Lord bless 'ee! we'm so happy together as the day is long, 'cepting when anybody troubles my missis with chatter, which they don't often now, for they sees that the proof o' the pudding's in the eating.

"Thic clergyman, to-day, he come'd down and spinned up a yarn, saying he wouldn't have us to Communion, which didn't trouble my missis, 'cause her don't concern herself with it, and her told 'en so. Then he said as we was living in sin, and how us should be lost everlastingly if us didn't repent and separate. Repent. . . . Aye! when the time comes. We'm none o' us perfect, and most o' us be drove. But separate. . . .

Us won't do it, and I'll tell 'en so if I sees 'en. That *would* be sin to take and go back as we was.

"Better to reel up they pollack lines. Baits be losted, I 'spect."

It was dark, but for the greenish after-glow in the northern sky. Tom took up the oars; laid them down again; leaned forward and put his hand on my arm. "It has turned out for the best in this world," he said impressively. "That I'm sure. But how about the next? There's Mary. . . . Thic parson. . . . 'Tis all right in this world, us knows, but *what about the next?*"

"Nobody can tell," I said. "But," I added, "it seems to me simply an unofficial divorce."

"That's it! You've said it!" shouted Tom, urging the boat forward with his most powerful stroke, swinging to it, and talking in spurts. "'Tis said, isn't it," he went on, "that chil'ern is God's blessing. Blessed is the man that hath his quiver full. Well, Harry and me have both had chil'ern by our missises, and nuther one o' us had any by our wives. I dearly loves little chil'ern. . . ."

Noises from the town floated out to us over the calm sea. There was smoke in the air of wind coming off land—smoke from people's fires. "Can 'ee smell it?" asked Tom just before we beached. "Her's waiting in there wi' a bit of supper ready. Will 'ee come? Come and tell her what you've a-told me, about its being an unofficial divorce. 'Twill comfort her."

THE ENGINEER'S KISS

"You wouldn't think," said the chief engineer, "that I've had three proposals of marriage on one voyage!"

It was getting on for midnight. The powerful engine-room lamp swung lazily above our heads. Just as I was snuffing the fag-end of a Corsican cigarette on a convenient part of the American drill, his bare chest touched my elbow, his scrubby moustache tickled my cheek, and he shouted that surprising bit of history twice into my ear. Shouted, I say, for the engines were pounding away not two yards from us at Full Speed Ahead, high-pressure steam was blowing from a badly packed gland, and our quiet little talk was in reality a quiet little shout. Promotion, pay, work ashore, hasty marriage without a honeymoon —wedged in between two voyages—youngsters, letters from home. . . . We had been exchanging confidences about these matters at the very top of our voices. There was a softness in his eyes, as of a man whose work is a cage to keep him from what he thinks about. So speaking, we had come to an end, face to face with things hardly to be discussed even over midnight cigarettes. Then it was that he approached and shouted into my left ear : "Wouldn't think, to see me like this, that I've had three proposals of marriage on one voyage? Yes!"

But I could think so. He was fond of his engines, worked with a will at them, and nothing suited his clean straight figure so well as oily trousers and an open shirt. Never did his quick, thin face look better than when it shone with sweat.

Therefore I shouted back a questioning "Oh ?"

"On an Atlantic liner ; not one of these round-bellied tubs o' tramps," he continued in loud jerks. "Was third engineer there. Carried nine engineers and four greasers."

"Any of 'em eligible, the fair proposers ?"

"Don't know. Weren't all fair. Fell in love with our uniforms, I s'pose. Wore uniforms off watch. Not like here. Smart there, I can tell you."

"You should have inquired their fortunes."

"'F all the officers on those boats that get proposals married, they'd have harems, by Jove ! When my little girl had me 'twas a case of love on both sides," he added in a quaint and serious shout.

"You might have married a rich old one ; smoked cigarettes and drunk phizz or golden pekoe ever after."

The temperature of the engine-room that night was 113° F. But even the idea of continual refreshment did not shake him into regret. "No thanks," he said. "Not me ! "

He pulled at his crumpled cigarette.

"Out? Want a light?" I asked. "Here's matches."

"Wait till I've greased her." He proceeded to oil the revolving cross-heads of his engine. "Thanks."

"Ah!" he began shouting again, "but I did fall in love that voyage. Lovely piece. Strapping Irish girl. Young. Blue eyes. Nice rosy cheeks on her. Hair! Walked like a cloud in the wind. Didn't wear those stay-things, I 'spect. Held her head sideways, so, when she laughed. White teeth. Talked the brogue. Pretty. Can't do it."

"And you didn't marry *her*, either?"

"Going out to marry a fellow in Canada. Big lout of an Irishman, curse him! But I had a kiss!"

"Oh?"

"Thought I never should get it. Everybody trying all they were worth. The only one. Me!" He patted his chest. "Like this. Was ready to go on watch at eight bells—not in uniform. Saw Mary sitting aft, her head bowed down low. Think she was crying. So down I sit by her:

Oh, kiss those tears away!

"'S that right? Eh? 'Not turned in, Mary? Crying, Mary?' says I.

"'Sure, and I'm after longin' for Oireland again,' says she.

"So I took her hand, like this. Didn't say

anything till she'd got quiet. Then—'Give me
a kiss, Mary,' I said.

"Took her hand away as quick as anything.
'Give me a kiss, Mary,' I says again.

"She started to go. Made her sit down again.

"'Just one, Mary.'

"'And fwat would my Pat be saying when
I get there!'

"'How'd he know?'

"'S'pose he wouldn't marry me, and I would
be all alone there?'

"Began crying again. Quite soft. Nestled
up to me. Felt her warm shoulder through my
shirt-sleeve. Hope, thinks I to myself. 'Mary,'
says I, 'I'm going down below to the hot engine-
room all night. Just one before I go.'

"Turned her head away. 'Not 'fore I go
down *there*, Mary, below water? S'pose the sea
came rushing down there. I'd be drowned for
certain while you were being saved up here.'

"She wouldn't give me a kiss. Not a bit of
it! Thought to myself, 'All's fair in love and
war,' thought I. Spoke very seriously, like a
sermon: 'Mary, if it wasn't for us engineers
down there, ship might go to the bottom of the
sea and no one be any the wiser. Got all the
power of the ship in our hands—seven thousand
horse-power! Break the engines, and she'd be
left floating in the middle of the Atlantic till
some one came up and took her in tow. And
nobody might come. We're off the regular course.
Icebergs! If I turned one valve. . . . You know
what power of steam we've got there.'

"Felt her shiver. Dark night. Sea very calm and black and quiet.

"'Mary,' says I, 'if you don't give me just one kiss, I'll blow up the ship in the middle of the night.'

"'No. . . .'

"'I will!'

"'Dear Misther Engineer. . . .'

"(Heard the order to strike eight bells.)

"'I tell you I will.'

"'I'll call the captain.'

"'He won't believe you. Knew me when you were a child.'

"'Oh, you're mad, mad!'

"'For a kiss, Mary. By God, I'll do it—I'll blow it up!'

"She flung her arms round my neck and gave me such a kiss. 'Thank God, I've saved the ship!' she cried. 'Oh, Holy Mither, fwat will my Patrick be saying?'

"And then she got up and ran down below like a rabbit. What d'you think of that?"

"H'm. . . . Have a last cigarette?"

"*Grazie.* Lovely girl!"

"Good-night."

"*Nos dawch*," he answered in his Welsh.

When I got on deck I looked down on him through the engine-room skylight. He was oiling his engines—glanced up and smiled very sweetly; and I'll swear he was thinking of his wife and those kids in Wales. For I know what thought it is which brings that particular smile to his face.

THE BEACHCOMBER

I

NOT one of the summer visitors was more faithful to Seacombe than the wrecked man of whom the fishermen said with kindly contempt, "He's a beachcomber, that's what Joe is." His other name was Jenner, whether by birth or by adoption scarcely matters.

We never knew for certain where he spent the winter. It was charitable to believe that every autumn he signed on for a voyage in some sailing ship—"Can't a-bear them stinkin' steamers," he would say—and that every spring he suffered dreadful wreck. Shrewd people favoured the idea that he went on the tramp, or retired to the shelter of some inhospitable workhouse, where the guardians of the poor allowed him to break stones, or to lend a hand with the oakum—both of which occupations must have reminded him of Seacombe beach. At all events, when sunshine made the shore a sun-bath, and the sea a glittering, lazily swaying stretch of harmlessness, Jenner so haunted the beach that we could not help wanting to know something about him. And we went on wanting.

Nearly every one found him interesting. He could narrate by the hour his real and fictitious adventures, speaking as if he were half ashamed that he, of all men, should be chosen out for such wonderful happenings ; and, moreover, he could fill in the details with a very fair consistency. Though he seldom complained of any definite misfortune or tribulation, except, of course, his shipwrecks—though he seemed to bear no ill-will against the sea for wrecking him regularly once a year, in the spring—he often bemoaned the general course of his shifty life, and spiced his monologues with the mild and resigned cynicism of a man who finds despair not entirely uncomfortable to live with.

"I can't 'elp it, you know," he would repeat. "Some people do 'ave somethin' or other always against 'em. . . . Do what they will, it's always the same. I'm like that. I can't rise nohow ; or if I does, down I comes again pretty quick. I *can* rise, but somethin' pulls me down again—often as not into the sea. It's like that with some people —somethin's against 'em—they can't 'elp it, you be sure."

The temptation was to smile unbelievingly at the biographical basis of his philosophy. But we learned to take care. He was one of those piteous, helpless people who always succeed in making one sorry for differing from them, whether they are in the right or the wrong, lying or telling gospel-truth. Conscience never reproaches us with such clammy persistence as when we have disbelieved to his face an unfortunate creature who, after all, may have been telling us the truth. We *had* to listen to him.

Usually, just at the dawn of some fine May morning, the mackerel fishers coming in would see his slouching figure waiting for them on the beach. He could be recognised afar off. His cranky bent knees and the way his coat stuck out behind, as he stood shivering, with his hands in his trouser-pockets, made him appear from a distance, and from the side, like a tall man seated on nothing at all.

"Want a hand?" he would say as the craft was beached, or as a boat shoved off to meet it.

"'Ullo! You back again! Were's been to this time, then?"

"Tramped from Portsmouth." (Or some other southern port.) "I've 'ad as bad a winter as I've 'ad. I've been. . . ."

"Yer! let where thee's been wait. Lend 'em a hand up there wi' the capstan."

Then Jenner would walk round and round with the pole, laboriously turning the old wooden capstan that slowly, and with creaks innumerable, hauled the drifter up the steep beach. This done, he would hang about for his tip or for another opportunity of lending a hand. Willingness was his virtue. As a fisherman explained, "Joe's always ready to lend a hand or do a job and that. But he can't do no heavy work. . . . 'Er an't got the strength of a mouse. Once I got 'en a job up Honiton way, diggin' a pond for a gen'leman. He went off there all right. The second mornin' Master Joe didn't turn up. Stayed in bed tired,

I s'pose. Anyhow, 'er come back yer, an' yer 'er is always ready to help." Joe was the incarnation of your very humble and obedient servant.

His earnings were the most variable thing about him. Some days he might pick up two or three shillings ; some days not enough for a bed. He could cadge skilfully when he had a mind to do so. Every fisherman received at one time or another a hint that his, the fisherman's, generosity must naturally, seeing he was one of the old sort, be greater than the generosity of every other man along the beach. Joe's expression, too, was excellent for begging. It seemed to have no gradations between that of a brazen rogue and that of a wretched, God-forsaken, uncomfortably pathetic creature. He was like an independent man who, finding independence a game not worth the candle, preferred to be miserably dependent.

He evidently sailed very close to the three primary facts of life : he had been born—though, indeed, it was difficult to imagine Joe as a baby ; —he found himself a living man ; and sooner or later—sooner, unless he got something to eat—he would have to die.

Meanwhile. . . . But that was it. He had mastered the art of living in the Meanwhile.

II

Last year Joe appeared to have aged considerably. A point about him in former years was, that he never seemed to get any older ; only to

become more decrepit.   Now, at last, age and
decrepitude had joined forces to make him look
more miserable than ever.   His eyes were almost
of one colour all over—bleary blue shot with red
—and his face had that thick, coppery tint that
one associates less with sunburn than with beer-
drinking and peripheral neuritis.   He had let
grow a stub of brownish-grey beard which, when
he walked along the water's edge at low tide,
searching for coins, made him look like a big
evil bird with its head bent down to pick up
garbage.   Moreover, he had a cough nasty to
hear, and in no way surprising, for his visible
dress—salted blue cotton trousers, a jersey which
hung loosely upon him, coat, scarf, old boots and
cap—seemed, from the way he shivered, to be all
the clothing he had.

In answer to the usual query : " Were's been
to this time, Joe ? " he had a long tale to
tell.

" I've been wrecked again—off the Scillys—
that's where I been.   The boat foundered and I
went in with the stewardess under my arm—great
big woman, 'bout as big as myself, and that's a big
woman to swim with.   Well, I did swim with her
for, I'd think, a couple of hours, thinkin' every
minute as I'd have to let 'er go and sink myself.
The water were that cold and 'twere that rough.
. . . I don't know 'ow I did do it.   Then we got
throwed up, flop ! against a rock—in the night
and dark as pitch.   'Owsomever, I managed to
clamber up that rock and drag 'er up with me.
'Twere God's own rock, that were."

The idea of God's own rock seemed to amuse him. He grinned.

" An 'orrible night it was, and I didn't know w'er the tide 'd come up and sweep us off, or w'er 'twas going down. In the mornin'—I never 'eard tell o' such a thing—we found we was quite near land, and I took 'er under my arm, like this, and swum in with 'er. She wouldn't leave me and stay behind while I got a boat. Not 'er ! She'd ha' chucked 'erself into the foamin' waters a'ter me—and not for me looks, you bet."

Then began his real tale of woe.

" We was back on land all right, but my foot were poisoned bad climbin' up that there rock, and I been in Penzance 'orspital with a cruel bad foot three months and a week and two days, I 'ave ! Can't 'ardly walk yet, no sense like. Now I've come up all the way from Penzance on my bad foot. That's where I been."

It was not observable that he walked worse on one foot than on the other, and when the news went round—" Joe Jenner, he've been wrecked again,"—it did not everywhere excite pity. All, however, wished to make him repeat his tale for their own private examination and pleasure in hearing. If nothing else, it was part payment in advance for sundry ha'pence which would be paid out during the summer for Joe's benefit.

He never explained the presence of a stewardess on one of his chosen sailing vessels, nor, curiously enough, does any one seem to have thought of asking him.

III

When the mackerel boats went out in the evening, just before sunset, Joe never failed to be on the beach. About the end of July, after he had finished helping shove a boat down to the water, and as the fishermen were discussing whether or not a fresh sou'westerly breeze was going to spring up in the night, Joe said very disconsolately, yet as if his misfortunes made him in some way superior, " You'll be snug enough out there, lyin' asleep in the cutty. Me! I an't got enough for a bed."

Usually, when he said that, he did succeed in finding the pence for a bed. No one, therefore, took much notice of him.

It both rained and blew in the night. Out in the Channel the sea boiled, and the spray of white horses could be heard in the darkness, racing the waves and scudding from crest to trough. On shore, the wind, with rain in it, blew in gusts, and everything was hidden in the murk, except when, in lulls, the fast-incoming waves could be seen making a band of white surf along the beach. Daylight was late. Joe was on the shore. His clothes were darkened by rain, and his cough was shaking him as a terrier might shake a rat. When the boat he was awaiting grounded on the pebbles and slewed round, they threw out a dog-fish.

" How'll thic there dun-cow suit 'ee, Joe ? "

Joe kicked it into the water, saying contemptuously, " That's what they gives you in the village when you asks for fried fish."

He stood, an abject figure, looking sullenly at the dog-fish which the sea was washing off from the beach.

"Now then, Joe! Give 'em a hand wi' the capstan there. We'm going to have the boat stove in, banging round like that. Hurry up!"

He climbed slowly up the beach, took hold of the pole, and was at once doubled up by another fit of coughing.

"Get away with 'ee!" said one of the other men at the capstan.

"An't got the strength of a mouse," they repeated among themselves.

As for Joe Jenner—after stumbling a yard or two, he fell forwards down the beach. Seeing he did not move, one of the fishermen left the capstan and went to look at him.

"Hi, yer! Joe's took bad," he called out.

Blood, in fact, was running from his mouth, staining his beard and the pebbles under his head.

They formed a little circle around him. In the yellowish-grey twilight of a cloudy dawn, they looked like ghosts receiving a dead man amongst them.

"What shall us do?" said one. "We can't leave 'en here, that's certain."

"You three can wind the boat up, can't 'ee?" said another. "I'll carry 'en up home along, and take 'en in house. He's only a bag o' bones."

"All right. You do. We'll be up d'rectly. Take care not to shake 'en more than thee ca'st help."

"Right-o!"

Joe was carried into a cottage and laid on a bed. The fisherman (his wife refused to have anything to do with beggars in her bedrooms) waited for the others to advise him how to act; for country people have an almost superstitious dread of internal bleeding.

When all the men had assembled round the bed, Joe showed signs of reviving.

"What's to do now?"

"I don't know. Best give 'en a drop o' spirits, I should say, if thee's got any in house."

The spirits brought him back to confused consciousness. No one, however, could suggest what to do with him.

"'Er an't got no people—relations like?" asked one of them, putting forward a vain hope for want of a practicable idea.

"Got a wife or anybody, Joe?"

Joe looked suspiciously at them. Finally he grunted, "Don' know. Maybe." It was easy to see there was something he did not wish to tell.

"Where be 'em then?"

"They been a'ter he for to take 'en back to his lovin' wife, to help support her like. That's what 'tis. He won't tell thee nort—you see."

"Better put 'en to bed and send for the doctor."

So they took off his clothes. Instead of a shirt he had newspapers wrapped around his body, and the ink had come off on his skin. He was a horrid sight as he lay on the bed. They put out the lamp, and by the early morning light that filtered in through the window, he looked worse than ever—not unlike the dead dog-fish he had despised.

" Ain't he thin ? " said one.

" Poor devil ! " said another.

" Put 'en under the bedclothes," said a third. " You can always wash 'em."

They began to move him, and in so doing completely roused him.

"What 'ave I been doin'?" asked Joe. "Spittin' blood ?"

" Spoutin' it, more like."

" I s'pose I'm dyin'? "

" P'raps.   P'raps thee't pull round again."

" Pullin' round ain't my way. . . . Haven't 'ad such a bad time, you know. . . ."

Those were his last words. The same movement which thoroughly awoke him, the spirits probably, and the talking, brought on another sickening effusion of blood. He became unconscious and was dead before the doctor arrived.

He is gone from the sunny beach as if he never had lived. But his last words are remembered. " 'S thee know," the fishermen say, " what thic there ol' beachcomber said afore he died ? *That 'er hadn't had such a bad time, after the rate !* Do make a man think summut—that —from the likes o' he."

THE LOG OF THE *BRISTOL BEAUTY*

I

On a regular voyage it would have meant trouble for the engine-room. The old *Aganippe*, a steamer that had carried Royal Mails and had broken records in her time, was hove-to during fine weather—stopped for engineers' purposes on the high seas off the north-west coast of Spain. No harm was done this time beyond scaring the passengers, for the *Aganippe* was only wandering. She had been specially chartered by the Affiliated South Lancashire Literary Societies. "Where Lancashire leads, England follows," as they say in Lancashire. The Affiliated Literary Societies were bound for One Month's Co-operative Trip to Historic Spots of the Mediterranean.

"Funny! funny! funny!" was the second mate's verdict on the passengers. "There's only one fine piece among them, and she's always got that blamed sky-pilot hanging on to her skirts."

The passengers consisted of several young clergymen of various denominations, some older men not clerical, a bevy of pale, tousled women-students from the Lancashire universities and

technical schools, merchants' daughters putting
the final touches to their education, fathers,
patronesses, chaperons, self-improvement people,
and a considerable number of secretaries and organ-
ising persons.   They were all interested in liter-
ature ; therefore, theoretically, in human nature ;
and hence they were sharply divided in opinion
as to whether or no the somewhat shameless
encouragement given by Miss Alice Kirby (the
one fine piece) to the second mate involved the
jilting of the Rev. Mr. Titwell ; provided, of
course, that there really was anything between
Miss Kirby and Mr. Titwell.

It was the finest of days when the ship was
stopped, but under the circumstances very trying
for bad sailors.   The *Aganippe* was lying broad-
side to the sea a mile or two from Cape Finisterre.
Though there was no wind, she rolled gently and
decidedly on the long smooth swell that breaks
against the western coasts of Europe in all but
the most long-settled calm weather.   A few gulls
from the cape flew round about the ship, screeching
mournfully.   In the hot sunshine her decks reeked
of pitch.   There was no cool, steadying breeze
for squeamish heads ; only the sickening roll.

Most of the passengers were on the port side,
spying at the lighthouse on Finisterre, flinging
poetic quotations at the purple Spanish mountains,
or talking ship's gossip and weather.   In the
starboard alley-way, however, almost under the
bridge, a troubled young man grasped a stanchion
with one trembling hand and looked most earnestly
over the ship's side.   The Rev. Mr. Titwell, a

great favourite among the ladies so long as there was not an officer of the Mercantile Marine standing by to eclipse him, was one of those modern Nonconformist ministers whose silky clericals, clean-shaven manner, and ascetic countenances render them almost indistinguishable from the High Church lads fresh from Oxford. He appeared now to be meditating on the profundity of the sea and the astonishing number of little fishes therein.

The second mate leaned over the bridge.

" Well, Mr. Titwell ? "

" Mr. Roberts."

" How's this for you ? "

" I thought you said that as we had it so rough in the Bay of Biscay we should have it fine on the Portuguese coast."

" What d'you call this, then ? A hurricane ? You wait, Mr. Titwell, and see if we have a northerly wind in the Gulf of Lyons. It does blow there ! Have you seen Finisterre ? "

" Yes ; I *have* looked at it, thank you. Don't you think the ship is rolling rather ? "

" Are you going to feed fishes, Mr. Titwell ? "

" Feed fishes ? Is that a nautical phrase ? "

" Be sea-sick. Are you feeling sick ? "

" I—I don't know. I thought I had been."

The poor young man gazed still farther into the profundity of the sea, grasped the stanchion yet more firmly, and proceeded to feed the fishes. Miss Kirby, peeping into the alley-way, began : " Mr. Titwell, come and. . . ." Then she saw what Mr. Titwell was about, smiled confidentially, not to say intimately, at the second mate, and ran away. Her aunt and chaperon, Mrs. Kirby, a youthful old lady renowned as a singer of sentimental songs at Manchester slum concerts, came searching for her niece and found only Mr. Titwell.

"Have you seen my niece, Mr. Titwell?"

"No."

"I wanted her to accompany me through a new song for this evening. Will you, Mr. Titwell?"

"I'm afraid. . . ."

"Now, I know you can. You play quite well enough for that."

"I'm afraid I'm being sea-sick."

"Oh!"

Mr. Titwell ruffled his lanky hair despairingly. What his face was like only the little fishes saw.

The second mate heard his own name called in a small voice. Thinking it was only Mr. Titwell's anguish, and not being a steward, he took no notice.

"Mr. Roberts!" he heard again, in a stronger voice. "Here's something in the water."

"What?"

"Here's something floating in the water."

"Ay, ay!"

"It's got some letters on it. It's got the letters L-O-G on it."

By the time the second mate had swung down the ladder from the bridge Mr. Titwell felt almost well again.

"What does L-O-G stand for?" he asked.

The flat piece of wood was drifting slowly astern.

"Why it's a ship's log in wooden covers. Can't you see? Sufficient reason for launching a boat, that. Keep your eye on it. Don't you let it out of sight!"

"What is it, then?"

"It's got a ship's log in it—or ought to have."

The mate was called. A boat was hurriedly launched.

"There it is!" yelled Mr. Titwell, keeping his finger directed towards the drifting object.

"Ay, ay, sir!" responded the boat's crew.

The passengers forsook the purple mountains and crowded to starboard. The captain appeared at the door of the chart-room.

"What is it?" inquired the passengers. "Oh, I hope there's nothing more the matter."

"I've sighted a log," Mr. Titwell explained.

"A what?"

The log was brought on board and delivered to the captain.

"What is it, captain? Oh! do let us see."

"It appears to be a ship's log, madam."

The captain went back to his chart-room and banged the door.

"How rude these sailors are!" remarked Mrs. Kirby.

II

Dinner that evening was an exasperating meal for the captain of the *Aganippe*, who, though kindly and jolly enough personally, was apt officially to be formal and somewhat irritable.

" What was it they fished out of the water this afternoon, captain ? Was it only a piece of wood ? "

" A ship's scrap log, madam."

" Did Mr. Titwell see it first, captain ? "

" So I understand."

" What is a scrap log, captain ? "

" It is a rough log for the mates' use."

" What is it used for ? "

" To record the distance steamed by patent log, the ship's course, wind, the weather. . . ."

" How did it get into the water ? "

" Ladies and gentlemen," said the captain, " let me tell you all I know at once. We have this afternoon, thanks to Mr. Titwell, picked up the scrap log of the cargo steamer *Bristol Beauty*, of Bristol. It is almost uninjured, written in pencil, and enclosed in neat painted wooden covers—from which I gather that they had more leisure in the *Bristol Beauty* than we have here. The ship appears to have met with bad weather. The log may have been washed overboard. We launched a boat for it because ships' logs are important, greatly used in Board of Trade inquiries. I have also signalled to Lloyd's Station on Finisterre. If there is any other information. . . ."

" Was the *Bristol Beauty* wrecked, captain ? "

" She met with gales all the way out."

" How dreadful ! Do *you* think she was wrecked ? "

" How can I say, madam ? "

" Will you let us see the log, captain ? Will you read it ? "

"Yes. Do! Please, captain!"

He refused to continue the subject, and probably that would have been the end of it if Mr. Titwell and Miss Kirby had not succeeded in catching him alone immediately after dinner.

"Do, please, read the *Bristol Beauty's* log, captain," Miss Kirby implored.

"No, no."

"But Mr. Titwell wants to hear it, and it was his find, wasn't it?"

"Yes, it was my find, captain."

"D'you want to hear it so very much, Miss Kirby?" asked the captain.

"Oh, please!"

"Well, we'll see what we can do."

"When? When, captain?"

"When dinner's cleared away, shall we say?"

"Oh, *thank* you, captain!"

Miss Kirby ran off with the news, which, if anything, travelled still faster. Hardly was dinner cleared when the passengers began to re-assemble in the saloon. The questioning became a fusillade, directed mainly at the little group which included Mrs. and Miss Kirby, the second mate, and the Rev. Mr. Titwell. A few superior people affected to discuss other subjects, but they found nobody to talk to, and, as usual, they didn't much want to talk to one another.

"Did Mr. Titwell really see it first?—Miss Kirby got the captain to promise.—He wouldn't do it for anybody else.—Not quite nice of her, d'you think?" Such was the conversation when

Captain Cornish entered the saloon with the log-book under his arm.

A hush !

" Ladies and gentlemen," began the captain.

" The old man's no hand at talking," whispered the second mate to Miss Kirby, " but he's great at speechifying."

" —the scrap-log which we picked up to-day belongs, or belonged——"

" Good again ! " remarked the second mate.

" —to the *Bristol Beauty*, a ship of about a thousand tons registered, so the mate tells me. I don't think I need go into the details of stowing the cargo."

" Please, captain."

" Well, she took in three hundred and fifty-two tons eight hundredweight of bunkers."

" Coal for the engines," the second mate explained to Miss Kirby.

" Then," continued the captain, " early on Tuesday morning, the log goes on to say :

> This day commenced with a whole SW. gale and frequent lightning in E. quarter— heavy showers and hailstones at intervals. Barometer low.

They made all prepared for sea. Dock and channel pilot came aboard. They unmoored and got clear of the dock gates, pilot in charge. They proceeded down the Bristol Channel, discharged pilot, and set the course to west-half-south. Engines full speed ahead."

" Where were they going to, captain ? "

K

"Bristol towards Lisbon, then on to Corsica for bark extract."

"Where we are going?"

"Exactly. The weather, a heavy SSW. gale and showery. They streamed the patent log. The rest I will give you in the words of the log-book itself, only omitting nautical details of no interest to you:—

Tuesday, 4 p.m.—Wind W. Heavy gale and high head sea, steamer pitching and labouring heavily, engines racing considerably.

8 p.m.—Strong gale and clear. Passing showers.

10.35 p.m.—Lundy at 3 m.

12 midnight.—Similar weather.

Wednesday, 4 a.m.—Wind NNW., fresh breeze, and clear weather; rough sea gradually moderating.

5.40 a.m.—Trevose Head at 8 miles.

8 a.m.—Similar weather.

12 noon.—Strong breeze, high head sea, steamer labouring heavily."

"Poor things!" sighed one of the lady passengers.

"3 p.m.—Wolf at 6 miles. Patent log $75\frac{1}{2}$, reset to 0.

4 p.m.—Hard gale from S., with terrific rain squalls; steamer labouring severely and shipping immense quantities of water; several empty casks washed overboard."

" Oh, Mr. Roberts ! " exclaimed Miss Kirby. " How lucky it was not the crew ! "

" It was the casks, Alice," said Mrs. Kirby. " What a pity it is that England's brave sailors drink so much ! "

" Too true, I'm afraid," added Mr. Titwell.

" The casks," the second mate explained, " were deck cargo, going back empty for bark extract for tanning—first-class passengers, we call 'em—not liquor for the crew. We don't drink bark extract, anyhow."

" Indeed, Mr. Roberts ! " said Mrs. Kirby with dignity.

The captain read on :—

" 8 p.m.—Moderating wind ; hauled to west.

12 midnight.—Wind NW.   Strong gale and high, confused sea ; steamer labouring, straining heavily, shipping heavy water ; empty barrels washing about decks, and engines racing fearfully.

Thursday, 4 a.m.—Wind W.   Hard gale with terrific squalls and high seas ; steamer labouring."

The sound of " Ah-h ! " ran around the saloon —a sound between pleasure and pain, or compounded of both.

" 8 a.m.—Heavy SW. gale, and sea running mountainous ; shipping heavy seas fore and aft ; several empty barrels over the rail."

" How terrible ! "

" 12 noon.—Similar weather."

" Oh, poor things ! "

"4 p.m.—No change to report. High, dangerous, and confused sea running ; shipping heavy seas fore and aft. Empty barrels continue going overboard.

8 p.m.—Similar weather, with terrific rain squalls, thunder, and lightning. Wind shifted to west."

" What terrible *similar weather* they seem to have had ! " exclaimed an elderly lady, who was slightly deaf.

" It's like the fourth act of *King Lear*, on the heath," remarked a woman student.

" Friday, 4 a.m.—This day begins weather as before. Vivid lightning all round horizon ; high cross-seas running ; deck constantly full, washing all movables about.

8 a.m.—No change.

12 noon.—Similar weather.

4 p.m.—Ditto.

5 p.m.—Wind shifting to N.

8 p.m. — Terrific northerly gale ; high, following sea.

12 midnight.—Ship pooping seas."

" What is pooping seas, Mr. Roberts ? " Miss Kirby asked.

" Big seas breaking in over the stern. Some skippers run before stern seas till it's too late to turn round, and then they can't."

Mr. Titwell wished for something in the log that he, too, could explain.

> "Saturday, 3.10 a.m. — Huge sea broke over the stern, washing away the flagstaff and after-deck compass-stand and damaging the after wheel. Several barrels overboard.
>
> 4 a.m.—Similar ; no change ; still pooping seas and decks flooded. Crew employed trying to secure empty barrels, but to no avail ; still washing same overboard. Fear cargo adrift in No. 2 hold.
>
> 4.15 a.m. — Tried to turn head to sea. Shipped immense sea. Wheelhouse door broken, lifeboat washed on to engine-room skylight.
>
> 4.40 a.m.—Again tried to turn head to sea ; impossible. Pooping huge seas. Steam steering gear jammed. Position of ship ﹐ dangerous.

That, ladies and gentlemen," said the captain, "is the last entry in the scrap log of the . . ."

Exclamations of pity from all quarters of the saloon drowned the captain's voice. Mrs. Kirby was fingering the piano very softly. A lady near her caught the tune and hummed it.

'Twas the rather nasal, but beautiful, melody of the hymn "For those in peril on the sea." Mrs. Kirby played with more and more confidence. She broke into song, *con molto sentimento*, and in a moment all save the superior persons were singing or humming plaintively—

> " Eternal Father, strong to save,
>   Whose arm hath bound the restless wave,
>   Who bidd'st the mighty ocean deep
>   Its own appointed limits keep :
>   O hear us when we cry to Thee
>   For those in peril on the sea."

The captain retired hastily to his room. Sundry passengers wept and were unashamed. Miss Kirby felt ill—quite faint. The second mate and Mr. Titwell competed to support her.

III

The names the captain called himself, and those his officers called him, for reading the log were not polite. A breeze sprang up while the passengers were turning in. After the manner of breezes in the south, it began as suddenly and forcibly as it continued. A long whistle in the rigging, an aerial push against the ship, and it was upon them. It was only a moderate breeze, and short-lived, but it caught a ship already rolling, and the passengers' minds were full of the *Bristol Beauty* and the perils of the sea. A number of them wished to be brave and to stay up all night. Miss Kirby and the Rev. Mr. Titwell actually did sit together on a coil of rope till nearly midnight.

Within two days, however, the *Aganippe's* passengers were at dinner in Lisbon Harbour, talking, not now of wrecks and storms and perils, but of Lisbon and the lazy Portuguese. Just as cheese was being handed round, the head steward came behind Mr. Titwell and whispered : " You remember that log you sighted, sir ? "

" Yes, yes."

" Mr. Roberts has met the captain of the *Bristol Beauty* ashore and brought him on board."

" What ! "

Almost before the innocent expletive was out of the young clergyman's mouth, the second mate burst into the saloon, half leading, half dragging a round, ruddy, twinkle-eyed man, whose gait was compounded of sea-legs and Portuguese wines.

" Sir," said the second mate, " here's Captain Jones, of the *Bristol Beauty*."

" Oh, here's the captain of the ship that was wrecked.—Here's the dear captain !—What he must have been through !—He doesn't look it, does he ?—Poor man !—Not a gentleman, evidently.—Will he tell us, d'you think ?—Speech ! speech ! "

As he walked up the saloon one pale young lady plucked his sleeve : " Thank God you're safe, captain !   We prayed for you."

" Did ye, miss ? "

A place was laid for him to the right of Captain Cornish. He was urged to speak—to explain how he was saved.

" Ladies and gentlemen," said the captain of the *Aganippe*, " perhaps Captain Jones will make a speech when he's had something to eat."

" Have I *got* to ? " asked Captain Jones.

" Yes, you must."

" Let's get it over, then."

He was rapturously applauded.

"Ladies and gentlemen," he began, imitating his fellow captain in a way that made the superior persons smile. "You found our scrap log. I don't know why—what—that is, you want to know. . . ."

"The terrible weather you had."

"We did have it roughish across the Bay."

"And the dreadful entries in your log. Pooping!"

"Not my log; the mates' log. That's easy explained. Don't know that I ought to, though. Never mind. You see, 'tis like this. We're between the devil and the deep sea—the owners and insurance people, and the sea. Owners spend their money insuring, instead of making their ships seaworthy. Insurance people never want to pay up, of course. Suppose we get cargo injured—deck cargo—no fault at all of ours—and can't prove it's the act of God—storm, fire, lightning, ancetera; then insurance people won't pay, and owners give us the sack for careless navigation of their scrap-iron. Besides, Board of Trade might hold an inquiry and give me a year's holiday—compulsory holiday—take away my ticket—my certificate. So, if we meet with bad weather, we take the log and write up damn bad weather—worse weather, that is. Self-protection, I say, with a deck cargo like ours. We did have dirty weather. Seen worse. . . ."

"But pooping seas?"

"Pooh! Steamers nowadays is only floating warehouses fully insured—sterns like tubs—ship

seas like rafts and roll like barrels.   I've navigated
the little *Bristol Beauty* through worse weather
than we've had this voyage—worse, aye, hurri-
canes !   If you've been making a fuss over our
log and singing hymns and suchlike, then, 'strue
as heaven's above, you've been done brown.
Beg pardon ; you was had.   See ?

"Thank ye, sir.   Soup, please."

The Rev. Mr. Titwell was perhaps the least
dissatisfied of all the passengers, for he observed
that the uproarious laughter of Mr. Roberts, the
second mate, brought severe frowns upon the fair
forehead of Miss Alice Kirby.   She told him
afterwards, while they were hand in hand on deck,
watching the lights of Lisbon Harbour, that in
her opinion sailors had no hearts.

Mr. Titwell had.

ROBBERY ROBBED

I

HIS grey cob was of the sort described at sales as " useful." His dog-cart, smartly built, now had painted on its scratched varnish, THOS. J. SHINNER, CORN FACTOR AND COAL MERCHANT. His clothes were more gentlemanly than his rather well-fed person. Under the wide and cleanly sky of the downland his neat driving did not remove the impression of fussy smallness. Pretty obviously, he was one of those up-to-date, business-like tradesmen who still, by fair means or foul, make money among the stagnant industries of the countryside.

On one side was the great green escarpment of the chalk hills. Stretching far away below were the fat dairy pastures. The larks' songs descending from above mingled with the grunts of the cottager's rent—his pig, that is—ascending from the earth.

Along the road which meandered about on that ledge of poor land, were many scattered cottages. Most of them possessed ramshackle outbuildings or pig-sties ; on some of the latter

swine-fever notices were posted. Thos. J.
Shinner called at nearly every cottage. The men-
folk, of course, were at work in the fields. He
knew that. He almost ran from his trap to the
doors. Small chance was left to anybody of
escaping his visits.

Mrs. Slade received him respectfully. "No,
sir, we don't want no barley meal, thank you
kindly. They've a-killed our old sow, all 'cause
they says as one o' the little 'uns had the fever,
though 'twas only an inflammation, that I'm
sure."

"Any coal, Mrs. Slade?"

"No, sir, thank you kindly."

"How much have you got?"

"Well, sir, we ain't got hardly a hundredweight, but we be trying to put by a little towards
a hen and a sitting of eggs in place of our sow, so
we ain't going to have no more coals just yet."

"I'll send you out three hundredweight—
cheap—pay weekly. Your husband's earning
seventeen shillings a week, isn't he? You can
afford a shilling a week. Good day."

Mrs. Slade sat down helplessly and plucked at
her apron, whilst Mr. Shinner rested his pocket-
book on the garden gate and made a note.

Mrs. Churney at the next cottage worked with
her husband in the fields. Their door was closed
and locked. Mr. Shinner, therefore, went round
to the back premises, inspected the sty, the meal
bag, and the coal house, and again made a note.

He jumped out of his trap fifty yards from the
cottage of Squire Rodden's shepherd, and, creeping

along under the hedge, he arrived at the door
very suddenly. Though he thought he heard a
movement, the place was empty except for two
sick lambs before the fire. "Mrs. Drake !" he
called. "Mrs. Drake !" he shouted upstairs.
"If your husband doesn't pay by next week I
shall sue him. D'you hear ? County court !"

Once more he made a note. (Mrs. Drake
watched him do it from behind the curtain of an
upper window.) He took up the reins to drive
home ; and then, thinking better of it, he turned
towards Squire Rodden's—towards the big red
farmhouse that stands alone in a field beneath
Acster Beacon.

II

The Squire, an old tenant farmer whose force-
fulness had earned him that title, was suffering
from a touch of the gout, and sat with his foot up
in a room whence he could look out on some of
his arable land, on most of his pasture, and at his
stables. Before Mr. Shinner was shown in he had
been tugging his white moustache over the turf
columns of a newspaper.

"How am I ? Bad !" he wheezed, in answer
to polite inquiries. "Gout, always, and now
bronchitis too. Shan't last out the winter. An
oppression here." He slapped his broad chest
vigorously. "Get out the whisky, my dear."

"No, thank you," said Mr. Shinner.

"Yes, you will," snapped the Squire. "My
doctor says a glass or two. . . . One minute."

He rose quickly, threw up one of the windows, and roared out : " Take that mare into her stable, fool! Can't you see she's sweating ? "

Mr. Shinner glanced at him keenly and accepted the whisky.   Then he unfolded his business, which was, in brief, that Squire Rodden should stop out of the shepherd's wages what the shepherd owed to Mr. Shinner.

" What's that ?   Reuben Drake in your debt ? Several pounds ?   Oh !   He's got two strapping daughters at home that ought to be out in service, but he's a good shepherd.   Repeat what you said."

Mr. Shinner amplified his offer to the extent that if the Squire would pay then and there the shepherd's debt, he should be allowed a good discount, and so himself would gain a profit out of the shepherd.

The Squire rose again, very quickly. " You trick my labourers," he shouted, " into buying your bad goods at top prices when I know, and they know, and you know, they can't afford it, and then you dun 'em.   You cheat my men, but you damn well shan't cheat me.   Get out of my house, you dirty little cad ! "   Whereupon he took Mr. Shinner and kicked him out of the front door.   Had the gouty foot not kicked so well, the violently slammed door would have smashed Mr. Shinner's skull.

On arriving back at his office, Mr. Shinner directed his clerk somewhat thus : " Slade of Acster, three hundred of smalls.   Pay weekly a shilling, and see they do.   Charge on arrears.

Churney, two hundred of kitchen, and a half a
sack of meal, seconds. Call for money. Drake,
Rodden's shepherd—see what a typewritten letter
will do, and if we don't hear, take out a summons
next week."

Then Mr. Shinner signed his cheques, two of
which were for religious subscriptions.

III

A night-flitting under the dark massive
hills. . . . By the light of two or three stable
lanterns the shepherd's more portable and less
worthless household goods were being carried
out to a wagon of the old-fashioned build that
Squire Rodden swore by. And the voice which
said : " If you don't hurry up, Drake, you'll
miss the early train, and be nabbed," was that of
the Squire's fourth son. Money chinked. The
wagon with its piled-up freight of goods and
children, but without any light, lumbered into
darkness, and under the hills all was quiet again.

Next morning the Squire betted his son twenty
to one that Mr. Shinner would be out at Acster
within two days ; and Mr. Shinner, owing to his
relations with the railway station, did hear of the
flitting, and did hasten out to Acster.

Squire Rodden, who was on the watch, flung
up his window. " What the devil d'you want
now ? "

" Where's Drake ? "

" Drake's gone. And it's no use you running
after him, because he's saved enough to make him-

self bankrupt under the Small Debtors Act.   I
made up the amount myself, by allowing him
Michaelmas money that was't due yet.   Put that
in your pipe and smoke it, you little scoundrel !
And get off my land, or I'll call my boys to chuck
you into the pond.   Come here again, and see ! ''

The window banged down.   Stalwart sons
began to gather round.   Mr. Shinner removed
himself from the Squire's land.

He directed his clerk to write off the debt, for,
being a good business man, he realised the useless-
ness of pursuing a debtor who would simply make
himself bankrupt, and would pay, probably, next
to nothing in the pound.

And then—being, as I say, a good business
man—he left his office early, in order to preside
at a tea-fight.

MRS. TRIPP'S FLUTTER

*And, with the voice of these subdued soundings, the
Angelet sprang forth, fluttering its rudiments of
pinions—but forthwith flagged, and was recovered
into the arms of those full-winged angels. And a
wonder it was to see how, as years went round
in heaven—a year in dreams is as a day—continually its white shoulders put forth buds of
wings, but wanting the perfect angelic nutriment,
anon was shorn of its aspiring, and fell fluttering
—still caught by angel hands, for ever to put forth
shoots, and to fall fluttering, because its birth was
not of the unmixed vigour of heaven.*—(Charles
Lamb's The Child Angel.)

I

Miss Jane Benson, when she became Mrs.
Thomas Tripp, married below her station. The
unforgettable home of her maiden days was a
back-street shop in the window of which was dis-
played an assortment of goods, ranging from
bacon and cheese to ha'penny sweetmeats, with
pots, pans, and a selection of underclothing thrown
in between. Children flattened their noses against

the glass.   Little Jane Benson called them street-children.

Young Tom Tripp had reminded her of village blacksmiths, and spreading chestnut trees.   He was foreman to a Manchester chimney-sweep, and possessed a nice taste in presents.   He assured her that soot was healthy, and did not stick like some sorts of dirt he knew ; and soon after he had set up on his own in business, they were duly married.

Had Miss Benson remained single, she might, with her natural gifts, have risen to a position far above her pa and ma's.   As it was, she spent the greater part of her mental and vocal talents in trying to rise only to her maiden altitude in life, and in trying to carry up with her Mr. Tripp and all the little Tripps.   Well that there were angels ever ready to receive the oft-descending Jane Tripp—not real angels, but something far better, the pickled memories of her birthplace and her parents.   She never made a long stay in her heavens on earth.   But, like the Child Angel of Elia's dream, she had some glorious flutters.

Her first six attempts at flight had to do with Tripp's concerns.   Unfortunately, he was such a contented lump of a man.   He wanted home comforts, rather than more chimneys than he could himself sweep.   Still less did he want more fashionable chimneys.   "They don't pay cash, them sort," he held.

Prince Albert Grove, from which he resolutely refused to move, was a wretched place, dismal and incomplete, only half a street and nothing at all of

L

a grove. It consisted of thirteen five-and-three-penny houses, each of which possessed in front of it a garden where the cottager might grow pansies, cabbages, roses, and other green things on twelve square yards of dirt and a path. At the time of Mrs. Tripp's seventh flutter the gardens were thirteen railed-in mud-pie grounds, and the front windows looked out on the blank back-yard wall of a row of six-shilling houses. Three decorations this naked wall had on it—three police notices to the effect that whosoever should cast vegetables, fish offal, or garbage of any description into the roadway would be liable to a fine not exceeding forty shillings, or, in default, to six weeks' imprisonment. As Mrs. Tripp remarked : " England ain't a land of the free when things like that is stuck about. This ain't no place for a respectable woman, I say. And I'd move to-morrow, I would, if Tripp was willing."

In places like Prince Albert Grove there are two social functions a day, the morning step-washing and the evening gate-standing. House-visiting is not the thing, except in the case of interesting illnesses or beautiful bereavements. Conversation, therefore, is semi-public.

Mrs. Tripp's voice was well and often heard in the Grove. She had some reputation as a talker who could be both vivid and convincing, without the use of words unbefitting a grocer-draper-ironmonger's daughter. The strength of her voice, not of her language, did it : for had she not called a section of her nine children home to bed every night for a dozen years or more ?

At the age of thirty-seven, she was tall, bony,
prominent as to the nose and yellow in the face,
and her voice was as aforesaid. If you do not
appreciate the burden of a family of nine children,
think of seventeen times three hundred and sixty-
five (or six) nights with a baby, or babies, crying
in each.

II

One morning, Mrs. Tripp and her next-door
neighbour, Mrs. Maslen, raised themselves up
from their half-washed doorsteps. They had
plenty to say, and while their bare arms dried in
the sunshine, they said it. For the moment,
Mrs. Maslen was leading lady of the Grove.
Two evenings beforehand, she and Mr. Maslen,
having gone out together as in love's young days,
had indulged in the middle of the Grove in a
violent and unsober quarrel, which led to a bleeding of Mrs. Maslen's nose and a black eye for her
husband. She had been treated shameful according to some, and had got just what she wanted in
the opinion of others.

Mrs. Lowman, a plaintive mother of five, had
been publicly buttoning up her bodice on her
doorstep. Being more than interested in the ups
and downs of matrimony, she turned within to
put on a hat and shawl, and so protected against
cold, she took a dozen steps to Mrs. Maslen's
railings. Miss Tripp also joined the group.
Miss Tripp did not relish being told she was just
like her ma ; and usually she was as frowsy and

blowsy in the morning as in the evening she was elegant and beauteous by reason of three rings, two bracelets, and a princess fringe. This morning her hair-curlers shone like a diamond tiara, and Mrs. Tripp thought her daughter far too ladylike for Prince Albert Grove, although at other times she could reproach her for being too ladylike by half.

"Beautiful morning, is it not, Mrs. Maslen? Almost too nice for sand-bricking doorsteps?"

Some of Miss Tripp's remarks had been known to leave stout Mrs. Maslen, as the saying goes, with a flea in her ear. She therefore replied warily: "Yes, feels like real summer, don't it? Aye, let them enjoy it as can—like you, Lily Tripp. I ain't got no stomach for nothing nowadays."

"No more haven't I," added Mrs. Lowman.

"We all have our worries," said Mrs Tripp.

"I do!" Mrs. Maslen declared.

"Me too, I'm sure," Mrs. Lowman whined.

"How'd you like to live in my house with eleven in family, counting me, and only two bedrooms? And all the cooking and the washing and the scrubbing—and I can't keep 'em as clean as I wants to."

"You want a bathroom, Mrs. Tripp; that's what you want. Then you might be able to keep 'em clean—which they aren't now. 'Twouldn't be a bad thing for Mr. Tripp neither."

"Let people talk about their own husbands, Mrs. Maslen."

"Talk to 'em's more your line, ain't it?"

"Ma does do it in her own house," said Miss Tripp.

"Aye!" Mrs. Maslen went on. "This place ain't good enough for you, Mrs. Tripp. You'd better go across the road, or else up to Larch Avenue. New eight-shilling houses, them— pawn a bit of your Lily's finery—with bathrooms, Mrs. Tripp."

"Larch Avenue off Snow Street?" Mrs. Tripp inquired.

"And three bedrooms. . . ."

"I've been up there."

"And a bow window. . . ."

"It's a nice sort of neighbourhood."

"And a back door. . . ."

"Tradesmen's entrance!" remarked Miss Tripp.

"And them as lives there has afternoon tea in one another's houses, in turn, week by week. They don't wait there till their husbands comes home."

"You seem pretty anxious to get rid of me," said Mrs. Tripp. "And I *have* got a good mind to move out of this. . . ."

The vision, in fact, of a house in Larch Avenue was fast taking hold of her imagination. She was tired of the rough and tumble necessary to keep up her social standing in Prince Albert Grove; and besides, as she told the assembled housewives: "I've got a lot of furniture what pa and ma left me. It's too good to sell; which I shouldn't like to. I could well-nigh furnish an eight-room house—like ours was—I could do it easy. And 'tisn't right for people what want Tripp to have to come to a place like this. And the children do get that dirty here. . . . Oh, Willie, Willie! Just as I was saying! What *have* you been doing? You little torment! Come here this minute. Your clean clothes and your new shoes!"

Willie had proved that the six-shilling houses, where he had been playing, had also their mud-pie grounds. He was carried, crying, into the house and commanded to sit still near the coal-box. Before Miss Tripp followed her mother and William James, she observed maliciously: "Your step *will* look nice, Mrs. Maslen—when it's done." And Mrs. Maslen knelt down to it, retorting: "Do your own step, you proud hussy!" Mrs. Lowman, who couldn't abear Mrs. Maslen, in the absence of Mrs. Tripp to keep the peace, retired to suckle her latest-born.

The Grove was empty.

III

But Mrs. Tripp's brain was full. New pinions for another attempt at flight were sprouting with such rapidity as to be able, that same evening, to make no small rush, whirl and flapping around the inattentive ears of Mr. Tripp.

Small matters, the formal whipping of William James, for example, were always referred to Mr. Tripp. In questions of ordinary importance and everyday occurrence Mrs. Tripp's lead was un-disputed, except by Miss Tripp. But on really

critical occasions, Mrs. Tripp was obliged to bow
before her husband's blunt decisions.   Nevertheless, Mrs. Tripp's flutters, coming as they did
in neither the second nor the third class of events,
but between, seldom took place without considerable stress and strain in the bonds of household
peace.   Tripp was so slow in understanding what
was best for himself, his wife, and his nine
children.

On the first day of the seventh flutter, Tripp
returned about William James's bedtime.   Mrs.
Tripp, who had prepared him an extraordinarily
good supper, went to the door to call William
James home to bed.

"Willie !   Willie !   Will-yum !   Will-y-am
James !"

When his mother's voice was already cracking,
and her threats had become almost inhuman, let
alone unmaternal, William James carefully raised
himself out of a hole at the end of the Grove.   If
possible his state was worse than in the morning.

"Oh, Willie, Willie !   You dirty little wretch !
I'll teach you !   I'll teach you, I will !"

Mrs. Tripp raised him upside-down in her
arms, and punctuated her remarks with the hand.
Willie squealed.   His mother slapped.   Tripp's
first inquiry was an epitome of his life and his
surroundings.

"What's the matter now ?" he asked.

And Mrs. Tripp's reply was addressed to
Tripp, to Willie, and to the whole of this hard
world.

"Did you ever see. . . . You naughty boy !

Will you stay still! One thing after another. . . .
I'm always putting him on clean clothes, and
he gets as dirty as a nasty little gutter-boy.
People wouldn't think he was a respectable person's
child. You'll be the death of me ; and you'll be
sorry for it when I'm dead and gone, you will ! "

Tripp had been going on with his supper.
" When I'm dead and gone," was usually, in his
wife's speeches, followed by a slight pause. He
took advantage of it to say for quietness' sake :
" You won't do it again, will you, Willie lad ? "

" Won't he just ! You'd better take him in
hand ; *I* can't do nothing with him."

" Aye ! but boys must play about, Jane.
Mustn't they, Willie ? "

" They needn't play in the worst muck they
can find. I never had to have clean things two
or three times a day when I was a girl. Willie
takes after you ; that's what it is. Look at him !
I can't keep him clean. . . ."

" Then you'll have to let 'en go dirty."

" Let 'en go dirty ! " repeated Mrs. Tripp with
scorn. " We all know what people's children gets
like when they lets 'em go dirty. Look at Mrs.
Lowman's ! I'm surprised at you, Tripp, I am,
when I've been working and washing and cleaning
for your children all those years, and got nothing
but worry for it. I'll not be able to do it much
longer. I've got a pain in the pit of my stomach
now. How can you expect me to keep 'em clean
and nice in this dirty place ? Why can't you
move into a better street ? That's what you
ought to have done years ago."

"What do we want to move into a better street for ?"

"'What do we want to move into a better street for'! Haven't I just been telling you? It's pigs as lives in pig-sties! Besides you'd get more chimneys to do."

"And not have time to do 'em! We can't afford a better house. How much is it?"

"Only eight shillings. . . ."

"Eight shillings—five and three—two and nine more. It won't run to it. Now will it, Jane?"

"If 'twon't, then we'd all better go to the workhouse straight off, I say. We shouldn't need to in Larch Avenue. And I've got plenty enough things to furnish a bigger house—thanks to pa and ma. There's bathrooms in Larch Avenue. That wouldn't be a bad thing for you, Tripp."

"No more it wouldn't. But don't you go setting your heart on what you can't get, there's an old girl."

"Old girl indeed! I shan't stay here all my life, and don't you forget it, Tripp."

Mr. Tripp, still wishing to smoke his pipe in peace, tried to dodge the trouble. "I'll tell you what," he said. "You find the extra rent, and then we'll all move off there.—No, I shan't have a lodger.—I ain't partic'lar keen, but you do seem a bit anxious like. You get the extra money, and I'll go."

"Very well, I'll take in washing, and hold my head over other people's dirty clothes week in and week out."

"No, no, my girl. You've got more'n you can do now. We shall be able to run to it when we get some of the children off our hands. For now, I tell 'ee, 'twon't run to it—an' that's enough."

IV

Tripp's decision, however, was not enough. He had left open the cage door, through which his wife might flutter.

But how find the money?

Mrs. Tripp thought earnestly of many different things, from dressmaking or selling sweets to Lily's winning competitions or getting married to a gentleman of means. She thought till her mind became misty, full of the unknown, unfound something needed. The new house depended on her power to juggle with shillings and pence.

Suddenly the mist cleared off. Like an angel from heaven there appeared to Mrs. Tripp the figure of her not very well-beloved brother, Alfred Benson, a butcher's salesman. She saw him under the oil flares, clad in a meaty white overall. She saw him going home to a street not unlike Prince Albert Grove. And she knew that if anything is worse than living in such a place, it is lodging in it. Lastly, she pictured him taking his evening meal in the new house of Tripp, and for that and other great comforts, paying at least twelve shillings a week towards the household expenses —towards the additional rent. "I felt," she confided to Mrs. Lowman, "I don't know how

I felt. Tripp can't have no objection to Alfred, seeing he's my own brother. We shall only have two bedrooms still, 'cause Alfred 'll have to have one to himself; but the rooms is bigger, and there's a scullery and a wash-house and a yard. Tripp won't have to keep his soot-bags in the kitchen. And there's a bathroom. Tripp'll like that."

And Mrs. Tripp felt flattered when Mrs. Lowman echoed : "Of course he will. I only wish I had your chances, Mrs. Tripp. But where I am, there I stays, I do."

Tripp's consent was certainly a little grudging. He thought Alfred Benson a bit hard to get on with, not so sober as he might be, and unmarried at an age when any respectable man should have got his young woman and be settled down.

But moving from and into weekly houses is not a matter of months and quarters. Before three weeks were out, Mrs. Tripp carted all her goods, chattels and children, and her pa and ma's furniture, to No. 67, Larch Avenue. Alfred Benson had been a little unwilling, to be sure ; but when Mrs. Tripp had promised him a room to himself, the second latchkey, and meals at his own time, he told his old landlady to go to the devil, and followed his sister.

Larch Avenue may be described as the most superior of those quarters in which the morning step-washing and the evening gate-standing are important social functions. Had the rent been twenty pounds sixteen shillings a year instead of eight shillings a week, it would have made all the difference. The two long rows of houses, for ever staring at one another, were built of bright red brick, and in spite of their newness the street already suggested premature decay and falling rentals. Larch Avenue would never mellow with antiquity. Its window-curtains were the one sign of its superiority.

At an evening gate-standing shortly after Mrs. Tripp had joyfully moved house, all the heat of the day was lying stagnant in the street. Patches of sun-fused tar ran down to the gutters in treacly streamlets. Miss Tripp pointed out to her mother a little girl on the opposite side : " Look at that little girl, ma. She's making tar snow-balls. She's covered with it, worse'n our Willie." Groups of women, their hair just rid of curlers, stood at the gates, wallowing in their own and each other's petty misfortunes. Certain phrases made themselves heard through the hum and cackle : " I said. . . . She said. . . . He told me. . . . I never heard of such a thing. . . . It's a shame, that it is ! " And meanwhile, through open doors and windows, the cries of babies could be heard : " Mum-ma ! Mum-ma ! Mum-mum-mum ! "

Mrs. Tripp had been living such a short time among the elect of Larch Avenue, that the strange joyfulness she felt on realising that she was moved into a better street, made her slightly shy. It is true that the furniture was not yet put straight ; that old newspapers took the place of window-curtains : and that Tripp's sole advertisement took the form of a sprawling

MR. TRIPP, chalked on the lintel of the front door.   But the chimney-sweep's signboard was at the painter's, where, following Miss Tripp's patriotic and enlightened advice, the threefold announcement

THOMAS TRIPP.
CHIMNEYS SWEPT
MODERATE.

was to be coloured red, white and blue, on a royal purple background.

For the first few days, indeed, Mrs. Tripp was supremely happy.   Not only did she feel the glow of having risen in the world ; her brother appeared to be content, Tripp to have settled down, and William James to love dirt a shade less.   She talked much with a childless Mrs. Arter, who was often quite pleased to take charge of William James, and to amuse herself by putting him clean.   By Mrs. Arter she was introduced to the afternoon teas, and she found the conversation there to be of entrancing personal interest.   Mrs. Lowman was invited to tea, and left saying : " Aye ! Mrs. Tripp, but you're one of the lucky ones."   Whereat, Mrs. Tripp, failing to distinguish between luck and reward, was much pleased.   Her pa and ma's furniture fitted so well into the new house, and reminded her so much of her childhood, that she soon felt doubly at home.   And in the evening time Miss Tripp played tunes with one finger on her grandmother's harmonium.   Mrs. Tripp was so pleased and proud that she spent more time in thinking how to do things in correct and seemly fashion than she did in the doing of them.

V

The flutter was slow; the fall quick.

On the second Monday morning in the new house, Tripp returned from sweeping chimneys at breakfast time. Alfred Benson was at table in a clean white overall which Mrs. Tripp had herself starched. They all sat down most pleasantly. But alas! while they were eating, William James found out the soot-bags in the back yard. Thence he went to the breakfast table to beg a little of his elders' food. His mother got up to slap him. He fled to the protection of his Uncle Alfred. Some of the abundance of his soot came off on his uncle's overall, and Alfred Benson's language was worse than Mrs. Maslen's at her worst. Mrs. Tripp turned from her son to her brother. "Pa would have beaten such language out of you," she said.

"Well! look what a mess the little beast has made me in. I'll wallop him!"

"Can't have your language here," said Mr. Tripp. "We ain't used to it, not with the children about."

"You won't, won't you? D'you think he's going to plaster me with his nasty soot whenever it comes into his dirty little head? Hanged if I'll stay in your sooty house!"

"Then you'd better go," said Mr. Tripp.

"Alfred!" exclaimed Mrs. Tripp. "Alfred!

I can easily give your overall another wash. But you shan't teach my Willie your language, and don't you dare to hit him ! "

"No, I'm blowed if I will ! I'll shunt to-day. I never been in such a squallin', sooty house, and I ain't goin' to stay. Look how the brat's squallin' now—like a stuck pig. Think I'm goin' to stand that ? Blowed if I will ! "

Alfred Benson left the house. "Good riddance ! " said Mr. Tripp, and then he, too, went out.

Mrs. Tripp knew she could no longer depend on her brother for the additional rent. She decided that she must take in washing ; looked forward with fear to the time when she would have to get Tripp's consent, yet leave unroused his persistent, if silent, desire to be back in Prince Albert Grove. "Anyhow," she thought, "we shall have a third bedroom." But Miss Tripp's promise to help with the washing was obtained only on condition that she should have the third bedroom all to herself.

"'Tisn't as if we were in the Grove," said Miss Tripp, and her mother gave in.

Later on, that same morning, the landlord came in person to collect his rents. Mrs. Tripp, when she fetched her eight shillings, thought with shrinking of the clothes that must be washed to earn eight shillings.

"Good morning, Mrs. Tripp. Fine morning," said the landlord, who was either excessively civil or extremely blunt, partly because it was his nature and partly because it was advisable. "Thank you," he continued, filling in the receipt. "Mrs. Tripp—one week in advance—eight shillings. Much obliged. Do you like the house, Mrs. Tripp? Getting on all right?"

Some of the neighbours had not failed to discuss the new-comers, and also to mention the ordinary state of William James. In Larch Avenue the parents liked to keep their children rather more spick and span than they troubled to keep themselves. Hence William James was very noticeable, and it had been hinted to the landlord that the street was already beginning to "go down."

Mrs. Tripp answered with pleasure, "Nicely, thank you, sir. We shall soon be quite settled, when we've got this fixed up over the window." She brought forth the red, white, blue and royal purple signboard to show him. "Isn't it pretty, sir?"

"But, my good woman, you can't put that up here—you really can't. This is a residential property, and signboards of any description are strictly prohibited."

"But, sir. . . ."

"I repeat, I can't allow it. This is not a business street. It is residential. Don't you see, Mrs. Tripp, if I allowed that, there's no knowing where it would end?"

"I don't see. . . . Tripp won't stay here if he can't have his sign out, fresh painted and all. What's the good?"

"Well, he can't have that, Mrs. Tripp."

"Then Tripp won't stay."

"Do you wish to give notice?"

"What's the good of staying, if Tripp can't have his sign?"

"You wish to give notice?"

"Tripp *will* have his sign."

"Come, come, my good woman! You do give notice?"

"I . . . Yes!"

"Good morning, Mrs. Tripp."

But Mrs. Tripp had gone swiftly indoors muttering: "It's a shame, a shame, a cryin' shame!" She dropped into her pa's armchair, and wept. Willie wept with her. On hearing him she regained her self-control, and, in some mysterious way, she calmed herself by rocking him and repeating: "Poor Willie! poor Willie! my poor Willie!"

She washed him; then put on her hat and shawl, and went to see Mrs. Lowman, who, she knew, would at that time be washing her door-step. The old house was still empty.

Mrs. Lowman was taken aback. "Well, Mrs. Tripp! Well! I didn't think to see you now. Do you still like Larch Avenue? It's weary work settling in a new house, though I've never had the chance of doing it. Are the curtain-rods all right now, my dear?"

"No, love! We've got to go! We'll be coming back!"

And to avoid breaking down before such a weakling gossip, the broken-winged woman left abruptly.

Throughout the day, Mrs. Lowman, ignorant

M

of all reason for the fall, and supposing it to be due to Tripp's cruelty, continued to murmur: "Poor woman! We all have our trials. Poor woman!" She thought she'd just tell Mrs. Maslen. "Jolly glad the proud thing's got to come back," said that lady. "And I'll let her know it too!"

One rainy evening, being the following Saturday, Mr., Mrs. and Miss Tripp, and some of the children, journeyed many times to and fro, removing pa and ma's furniture, and everything else back to Prince Albert Grove.

When it was all finished, Mrs. Tripp felt ready to drop. She wondered what her pa and ma would have said, and wept awhile. And she wept again when Tripp tried, in his offhand way, to comfort her.

Yet, this the seventh, was by no means Mrs. Tripp's final flutter, nor her last fall. Like the Child Angel, continually she put forth fresh buds of wings, but anon was shorn of her aspiring, and fell fluttering into the hands of those full-winged angels—the memories of her genteeler maiden days.

TURNED OUT

ONE evening in early autumn the sun was low down between Morgan's Mount and Oliver Cromwell's Camp—sinking, as it were, behind the edge of the Downs. All the west was overspread with flaming clouds, which changed their colours with the sun's decline and their floating faery-like forms with the light winds of the upper air. Tongues of heavy grey broke from the clouds that made a canopy above the sun ; the west was gloomy in its fierce intensity. Underneath, the trees on the distant horizon burnt with a lurid red—it might have been the mouth of hell. Some of the splendid light overflowed into the east and tipped its feathery cirrus clouds with gold ; whilst the hills shone with radiance, or seemed grey and grassless under deep shadow. There was no sound save the melancholy cry of the peewits, and the rush of wind through the grass like the sound of the sea on a far shore.

A woman and a dog were alone on the hills. Silhouetted against the sky, they looked black and meanly small. The woman was evidently of the country. She was soon to become a mother.

Sorrow, felt rather than thought of, stared from her tearful eyes, and her face suffused with a uniform flush of redness. She was wrought upon by her destitution and the fear of her coming pain, and she had no relief by thinking on the after-joy of mothers, for she knew that she could but add a living burden to her heavy life.

As they walked over the down the dog put up a hare, and was called in by the woman. Then, while he looked up at her with eyes seemingly full of a sympathy which asks no questions, gives no advice, she vaguely felt that he would understand, and told him about her sorrow.

"Poor Bruno! your master's gone back to London and only left me you—and this. What shall we do now his father's turned us out?

"He's gone back to London, where he was married before, and nobody but me—not even his father—has got to know. What shall we do? Oh, Bruno, not but a week or so left!

"I was happy for a month, Bruno—so happy! And now we've nowhere at all to go to. But I'm glad I was happy.

"Bruno, I loved your master! He doesn't love his church wife a bit—I'm sure he doesn't. He'll be unhappy now, like me. Oh, if he hadn't been and got married! We'd have gone to London with him.

"You might have got lost or been poisoned there, Bruno.

"What can we do? In a week's time it will all be over. We may be in the workhouse. The

old man said we could get off there, and if they
find us they'll want to send us to it. I won't go
—and they'd take you away.

" His father used to be kind to me—before he
said he wouldn't have no brazen-faced hussies for
servants. I wasn't a servant—not a real one. I
was a help. He swore, by God, he wouldn't have
me in his house again. If he's sold the pigs well
and isn't drunk, perhaps he'll do something when
he sees me out here.

" 'Twas *his* son, anyhow. . . .

" The later he is from market the more he's
likely to be drunk.

" It's getting late now. It's cold up here.
Poor Bruno ! Lie down then."

She shivered, and sat down on a heap of chalk ;
the dog lay on her skirt. All around the Downs
looked grey ; for the sun was now below the
horizon, and the glory of the sunset was shrunk
to a nightcap cloud.

The wind, unwarmed by the sun, still rushed
through the grass. The peewits had gone, and
only the hoarse corncrakes croaked loudly in the
fields over the brow of the hill. The woman felt
the cold air cut her like a knife as she waited by
the side of the road.

Presently, in the dusk, a heavy dog-cart came
along the white chalk road. Two men were in it.
The elder, the old farmer, held the reins ; but he
was rather guided by the horse than guided it.
His red face and bloodshot eyes contrasted, even
in twilight, with his stubby white beard. He was
market-day drunk.

When the cart approached the chalk-heap the dog barked and roused the old man, who, seeing the woman, gave his companion a heavy nudge. He drew himself up and pointed to her, and his laughter went round the hills in a hoarse loud cadence.

"Ha, ha, ha, ha, ha!　'Twas she as fooled my Joe!"

But he drove on, and then whistled for the dog.

"Bruno, yer!　Bruno!"

Bruno ran a short way after the cart, turned, looked back at the woman.　Fearful lest he should return to the farm, afraid to face the night alone, she cried out shrilly, and he went to her.

"Damn you!" roared the farmer.

He whipped up his horse.

Then the woman lost all hope.　She stumbled to the edge of a small pine wood.　There she sank to the ground in a black heap, at which the dog sniffed and whined.

It grew still cooler; and, as the moon rose in a clear sky, an autumn frost spread over the Downs. No one of the few passers-by saw the stricken woman.　In the cold deceitful moonlight the little group looked just like a tuft of stunted furze-bush.

In time the wind bore with it a woman's groans—for a few minutes a human being's first cry on earth; and again it rushed alone through the grass, and made a deeper sound amongst the pines.　The woman lay unconscious on the ground, while the dog slept by her or prowled along the edge of the wood.

Next morning the sun rose with a clear and hopeful splendour, giving a fresh brilliance to every blade of frosted grass. But through his absence only the dog had lived. A shepherd found the woman and her child sodden with the white frost-fog, dead, and stiff; and they were taken to the workhouse mortuary.

SILLY SALTIE

I

" HULLO, Silly Saltie ! You *be* here then. What's got for the c'lection bag, eh ? "

Most of the labouring people threw a kindly jeer at him as they walked stiffly into Lincombe Church for the Easter morning service. Silly Saltie chuckled back at them ; but to the few farmers and their wives (more wives than farmers) he touched his cap and called out in a high-pitched monotone : " Gude morning, sah ! Morning, m'am ! Fine morning, sah ! "

" Not late this morning, Silly Saltie ? "

" Aw no, sah ! Never late if I can help it, sah."

Silly Saltie's words tumbled out of his mouth as if, once formed in his throat, he had no further control over them. In boyhood he had been known as Lizzie Salter's Wallie. Because he was too stupid for labour, and for a carter's job was too cunningly cruel to horses, his mother sent him to sea under a cousin of hers, a coasting skipper out of Plymouth. He soon returned, hugging a small French-made box which he hid away without showing its contents to anybody.

168

Dubbed the Silly Salt, he became known, jocularly at first, and afterwards by everybody, as Silly Saltie. He did not appear to resent his nickname. It was a good joke in Lincombe. So was Silly Saltie himself.

One day a Lincombe man met the coasting skipper on Plymouth Barbican. " Silly Saltie— Lizzie Salter's boy to Lincombe ? " growled the skipper. " Sending me a damn'd idiot like that ! And I could tell 'ee more if 'twasn't that his mother's related to me and you come from the same place." The end of it all was that Silly Saltie's mother supported her son by cleaning the church and scrubbing at the vicarage, whilst Silly Saltie earned ha'pence at odd jobs and blew the organ. It was even said that he was well off. Twice in three years he had changed half a sovereign. " 'Tis won'erful," some said, " how they sort gets hold o' money an' puts it away —them what's something lacking in the head." Silly Saltie's reputed wealth earned him a sort of respect. But everybody laughed at him. And he had the laugh of them all, simply because his laughter was an irresponsible cackle, impossible to stop till it had wearied itself out.

In the churchyard this Easter morning the news quickly spread that Captain and Mrs. Kelland, Lincombe's Lord and Lady of the Manor, had their son home—" Master Herbert " to Lincombe people, Lieutenant Kelland, R.N., to the world at large. Presently they came, all three of them, out of the only big house besides the vicarage. The organist beckoned to Silly Saltie from the

vestry door ; his mother ran out with a feather
dusting-brush in her hand and clutched him by
the arm. "Whatever's thee at, Wallie ? They
won't hae no music to welcome 'em in if thee
doesn't stir thyself. Oh my dear soul ! if I an't
got me brush in me hand, Sunday an' all."

The little work-worn woman hastened within
again. Silly Saltie followed, talking to himself.
"Aw ! he'll be playing loud to-day. Blow, blow !
' When I plays loud you blow hard, but if I plays
soft don't you bust 'en ! ' That's it."

Happily for the village sense of the fitness of
things, the Kellands lingered in the churchyard to
gaze down the combe. Fields, just beginning to
grow green in the spring sunshine—dotted with
leafless stunted trees, with patches of dead bracken
and bright yellow furze—slanted in a great open
curve down to Lincombe Brook. At Linnicombe
Ope, the cliffs, throwing themselves back, revealed
a U-shaped piece of sea, blue and sparkling close
to shore and on the horizon of a dull bluish
mistiness that was hardly distinguishable from
sky.

While the Kellands were walking to their pew
the organist played very martial music, for theirs
was a naval family and "Master Herbert" had
been seeing some active service. Silly Saltie's
rackety blowing was distinctly audible through
the music. People smiled.

Outside, all was sunshine and shimmer and
peace. Lincombe lay at the top of the combe
as if asleep in the earth's arms.

The service proceeded, a thing, seemingly,

half of this world and half of another, so little did
the voices of the congregation fill the church,
so hollowly did the singing echo about the walls
and in the oaken roof. Soon after the vicar had
begun his sermon, a face looked out from behind
the organ and remained peering into the church
—a face most delicate in the curve of the nose
and of the thin lips, though discoloured by sun
and rain, and encircled by a straggling picture-
frame beard—the face of an ascetic, of a saint.
But the eyes, on the contrary, were those of a
bird which is wondering whether it dare hop
down from a roof and carry away some tit-bit.

It was Silly Saltie peeping. Again people
smiled. At the back of the church they nudged
one another.

In compliment to the Kellands, the vicar spoke
in his sermon of bloodshed and death on the field
of battle. "Think, too," he said, " of the stokers
in our battleships, drowned unawares in the midst
of their duties, sunk with their ship in the din
of battle, dead without a moment to repent
themselves. . . ."

" Aw, what a pity, sah ! "

Aw——*what a*——*pit*——*ty*——*sah !* was how
Sillie Saltie bleated it out. A hand dragged him
back behind the organ. There were more smiles.
Laughter was heard from the Sunday School
pews.

"Why two, my dear ? " Captain Kelland
whispered to his wife when, during the last
prayer, she took two five-pound notes from her
purse.

"Herbert's home," she replied, touching his hand with a dainty, pathetic gesture.

It had been her custom, ever since her son went to sea, to place five pounds in the poor-box at Easter. 'Twas her intercession of the saints. Waiting till the congregation was out of church, till in fact the organist had ceased playing, she doubled up the notes and pushed them into the box.

Silly Saltie was peeping again, more saint-like and bird-like than before. Mrs. Kelland caught sight of him. "Give Walter Salter something," she said to her husband. "He's been to sea, too. —You give it to him. I don't like going near him."

Captain Kelland held out both hands in front of Sillie Saltie, a half-crown in one and half-a-sovereign in the other; "Which will you have, Salter?" he asked.

"Aw, sah! Don't like to be greedy, sah. I'll hae the little 'un, please sah. Thank ye, sah."

So Silly Saltie took the half-sovereign, leaving the half-crown in Captain Kelland's other hand. Father and son laughed freely, but while Mrs. Kelland was walking home she heard Silly Saltie cackling and gloating over "the little 'un," and she shivered.

II

At the Easter vestry meeting the poor-box was opened and its contents counted.

Captain Kelland said nothing at the time.   In true West Country fashion—when there is business to be done—he dropped across the vicar as if by chance.

"Didn't you make the poor-box four pounds seventeen and threepence-farthing?" he asked.

"Yes. Why?"

"Well, my wife. . . ."

"I was wondering to myself what had become of her usual five-pound donation. I knew, you know, whose 'twas. How is she to-day? If the box had been five pounds odd I should have concluded that the five pounds was hers and the odd everybody else's."

"But she did. She put in two five-pound notes this time, because Herbert is home."

"She couldn't have. . . ."

"I saw her do it—saw the notes."

"I must find out. Thanks."

That was all. The two men were so used to settling between them the affairs of the universe in their own parish that of course the vicar would find out.

In consequence of his rather unguarded inquiries as to who had been in the church, and at what time, it rapidly became known throughout Lincombe, even to the outlying farms, that the poor-box had been opened and from three pounds to three hundred stolen out of it. The villagers appropriated suspicion to themselves. It might have been the tramp who had a pinch of tea at Mrs. Finzel's, boiling water at Miss Prowse's, and bread at Mrs. Salter's, but the village felt itself none the less suspected because it heartily blamed those ladies for encouraging tramps.

At last, after several street-corner meetings among the men, Jacob Nosworthy, carpenter and leader of the choir, carefully arranged that he should be dropped across by the vicar.

" Have 'ee found out anything, sir ? "

" What ? "

" 'Bout the poor-box."

" No, I can't get a clue."

" Sure 'nuff you can't, sir."

" What d'you mean, Jacob ? Do *you* know anything ? "

" No, *I* don't, sir ; leastways, I'd rather not say. . . ."

The vicar waited in silence.

" Didn't ought to have thic Silly Saltie about the church so much, sir."

" Nonsense, Jacob ! Why ? He's harmless enough. His mother cleans the church."

" I knows her do, sir."

" Besides, nothing more has been taken from the box."

" Do 'ee know that, sir, for sure ? "

" Look here, Jacob ; what are you driving at ? Do you think it's Silly Saltie ? Have you got any proofs ? "

" No, *I* an't got no proofs. But I've a-seed they mazed articles a sight artfuller with money than you nor me nuther, sir. An' I tell 'ee, sir, what 'tis : if you don't keep Silly Saltie out o' the church, me and the others what sings in the choir, we'm agreed not to sing any more, 'cause, you see, sir, *we* goes into the church too, an' 'tis a shadder, like, over the lot o' us."

Then the vicar exercised the tact which underlay his shortness of manner. He could not bar Silly Saltie from entering the church, partly because he scrupled to do so, chiefly because no other man could be got to blow the organ on week-days, and every one knew how much the organist needed all the practice he could get. The vicar suggested, therefore, to Nosworthy that they should let matters stay as they were until they could find out whether or no the poor-box was still being rifled.

Nosworthy was very willing to undertake the work of finding out. He knew that the vicar and Captain Kelland had the only two keys in the village that fitted the padlock, and he also remembered that instead of dovetailing in the bottom of the box, as well as the sides, he had merely made it fast with four thin brass screws.

Very warily he filled up the gullets of the screws with beeswax, pressed it well home, and polished away the smudges. "Nobody can't unscrew they without disturbin' thic there wax," he said to himself.

Within a few weeks he was able to prove to the vicar that the box had been opened from the bottom, and, as he had anticipated, the vicar's interest in the main point caused him to overlook the slack workmanship of the box.

"Don't you take ort out, sir," Jacob recommended. "You jest count the money from time to time, like,"

The vicar did. First he found that the sum in the poor-box diminished, and then he noticed that the number of coins remained nearly the same. Coins of less value were substituted for coins of higher value, shillings for half-crowns, sixpences for florins, and so on. He noticed with surprise how seldom threepenny-bits were to be found in the box.

Finally, he marked all the coins, and shortly afterwards, a marked half-crown was changed at the village post-office shop by Silly Saltie.

The vicar set out on the warpath. It was perhaps as well that he met Jacob Nosworthy on the way. "No, don't you tackle 'en now, sir. Just you wait an' see where he stows it away. They mazed articles, they hides things away like dogs hides bones. You won't never get back what he've a-took if you fronts 'en wi' it now. You wait. You been watching the poor-box; now you watch Silly Saltie, sir."

Late one evening, Nosworthy came to the vicar. "I've a-see'd 'en 'long wi' a screw-driver," he whispered.

III

Half a gale of damp southerly wind was blowing gustily up the combe from the sea. It rustled in the trees, then rushed, then tore at them, and underneath its many sounds a savage ground-bass could be heard—the pounding roar of surf on the shingle at Linnicombe Mouth. One of those nights, it was, when the clouds which hide the face

of the moon are not so thick but they allow
its light to soak through ; when the light itself,
though faint, yet has a certain glare in it.   The
vicar and Nosworthy could see where they were
going ; they did not stumble, but they did lift their
feet higher than was necessary, like drunkards
indeed, except that the lurch came after the step
instead of before it.   They could not, for the
drizzle, see the top of the church tower.   But the
jackdaws saw them and chattered.   Nature was
wakeful.   Nosworthy wished himself snug in bed.
He even remarked to the vicar, " P'raps 'er won't
come, sir."

Entering the church by the south door, they
crept (there was no real need to creep) up to the
chancel, and seated themselves side by side where
they could peep through the wooden tracery of
the screen.   Strange how many little noises there
were !   The high unstained leaded south windows
appeared to be bulging inwards, but that was doubtless an illusion of the dim variable moonlight.

Presently, nearer eleven than ten o'clock,
the vestry lock snicked and the door creaked.
Nosworthy edged closer to the vicar.   A man,
a shadow, a blackness in the air, was moving
slowly along the wall towards the poor-box.
Something rattled.   A match was struck, carefully shaded between two root-like hands.   A
candle in an old stable lantern was lighted ; a
broken bowler hat placed over it.   But there was
light enough to glint on a steel tool ; to shine
through a scrappy fringe of whiskers ; to outline
Silly Saltie's delicately shaped features.   " Very

N

still, like a ghostis's count'nance," Nosworthy says it was.

The bowler hat was tilted so that the lantern shone on the wall and on the bottom of the box. It also shone full on Silly Saltie's face. The vicar declared more than once afterwards that he never in all his life saw eyes so rapacious and cunning, so meanly devilish. He confesses to having been afraid, not of Silly Saltie, but of something unknown that Silly Saltie's face suggested to him. And Nosworthy, too, never talks about that night without saying : " You should ha' see'd how thic Silly Saltie looked. I tell thee what 'twas like—you knows when you be so quiet as death an' the rats comes out to hunt for crumbs an' keeps their eyes on 'ee, seems so, all the time —well, 'twas like rats' eyes, hisen ! '

" Tssh ! tssh ! tssh ! " went Silly Saltie with each turn of the screw-driver. He drew, one after another, the thin brass screws and lowered the bottom of the box gently in a piece of cloth. He peeped silently into the cloth, then carried it together with its contents into the vestry, because, no doubt, he understood that its single small window was turned away from the road and could not in any case show much light. Though the wind still blustered outside, the church inside became entirely soundless except for the clink of coins and an occasional cooing noise, like the satisfaction of a fed baby falling asleep.

The vicar and Nosworthy took a long step into the aisle, tip-toed along the red carpet, out at the south door, and crouched down behind a tomb-

stone near the vestry ; then waited what seemed a
very long time. The clouds had thinned to a
driving rack. When Silly Saltie came out, for all
the world as if he had been helping his mother at
cleaning the church, but with his French-made box
under his arm, they saw him hide away his lantern
within a broken square tomb. They followed him
out at the lychgate, down the lower lane, across
the brook by footbridge, along a field-road, skirt-
ing the farmhouse, and so, always slantwise and
upwards, to the edge of the cliff. Whereupon
Silly Saltie disappeared. Gulls flew screaming
from the ledges below. " He's gone ! " the vicar
exclaimed.

"*He* an't falled," said Nosworthy. " He be
gone down along to the Man o' God. You
follow me."

Nosworthy led the vicar down a couple of
hundred feet to the cliff gardens which were made
long ago on a wide shelf three-quarter ways up
the otherwise sheer cliff. Thence they climbed
up again till they stood just below a pinnacle of
harder sandstone which the weather had separated
from the cliff, leaving only a narrow neck of cliff-
rubble to connect the two. It was the Man
o' God rock—the weather-worn, twisted and
grotesque image of a gigantic human being.

Silly Saltie — like a misshapen animal — was
crawling along the neck of weed-grown rubble.
Dislodged stones scuttled down and hit the beach
far below. Arrived at the Man o' God, where
the neck broadened again, he rose upright and
rested his box on a projecting slab of stone that

was formerly called, when the place was more
accessible, the Man o' God's Dinner Table.
Then, in the strengthening moonlight—for the
rack was blowing off the sky—the vicar and
Nosworthy witnessed a ceremony at which they
hardly knew whether to laugh or shudder. Before
his box, at the feet of the Man o' God, Silly Saltie
bowed, genuflected, knelt and prayed, his arms
outstretched in supplication, his head lowered
reverently between them. The vicar recognized.
. . . His every action at Choral Celebration was
being faithfully reproduced. The soughing wind,
the mewing of gulls, the roar of invisible surf
hundreds of feet below, made a weird music for
Silly Saltie's ceremonial. He stood up, he lifted
the box on high in worship ; and on his raised
face and in his eyes, too, so far as they could be
seen, there was once more the ecstasy of a saint.
It was his *Gloria in Excelsis !*

Silly Saltie took something bright from his
box. Involuntarily the vicar called out.

Silly Saltie listened, banged the box-lid, and
ran.

"Come on !" cried Nosworthy. He pushed
and pulled the vicar to the neck of land, and,
having run back a moment to pick up something,
edged him along to the top of the cliff. "Here's
three threepenny-bits anyhow," he said, "on the
Man o' God's Dinner Table. Lookse ! There
he goes !"

A figure was running, or rather tumbling,
down the steep coastguard path to Linnicombe
Ope. Nosworthy and the vicar chased it, gaining

when the figure fell and had to grope round for its box. They followed into the deep-cut bed of Lincombe Brook and some way up the tunnel which is formed by the thick bushes overhead. There they gave up the chase : the path was too stony and wet and dark. But on coming to the churchyard, they caught sight of Silly Saltie clambering over the far wall, and, on looking into the broken tomb, they found his box. It was of beautiful workmanship, and inlaid with silverwire. The vicar took it home.

He was tired beyond measure, yet could not sleep. He seemed to have been present at some wicked rite of the dark ages that he could not get out of his mind's eye.

Besides, what was he to do with Silly Saltie?

IV

The vicar of Lincombe was not one of those parsons who send for a policeman as soon as a call is made upon their Christianity. Instead, he sent next morning for the thief himself, who appeared most humbly and respectfully, exactly as at other times.

"This looks bad, Salter," said the vicar sternly, pointing to the French-made box. "How long have you been stealing from the poor-box in the church?"

"Aw, sah! Sorry, sah! Fust time an' all, sah!" blabbed Silly Saltie.

"Where is the key, Salter?"

"Aw, sah! How be I to know, sah?"

"Give me the key, or I shall have the box broken open."

"Pity, sah. Pretty, sah. I didn't break the church box. I an't got the key, sah."

The vicar sent for Nosworthy; then turned again to the cringing Silly Saltie : "I shall not have you enter the church at all—d'you understand ?"

"Aw, sah! An' I blows the organ, sah."

"I don't think you quite know the wickedness of your crime. I will pray for you, Salter."

"I'm sure I thank you, sah. Parsons' prayers be good, sah."

"D'you understand ? This would send you to prison. . . ."

"Aw, sah! What a pity, sah! Should *you* like to go to prison, sah?"

Thinking it was perhaps necessary to speak to fools very strongly and loudly, the vicar shouted with decision :

"You'll go to hell!"

Silly Saltie jumped. "Aw, sah! Hot, ain't it, sah? Shall you like it, sah?"

"But I haven't committed sacrilege. . . ."

"An't you, sah?"

Silly Saltie's gibbering suavity nonplussed the vicar. Nosworthy came in, and while he was prising open the box, Silly Saltie looked on miserably, as a helpless child looks on while a favourite animal is being slaughtered.

Mrs. Kelland's two five-pound notes, together with thirteen pounds odd, mostly in silver, were found inside. Very strangely, for money given in charity, there were no threepenny-bits.

"Did you get all this money from the poor-box ?" the vicar asked.

"How be I to know, sah ?"

"Well, I shall keep it : d'you hear ! "

"Aw, sah ! What a pity, sah ! Poor man an' all, sah. Siller an' gold. 'Twouldn't ha' mattered if 'twas pennies, sah."

"You can keep your box."

"Aw, I thank you, sah."

"Now go, and don't you ever let me see you near the church again. Go now. D'you hear? "

Silly Saltie took his box into his arms. He fingered it tenderly, raised its broken lid. "Aw ! Wicked, sah ! " he said. "Pretty box ! Poor man an' all, sah ! "

Weeping quietly, bent almost double, like a suffering saint, he tottered from the vicar's study, out of the house, and down the lane to his mother's cottage.

The vicar had no sense whatever of triumph.

Nosworthy went again to the Man o' God and found, hidden away in an old church collection bag at the back of the Man o' God's Dinner Table, a large number of threepenny-bits. In the vicar's opinion it was an idiot miser's hoard, but Nosworthy always declares, not without reverence, that it was Silly Saltie's offerings—whether to God Almighty or to the Man o' God rock, who knows ?

A LOVE'S HUNGER

"The voice of my beloved!"—*Solomon's Song.*

ONE evening in the earlier half of last century, Matilda Hennyker, at that time frail-looking, thin-faced, and very young, was clambering through a hedge in order to cross the turnpike road which ran by her estate. Suddenly she heard a sharp knock, a scuffle, and many oaths fluently rapped out by a deep angry voice. Fearing some mishap, she hurried round a bend in the road, to the place whence the sound had come. And there she saw a chaise and a barouche with their wheels fast locked together. A gentleman held one horse's head and a loutish stableman held the other's. Meanwhile, since neither could move from his horse's head, the gentleman was rating the stableman with a torrent of forcible language which startled Matilda quite as much as the accident itself. Seeing her, he raised his hat and bowed, hoping she had not heard what he had been saying, and put an end to his apologies by pointing out that the stableman was drunk. Without exactly meaning to tell a lie, Matilda managed to convey to him that she had not heard

184

what, as a matter of fact, she had heard very plainly. She held his horse's head while he guided the unlocking of the wheels, and, after short but evidently sincere thanks, he wished her a very good evening.

This encounter remained the uppermost subject of Matilda's thoughts. She was living almost alone, in a part of the West Country where there is little to talk about and less to be seen ; and she could not help welcoming contact with a man who was neither a hind nor a sporting squire. Without any close friends to sympathise with her longings, she had become like a climbing plant that has no support for its tendrils ; and this gentleman had impressed and attracted her as no other man had done. She decided that she liked his eyes and smile, which were dependent one on the other. She liked also his words, which, however inadequate by themselves, were to the point. His face, as strong as his body, and expressive, helped out his meaning ; he looked at her with meaning—that was it. She very soon felt as if she had been acquainted with him before, as indeed she had in mind, in her castles in the air, though she had never seen him in the flesh.

" Do you know who that was ? " she asked the maid who had been attending her while she was out walking.

" He's the new doctor, ma'am, that's come to take old Mr. Tillet's place."

" The doctor. . . ."

" Yes, ma'am ; and they do say he've worked a wonderful cure with Mrs. Burbage's jaundice."

Matilda was interested in doctors and their profession. She would have liked to know this one, the first real doctor who had ever come to live in that part of the country.

Not many weeks after the accident the wished-for opportunity occurred. She was ailing, and sent for him to bleed her. The operation was done with delicacy; but when she would have kept him by her for a little conversation not directly bearing on her ailment, he quickly and somewhat awkwardly took his leave.

She was very greatly impressed. Unlike most men of few words, he had not spoken at all brusquely. His voice had been quite gentle; it was his silences that were violent. She judged from his face that he had much to say if he would only say it. She felt a strange kinship with him; as if much would result from the breaking down of his reserve; as if she must struggle to break it down. Besides this, she was frankly attracted by the outer man. If only he would speak. . . .

Until she could invite him openly to little parties at the house, her health was apt to be more troublesome than God made it. She determined to gain his friendship. Nor was she frightened when she found she was gaining a lover. His reserve persisted; it became, in fact, another basis for admiration. All in a flutter she talked to him; monosyllabically and facially he showed her that he understood. The course of their love ran smoothly enough, but silently. She began to look forward to the time when he

would speak in asking her hand. She imagined
a terrible and beautiful explosion of pent-up
passion.

In hope of meeting him she often walked
abroad unattended by her maid. Especially would
she make a point of going for a short walk while
the sky above the western hills was lighted up by
· the after-glow of sunset. At such hours the
black-green pines on the hills stood out against
the greenish yellow of the sky with a poignant
contrast of colours not otherwise to be seen in
nature. The voices of men, the twittering of
birds at roost, the noises of cattle, even the
rustling of the trees, sounded so clearly in the
still twilight that they became spiritualised and
unearthly. It was, to Matilda, as if the general
restfulness seized on her lower self, and left her
imagination to wander through an immensity
peopled with the shadows of beautiful things.
Her love and her yearning would almost overcome her. Courage and hope would become
powerful within her. She would be caught up
into that exaltation which is of the spirit of
nature.

On such an evening the doctor met her and
asked her in marriage. The glory she had been
watching shone in her eyes, and, because the
exaltation was still upon her, she could not at
once bring herself to keep up the burden of a
one-sided conversation. "It is beautiful," she
said, with her face towards the west and lighted
by it. Then they were both silent.

The light went on fading until it was in the

sky rather a pledge of the morrow's sun than reminiscent of the day. Nevertheless, instead of going their ways, they remained together. He wished to say something, and by her sympathy with his thoughts she knew it. At last, in the sorriest fashion, he spoke.

"Miss Hennyker, will you permit me to address you ? Will you give me. . . . " He ceased, and looked at her. It was unlike him— forced; and came to her like a sorrow. But when he blurted out : " Matilda, will you marry me ? Eh ? " she felt like one star approaching another in the night, and thought forsook her.

Most pitiable he was—and said no more. Their kiss took her further than her dreams. She hung on the sound of his voice, to hear him tell her how he loved, and he made her know it without telling her.

But she lived in expectation of his speaking. In her mind she made for him strange passionate words of love, which were surely to come to her ears. She bowed down before him as if she were worshipping the god Apollo, stringing his lyre ; her lover's presence seemed to draw out of her something which surrounded them like the scent of a flowering tree ; and her imagination went forward towards their marriage, when, at last, he would surely tell her all she wished, and all she knew from his face and from the tone of his few words.

Their marriage was a gladness, the going from a great joy unto a greater ; but it was a silent gladness. Though she doubted nothing of

his love, the ritual of love, with all its songs,
was dear to her. Nay, it was necessary. She
hungered for his assurance, but she had no more
than was in his embrace and in the tenderness of
his face. She spoke, and she knew that he heard
and remembered. The course of his thoughts she
could follow only by her sympathy. She suspected that his reserve was a part of himself—that
he could not speak what he wanted ; but her great
desire never ceased to await a miracle. Always
she waited on events, saying within herself:
"Now surely he will speak." And he showed
his love in all ways except by the words she
longed to hear. His smile of greeting was like
the smile with which the sun at dawn greets the
earth ; but, after a while, her smile became wan,
like the smile with which the earth greets the
sun.

The years went by as a note of music that is
honey-sweet and swells with pain and dies away.

They had one child, and much of her great
hope fastened on it. But, before it learned to
return its mother's prattle, it died. "Nothing is
like the death of a child," thought the mother ;
while the father wept quietly, as much for his
wife as for the child. Matilda clung to her
husband for sympathy and strength. All that he
could give her by look and tender caress, that he
gave.

They went home together after the child's
funeral, and sat in a room that was full of sorrow
and the scent of roses. Matilda wept, not less
because she had no words of consolation from her

husband than because of her child ; for now, as
the greatness of her grief deadened her by its
intensity, so she turned to her husband. And, as
she waited, he gazed at her ; and then he burst
out neither into sorrow nor into consolation, but
into furious anger against God. Matilda was
frightened by his anger, and tried to calm him,
and to that end whispered many empty things
that assuage by their emptiness.

When he was calmed he became silent.

Not many years ago, one of those lingering,
sleepless illnesses that make ready the old for
death, killed Matilda. She was still waiting, and
in the silence many sayings about death and its
inevitableness took life and struck her. But she
struggled to wait yet a little while longer, so that
she might hear of her husband's love and of the
well-remembered love of their youth, about which,
she thought, " He will surely tell me before I die."
In her pain she called so for her husband that,
towards the end, he sat by day, and slept or
watched by night, in a chair by her bed. From
time to time she called him nearer, and when he
was asleep in the chair by her bed, she asked
momently : " How long do you think he will
sleep ? When will he wake up ? " And then,
sure of what was to come, she would desire him
to sleep on.

Finally, death made an end of her hope.
Perhaps she knew before death that he had
utterance only when he was angry : perhaps she
died unknowing. She had never angered him ;
she had loved him too clingingly for that. She

would have felt the first oncoming of his anger, and would have known how to turn it.

It is but a short time since her husband also died. He called on his wife as a man might call on God for succour; but she was beyond hearing.

DEAR PAPA'S LOVE STORY

ASKED how the home folks were, Nell Pritchett burst out laughing.

"Why, my father—haven't you heard? My dear papa. . . . I'll read you my sister Caroline's letters."

Hereunder are the letters as she read them :—

Letter I.

To Miss Helen Pritchett,
  2 Sunnyside Studios, Chelsea, S.W.

THE ORCHARDS, *November* 11.

DEAREST HELEN—Margaret says she is too tired to do anything, so I snatch a few moments to write to you before dear papa comes in and wants me to read the Parliamentary News to him. He is out in the West Orchard planting young apple-trees, of a very new superior sort, by lantern light. You would say that papa and the men looked like Pixies among the stems and branches. He said he would not come to a "cackling" working party, and he *would* have the new trees in to-day. John and Jim will grumble so and want supper and overtime. The roots have to be horizontal

to the ground, or something, I think, and well
mulched, so it is long work.   Papa becomes more
and more devoted to his trees.   He says they
are good company.   We had a working party
here this afternoon and cut out and sewed quite
a lot of things for the Church Bazaar, and the
Rev. Septimus Brinkworth read to us from a
beautiful book about a very good sincere clergyman who put down smoking among women and
did such a great deal of good in the world.   We
were glad to see him (Mr. Brinkworth) make an
excellent tea and eat seven of Margaret's Fairy
Cakes ; we do not think his landlady gives him
good enough food for a young man who works
so hard, or he fasts too much, he is getting so
thin.   We like him very much, though he is
Higher than we have been used to.   But the
Rev. Septimus Brinkworth seems to feel instinctively the spiritual needs of the parish, and it is
a treat to hear him read at the new week-day
services he has started, though the congregations
are so small.   The day before yesterday dear
papa went to the new Mayor's dinner, came back
very late in the evening singing in a cab, and
yesterday he had a bad bilious attack, we think,
which makes him extraordinarily irritable.   He
must be careful what he eats at his age, and not
tempt the night air.   He is fifty-nine this
winter.   Margaret's heart is better, though she
is always far from strong, poor thing.   She sends
her love and wants to know when you will come
home for a visit.   I am well except for a little
rheumatism.   Fancy Mr. Jones being made

Mayor. I remember when his father had a shop in Back Street, and his wife was once in service, you know. What are we coming to? Ever your affectionate sister,

CAROLINE KIRBY PRITCHETT.

Letter II.

THE ORCHARDS, *November* 30.

DEAREST HELEN—I should have written yesterday, but we went to a concert at the schools in aid of the Church Surplice Fund. It was very successful. The Rev. Septimus Brinkworth sings charmingly, and they made over four pounds, £4. But still Margaret and I think that people ought to support the Church without entertainments. I grieve to say that dear papa seems very unsettled since Mayor's Day. He has been staying out till after eleven at night, and Ellen's young man told her that he has been to the Lion Hotel bar, talking about apples with a Mr. Robertson. His brother heard him. There is no need, my dear, for dear papa to go to those places, frequented by tradespeople, when he has a comfortable home. Mr. Robertson could come here if he is fit for ladies' society. Two days ago I said we would sit up no more till half-past eleven, so I locked and bolted the door, and we went to bed. But Margaret heard his footstep in the road and went down to the door. Next day I kept her in bed till dinner-time with a cold, caught by getting out of her warm bed to go to that horrid door. I told dear papa, and he ordered me to have another latch-key made for him, but I could not go to bed unless the door was properly locked and bolted. . . .

I am sending you last week's *Arboricultural Weekly* with a photograph of dear papa in it. They say that Pritchett's Pippin is *the apple of the year*. Ever your affectionate sister,

CAROLINE KIRBY PRITCHETT.

Letter III.

THE ORCHARDS, *December* 24.

MY DEAREST HELEN — Doubtless you have received Margaret's and my little present. Dear papa wants to know if you have enough garden for apple-trees. If so he would send you two or three young trees of Pritchett's Pippin, *the apple of the year*. But perhaps the London smoke would kill them. He has been receiving large square envelopes with letters inside them. Margaret says they are forwarded letters—about prize apples, probably — though we do not see why they could not be re-addressed on the same envelopes or sent direct. He is very impatient for his letters in the morning, and told Ellen to take them up to his bedroom ; but, of course, we could not have that. It makes breakfast so late to have one's letters in bed. There is nothing to hurry downstairs for. I caught a glimpse of the handwriting on one of the inner envelopes, and it was like the pointed Italian hand old Miss Vegg used to teach us before we went to the Academy, but not so good as Miss Vegg's. . . .

That every blessing and prosperity may be yours
is the wish of your affectionate sisters,
  MARGARET AND CAROLINE KIRBY PRITCHETT.

Letter IV.

THE ORCHARDS, *January* 1.

MY DEAREST HELEN—. . . Dear papa has been
to Bristol about the advance orders for this year's
Pritchett's Pippin. He had a letter this morning
marked "Private," and I am sure it was the same
writing that came in the big square envelopes and
in a woman's old-fashioned pointed hand. The
postmark was Clifton. He did not open it at
breakfast, but took it into the South Orchard to
read, in spite of the bitter north-east wind which
has been blowing for some days. He seemed
unusually pleased. We cannot think what it is.
. . . A Prosperous New Year from us all.
Ever your affectionate sister,
  CAROLINE KIRBY PRITCHETT.

Letter V.

THE ORCHARDS, *February* 15.

DEAREST HELEN—We think you certainly
ought to know. We have begun our spring
cleaning early as usual, especially as Margaret is
rather well for the season. I think people leave
it far too late nowadays. We *never* have.
When Ellen was tidying the top drawer of dear
papa's dressing-table she found a horrid paper
called the *Matrimonial News,* and brought it to

me. I was just glancing at it before telling Ellen
to put it in the fire, when a mark caught my eye,
and I read——oh, Helen, dear ! Can it be papa ?

An Elderly Gentleman owning a small
Estate and a small but sufficient Income would
like to correspond with a Widow, having small
means preferred (middle-aged, Protestant), with
a view to sharing his life and interests.
Enthusiastic arboriculturist. Two unmarried
daughters only encumbrance. Write in strict
confidence to J.P., Box 4091, 102 Derby
Street, W.

I do hope Ellen did not read it. If it got
about I should not be able to walk up the aisle
for shame. And I cannot ask her if she saw
it, for fear she didn't. It looks so like dear
papa. "Two unmarried daughters only encumbrance." Margaret and me encumbrances, and
we have kept house for him and contributed out
of our little to the household expenses ever since
poor dear mamma died. But the widow's small
means would make up for ours. J.P. does look
like James Pritchett, but, as Margaret says, it
might also mean Justice of the Peace. I wanted
to tax him with it, but Margaret says we had
better wait. "Everything comes to him who
waits." And it may not be him. She persuaded
me to put the dreadful paper back in dear
papa's drawer, which I did, and tidied the drawer,
and then she went up (I looked afterwards) and
made the drawer untidy again on purpose.
I thought of asking the Rev. Septimus Brink-

worth's counsel, but Margaret says that though we ought to open our hearts to the Church, we ought not therefore to open the heart of our family. Our best love. What shall we do, dearest Helen, if it is dear papa ? It can't be.— Ever your loving sister,

CAROLINE KIRBY PRITCHETT.

Letter VI.

THE ORCHARDS, *March* 17.

MY DEAREST NELLIE—The worst that we feared has come true ! Dear papa, who never visits, has been away for a week. I told him that he ought not to have carried his bag up from the station at his age, and he said I was getting particular and old-maidish, and that he felt a young man again. We sat down to supper. Papa ate ravenously. I was obliged to warn him against one of his bilious attacks, when he becomes so irritable ; and between two mouthfuls he said, " I'm going to bring home a new wife to look after us all." Our worst expectations fulfilled ! There was a scene, almost. Margaret stood up and I stood up, but dear papa only went on eating. I thought Margaret was going to faint and supported her out of the room. It is so bad for her heart. And then I went back and demanded of papa, " What do you mean ? "

" I'm going to be married to Mrs. Salter. You had better write and tell her you're pleased. Her address is 5 Lake Road, Clifton—a very nice capable woman."

I remember every word. "What!" I said. "Write to her! Me! Have you forgotten the memory of our own poor dear mother?"

"Now don't carry on, Carrie," he said with one of his horrible puns—at such a time too! "Give me another slice of undercut and pass down the walnuts, my dear."

I slammed out of the room and found poor Margaret prostrate. She tried to laugh and say, "There's no fool like an old fool."

"We can't stay here," she said. "We must leave home like Helen—after all these years."

Oh, it is ungrateful! Encumbrances! It is wicked after all these years to bring a strange woman into a respectable united family. Papa seems to rejoice in his wickedness. I have not spoken to him since. We shall not stay.—Ever your loving sister,   CARRIE.

P.S.—Do you know any one who knows a Mrs. Salter, of 5 Lake Road, Clifton, Bristol? I have written to Fanny Jameson, who has been living in Clifton since her marriage.

Letter VII.

THE ORCHARDS, *March* 25.

DEAREST NELLIE—How shall I bring myself to tell you? Fanny Jameson, who has three little children now, has written that the woman was housekeeper at Budleigh Grange, quite near here, and retired ten years ago to Clifton with enough money to buy an annuity. Gentlemen's house-keepers get plenty of perquisites and tips and other things. A housekeeper, my dear ! I shall never hold up my head again. I said to dear papa, " Do you know that Mrs. Salter has been a housekeeper at Budleigh Grange ? "

" She told me all about it," he said. " That's what made her so capable."

" Margaret and I will not be able to stay here with her, and it will kill Margaret, with her heart, to leave home," I said.

" Fiddlesticks, my dear," said papa. " You and Margaret will be very fond of her. I'm going to be married next week, and I know how fond Margaret is of this place and that 'twas your mother bought it, so I've been up to the lawyer's and settled it on you and her. It's yours, except that I have the life-interest. What do you think of that ? *She* put the idea into my head."

All I wanted to say went away from me. I know it would kill Margaret to separate for ever from the Orchards. But we cannot live here with that housekeeper woman. We are quite decided to leave home, like you. We still think you were wrong to go, though you have had pictures in the Royal Academy and the Christmas numbers, because you might not have been so successful. Now we shall all be exiles.—In sorrow, ever your loving   CARRIE.

Letter VIII.

THE ORCHARDS, *April* 1.

DEAREST NELLIE—Papa has gone away to be married to that woman. Oh, the shame of it !

He told me and Margaret before he went to have the house nice for "the future Mrs. Pritchett," and more flowers about because she is fond of them. As if the house was not always nice. And flowers drop and make such a mess. I did not tell him we shall not be here when he returns, but we are quite decided. We shall pack up and he will find us gone. The fewer words the better, Margaret says. The house is ours, it is true, or will be (the deed is signed and in the bank for safety), but a house is not always a home, and our home is broken up for ever. We shall have only enough to live on if Margaret does not get worse, but we shall receive help and comfort in our affliction. I could cry, Nellie.—Ever your
                                              CARRIE.

Letter IX.

THE BURRIANA BOARDING ESTABLISHMENT,
WESTON-SUPER-MARE, *April* 15.

DEAREST HELEN—We are here, and what do you think ? We saw the Woman in the train. Margaret was so unwell, and we were so loth to leave the old place, where we have spent so many happy, profitable years, that we only had our packing done in time to leave the station by a train which goes out about the same time as the one by which papa returned comes in. Their carriage stopped at the other platform almost opposite ours, and we saw Her. She is a big fat woman with a vulgar red face, and such a bonnet—overloaded with flowers and ribbons like a straw-wagon. They travelled first, just like a silly young honeymoon couple, Margaret says. She (Margaret) is not at all well. I do not think she would have come away in the end, but I was quite determined. She cast such longing eyes at the Orchards as we drove off. This boarding establishment is most respectable. . . . Ellen will forward letters.—Ever your loving sister,

CAROLINE KIRBY PRITCHETT.

Letter X.

THE BURRIANA BOARDING ESTABLISHMENT,
WESTON-SUPER-MARE, *April* 21.

OH, MY DEAR NELLIE—It was wicked of papa to turn us out of our home. Margaret is very ill, I fear—the doctor here says her heart is in a delicate state. I hear her stifling dry sobs at night, and she has no distractions here. I think she will hardly survive this transplantation. And I have heard from Ellen, who says (I copy her letter), "The master carried on dreadful, Miss (and you know what that is like), when he came home and found you and Miss Margaret was clean gone. He said as you should never have the trees, if the house was yours, and he has dug up and cut down all the apples which is bad, and the orchards look that bear (bare), and he would not take no holding back when the new missis tried to stop him." It is a sin and shame, his behaviour! I have written to tell him he is killing Margaret.—Your   CARRIE.

Letter XI.

THE ORCHARDS, *April* 24.

DEAREST HELEN—We are home. I told you
I wrote to dear papa.   Two days afterwards the
same homely figure that we saw in the railway
train (and the same bonnet) burst into the saloon
of the Burriana Boarding Establishment, where
Margaret was lying on the sofa, and ran up to
her and kissed her, and said, "Now, my dear, do
'ee come home 'long with me, and be comfy in
your own house."   It was so like poor dear
mother's old-fashioned way of speaking that my
heart melted, and I could have loved her on the
spot.   It was the echo of our dear mother!
Margaret wept real tears, which I think relieved
her.   We all cried together.   And though I could
not tell you how it happened, Mrs. Pritchett
brought us home with her, and dear papa only
called us "silly children."   She is so kind and
good to Margaret.—Ever your affectionate sister,

CAROLINE KIRBY PRITCHETT.

P.S.—He has not mentioned the trees.   They
are all lying dead in the orchards.

Letter XII.

THE ORCHARDS, *May* 3.

DEAREST HELEN— . . . Dear papa says poultry
pay better than arboriculture. Polly (she has asked
us to call her "Polly" as there is so little difference in our ages) used to have 400 chickens to

look after. . . . Margaret seems better than she has been for a long while. She is trying a special diet that did the late Lord Budleigh so much good when his heart was bad. . . . No one has found out that Polly was at Budleigh Grange as housekeeper. She is going to help dear papa with the fowls and garden, which she is clever at, leaving me the housekeeping that I am used to. . . . It's an ill wind that blows nobody any good, Margaret says. Our love. When shall we be seeing you ? —Ever your loving sister,

CAROLINE KIRBY PRITCHETT.

P.S.—Thank God.

A MARRIAGE OF LEARNING

I

THERE are in these latter days independent strenuous women who, devoting themselves to knowledge, instead of men, succeed in embracing the skeletons of all arts, philosophies, and sciences. Bertha Œnone Smith, B.A., was one of them. Her learned independence revealed itself not so much in her reposeful, boldly-cut features, and her somewhat untidy hair, as in the peculiarly assertive swing of her skirt as she walked. She was full of reason ; passionate, and a woman withal ; a packet of reasons in a whirlwind.

One notable evening she was seated with her aunt before the drawing-room fire. Although a book and a notebook were on her lap, she did not read. The saints forbid that we should accuse so rational a person of building castles in the air ! Yet that is what she was doing. (Excuse her. She was recently engaged.)

Presently she returned to workaday life.

"I think," she said, "I will go up into the study."

"But, my dear, it's much too cold."

"I have had the fire lighted."

"And didn't you say Mr. Thornbury was coming? I can't let you two sit up there."

"There's not the least reason why. . . ."

"But I'd much rather you didn't, dear."

Bertha might have given way, but for a plan she had in mind : a moonstruck plan, she knew it would seem to others. So she stopped her aunt with a phrase in quality like lemon-juice. "My dear aunt, you know perfectly well that I should not wish to do so without a reason."

"Very well," returned Miss Smith. "I hope the fire has burnt up."

"I superintended the laying, and, given favourable initial conditions, a fire *must* burn."

Poor, kindly aunt! It is no light task to bring up a child that insists on bringing up itself. Yet, by a dexterous, half-unconscious use of her helplessness, Miss Smith managed to exercise some sort of authority over her niece, except when the latter transformed herself into a porcupine, armed with a thousand quills, each of them ready to prick a different and conclusive reason into every dissentient.

II

THE SPIDER AND THE FLY

Bertha waited by her fire, and finding that a certain amount of excitement was threatening to invade her most ordered thoughts, she reached down a very original hash of various sciences and ancient philosophies, a bulky volume *On Soul and Spirit referred to the Brain, and the Brain considered Mechanically*.

Ralph arrived. Bertha rose to greet him, and the philosophical tome fell into the fender.

"So you have come, Ralph."

"Yes, here I am—my darling !"

She felt that her welcome was outdone, unworthy of the occasion, empty as a scarecrow, fit only to frighten Venus's doves. This for a moment while she received one of his most possessive kisses. Then she recovered rapidly, caught sight of the tome, lying lopsidedly in the fender, and tenderly picked it out.

And yet she was really in love after her own fashion. Ralph Thornbury, B.Sc., Ph.D., was as suitable a mate as she might have found in fifty years. He was one of those easy-going men in whom the pursuit of science develops a most obstinate tenacity—which, notwithstanding, remains well under control unless it is especially roused. What matter that he looked like a man who had to thank his clothes for holding him together ? He, with his large head, clean-shaven raw-boned face and thin mouth, had quickly become the incarnation of Bertha's ideal of the preponderance of mind over matter. A little shyness, an awkwardness or two, did but confirm the impression. She felt sure that there was in him more than eye could see. He had to work for his living. She had money. That also pleased her.

It was not long before the love-formalities,
which even a couple such as this must use, were
done away with to make room for Bertha's match-
less plan ; in token whereof she removed herself
to the opposite arm-chair.

"You were speaking about the day. . . ." she
began.

"We needn't wait," said Ralph.

"I see no reason for delay," assented Bertha.

"Not a bit!" exclaimed Ralph, drawing near
for a kiss.

She withdrew into the farthest depths of her
easy-chair. "I thought we were going to talk
sense," she said bitterly.

The deluded young man asked: "Weren't we?"

"I've been thinking a great deal about
marriage."

"So have I, dear."

"And I don't think even now that it is an
unmixed advantage. What I want to say is this :
Schopenhauer says that when a man marries he
halves his rights and doubles his duties."

"But it doesn't follow that that old bachelor
knew everything."

"No," she said. "Precisely. A woman is
likely to do the same, and for each child to halve
the remainder of her rights and double the sum of
her duties. But what I really want to say—we
see it all around us—after marriage men and
women cease to gain in individuality. And—
worse still—a woman becomes a baby-washing,
small-talking phonographic machine. With a man,
things go in at one ear and out at the other :

with a woman, they go in at two ears and rush
out at the mouth. And I can't help thinking
that this is due to. . . ."   Ralph was preparing for
another kiss. " No ! That this is due to a too
close proximity of husband and wife. A person's
individuality is the sum of his (or her) abnormalities, is it not ? Well, then, they neutralise each
other's abnormalities."

" You mean," said Ralph, uncertain whether
to laugh or not, " that husbands and wives are
like acids and alkalis. Put 'em together, and you
get a neutral salt."

" Exactly."

" Which is which ? and how about the right
proportions ? and how about those substances that
are both acid and alkaline in their reaction ? "

" Now you are trifling, Ralph."

" I didn't mean it," he said.

" I know you didn't," she replied, appeased.
" What I have all along been wanting to say is
this. In order to prevent our spoiling each
other's work, and yet, at the same time, to allow
us to have the benefits of mutual encouragement,
I propose that we take two houses. . . ."

" What ever for ? "

" Listen, and I'll tell you," said Bertha, taking
some sheets of manuscript from the philosophical
tome. " I have been writing an opening for our
next debate, on *The Rational Utopia*, which enters
into the whole matter. The section on marriage
will run something like this :—

Marriage has not hitherto been considered

sufficiently as a means for the benefit of the whole commonwealth, actual and potential. It has had a retrograde effect on civilisation and knowledge. In the Rational Utopia the husband and wife are not permitted to interfere with each other's work. They live together for one month, and live apart, and pursue their work independently the next month ; and so on, alternately, month by month. Moreover, in the periods of separation, the offspring live first with the wife, then with the husband, and so on again alternately. Thus does youth become early habituated to an atmosphere of strenuous work as well as to the amenities of united family life. Thus does the Rational Utopia preserve all the advantages, and few of the disadvantages, of the institution of marriage."

" Preposterous ! " exclaimed Ralph. All through the harangue his lips had been making spasmodic jumps at the formation of words that never came. " Preposterous ! " he repeated, with more emphasis than before.

But Bertha, being determined to try her experiment, and feeling no doubt that a fly in the web is worth two in the air, struck her last and none too fair stroke. " I intend to get two houses, and if you want me to look after the larger central house, then you will have to go off every other month and live in the smaller."

Of course she could spend her own money as she liked. Ralph Thornbury was obliged to give way, or to lose her.

"And what am I to do in the little house?"
he asked.

"Do as you do now: live *en garçon*—and
work."

"I don't half like it—your plan. It's not
natural."

"What is not natural? Man, to be natural,
must adapt himself to advanced civilisation."

"I don't half like it," Ralph repeated.

"We can never tell with absolute certainty the
result of an experiment," added Bertha. "I *may*
be wrong, but. . . ."

The porcupine again!

Ralph sat silent and unwilling before the re-
doubtable animal. Had a servant not interrupted,
to say that coffee was served in the drawing-room,
he might have taken steps once and for all to
conquer, or else to retire from the field. From
a habit of reviewing scientific arguments on all
sides, he was given to repetition. He said for
the third time, "I don't half like it."

The fourth side of the matter was yet to be
viewed; and of that he might say, with fine
masculine emphasis: "I won't have it!"

Though easy-going, he was always capable of
that.

III

THE FLY FAST BOUND

Miss Smith, the elder, always had a very
present fear of what Bertha was going to do next.

She was, this evening, anxious to know what was meant by her niece's secrecy, and also it was on her mind to give Ralph at least some notion of the difficulties of his undertaking. Bertha was triumphant; yet not wholly. Ralph was like a cat on hot bricks, with a pressing desire to cool his toes by climbing up Miss Smith's sympathy.

"Has Bertha told you what she is going to do?" he hazarded.

"Oh, I know nothing," Miss Smith replied. "Have you settled everything?"

"Yes, aunt," said Bertha.

"And when is it to be? I *shall* miss her, you know, Mr. Thornbury."

"Oh, we haven't settled minor details like that," exclaimed Bertha.

"Then what have you settled, my dear?"

Ralph interposed. "She says she is going to take two houses, and that we are to live separately during every other month."

"What *do* you mean?"

Bertha took up the tale. "We shall go abroad for the honeymoon—shall we not, Ralph?—and, having found a little house and a big house. . . . What is the matter, Ralph?"

Little house, big house, pigsty, barn, was running through his mind; but he answered: "Nothing. Go on."

"Well then, aunt—when we get back, we shall settle down for a month together in the big house. Then Ralph will go off for a month's uninterrupted work alone in the little house; then a month together, then a month apart, and so on, alternately, month by month."

" But, my dear, it's absurd. And your husband ? "

" He's agreed."

" Every one will laugh."

" Then never mind if they do," said Bertha. " They laughed at Darwin : let them laugh at me."

" And—and if you have any children ? "

" That would easily be settled. But with regard to the date ? I'll go and get an almanac."

While she was gone, Miss Smith gave Ralph the results of her experience. " You'd better allow her to have her own way, perhaps. You can see about it afterwards, you know. The kindest way of ruling people like Bertha is to let them have their own way till they're tired of it."

Bertha returned. " How will the 10th of May suit you, Ralph ? "

" What for ? "

" The ceremony, of course."

" So far as I know, 'twill do very well."

" Then I'll look for the houses to-morrow."

Ralph felt like a mouse caught by the tail ; and it is not every mouse that has the courage to gnaw off its own tail. He went to his lodgings filled with meditation.

Very soon Bertha herself was reduced by the curiosities of domestic architecture to a state of great irritation. She had the choice of several big houses ; but a little house, to suit her, she could not find anywhere in the district. Finally, she paid one of her own tenants to turn out, discovered that the hygienic condition of her property was deplorable, rated her agent, and had a great many workmen in for a great many days. When the place was finished, she took her aunt to see it. Miss Smith was quite pleased.

Very shortly afterwards, the Experiment was set going before a large and inquisitive congregation, by the marriage of Ralph Thornbury, B.Sc., Ph.D., and Bertha Œnone Smith, B.A. The bride was dressed in a plain dark-blue tailor-made travelling costume, with a dainty appliqué collar. Her hat does not call for notice.

IV

SEGREGATION

Among the mountains of Switzerland it was easy enough not to call to mind the two houses that were waiting for them. Ralph imagined that Bertha had given up the plan ; while Bertha, on her part, thought the arrangement so settled and confirmed that there was no need further to discuss the matter. In consequence, she was at her quietest and best, and her husband enjoyed much peace. It seemed, indeed, as if the adage of *The wilder the filly, the better the mare* was about to receive fulfilment.

After their return to England they abode together a calendar month in the big house. Ralph continued carefully to avoid mentioning the Experiment. He even decided that an empty house might well be the price paid for ignoring it. But one evening he found his wife's work-table in the study as tidy as if she had never used it.

"What have you been doing to-day, dear?" he asked, with the care of a newly-married man.

"It was time to begin putting the other house straight for you," replied his wife.

Still only an experimental husband! There was no escape. The preparations went on apace. By giving way now, while still determined that the plan should eventually be put to death, he caught a remnant of the peace of his honeymoon—peace under an umbrella with a rain-cloud overhead.

All their last evening together Bertha was as sad as her namesake, Œnone—about to cry heart-rendingly to her gods for a month:

> "And I was left alone within the bower;
> And from that day to this I am alone,
> And I shall be alone until

the end of this conjugal month!"

As for Ralph, he wandered about the hearthrug.

A cab (which Bertha had ordered in unsentimental daylight) drew up at the gate. The Experiment was in its first fizzle. But sentiment would not utterly be quashed. They went hand in hand to the hall.

"I don't think I like it just at the time," said Bertha.

"Nor do I," Ralph returned hopefully.

"We will be brave and carry it out, won't we? It's for our good, and for the good of the human race."

"So it may be."

"Good-night, Ralph."

"I've forgotten my hat.   One moment.—
Good-night, Bertha."

"Good-night."

They kissed and parted.

May the goddess of Truth be with us !   Bertha
went through a swift syllogism :—" My husband's
on the garden path—the letter-box looks out on
the garden path—therefore my husband can be
seen through the letter-box."

She looked through the letter-box.

How the cab-door banged !

Loneliness descended on her like a frost-fog.
She went back into the study and dropped into
her husband's arm-chair.   So strong was her dis-
inclination to read, that she wrote to three friends
of her schooldays, and tried, unsuccessfully, to
alter the trimming on a hat.

In the month of disunion both of them learnt
many things.   Bertha was the more disconsolate ;
but she held her head up, and her nose high, and
went her solitary way ; and she showed her feelings
no otherwise than by snubbing all who inquired
after the Experiment.   Miss Smith's house was
the neutral ground where Ralph was allowed to
meet his wife.   The first time he saw her there,
he inquired : "You're not going to keep up this
absurdity any longer, are you, Bertha ?"

"I don't know what you mean by *absurdity*.
If you mean our plan of life, of course we are
going to *keep it up*."

"But, Bertha, can't you see I want you to live

with me ? I'm asking you because I want you."
He took her into his arms.

For the moment she yielded ; then she shook
him off and stood angrily behind a chair. " I
shall call aunt ! "

" I didn't know you believed in chaperons,"
he retorted, leaving her to herself.

But as the months went by he found it easier
to take up the thread of his single or of his
married life, and he recognised that each state had
undeniable advantages. He never thought to
live all his days like a moth round a tallow
candle ; yet it did seem as if this sorely self-tried
couple had settled down to a life of unsettlement.

V

THE OPPORTUNE ILLNESS OF THE BABY

The year after their marriage, when the trees
were budding, Bertha developed a new phase.
The same day, it so happened, was the last of the
conjugal month, the one on which Ralph was due
to move into the little house. Late in the evening
he was told that he might go upstairs and see
his little son. Curious word to Ralph, *son*—
a mysterious affair. Mystery points to the tiptoe
method of walking, and in that undignified way
he crept into the room, bent over the bed and
reverentially kissed his wife.

" Wouldn't you like to look at him ? " she said,
turning her head towards the cradle.

Ralph looked. He saw a red and wrinkled

face, distinguishable only by its puckers from
an equally red scalp. It squeaked—it made him
feel shy. "Isn't he lovely?" said his wife.
"He's like you."

"Yes," replied Ralph,—"I suppose it is."

"Now you must go home, dear."

"I'm not going there to-night," he said
stoutly.

"No, Ralph. You *must* go now. You're
taking an unfair advantage. . . ."

The nurse intervened : "You must go now,
please, at once. You may say good-night and go."

He set out for the little house. "Turned out
neck and crop," he thought bitterly. "I *will* put
an end to it. Oh! curse it!"

Henceforward the big house seemed home to
him, but he could not return to it until Bertha
was almost recovered. He thought her a good
mother up to the day when she began to speak of
weaning the child.

"They don't wean babies eight weeks old,
do they?" he asked.

"No, not usually. But *his* life is conjectural,
ours are certainties. He must not be let interfere
with our work." She kissed the baby, and said
to it : "Oh, you must go and visit your father
for a month. Your father will keep you all to
himself."

Ralph noticed that she clung to the child
convulsively, almost too strongly, in his opinion,
for its little body. He saw a chance of escape
from the Experiment. "Very well," he said ;
"he shall come with me to the little house."

So, at the end of that conjugal month, he went off with a nursemaid, a baby, a perambulator, a bottle and other impedimenta. He pictured his wife in the big house—twice as lonely this time—and was very near saying, " Serve her right ! " On their arrival, later than the baby's bedtime, they discovered that the cradle was left behind. It was a happy chance. Ralph would see if a man could take the place of a mulish mother ; he himself would put the baby to bed.

He took it to his own room, lighted the fire and got the bath ready. After tearing one or two upper garments, he turned the child round and round until he had taken out all the safety-pins he could feel ; whereby the process of undressing was much facilitated. Then he bathed it as tenderly as if it had been old china, wondering the while how womenfolk can pull babies this way and that, turn them up and turn them down, and hold them up by their feet. His little son cried, of course. Men have a curious notion that when babies cry they have something to cry for. Ralph decided that it was a matter of nutriment. He made a bottle of food according to the directions on the tin, with as much care as he would have used in a chemical experiment. This did quiet the baby, but no sooner was it finished than the cries began again. It might be good to imitate the women further. . . . He waved his hand above his son's infinitesimal nose, then suddenly gave it a timid dig in the ribs. The end was vocal. He patted it on the chest ; it squalled the more. He grasped its night-dress, and, by

alternately pulling and relaxing, he made it rock
nicely on its rotund little back.   What followed
was horrible to hear and see—ear-piercing shrieks,
furious clawings of the air, extreme redness of the
face.

But they sing to babies. . . . Ralph could not
sing.   But he was desperate.   He made a dash
for it.   There was only the child to hear.

He sang. . . .

" Oh, sir ! "   It was the nursemaid with the
cradle.

" See to him," said Ralph, retreating, " and
tell me when he's asleep."

He went down to his study thoroughly
exhausted, and meditated on the infrequency
of infanticide.   The nurse came in on her way
to supper, and told him that the baby was nicely
asleep, little cherub !   He crept up to see.
There was the child, sleeping peacefully.   Only
his fists, clenched on the coverlet, showed the
force that was in him.   Ralph, as he stood over
the cradle, thought not so much of the child as
of his wife.

A beam of light fell on the baby's face.   It
stirred.   A hand unclasped itself with frightful
clawing motion.   A turn, a whimper. . . .

Ralph fled.

Very frequently in the night he heard cries.
Next morning the baby was still more fretful.
It made noises like the squeaking of a beaten
dog, like fowls, like parrots, like pigs, like cats.
The nursemaid would have sent for its mother.
" The missis was in the garden, right under the

nursery window, last night, sir. I thought as
'twas a ghost. It gave me such a fright. Shall
I fetch her, sir ? "

"No. Go and fetch Dr. Blakey-Jones."

His counter-plan was working !

The doctor affirmed that babies don't cry like
that when they are really ill, deprecated early
weaning, recommended a boat-shaped bottle, and
said he would call again. Ralph determined to
go on.

But if the baby died. . . . Oh, no ; it would
not die.

Most of the day, therefore, he sat and smoked
in his study. Most of the day he bore with the
cries of his firstborn. If there was an interval,
he awaited the next outburst with an ear painfully
alert, and heard cries when there were none.
He thought the frail little body could not
possibly hold out much longer. He even fell
to calculating whether or not the cries came in
series, like waves, each seventh, tenth, or thirteenth
paroxysm the loudest. His brain became doughy.

In the evening, the servant being out with her
young man, he once more took charge of the
baby, in order that the nursemaid might fetch
Miss Smith.

VI

BERTHA BECOMES TRAGICAL AND WINS DEFEAT

Excitement lent fleetness to the nursemaid's
feet, breath to her lungs. She hardly noticed
that a soft summer rain was falling on her hat.

After peeping into the kitchen to say, "Baby's dreadful ill!" she rushed into the drawing-room, and, without noticing Bertha, she blurted out: "Please 'm, master sent me will you come 'cause baby's ill and we can't quiet 'im."

"Get your breath, Annie, and tell me quietly," said Miss Smith.

"Please 'm, we don't know 'xac'ly."

Meanwhile Bertha had gone quickly from the room. Snatching a hat from the stand, she set off down the road more rapidly than the servant had come. She was, as it were, gyrating on the slopes of a whirlpool up which floated the words, "Baby! baby!"

Ralph, from the nursery window, saw her approach. Upheld by the dictum of the doctor, that babies do not cry lustily when they are dangerously ill, he ran downstairs and saw that the doors and windows were bolted.

It was almost twilight when Bertha ran up to the door. The rain had stopped; the air was full of the scents of night-flowering plants. A cockchafer buzzed into her face. She turned the handle of the door; turned it again the other way round. Her knees bumped against it. She rang the bell—once, twice, thrice: it was useless. Only the baby's cries echoed in the hollow house. She wondered whether Ralph had left the baby alone: she knew he would not do that. Then it suddenly struck her that she was locked out. She went and tried the back door. Yes; she was locked out. She stood on the flower-bed beneath the nursery window and called loudly : "Ralph ! Ralph ! Let me in. *Ralph !* "

Ralph, however, was too thoroughly roused for anything less than a complete victory. Bertha called out a second time. She trampled the flower-beds. Then she saw the lamplighter looking over the gate, and his light glowing like a couch-flame through the branches of a hawthorn ; and she called out no more. Instead, she made one of her swift syllogisms, the result of which was that she went to a corner whence she could see the front door and yet be hidden in a leafy triangle formed by the ivy-covered wall and a couple of laurel bushes. The rain-water dropped on her hair and soaked through until her head was chilled ; but she waited on. Miss Smith was certain to be coming, and the door would be opened for her.

Presently the nursery window became lighted up. It threw across the lawn a ghostly beam of light in which the moths danced a moment and were gone. Bertha heard the baby crying and her husband singing. Such singing ! It was idiotic. She laughed outright. Becoming savage again, with her own laughter still in her ears, she tore out of the ground a tobacco-plant, the sickly perfume of which was blown into her face, and crushed its white blossoms in her fingers. The dancing moths mocked her. Insect noises shared possession of the air with Ralph's uncouth singing. She was all of a tremble from excitement and the damp.

She saw her aunt coming, saw Ralph look out

of the window, and heard the key being turned.
She burst out of the shrubs, rushed up to the
nursery, nearly overturning Miss Smith on her
way, and flung herself on the baby, who, failing
to recognise a loving mother, screamed with terror.

"You'll kill the child!" exclaimed Ralph,
following her into the room. "Come away."

He took her by the wrists; forced her into a
chair. She broke down, and wept with heavy sobs
and loud indrawings of breath. Ralph continued
to hold her hands, and murmured: "Sh! sh!"
as if she had been the baby.

"Take the child downstairs, will you?" he
said to Miss Smith; and to his wife: "Sh!
Bertha! You'll only upset the child more.
Bertha! Sh! Pull yourself together, Bertha!"

"I want to see my baby. Do let me. I know
—it's not—my month. Let me see—my baby."

"You shall see him, only you mustn't be like
that."

"I was afraid—he was—going to die!"

"No, dear. Not much the matter. Stomach:
that's all."

"Let me see my baby, Ralph."

She wept afresh, but in a short time the sobs
became fewer, then ceased; only the catching for
breath remained.

Ralph kissed her softly. "Let me help you
off with your blouse," he said. "You are all
wet, and so cold. There! I will go and get
one of my coats and bring up baby. We'll stay
here to-night, and all go home to-morrow, won't
we?"

"Oh, Ralph !   I. . . ."

"Sh, dear ! "

Wearing a man's coat that smelt of stale tobacco, she took their baby into her arms.

The Experiment was at an end.

II
KIDS AND CATS

MAY-BABIES

"CHIL'ERN, I reckon," Mrs. Bunter has said more than once, "didn't ought to be too forward in getting on. What's all right in a man isn't fitty in a kid."

Her own Johnny is a case in point. And maybe she knows it, for in speaking of the child to her husband she always calls him "Thy Johnny."

Whilst the children—ten or a dozen of them —were on their way to Lincombe Woods to find branches for their May-Babies, Johnny pushed to the front, and, looking back, said : "My May-Baby's going to be better than any of yours."

" 'Twon't !" snapped his sister Liz.

"I tell 'ee 'twill."

"Why for ?"

"You see then. I'll gie 'ee a penny out o' what I gets if mine isn't the best o' the lot o'em."

"How'll you know if 'tis ?"

" 'Cause I'll get more pennies give'd me. You see. An' you gie me a penny if I don't."

"Git 'ome ! If thee's get more pennies 'n us do, what do 'ee want mine for ? Always a'ter pennies, you be."

229

In the woods they ran hither and thither, tearing down branches as carelessly as nature had grown them up. When one child found that nut was easy to break off, and smooth, they all chose nut, except Johnny, who separated from the others and returned dragging a piece of oak just coming into leaf. "C'ooh, 'tis a rough ol' thing you got!" said Liz.

For answer, Johnny made a grimace, and showed her three neat bunches of flowers—Red Robins, Milk Maids, and Blue Bells. The other children had simply grabbed up some of the primroses that were like sunshine on the slopes of the shady wood.

"Lend me your khaki doll for my May-Baby," Johnny asked his sister on the way home.

"What's think! I want it for mine."

"Mother won't let 'ee hae it."

"N'eet you nuther then."

"Shan't let her see it till we'm all finished. I'll gie 'ee my pocket-knife what I found wi' two blades. One o'em isn't broke. 'Tis sharp's can be."

"You always gets everything you wants, Johnny Bunter. When will 'ee let me hae 'en?"

"T'morrow—after us been round wi' our May-Babies."

The branches were stacked in the scullery and the flowers put in water. Johnny hid his behind a pile of unironed linen in the front room. Next morning, long before their mother was down, the children were routing for ribbons

in the kitchen drawers and in the cupboards underneath the dresser. Unable to borrow from his
sisters any of their hair-ribbons, Johnny snatched
up something from the arm-chair, stuffed it under
his coat, and with his oak branch retired to the
linhay at the top of the garden, where, if any of
the children tried to see what he was doing, he
flustered at them as a broody hen will do when
you try to take an egg from under her.

"Be you coming, Johnny?" they called up to
him later.

"Where's mother?"

"Gone upstairs to fetch Baby down."

Johnny came out of the linhay. He had tied
to his oak branch little bows of red, white, and
blue rag, and little bunches of Red Robins, Milk
Maids, and Blue Bells. In the centre, where the
twigs branched off, was Liz's khaki doll, veiled
with a toy Union Jack.

"You'll get it!" cried Liz. "That's Baby's
skirt you've tore'd up for your May-Baby."

"G'out!" said Johnny. "'Tis only an ol'
thing. 'Tain't wuth so much as the pennies I'll
get. You see."

They started out. Perhaps it was only the
expectation of collecting pence in a time-honoured
fashion, but more likely it was a tradition, handed
down among children, of the old pagan May Day
ceremonial that led them to prance up the street
rather than walk. Very lightsome, even starlike,
were the nut branches, with their leaves, primroses, white ribbons, bits of golden tinsel, and
little bells. Inside the dancing bowers were the

veiled May-Babies ; through the twigs children's eager faces peered. Johnny's splotches of red, white, and blue, and the sickly green of his young oak leaves, looked dowdy among the rest, yet without dispute, without the others knowing how, he edged his way to the middle and front, so that, grouped around Johnny, they all chattered and laughed their way through the old town.

" Will 'ee gie us a penny to see the May-Babies ? " they asked every one they met.

In the Upper Fore Street a lady stepped off the pavement and stopped them. " What have you got there ? " she asked Liz.

" 'Tis our May-Babies, please. People gives us a penny for looking at 'em."

Johnny spoke up. " Mine's an Empire May-Baby," he said.

" What d'you mean ? "

He unveiled Liz's khaki doll, which had tiny flags sewn to its dress. " 'Tis Empire Day this month, an' we got a paper to learn—how many people there is in London an' Calcutter an' Liverpool, an' how many miles the British Empire is, an' who the King is that we'm subject to ; an' teacher says us ought to hae flags, an' red, white, an' blue, 'cause we'm the biggest empire that ever was see'd ; an' they'm going to gie us prizes for who says it best. I knows how many people there is in the British Empire—what us got to learn."

" So you have got an Empire May-Baby ? Was that your own idea ? "

" Yes 'm. Please, I dressed mine by meself."

" What an intelligent little boy," exclaimed the

lady, "and patriotic! I didn't know May Day was still kept up. You all look very pretty. Here's something for your May-Babies."

She put half-a-crown into Johnny's hand. With that the children all turned homewards.

They met Johnny's Uncle John, his mother's brother, after whom he was named. "Gimme a penny, Uncle John."

"What for?"

The other children clustered round.

"'Cause I've got an Empire—red, white, an' blue—May-Baby," Johnny replied.

"Why an't the others got red, white, an' blue May-Babies then?"

"'Cause they didn't think o'it—an' I didn't let 'em see."

"Get 'long wi' thee," said John angrily, to Johnny's great astonishment, "or I'll gie thee a good clout. Thee't just like thy blooming father. Always starting some new idea, an' then everybody has to follow suit, or else 'tis said they'm behind the times; an' then he starts something else new, not contented wi' that, an' with the same, everybody has to follow suit again, an' nobody ain't a bit the better for it when 'tis all done. They sort makes more misery 'n enough, an' you'm one o'em. I shan't gie thee nort for thy May-Baby. Get 'long home to thy father!— Here's tuppence for the rest o'ee to buy some sweets wi', an' don't you let he see they."

"I don't care," Johnny said. "I've got the lady's half-a-crown. I shall buy a whole pound o' sweets!"

"No, you an't.   'Tis between all o' us."

"No, 'tisn't.   Her give'd it to me."

"Her didn't."

"Her did ; an' I got it too."

Mrs. Bunter put an end to the squabble. "Just you give thic half-crown to me," she ordered, "an' I'll put it by for a pair o' boots for 'ee."

"Oh, oh !   Shan't !" cried Johnny.

"You won't go for the Foresters' excursion if you don't.   You won't hae any boots to go in."

"Aye !" assented Johnny, quietening down at once.   "Then I *be* going, bain't I ?—If I buys sweets wi' it, you'll only take 'em away an' share 'em out to all o'em."

Johnny will make his way all right.

TWINSES

I

ETCHILCOT, Wilts, has been described as : " Down a hill and round the corner." Down the hill are the boxy, creeper-covered houses of the village gentlefolk. Round the corner are Etchilcot Brook and the labourers' cottages, some on the road and some behind, all facing different ways. Down the hill Etchilcot is very clean, bright, and hot. Round the corner it is unclean, huddled, and damp. Nellie Giles lives round the corner.

One summer's day the air was shimmering with heat. A very old woman, wearing a woollen bonnet and shawl, and bowed with rheumatics, shuffled round the corner. Her stick tap-tapped on the empty silent road. The hill, with sunshine blazing on its whiteness, was much too hot for such an old woman. Grandmother Giles (Nellie Giles's husband's mother) stopped a moment or two, breathing hard, mumbling, dribbling a little, and leaning on her stick. Then she hailed a woman who was hanging out clothes to dry.

" I jest been up Piggy Lane to break it to our Mary as our Nellie got twins—boys as won't be

no use till they be out to work.   '*Tis* so bad.
She hadn't hardly got enough for one, an' now
she'll want two lots o' clothes, an' all."

"Law, Mrs. Giles!" said the other woman,
cheerfully.   "You must try and bear up.   P'raps
'twill please the Almighty to smile down and take
one on 'em."

II

Grandmother Giles was nearly weeping.   Nevertheless, she toiled on up the hill until she came
level with the discreet house of that pious retired
tradesman whose bounty keeps the church, the
Sunday schools, the institute, the churchyard, the
club, the mission, and the magazine all going.
There she rested again.

A man leant over the wall above her head.
"'Ullo, Mrs. Giles, 'ow be 'ee?   'Ot?"

Mrs. Giles gathered together all her forces
before replying: "S' thee know poor Nellie Giles
got twins—boys?"

"Well," said the man, "'er wanted a bwoy,
didn' 'er?"

"Yes, 'er did that; but 'er didn' want two."

"Well, 'er must put up wi'em now 'er's got
'em."

Mrs. Giles meditated aloud: "An' 'er's got
five girls. . . ."

Suddenly she lifted up her stick and pointed
up the road with it, at an old man who came out
of one gate with a wheelbarrow and went in at
another.

"An' that there man," she said with pride and astonishment, " an' that there man, as went along there, were *her* father ! "

III

The eldest of Nellie Giles's five girls ran into the cottage, stumbled over one of several half-starved cats, and said : " Blast the cat ! "   In the same tone of voice she shouted at the foot of the stairs : " Ou-er moth-ther ! The freckly Miss Dawkins be comin' 'long the road wi' the magazines."

An answering voice from upstairs shouted : " Voilut. Yer. I wants 'ee."

But Miss Violet Giles was already back, trying to dam up Etchilcot Brook, and the voice upstairs continued : " Voilut, y' little varmint ! I'll warm 'ee when I d' get up ! "

When, however, the freckly Miss Dawkins asked Violet how her mother did, the child curtsied and replied very civilly : " Yes 'm. She's doin' nicely, thank ye kindly, mum. And they's boy twinses."

Violet, civil child and sister of twinses, received one penny.

IV

Miss Dawkins, known to the poor people by her many small benevolences, and above all by her freckles, is a lady with a very rapid manner of speech and a very inconsequent flow of ideas.

She groped her way up the cottage stairs, nearly dropping her bundle of Church Magazines. She also knocked her head.

"Law, Miss; who's ha' thought to see you! P'raps you'll find yourself a chair. 'Tis twinses, and I be in a confusion like."

Miss Dawkins was pleased to sit in the centre of the room, her skirts well tucked round her, for Nellie Giles's bedroom was reputed, rightly or wrongly, among district visitors, to contain inhabitants other than human. In one corner of the stuffy little place were a mattress and a heap of bedclothes—Mr. Giles's temporary resting-place. In another corner was the bed (now occupied by the twinses) of the Misses Violet, Evelyn, and Lilian Giles. There was indeed confusion. It was Nellie Giles, on the big bed, her bright dark eyes, black hair and red cheeks—her jolly round face—who seemed, so to speak, to hold the room together.

"You'd like to look at 'em, Miss. Fine babies they be, both as big as one."

The freckly Miss Dawkins took a peep.

"My sister always says I like cats and dogs best, Mrs. Giles."

"Oh, Miss!"

"And how are you managing, Mrs. Giles? I've brought you your magazine, you see—killed two birds with one stone."

"I don' know how I shall manage, Miss. I be givin' Mrs. Ash a shillin' this week to come in marnin's and get the children off to school, and to come in evenin's and get Giles his supper, and to

do a bit o' cleanin' in the day. I don' like bein'
up here at all, at all. I don' trust nobody but
myself to do me own house ; 'tain't the same ; but
there, Miss, what can a body do when they has
twinses ?"

"I'm glad to see, Mrs. Giles, you've got them
in a separate bed. There have been so many
dreadful cases of overlaying in the newspapers
lately—mothers waking up in the morning and
finding their children dead underneath them."

"Good gracious, Miss ! Perty dears. But
that ain't 'xactly why for I done it, an' I never
see'd nobody else as has. You see, Miss, when
I d' put 'em both on one side o' me, I can't
manage 'em both, layin' down like, and they d'
make each other cry ; and if I has 'em one on
each side o' me, then when I d' try and turn one
way (my poor back bein' tired) I d' squeeze one
on 'em an' makes he squall, and when I d' turn
t'other side I d' lay on t'other on 'em, an' makes
he squall, too ; and my poor head can't stand
both on 'em at once ; so I says to our Voilut, she
got to turn out o' *her* bed. . . . You won't tell
the orficer we be overcrowded, will you, Miss ?
I'm sure I don' know where we should go if they
was to turn us out, and we be nine in fam'ly
now."

"Yes, just so. I've brought you your
magazine, Mrs. Giles."

"Thank 'ee kindly, Miss. I d' always look
for'ard to that, don' I, Miss ? If so be you'll
look in under the little chaney man on the
mantelshelf, as Giles says is like the vicar, savin'

your presence, you'll find the penny there waitin'
for 'ee."

Mrs. Giles lay quiet a moment before saying
confidentially : " What d' worrit me, Miss, that
I ain't got the money for Mrs. Teddington's
blanket club an' the rent as well ; an' if I borrows
a bed o' old Mrs. Giles for Voihut, an' lets the
twinses have Voilut's bed, then I shan't have
blankets for it wi'out the club blankets. You
don't think, Miss, you could get Mrs. Teddington
to break the rules a bit, seein' 'tis twinses ? "

" I'm afraid she can't. You see, each pair of
blankets cost seventeen shillings. You give
twelve shillings and Mrs. Teddington the other
five, as it is. If she made an exception for you,
everybody would expect the same, and there's no
knowing where it would end. It costs her a lot
of money now."

" Yes, Miss ; I s'pose it costises a power o'
money ; an' as I can't have rent an' blankets too,
I must keep the rent, so near rent day, an' all."

" I'm afraid that is so, Mrs. Giles. But I'll
send along a little soup and a rice pudding with
an egg in it. Good afternoon, Mrs. Giles. We
all ought to be thrifty. Has the vicar called yet ?
Good afternoon."

No sooner had Miss Dawkins gone than Nellie
Giles said something to this effect : " Dang her
ol' soup an' her rice puddin's wi' eggs in 'em !
She might ha' stumped up for they blankets,
seein' as 'tis twinses."

V

Hardly four days after the birth of the twinses, Nellie Giles was getting up in haste. Violet assisted her angry mother.

"Did you say, Voilut, as you saw Mrs. Ash a-takin' they there best pair o' sheets out o' the house?"

"Yes, mother, I saw her, I did, mother, takin' of 'em when she'd finished up here ; and I said as I'd tell my mother, and she put 'em back in the drawers and said she were only lookin' at 'em 'cause they was beautiful stitched ; and she did look at I, fit to frighten any one. . . ."

"I'll tell her what I thinks on her, stealin' people's best sheets when they's laid by wi' twinses. I've a-heard of her doin's afore this day, an' I'll tell everybody, I will. Gettin' me up when I didn't ought to. Mrs. Ash ! Good Lor' ! Who's she, I'd like to know ? A common thief, that's what she is !"

Followed by Violet, Nellie Giles walked rapidly off to Mrs. Ash's gate.

"Mrs. Ash, a word wi' you ! Mrs. Ash !"

"Law, Mrs. Giles ! How glad I be to see 'ee 'bout so soon !"

"You bad, wicked woman ! I spurns you ! Didn't you. . . ."

It must suffice to say that the conversation which followed was both long-winded and strong. Mrs. Ash's honesty and the state of Mrs. Giles's house, children and emaciated cats were all called

R

in question ; and the virtues and vices of all their
known relatives were discussed. When it was
over, neither side being victorious, Mrs. Giles
retired, saying to Violet : " Jest thee go 'n look
to they blessèd twinses, Voilut. I feel as there's
nothing 'll do I so much good as a pint o' old
beer. Sheets and blankets ! I'll have sheets and
blankets to make her beastly face turn blue, an'
I'll pay into Mrs. Teddington's blanket club, an'
I'll tell Mrs. Teddington why, an' I'll let the rent
take care on itself, I will."

All these things Nellie Giles did.

VI

She did not go to bed again—not as a mother
of twinses. She bustled about, put her house in
comparative order, and worried about the rent she
had paid into the blanket club.

Quarter day came and passed. " 'Tisn't like
she'll forget us altogether," said Nellie Giles,
talking to herself of Mrs. Whitton, the landlady.
She did not dare tell her husband about the
difficulty, because he had said distinctly, both at
home and at the " Waggon and Horses," that
one may have blankets, but one must have rent.

Next day, however, she was, as she said, fair
flabbergasted to see Mrs. Ash running up her
garden path.

" Mrs. Giles. . . ."

" Mrs. Ash ! "

" Here's Mrs. Whitton a-comin' round herself
for the rents."

MOTHERS ALL

"How is 'er now then?" Granny Noakes asked her daughter. Cheerfully she dumped down her basket upon the kitchen table, and from beneath her arm a pair of newly-soled boots fell noisily to the ground.

Young Mrs. Ferris, who was suckling her child on a low chair beside the fireplace, bowed her head and poked out her only spare finger for quietness. "He's going to get better," she whispered confidently; and as she spoke a she-cat which had been prowling round the kitchen, searching under chairs and pawing at the cupboard doors underneath the dresser, gave a pitiful long-drawn mew and jumped into the coal-hole on the other side of the fireplace. There it could be heard scratching and whimpering.

"'Tis the first time these three days," continued Mrs. Ferris, "as he've a-slept proper an' took anything into him to speak of. He's going to pick up now."

"I never thought no different."

"I did; an' I don't believe he would have if. . . . *Do* 'ee shut thic coal-hole door. I can't a-bear to hear Tab miawling like that."

Mrs. Ferris looked up at her mother with half-dry tears on her cheeks. Though she smiled, apparently with satisfaction, yet at the same time she shuddered and hugged her baby to her breast as if she had just rescued him from danger —from falling into the fire or from being run over. A black smudge, in which the tear-drops had made a kind of lattice-work, extended from her left eye to the corner of her mouth. In her attitude there was not only the patience of a nursing mother, but suspense as well.

Granny Noakes, when she had shut up the big dark coal-hole, stared keenly into her daughter's face. "Why, what, for the Lord's sake, 's the matter with 'ee ? " she demanded. "You'm all of a flitter. Let I go an' get 'ee a drop o' stout."

"No, don't 'ee. I don't feel like eating or drinking ort—not just now. Bit later, p'raps."

"What's the matter with 'ee ? "

"Go'n look out in the scullery sink," replied Mrs. Ferris, mysteriously.

"Casn' tell a body what's the matter wi'out all this yer miss-messing about ? There's nort 't all there 'cept a drownded kitten. Where did 'ee get thic ? "

"That's it ! " said Mrs. Ferris, again confidently. "Thee's know Tab had kittens last month. Her always keeps 'em in the coal-hole, among the litter back behind, what I been meaning to clear out. Jack, he scrawled about in there an' took an' drowned all o'em, as he thought, 'fore their eyes was open. I wondered why Tab didn't make so much fuss as her has afore now, an' yet, for all that, I couldn't make out why her sticked to the coal-hole so much.

"Well, 'twas just after then that Baby began to ail, an' I couldn't make thic out nuther. 'Twas as if he hadn't no spirit left in him to eat or ort, an' he got so thin an' soft too wi' it, in his little legs an' arms, I didn't hardly like washing o'en. Us thought 'twas teething, an' us had the doctor to 'en, an' he said 'twas weakness, which didn't get us no for'arder.

"By'm-bye, who should come in from the country but ol' Mrs. Ferris, Jack's mother. It just so happened when her was sitting there, where you be—so pleased an' proud her was wi' Baby 'cause Jack's her eldest—Baby, 'er went into the coal-hole, like he do, an' lugged out a kitten by the tail, Tab following. Up jumps ol' Mrs. Ferris. 'Law, my dear!' her says, 'if you rears that kitten 'long wi' your baby, 'twill draw the nature out o'en, 'twill suck his life away, so sure as eggs be eggs. 'Tis so good as murdering o'en to keep thic kitten. If I was Jack I wouldn't let 'ee to.'

"'G'out!' I says. ''Tis ignorance that, I reckon. No doubt if the kitten has a disease . . .'

"'Thic kitten,' her says, so solemn an' quavering, like, as if 'twas *Ashes to ashes, dust to dust,* 'thic kitten 'll bring your baby to his grave!' An' with the same her went out o' the house— offended, 'cause I said 'twas ignorance. Just like Jack her is.

"When Baby didn't get no better I thought

on ol' Mrs. Ferris's words. They stuck in my
mind like, an' at last I asked Jack to drown thic
kitten, not telling him for why. Howsbe-ever,
he wouldn't, 'cause its eyes was open an' 'tis
unlucky killing a kitten if it looks at you while
'tis dying ; which besides, Jack don't like killing
things. An' I couldn't bring myself to kill it
nuther, knowing how Tab'd miawl about after it,
an' me being fond of ol' Tab after bringing her
from home an' all. Baby, he was fair mazed over
thic kitten. 'Twas the only thing as'd keep him
quiet. 'Cat ! cat !' he'd go, knocking at the
coal-hole door if 'twas shut ; an' so soon as 'twas
opened, out did jump the kitchen, hoppety-hop
like a feather wi' blue eyes, an' Baby'd play wi'
it by the hour, an' pull it about an' hug it, an'
never once did it scratch 'en.

"All the same time, he was getting worse an'
worse, till come last night he kept me awake
every single minute, an' I could have sworn in
the dark—the lamp give'd out—as 'twas a kitten
miawling 'longside me. This morning, as he was
a-lying on my lap, crying all the time so loud as
he had strength to do, he wriggled down. 'Cat !
cat !' he called, making for the coal-hole ; an',
poor little mite, he fall'd flat along the floor, 'cause
he hadn't the strength left for to walk. 'Cat !
cat !' It reg'lar hit into me. ' 'Tis his death cry,
that !' thinks I, an' the thought o'it drove me
fair mad. I gropes in the coal-hole ; I finds the
kitten ; I fills a bucket wi' water ; an' cursing it, I
did, I holds the kitten under wi' my hand. I
felt 'en struggle an' I grips 'en hard 'nuff for to

kill 'en wi'out any water—aye ! squeezes the life out o'en till he gives a little shake, an', suddently, wi' a quiver like, goes all limp. Bubbles come'd up. An' there was poor ol' Tab alongside me, looking up wi' her eyes an' miawling fit to break your heart ! I turned that weak an' leery. . . . I washed my hands wi' soap, an' Baby, so soon as I came in house, he held out his arms, an' took to the breast, an' here he's been sleeping ever since. I do believe 'twas given him to know."

"Precious little bundle ! " murmured Granny Noakes.

"The thought was in my mind," the young mother added, " ' S'pose this one dies, an' I don't never have no more. . . .' "

"G'out ! Thee't hae 'em right 'nuff. More'n thee's want, I'll warrant.—Same time, it don't do to take no risks, what you knows *is* risks."

Whereupon Jack Ferris himself returned home ; which put an end to the tale, if not to the mothers' conviction.

THE POWER OF LIFE AND DEATH

I

THE Pinney children were clamouring for their breakfast. "Come on, Mam! Come on! I wants my breakfast. I be hungry. Hurry up!"

"If you'd come in proper time an' got yourselves ready for school, you'd have had your breakfast 'fore now," said Mrs. Pinney, holding out the frying-pan at arm's length and turning over some small frizzling mackerel with a bent fork. She was all of a caddle with cooking, kids, and the week's washing, and being late down was slightly angry with herself. She flung her fork on the littered dresser that covers all one wall of the kitchen, and fairly rattled the frying-pan over the fire. "Now, then, Johnnie," she shouted, "get yourself washed."

"Have!"

"What's say? Call those hands washed? Take off your coat an' slouze yourself proper, this minute.—Comb out thic hair o' yours, Susan. 'Tis like a fuzz-bush. You won't hae a clean apron. You should keep thic one clean.—Yes, you will, Artie, go to school in your old boots.

Dost think I got the money to let 'ee wear
new boots to school for to play football in?
I'll burn thic ball, if thee a'tn't careful!—Rosie,
Rosie! God bless the maid, her's got her hands
into everything! Put down! *Put* down!—
You'm old enough for to look after Rosie, bain't
you, Ruth, 'stead o' squat there in a chair, reading?
Casn't hear. Stir theeself. Lay down the knives
an' plates.—Rosie! *Rosie!* What 'tis for to
hae a parcel o' kids!"

Rosie, a fair-haired little baby-girl, dressed all
clean for the day, took not the least notice of her
mother. She had found the pan in which the fish
had been cleaned (Mrs. Pinney has no scullery),
and was trying to feed the mackerels' heads with
their own entrails, saying: "Poor fish! Fish
baddy, Mam!" She was just old enough to trot
steadily on feet that went like paddle-wheels, and
when the pan was snatched away she made a dash
for the front door, where she ran headlong into
her father.

"Whatever buzz is it here?" asked John
Pinney. "Is it breakfast, Mam?"

"Breakfast, aye! That's all you minds, feed-
ing your face.—Now then, you chil'ern, sit down
to table. Nuther one o' 'ee shan't hae a bite
till you'm quiet. Get up on your chair, Rosie,
an' see what Mam's got for 'ee."

John Pinney sat up to the table like and among
his children, and with them waited. He gazed
round on them; they were wriggling and chattering, well-grown and full of life; seen in the mass
they made their parents look rather small. "To

think," he remarked, " of all that's got to be wrenched out o' my ol' arms, slaving an' digging out, for to feed this here little lot ! What's hae 'em for, Mam ? "

" What's hae 'em for ! You ought to know that better'n anybody else," snapped his wife. " Thee dostn't hae to look after 'em, and do for 'em, else thee wousn't hae 'em, p'raps. An' thee dostn't lift a finger for to help a feller wi' 'em, squat there tapping wi' thy knife for summut to eat."

" You does it so nice, me ol' stocking, an' so quiet," said John Pinney, " an' I earns the money for 'ee to do it with. 'Tis won'erful," he rambled on, " what you gives life to in a lifetime, when you wouldn't, sometimes, if you didn't ; an' I don't reckon you finishes giving life to 'em when they'm born and weaned. . . ."

" What's mean ? "

" Well, I'm wearing out providing for 'em, bain't I ? An' I don't know w'er 'tis the last o'em yet. Dost thee, Mam ? Not that I be sorry. Nobody don' know what life is till they has a family o' chil'ern. . . ."

His discourse—a frequent one with him, for he finds his children rather overwhelming—was brought to a sudden end by Rosie. When the butter had been removed from reach of her fingers, she caught sight of the basin of castor sugar which Mrs. Pinney buys instead of lumps, so that the children cannot so easily carry it away in their pockets. With a side-glance at her mother, and a mischievous twinkle all over her face, she grabbed a handful of sugar and rubbed it over her brother Arthur's mouth. Then she chirped out in mockery of Susan, " Mam, thic Artie's at the sugar 'gain ! "

Mrs. Pinney tried to be angry, but cuddled and kissed instead. " Thee't hae a pretty handful later on," said her husband.

" So't thee ! " she retorted. " Shouldn't hae 'em ! "

Rosie, being proud of herself, took up a spoon and flung it across the kitchen. It hit with a clatter the right-hand cupboard door, underneath the dresser, where Mrs. Pinney stuffs away the old clothes and patching material. The children, Rosie included, shrieked with laughter, and so, in a moment, did their parents.

II

Suddenly the laughter died out, on a shrill note, unfinished.

All eyes, except her father's, had followed Rosie's spoon. The cupboard door against which it had hit was seen to edge itself open in little jerks, as if it were alive. The children's eyes grew rounder. Rosie pointed, with both hands held out. " What's up ? " asked John Pinney, alarmed.

No one replied ; they all stared at the cupboard door.

With a final jerk, it opened itself wide, and out of the dark stuffy hole stepped Tib, the cat.

On the height of her legs, carrying her tail

straight upwards like a mast, she walked slowly
into the centre of the kitchen. One long leg she
stretched out behind her, and then the other.
It was a stately progress. In her every movement
was cat's pride, and on her striped face a bland
cat's smile.

"If I don't believe," exclaimed Mrs. Pinney,
"that thic Tib's been an' had her kittens in the
cupboard after all ! "

Before she had finished speaking there was
a scramble of children to the dresser. "Let's
see ! " "Let I see ! " "Git out ! " "Git 'ome ! "
"*Well*, then. . . ." Clothes and old boots and
rags were all dragged out upon the floor. Three
small tabby kittens, hardly yet dry, were brought
to light. Rosie grabbed two of them so that they
squeaked. Ruth shook Rosie to make her put
them down. Rosie, in her turn, began to cry.
Mrs. Pinney drove all the children back to their
places at table.

Rosie was lifted upon her chair. She still
hugged one of the kittens in her arms, and was
trying to open its eyes, saying, "Poor pussy's
got baddy eye, Mam ! "

Meanwhile a round cat's head lifted itself
cautiously over the edge of the table, a paw was
stealthily outstretched, and Rosie's little fish, which
had been specially boned for her, was clawed off
her plate to underneath the table.

Rosie flung down her kitten and cried in
earnest till another fish was given her.

"A job for thee, John," said Mrs. Pinney,
"to drown they there kittens."

"Artn't going to let ol' Tib keep nuther one ?"

"Yes, Mam — do ! Mam !" pleaded the children.

"No ! Shan't ! They brings fleas."

"Well," said her husband, "*I* bain't going to drown 'em. That ain't my job."

"Yes, 'tis !"

"*I* bain't responsible for Tib's kittens, if I be for thy kids, like you says."

"Yes, you be. If you'd called Tib in night-times. . . ."

"Git 'long with thee ! Your mistress might just so well have tried to call you in early when we was courting an' used to stand in thic shadow round by double-doors. . . . *I* bain't going to undertake the job of killing o'em. My job's bringing things to life. . . . Rosie'll drown 'em for thee," he added by way of a joke. "Her's nearly done for one o'em now, looks so."

Rosie was on the floor, nursing her kitten with a love too hearty for it. Tib sat beside her, as if she were taking care of both. "Poor pussy !" the child was saying tenderly. "Poor pussy baddy ! Git 'ome, Tib !"

After the children were gone off to school, Mrs. Pinney asked Ruth, who had been kept home to take care of Rosie on washing-day : "Where's thic Rosie ? Where's her to ? Casn't thee look after her one minute ?"

"Her's gone into Mrs. Trist's wi' the kitten."

"Better to let her stay there, if Mrs. Trist'll hae her ; then us'll hae some quiet here. Now then, wash up they breakfast things."

John Pinney got up to go out. "See thee's drown they there kittens afore their eyes is open," he called back to his wife.

"Do thee git 'long," she replied, "if thee wousn't do it theeself! Dost think I likes drowning poor ol' Tib's kittens?"

III

When the children came home from school they could not find two of the kittens ; Tib, they were told, had probably eaten them out of their way, and they were threatened with awful things if they pulled abroad the cupboard again. And when, a little later, they were called in to dinner, Rosie also could not be found. "Her came in here a bit ago while I was emptying the water off the taties," said Ruth in self-defence, "an' went to the cupboard where Tib's got her kittens. I see'd her."

"Why dostn't go'n look for her, then," said Mrs. Pinney, who was busy piling plates with food. "How's thee know what horses an' motors there is roundabout outside."

"Well, her isn't outside. *I* can't see her."

"Her might be killed. . . ."

At that moment Mrs. Trist came in at the door, leading an unwilling Rosie by the hand. "Whatever . . ." shouted Mrs. Pinney. "O my dear life ! Whatever's thic maid been doing ? Why, her little skirt and sleeves is dripping wet, an' her hands is scratched. . . . Bide there, you little rat,

till I've a-quietened these here wi' summut to fill
their mouths up."

Mrs. Pinney went on giving dinner to her
husband and children. Mrs. Trist, instead of
going out again till the meal was finished, sat
down on a chair by the door, and waited—plainly
with a tit-bit of news on the tip of her tongue.

Then the child's wet dress was taken off. For
a wonder, she did not cry. Without help she
clambered upon her chair, and there she stood,
demanding her dinner too ; like a quaint china
figure in her little red stays with shoulder-straps,
but lively, even for her, and unusually self-
assured.

When a suitable silence occurred, Mrs. Trist
began to speak. "Dost thee know," she said
solemnly, "what thic child's been doing ?"

Mrs. Pinney looked round.

"I wouldn't," continued Mrs. Trist, "I
wouldn't never have thought it of her. . . ."

"What ?"

"Her's been an' drownded two of your kittens!
Her come'd out wi' one o'em, an' as it happened
my tin tub was under the terrace tap, half full of
water. 'Poor pussy baddy !' her says ; and with
the same her throws 'en into the water. An' her
holds 'en down wi' the bucket what was standing
'longside. I see'd her do it. Then her goes
off in here an' fetches t'other kitten, an' chucks
he in after the first one, but her couldn't lift the
bucket this time, 'cause her'd got some water in
'en, so her holds the poor little kitten down under
wi' her hand. And then—what's think ?—her

S

comes along to my house, saying : 'Rosie drown
your pussy, Missie Twist ! ' An' her was going
to carry my ol' cat off an' drown her too, only
mine was too strong for her an' scratched her
till her put 'en down. 'You little wretch ! Get
'long in home ! ' I says. 'You've a-drownded
two.' Both the poor little things was dead and
limp. . . ."

Rosie, while Mrs. Trist spoke, was rocking
herself backwards and forwards, was dancing, in
fact, on her chair with an innocent glee and
childish animation. She continued the tale
proudly : " Rosie drownded pussy under water-
tap."

" But you've killed the poor little pussies,"
said her mother.

" Poor pussy baddy. Pussy killed dead."

" Yes, pussy's dead. You won't be able to
hae 'en any more—nuther one o'em."

" Rosie get more pussies."

" There isn't no more."

" Rosie have a ha'penny an' buy another
pussy."

" But you can't buy pussies with ha'pennies.
Pussies has got to be born. . . ."

Rosie's face screwed itself up into misery.
She plunged towards her mother's arms. " Mam !
mam ! " she wailed.

" Git 'long ! " said her mother, pushing her
away. " You'm a cruel little girl, you are, to
drown the poor pussies."

Rosie was so surprised that she forgot to go
on crying. She thought for a minute with a

puzzled reproachful expression. Then, once more, her face lighted up. She banged on the plate with her spoon, spattering gravy over all the other children.

"Tib," she cried triumphantly, "Tib'll lay another one!"

A CAT'S TRAGEDY

I

NELLIE's family, with their dogs and her three-legged cat, had recently removed from their West Country farm to a villa just outside a Wiltshire town. Watching the railway trains became Nellie's substitute for playing about with the farm live-stock.

One afternoon, the express rushed whistling down the incline behind the house. Almost immediately a child's piercing scream was heard from the bottom of the garden; then "Mother! mother!" and again the wild scream.

The child's mother ran out.

Nellie was standing on the branches of a currant bush. She was looking wide-eyed over the green-grown fence at the railway lines.

"Nellie!" called her mother. "You know you have to go back to school to-morrow in that dress. Get down."

Another scream—angrier this time.

"What is it, my dear? Nellie—my child!"

"Tibby! Tibby! Where's Tibby? Mother, is that Tibby? Look! she's only got three paws and the train's been and runned over her."

The child's mother looked over the fence. "Come indoors, dear," she said, "and we'll ask father to go down and see."

Whilst Nellie walked round and round the tea-table repeating ; "How long is he going to be ! Mother, is it Tibby, is it ?" her father went down to the railway line, picked up two pieces of a three-pawed tabby cat, and fitted them together in a boot-box so that the join hardly showed.

"It's Tibby right enough," he said on his return. "She must have been on the other side of the line, catching mice, and when the train came and frightened her she must have jumped across just too late."

"Where is she ?"

"In the scullery."

"What did you leave my Tibby in the scullery for ?"

Nellie went out and gazed for some time at the cat crumpled up in the boot-box. A leg without a paw stuck out. Saying nothing, she turned away, and there was in her eyes an unmistakable look of defiance. Death affected her that way.

She was coaxed to the tea-table. "Come, dear," said her mother, "you must eat something because you've got to travel to-morrow."

"I don't want anything—thank—you. . . ." And then she broke down. "Oh ! *how* can I go back to school and Tibby dead ? What did we ever leave home for, to come and live in this beastly place ? 'Tisn't safe for cats ! O Tibby, Tibby ! You've been with me seven years, and

I've always loved you 'cept when you got caught in the rabbit gin and your paw rotted off, and I've never hit you, only once, when you eat your kittens. Tibby!"

The child's voice rose to a scream.

"Listen, my dear," said her mother, partly in pity and partly hoping to ease the child's sorrow by whitewashing her cat's memory. "Tibby didn't really eat her kittens."

"Where did they go to then?"

"They had to be killed."

"What for?"

"Because there were too many cats about the farm."

"You said she eat them."

"Yes, dear. . . ."

"You liars!" said the child sternly. "I always blamed Tibby for that, and now she's dead I can't tell her I'm sorry."

Till bedtime the child was not seen; she refused supper, and when, about midnight, her parents peeped into her room, she was wide awake and her pillow was very wet. "Nellie," her father asked, "when you go back to school to-morrow would you like to take Tibby home and bury her in the garden? You haven't left your old school, so you can do that."

"Yes," replied the child shortly, turning her face to the wall.

But before long she fell asleep.

II

Next morning, a very quiet, pale-faced and large-eyed child waited apart from her father on the station platform.   She carried in both hands a small box upon which was tied a bunch of arum lilies.   Still quietly and with composed steps, she entered the train ; and while they sped from end to end of the West Country, she kept the box on her lap and would not put it down either to eat or to rest.   " I won't have Tibby shaken," she said.

At the hotel, through which the news soon spread that she was going out to her old home to bury her cat before she went to school, two chamber-maids and a kindly barmaid accompanied her in procession up the stairs when, still with an aloof dignity, she carried the box to her bedroom and placed it on the luggage stool.   She shut the door on them, and that night she slept alone with the dead cat in her room.

With ceremony again, on the following morning, she carried the box downstairs, looking very frail in her white dress smudged with green, very unapproachable in her sorrow.   A pair of horses took her with her father swiftly up hills and down combes until they came out on a wide brown moor, wooded only with clumps of dwarf wind-gnarled trees.   They turned down a lane towards a farm-house that stood within a girdle of sheltering black pines.

The hind was set to dig a grave.   When it was ready, the child carried out her cat and told everybody to go away.   She opened a prayer-book

at the Burial Service, and, starting at the beginning, she read straight on, using both of the
alternative psalms because she had never been at a
funeral and did not know that one psalm would
do.   The sea-wind blew her short skirts about.
Driven rain wetted her hair.   Though her voice
was husky and small by the time she reached St.
Paul's Epistle to the Corinthians, she read on
nearly to the end of it, stumbling carefully over
the long words, until she came to the passage :
"*We shall not all sleep, but we shall all be changed,
in a moment, in the twinkling of an eye, at the last
trump (for the trumpet shall sound), and the dead
shall be raised incorruptible, and we shall be changed.
For this corruption must put on incorruption, and this
mortal must put on immortality. . . .*"

There she failed.   She went back, lost her
place, and broke into weeping.

"Oh, Tibby, Tibby !" she wailed.   "One *last*
look !"

She tore off the flowers, the string and the
paper, and looked.

Tibby had come in two again.   The inside of
the box was horrible.   It steadied the child.   To
the hind, who had run up on hearing her cry, she
said breathlessly : "Cover her up—quick !" and
she was led into the house crying pitifully.

During the drive back to the town and school
she nestled up to her father.   "Will you write,"
she asked, "and tell him to put stones on Tibby's
grave so that the pigs shan't root her up and eat
her like they did the roupy fowls we buried ?"

And again she asked : "Do you think Tibby

will be raised again, joined together, when the last
trumpet sounds ? "

"I don't know," answered her father.

"I do !" said the child.

III

About a week afterwards a letter in large
handwriting arrived from the school : "One of
the day girls has given me a kitten and Miss
Adela says I can keep it. Has Todworthy put
the stones on Tibby's grave ? The kitten is just
like Tibby only she has got a pretty white shirt-
front and all her paws. I think she will be as
nice as Tibby almost. . . ."

A KITTEN: THAT'S ALL

ONE evening Mimi-Meaow retired to her cupboard and gave birth to three kittens that were not wanted by anybody, except, it may have been, by Mimi-Meaow.

Next evening we went to look at them.

(Roses were blooming in the garden, and the air was fragrant with the scent of them.)

Mimi-Meaow gazed up at us with pleasure in her eyes, for she was suckling her kittens: with trust in her eyes, for she had perfect trust in us who always had been kind to her; and with pride in her eyes: you shall see a mother-cat's pride if you care to watch.

Two kittens were hidden in her fur, and her fore leg lay protectingly across the third. She looked at us with still soft yellow eyes, and purred.

"We must not keep them all."

"How many?" I asked.

"And she must have one for her health's sake."

"Then we must kill two."

"No. Let her have two. They play so prettily together."

" Very well."

" We will have the two prettiest.   Let us look at them."

I detached the kittens from Mimi-Meaow and placed them on the table.   Mimi-Meaow stood up in her basket, and looked at us, and looked at her kittens, and looked at us again—and purred.

Tabby kittens they were.   Two of them were sturdy, but the other was not.   Its legs were barer of fur, its neck was thinner, its blind eyes bulged farther from its head.   Its cry was weaker and more plaintive.   It rolled helplessly upon its side and back.

" That is the one."

" Yes," I said.

The weakling was chosen.

" Put it back for a last feed, poor little thing ! "

I put it back with the others.   It crept under Mimi-Meaow, who was purring still, for her pleasure, pride, and trust were great.

" Bring Mimi-Meaow to me, before you kill the kitten," I was told.   " She may follow you."

Therefore I took her from her kittens and left her in safe keeping.

I found a bucket in the scullery, and I found a piece of string, and I picked up a hollow stone.

I filled the bucket with water, and I took the weakling kitten (how soft it was !), and I tied one end of the string around the kitten's waist (being thin, it had a waist), and I made fast the other end to the stone.

While I did it the kitten clung to the stone with its weakly legs and soft claws.

It cried with a tiny voice ; but Mimi-Meaow was purring on somebody's lap, under somebody else's caresses.

Very gently I dropped the kitten into the bucket. The scullery was dank and dark, the water darker. As I looked to make sure that all was well, I saw the kitten sprawl down into the blackness of the water, as if into a dark eternity.

And then I went quickly to where Mimi-Meaow was in keeping.

" Have you just drowned the kitten, a moment ago ? "

" Yes," I said.

" Well, Mimi-Meaow stopped purring and gave such a start, as if she was terrified."

I knew then that I had done more than drown a blind, dumb, separate, soulless kitten.

Sadly I went back and took it out. How wet and limp it was ! I tried not to touch it, and I cut the string, and I dropped it into a little paper bag.

With a broken spade I dug a grave for it behind a dying laurel bush ; and covered it in, and stamped upon it.

And I went away, thinking to walk about the garden and to smell the roses and lavender and to look down the valley that lies between the garden and the plain.

But I saw the kitten, flickering on the blue haze with which the trees in the valley were wrapped about ; the kitten ever sprawling into blackness ; and I could not by any means or any thought put the shadow of it from me. The

kitten going suddenly to death, the dark water ;
where I looked, there they were—impalpable like
the blue haze—so that I wondered when the sight
of it would go from me.

I took three sprays of cluster-roses and wove
them into a wreath.   I laid them on the kitten's
grave, and in the centre I placed a red rose and a
white, and I left them on the ground.

I don't know why I desired to lay flowers there,
nor why roses ; three clusters of roses, a red rose
and a white.   I don't know why the shadow of
the kitten faded, nor why I was able to forget.

But I do know why I felt ashamed that Mimi-
Meaow still trusted me.

THE CITIZENRY OF CATS

An invalid, whose chair is the meeting-place for one lively black spaniel and two sedate long-legged cats, was explaining why she appeared to be fonder of the dog than of the cats. "I love dogs differently from cats," she said ; "and I think that cats require a less selfish sort of love than dogs. They take as much and give less. Cats are objects of love : with dogs one exchanges affection. It is no good being selfish with cats, and expecting goods to the value of your coin from them. You can make a dog devoted to you, and he'll jump round you and wag his tail and be pleased to see you all day long. (Down, Toby!) But cats make so little return for years of petting. They are never hail-fellow-well-met. They allow you to be kind to them. Perhaps they are devoted to you really, and don't show it —one can't tell. I know I make more of Toby. *He* makes more of me. But I love 'em all equally, different ways : don't I, Puss?"

She raised the head of the cat that was on her lap, and kissed it. Whereupon the cat purred— with self-satisfaction, so it seemed—while Toby gambolled at his mistress's feet and hurt her.

The love of cats seems mostly inborn, but a love for dogs can always be acquired.   Dogs are such jolly fellows, but cats :—

> Ils prennent en songeant les nobles attitudes
> Des grands sphinx allongés au fond des solitudes,
> Qui semblent s'endormir dans un rêve sans fin ;
> Leurs reins féconds sont pleins d'étincelles magiques
> Et des parcelles d'or, ainsi qu'un sable fin,
> Étoilent vaguement leurs prunelles mystiques.

Those who like grace, skilful stealth, still waters that may, or may not, be deep, a lazy voice containing the possibility of unholy noises, and quiet staidness coupled with ferocity ; those who find pleasure in exchanging their affection for a promise to repay, and are satisfied to let the debt run on, —are born lovers of cats.

Several of the milestones of my life are shaped curiously like cats.

Short and accurate catapults to pull back to the eye ; long, strong and swift catapults to pull back behind the ear ; catapult-guns, air-guns and rook rifles did I have as a boy.   I worked the hedges of many a country lane, brought down tom-tits with shouts of joy and hen robins with mixed feelings.   I peppered dogs (an air-gun is excellent for dogs, I used to think, because the light pellets failed to penetrate their hides and caused them to yap pleasantly, like animated bull's-eyes).   I smashed windows and paid for some of them ; I did much evil with many unlicensed arms, and am not very sorry.   Yet I never potted at cats—never, that is, till they kept me awake at night.

Neither, till then, do I remember the time when I had not a cat of my own, or had not borrowed some one else's. And that, perhaps, was the reason of my queer, unboyish forbearance.

First of the cats was a tortoiseshell, a reputed tom. One day he walked into the room where illness had kept me for a month, and stood hesitating between the foot of the bed and a table from which the smell of whiting bones, no doubt, was wafted to him. Being bored, and therefore scientifically inclined, I set his back on fire to see how it would burn, and when I had put it out, he retired, unhurt, from me and my memory too.

Whether the large white cat really did, or did not, say "Yes," when it was sitting by me on the sunny steps, it is now too late to determine. Birds talk. I am inclined to say he did.

Picture a small cat-lover's disappointment when his family, accompanied by all its furniture but none of its cats, removed into a rambling old house with long passages, dark nooks and corners, an acreage of roofs, and whole suites of attics. Picture again his revived enthusiasm on learning that there were three cats native to the place— a sandy Manx cat, a tabby and—above all things wonderful !—a wild cat. He espied the wild cat in the garden, watched her kill a bird and eat it up with one scrunch and a gulp. He laid in wait for that timid-fierce cat and (O day of triumph ! Something like a birthday or Christmas !) he found her in an out-house, reclining on a heap of turnips, caught her, and carried her off to the nursery. On promising that she should neither

get into the larder, nor prowl about the attics and
passages, nor caterwaul in the garden, on promising, recklessly, that she should be a bad cat never
any more, he was allowed to keep her ; and she
settled down sullenly in a dark corner beside the
wardrobe. He petted her, fed her, stroked her
under the chin and roughed her chaps. She stayed
on his knee at last and purred, and then—she disappeared. Some one across the road had poisoned
her, they said. But before a month was out " some
one across the road " had also poisoned both the
Manx cat and the tabby. Thus it was that a
small boy first learned to suspect his elders of
lying, and realised after a few days' pondering
that he had done what nobody else had been able
to do—had caught the wild cat for killing.

Ma, Pa, and Baby appeared before the nursery
fire. The deeds of Pa and Baby have left no
record, but Ma taught me much about life and
death. Early in the morning she was sleeping on
my pillow. She meaowed. I half woke and said,
" Don't cry, Ma," and turned over to sleep again.
And when I finally woke up, there was Ma, still
on the pillow, but surrounded by a litter of seven
kittens.

They said she ate them. . . .

It wasn't true.

One of the men and myself began to keep
pigeons—homers and fantails. A homer was lost.
It had flown away, we thought, until I found a
fantail half-sitting, half-lying on a flower-bed with
its feathers dishevelled, a wing broken, and an eye
out. Tenderly I picked it up. " 'Twas Ma,"

said the man. " I've seen her a-following them."
The pigeon was in my arms. " I wish Ma was
dead ! " cried I ; and in less than an hour Ma
was dead. Her beautiful tiger-tabby form was
laid out on the same flower-bed. I called the
man a Beastly Pig and ran away to a lonely room ;
but I knew then and thenceforward that *dead*
meant *dead*, and wept.

Some time went by before a successor to Pa,
Ma, and Baby was found. Then, one winter's
evening, after I had been kept in at school, and
was sitting over the fire, revolting against the fact
that there are many other causes of being kept in,
besides deserving it, a little kitten was brought to
me with permission to have and to hold it—my
very own. Black glossy Peter with the white
shirt-front and round white shoes—you had a
thousand tricksy ways ! How you used to
scamper up and down the green-baize doors !
And you settled down into as dignified and
comfortable a cat as ever was, yet not without
occasional resurrections of your sprightliness.
You lost the tip of your tail, adding to your
beauty, because you *would* sit underneath the
nursery fire. (Your own sister was squashed by
the butcher-boy's foot upon the parson's back-
stairs.) You were exclusive Peter, owning no
intimates but Nurse Polly and me. You used to
come every morning to the door of the night-
nursery to be let in, and bade us " Good morning "
with a regulation " Pr-r-r-r-rh ! " And when we
grew older and the night-nursery was broken up,
you slept on my feet at night. A little later you

used to greet me for the holidays, holding off a moment, sniffing, recognising, rubbing yourself against my ankles, purring with delight.   O Peter ! why do a cat's nine lives tot up to something less than one score years ?

Fourteen years or thereabout after you came and calmed my childish misery, and at a time when I was overclouded by an approaching examination, ill and unable to work properly, the news of your death was brought to me : " Peter died in fits the day before yesterday.—Your old nurse, POLLY." I went out into the murky Manchester streets and wandered about, wet-eyed, and drank two twopenny whiskies to your memory and to keep my spirits up—two vile mixtures of alcohol, water and fusel oil.

Am I poking fun at you, Peter ? Nay, Peter ; I am making fun of *us*.

Nomads in lodgings cannot, as a rule, have pets. Peter was the last cat of my own I ever had.   Of all the cats I have since been acquainted with, there are four that I shall not more than half forget—Kitty, Tibbie, Mike, and the living, beautiful Minnie.

Kitty's mistress was a fellow-lodger, a large gaunt old lady, dragged to failure after a life of work, who had seen her friends die off, and now was ending her days on a meagre pension dealt her grudgingly by some benevolent society. Kitty was her final link with earth. Did Kitty stay out for a time, she would rise from her big chair and throw up the window that looked out on a row of poplars and a sad suburban sky.

There was the echo of a life's tragedy to be heard in the sound of her broken, failing old voice when she called, " Kitty, Kitty, where are you ? Kitty ! Come to me. O Kitty, Kitty ! " Pathetic and comic it was when, on knocking at her door one evening, I heard in tones of extreme anxiety, " No, no ! You can't come in. You can't ! Kitty's having kittens ! "

Tibbie, on the other hand, was a little maid's cat, well-beloved and willing to stand any amount of inconsiderate usage. Once, after five days' absence, Tibbie returned with a foreleg broken and cruelly lacerated by a rabbit-gin. The little maid's wailing—" Oh, my poor Tibbie ! My dear, dear Tibbie ! Oh, the devils ! "—was liker mad than anything else. But presently the leg festered, and was noisome, so that Tibbie was shunned by her own mistress, who, nevertheless, would not consent to any sort of operation or treatment. Then half the leg dropped off, and the other half was discovered healed ; and thereafter Tibbie was received into grace, and followed her mistress everywhere, hoppety-hop, on three legs only.

Mike was a landlady's cat ; a lank, dirty white, morose creature, which had the uncanniest face I ever saw on a cat, and swollen lips. He used to take his first meal betimes, lick his matted fur, swallowing no inconsiderable quantity, and was just ready to be sick while I was breakfasting. He was not a nice cat. He had something lacking. His qualities were unbalanced. Cats can be very objectionable. I own it.

Not so Minnie, however. First declared a tom, and called Mimi-Meaow, or Mimi, her name slid into Minnie when beyond doubt she proved herself a lady. (It is *Min* when she stays out o' nights.) She is a mongrel—to use an ugly word unworthy of her—and has the tabby fluffiness of her Persian father, together with the amiability of her English mother. Her short-haired body is the setting, so to speak, for her broad, soft ruff, made of a flossier kind of fur, her rounded head and her daintily cobby paws. When she sits on my shoulder at dinner and, stretching forth a paw, competes with my mouth for tit-bits, it is graciously done. A *grande dame* is Minnie, with perfect gestures and the daintiest ways. She has driven dogs clean out of the house. What welcome is sincerer than the patter of her feet along the passages, to meet me! What trait more charming than her refusal to walk downstairs when my shoulder is there to ride on. She is a wife for Peter—born too late!

The end of it all is not a shadow-show of cats, playing in the box of memory. Their life endures for a short time, yet it is longer than the life of many human friendships. And *Whom the gods love die young* is not so inapplicable to animals as at first sight it would seem. To know a cat or two, and love them, is to gain acquaintances in whatsoever countries there are cats. Few of them but will come to me when I hold out a hand and call. Let me touch a cat and soon it will be purring. They have an instinct for friends. I am a freeman among the citizenry of cats.

It has been said—cat-lovers know otherwise—that only dogs, of all the races on earth, have broken down the barriers between man and beast, and have entered into companionship and friendship with mankind. There is, indeed, a similarity between the friendships of men and the friendship of man and dogs, for the greater number of human friendships imply subjection on one side or the other, and, more than all other animals, dogs are in subjection to the will of man. They owe their forms to breeders, and their keep to their usefulness, slavishness, or capability of winning prizes. They are trained to hunt, and are thrashed if they go a-hunting for themselves. But a cat, if she catches mice, does it incidentally for the same reason that she catches birds and kills canaries. Whatever *we* may think, the catching of mice is not done for us. It is a sport she follows, the benefits of which we may appropriate, so long as we do not eat her mice. She is bound by no duties, and will not be beaten into thinking that she is. Her independence is greatly to be honoured. Cats are never slaves. I say to my dog, "Go fetch ! Come here ! Up, then ! Down ! Good dog ! Bad dog ! Get to your basket, will you ! " He is my good and faithful servant.

But my cat's my equal in another line of life.

III

SMALL TRAVELS

AN OLD WOMAN

Our Old Woman—Madame Veuve X.—kept a little restaurant on the outskirts of the Latin Quarter. We never knew her name; she was one of those distinguishable persons who need no formal name. Down between the high houses, whether the narrow street was misty or clear, her light glimmered before men in a dim and dirty round gas-lantern, on which was painted, *Déjeuners et Dîners à* 1f., 1f. 25, 1f. 50. 'Twas a one-franc restaurant. For a dinner consisting of four courses and wine—we thought the red wine was less bad than the white—the equivalent of nine-pence three-farthings is not a great deal to pay. Sometimes we used to remark : " I wonder how the Old Woman does it. There's the bread, two sous—say a sou and a half. The serviette a sou, not a centime less. Then there are the three main courses and the dessert or cheese—and there's only twenty sous to the franc ! " It was impossible to see how the Old Woman could make any profit. And since she and her daughter did all the waiting, there were no *pourboires* ; no payments for extra civility ; no means of hurrying the service with a fatter tip. Economy was, at

first sight, the only recommendation of the Old
Woman's restaurant.

But there were other causes of attachment.
The spells of initiation are strong in Paris ; it is
a city of conscious habits. This was my first
Parisian restaurant. I felt at home, *chez moi*,
under its dingy lights, at its marble-topped tables,
with their coarse and soiled cotton cloths ; within
earshot of the culinary frizzling that went on
ceaselessly behind the matchboard partition ; in
the composite grey smell of the place, and under
the watchful eye of the Old Woman. We called
her *our* Old Woman less because she belonged to
us than because for several months we belonged to
her. She welcomed us, rain or fine, late or perhaps early, with a slightly grim smile. She asked
after Monsieur's cough—"But it would have
been worse in the fogs of England, *n'est-ce pas ?*"
—and prescribed for it herb-tea. On my part, I
told my friend, who often would have liked to
dine in the Boulevard St. Michel or on the other
side of the river, that the Old Woman's food,
though neither good nor plentiful nor varied, was,
I felt sure, unsophisticated. That was it. No
gratuitous messes ! No room for any sort of
gratuitousness ! There was a chance—it was not
lightly to be gainsaid—that the Old Woman's
cooking was unsophisticated.

All the while I knew at the back of my mind
that it was the Old Woman herself who attracted
me, not her food, still less her wines. I liked to
watch her tall stout figure promenading backwards
and forwards between the kitchen, the tables, and

the little zinc bar near the window. That must
have been her recreation and her rest. Her
hands reposed on the ample front of her. Talking or silent, her face, so brutally hard at times, so
pleasant and motherly at other times—the face of
a woman who has made her way and cannot, alive,
go back on it—seemed to beam quietly with a
confidence that I must, willy-nilly, enjoy what
she had provided. Who could profane such
confidence by rejecting a plate of over-stewed
shreds and bones? Who could change white
wine for red because the white was become just
too sour? It was enough to picture the Old
Woman at the markets, buying in her supplies
very early in the morning, or to wonder, with
something of her own anxiety, how much money
she had succeeded in putting by towards her red-
headed, pug-nosed, harsh-voiced daughter's
dowry.

I afterwards learnt, though not from her, that
she was by birth a German, or an Alsatian as the
Germans in Paris used to call themselves. When
I knew her she was very Parisian. She was as
much a Parisian as the girl who told me proudly,
with the gesture of a bird that has just preened its
feathers: "I am a Parisian, I am. I have never
been outside the fortifications, never—*jamais de la
vie!*" The Old Woman had forgotten Germany.
Ask for *sauer-kraut* and she would not understand
choucroute. But possibly her birth accounted for
her negligent dress. Always she wore the same
floppity slippers, the same grey stuff skirt and
dull black bodice, unfastened at the throat.

Sunday made no difference. Why should it? She worked every Sunday just the same. All day long she looked like a working housekeeper in the morning. Her essential dignity would have shone through sacking. The fashion-papers interested her not nearly so much as the obscene booklets which hawkers sold about her restaurant.

She was ready to take a friendly interest in any ignorant Englishman's pronunciation of French. Herself, she spoke with such composure that even Frenchmen could not always understand her close-lipped mumblings. As a teacher she was stern. Unhappy the day when I asked her for *un cuiller*! Never afterwards did I ask her for a spoon but she waggled it before my nose, enunciating "*Une cuillère! une cuillère!*" until I arrived at the pronunciation, and resolved never to forget that in gender, at all events, a spoon is female.

In the Old Woman's restaurant her regular clients could find a welcome and a dinner so late as ten in the evening. At such an hour she would stand mumbling over one's head, lifting first one tired foot and then the other—and the service was very rapid. Or she would turn down the gas till an odour-laden twilight was in the air ; the cook would cease scouring her pans ; a huge copper pot would be placed on a table near the kitchen, and then the Old Woman and her daughter and the cook would sit around, dive for savoury bits, chatter, and make merry.

At four next morning—to market. How the Old Woman must have haggled there! No doubt it was in the market, by beating down prices, that she earned her profits. She never could have earned them out of us.

For many, many years she had conducted (*conducted* is the word) her restaurant in the Latin Quarter. Six days in the week her customers hardly varied. Lovers dining out, perhaps, or a conscript and his friends, would drop in—birds of passage, reminders of elsewhere, and of other and better restaurants. A new cook must have been the Old Woman's greatest change. At this moment she must be talking to the consumptive man with the chestnut beard, if he is still alive. She *can't* be dead herself. I cannot imagine her death-scene. Let her live for ever !

Owing to an illness which made me fastidious, I stayed away for a fortnight, and fed somewhat better at a franc and a half. Consequently I was never able to go there afterwards. The illness broke the habit : I dared not break the absence. I knew how the Old Woman would look.

SELF-EXILED

The Grand Boulevards were full of people. Not that all the world was there. . . . Most of the well-dressed and over-dressed women, the badly, indifferently, and grotesquely dressed men ; most of the human beings, who walked almost stolidly at the slow pace of expectation waiting on chance, were very different from those who, living in the sunshine and sleeping in the quietness of the countryside, gain some of the flower-like calm of the fields. The greater part of the men and women on the Boulevards belonged to the world that pants. Beneath and between the houses of Paris they reminded one of rats, now still, sniffing the air, now darting about in search of prey in a ditch lit by glow-worms. Eyes, the windows of strange, haunted houses, were feverishly active. Furtive glances revealed love or vice, or, it may be, a mixture of the two. Whoever wished could see that the boundary between them is a sinuous writhing line, as deeply hidden and indeterminate as the boundary between altruism and individualism, or between the earth above and hell beneath, when earth may be a hell, or hell a refuge. Death showed himself ; but it was life which made him visible.

The great cauldron of humanity seethed and hissed : its lid was of human faces.

I turned into a side street, where, but for people hastening to the Boulevards and others walking from them, all was tranquil.   Thence I found my way to a certain little wine-shop, partly café, partly restaurant, mostly *cabaret.*

It was a quiet place.   The *patronne,* with an old grey cape about her shoulders, looking always cold, sat at her desk beside the polished zinc bar. What there was to be seen through the window she did not fail to notice.   She lived half— possibly the more important half—of her life in the street outside.   The *patron*—fat, his bullet-head closely cropped—stumped about his shop chewing the end of one of his best cigars.   The *garçon* sat at one of the marble-topped tables reading the *Petit Journal.*   At another table a man, whose face was like freshly-washed chamois leather, lazily played dominoes with a woman who may have been his wife.   The quiet of the place was disturbed by his voice, which was as harsh as the whirring of a steam-saw.   The woman's beauty was a souvenir—like the albums of faded photographs of sun-bathed sea-side places.   The voice, the faded beauty, and the mirrors which lined the walls, were all that recalled the noise, lamps, and disorder of the Grand Boulevards, not many yards away.

I ordered a glass of coffee, and then I noticed a middle-aged man who was seated in a mirror-encircled enclosure—an inner café—the other side of a partition which extended almost across the shop. I saw at once that he was one of those solitary, uncared-for, naturally neat men, who carefully brush their more or less aged clothes, yet never depart so far from their daily routine as to clean out grease spots. Spotted clothes, hair turning grey, a face with a few heavy lines, especially about the eyes and mouth, sunken tired eyes. . . . He lolled behind his table with an almost vacant expression, neither regarding anything in particular nor demanding notice.

Red matches were strewn on the floor around him. It was that which drew my attention. The man himself was not extraordinary ; but in France sixty red Swedish matches cost a penny. As I was looking he threw under the table an empty match-box. Was he drunk ? Apparently not. Then why. . . .

Whilst the *garçon* was pouring out my coffee the man told him to go to a tobacconist and buy another box of Swedish matches.

" *Tout de suite, monsieur,*" said the *garçon*, who was attending to me.

I nodded my head towards the scattered and charred matches, and asked, " *Pourquoi ça ?* "

The *garçon* smiled tolerantly. " *Demandez-lui, monsieur. Il vous dira, peut-être ; il est Anglais— un original.*"

An Englishman and an eccentric. . . . I was interested now in the man himself. I did wish to ask him why he wasted comparatively expensive matches. But how ? I remembered that I had in my pocket an almost new box, and made use of the opportunity. Before the *garçon* had returned I went into the enclosure and said, "Excuse me ; can I let you have any matches ? "

The Englishman looked up keenly. He had a habit very common amongst thinkers and those who expect always ; I was in the direct line of his sight, yet both his eyes did not appear to be focused on me for more than a moment. He seemed to be scrutinising me, and, at the same time, to be looking at, or for, something indefinitely far behind me. He used his eyes like a man who is examining an object through a microscope : one eye looked at the object—at me—and the other eye looked anywhere or nowhere.

"No, thank you," he replied at last. "You are very kind, but I can wait a minute. . . ." He spoke almost as mechanically as a gramophone. "And here comes the *garçon*."

"Are you English or American ? " he added.

"English."

"Ah ! Will you have your coffee over here ? "

He gave the order ; eagerly, I thought, and my glass was brought to his table.

Then he turned to me. "Now, don't think me too inquisitive. . . . What part of England do you come from ? You speak like a Southerner."

"Wiltshire."

"That's not far. Do you know Bath ? You don't know Bath ? "

"I'm afraid I don't. I have been there : that's all I can say."

"Then you won't know any Bath people ? You don't, do you ? "

"No, I can't say I do."

U

Straightway I seemed to drop out of his interest. He took four of the matches which lay on the table in front of him. Two of them he inserted a little way down the sides of the box —between the sides for striking and the corresponding, longer, sides of the inner box. Between the other ends of these parallel matches, which projected equal distances, he lodged a third, which was kept tightly in position by the spring of the first two and of the sides of the box. With the fourth match he set light to the centre of the third, which burnt quietly for a few seconds and then, giving way under the pressure of the two parallel matches, described a curve in the air, and fell burning to the floor. It is a common trick, naturally more so in England than in France, but he did it with all seriousness, placing his matches with the greatest care, and following exultantly the course of the burning match as it sprang forth all alight and dropped. When it was done he disturbed his arrangement, took two fresh matches from the box and performed the whole trick over again. His hands shook slightly, whether from debility or excitement I could not tell ; he was by no means old.

Every time he gave the same care to his preparations, exulted while the match burned, with a curious, somewhat unpleasant expression on his face, and leaned back contentedly when it had flickered out on the floor.

"You must waste a lot of matches like that," I said.

"A good many, perhaps. It's worth it. Look.

"You put them like that and light. There. See how quietly it burns. See what a snap it makes as it springs gracefully away, burning. Besides there is always an off-chance of setting the place on fire. . . . You've heard of people snapping their fingers at some one. Done it? I used to do it, metaphorically and really, until I saw some one playing this trick with matches— even afterwards, in fact, until I saw the possibilities which lie in a box of matches. But see. . . ."

He did it yet again.

"There! That beats snapping your fingers. It is a perfect, burning expression of contempt. Perfect! Do you understand symbols? The snap, as the match gives way, symbolises contempt; the flame, hate. It is complete. Absolutely!"

I wondered if he was mad, saying: "But I don't understand. . . ."

"You don't understand contempt, I expect. No use for it—eh? I have. I'll tell you. You may be glad some day.

"When I first came over here nearly fifteen years ago I left behind me in England my home, my family and my fiancée—my 'financy,' as my little sister used to call her. The usual sort of things a man does leave behind him, you know; —father, he died soon after,—mother, to kiss the place and make it well—eh?—a sister and a brother or two, various friends and the girl. A young man generally leaves 'em behind. Good job too! Very right and proper thing to do. God knows what'd happen if he didn't.

"I didn't talk like this, then. People don't

talk the same all their life through. We've got
to provide amusement for angels and those gone
before and all superior beings like that, whether
we like it or not. Absurd to suppose they don't
snigger at us! How can they help it?

"However, you'll say I'm bitter. Because I'm
done for? So I may be. Some things blast,
kill, damn; other things only deform, little by
little, slowly and quite surely—make the feet of
our soul into Golden Lilies, so to speak—when
they don't go further.

"Anyhow, I came over here, eager, rejoicing.
In England there was home: in Paris there were
a good many substitutes—admirable substitutes,
for a time. But to a country-bred person a city is
a vampire; nothing more or less. After the first
freshness had worn off I always felt glad—very!
—that I had a home in England; exactly as a
Christian, I suppose, likes to feel that there is
a God, more merciful than just, behind everything.
I used to write home—long letters, diluted appro-
priately: people *will* worry over what they can't
help. Doubtless my letters were very interesting,
but it goes without saying that they tended to
become less so. However that may be, they
didn't write so much from home, sending love
and kisses, and asking for news of me. In fact,
they wrote very little. You know the sort of
people whose daily affairs are the important and
inexorable things of life, and whose loves and
affections are—well—so-so, incidental; people who
won't budge to please or to increase unnecessarily
the comfort of any one, because they've got a

pudding to make, or it's a fine day to dig potatoes, or they want to do this, or that, or the other little thing. Glorious majority ! see how the exceptions stand out !

"One by one my friends and relations left off writing to me. My ' financy ' wasn't the last. I raged over her, heard she was much taken up with some one else—they told me that—very natural of her, I suppose. We had sworn all sorts of eternal things. It was impossible for me to leave Paris, and finally, thinking I had always a home, at any rate, I managed to recover pretty successfully. Then my sister and brothers began putting notes into other people's letters. It was very nice to get a sort of family round-letter, or it would have been if they hadn't soon stopped writing altogether. They all owed me a letter — do now ; but I *will* not write to people who won't answer. I stuck to my principle.

"Last of all my mother left a letter un-answered. She was always an expert at pro-crastination ; but one doesn't expect a mother to exercise it on her children. I broke my rule and wrote a second time. At last she replied. She was afraid she had failed in her duty as a mother —her own words, *duty as a mother !*—she would try not to do so in the future. Who wants duty-letters ? I don't. I wrote and told her so. Whether she found she could write to me nothing else but duty letters, or whether she meant, at first, to punish me, and then forgot all about me, I don't know. Unanswered letters become increasingly difficult to answer, until there comes a time when one can't.

"Of course, something may have happened to her, only I felt that I couldn't write and ask. I was very lonely, and always expecting a letter. My *concierge* must have known my face; I used to peer through her window every time I went out and in. There was never a letter, and it always made the five flights of stairs seem dreadfully high. The heart and feet aren't so very far apart.

"When home is gone, one seems to be floating in chaos. I made no friends in Paris. . . . No place like Paris for making no friends —good God, there isn't! Even the dogs are exclusive, stand-offish. In those days I used to ache for news from home, and every barren post added another little to a weight which pressed on my brain. As I said, there are some things which deform and kill, very, very slowly—soul and brain first.

"Well. . . . After I had been here about seven years I got a good chance of going to England. I can't tell you how excited I was—enough to make it seem like a dream—or a nightmare. The evening train crawled to Dieppe, and after living so long cramped up in Paris, I went on board sniffing the night sea-air.

"For some reason or other my spirits fell steadily all the way across. It may have been the cold desolation of the sea by night. (I stayed on deck.) When I stepped on the quay at Newhaven, in the morning, long before dawn, it was

raining, and the dismal shanty of a station, badly
lighted, with the almost sepulchral porters, made
me feel. . . . I don't know how.   I went to the
refreshment room.   Bad coffee and tough heavy
bread took away all the rest of my courage.   The
rain beat against the windows.   How sodden and
cheerless England can be !   'All hope abandon
ye who enter here,' the place seemed to say.

"I could not go on ; couldn't !   My people
might have been dead and gone.

"The end of it was, I waited about the quay
and took the day boat back to Dieppe ; and going
into Dieppe station was like going home.

"When   I   was   back   in   Paris   even   the
boulevards   seemed   homelike—and   you   know
what the boulevards are like.   Then a curious
change came over me—a change which I can't
explain. . . .

"We are absurdly like pigeons—ever seen a
pigeon's courtship ?—and you know how automatic
our homing instinct is.   We have nothing to do
with it ; there it is : the instinct controls us ; it
seems to be an outsider dwelling in us, not to be
dislodged without tearing away some of our vitals.
'Distance lends enchantment,' they say.   I think
this applies, above all, to home.   How keenly I
used to feel it !   But, quite without any help
from me, unbidden by me, quite automatically,
as it were, my feelings underwent a change ; they
performed a *right-about-face*.

"I began to hate home and all in it.   The
longer I was away the more my hate and contempt increased.   I snapped my fingers at the

whole lot of them. Sometimes to think of it made me even breathless. Now I have had my contempt for such a long time, and it grows so nicely, that it has gained refinement of expression.

" This is perfect. . . ."

Again he did his match trick. I watched him. Just before the burning match sprang out he looked no longer semi-inert ; he looked devilish ; but, at the same time, the pitiful hungry longing of which he had spoken showed itself in his face. Whether, or no, the longing had really disappeared, as he said, and the expression of it was but a habit which the wrinkles of his skin and flesh had acquired in earlier days, I do not know.

It was nearly twelve o'clock when he had finished his tale. He turned to me : " Now, you see, I do the same things every day. No silly expectations ! Here is my comfort. . . ." He indicated the wretched cabaret. " There is my joy in life. . . ." He pointed to the match-box.

" It must be very dull," I said.

" Horribly ; and yet it isn't. I have some variety. . . . The moments when my hate and contempt bubble over vary from day to day both in time and number. They really vary most extraordinarily. I might classify the things that set them going. That's my interest. One discovers all sorts of curious associations. I'm almost afraid of a postman ; I can't bear to hear a gate clang, as ours at home used to do when the post-man came up the path ; and I absolutely fear the seventeenth of September, the anniversary of my last letter. I'm lonely enough, but that keeps me from being exactly dull. Otherwise, I'm mostly dead."

There was nothing more to say. I knew that I was in the presence of slow tragedy, a cancer of the spirit, most deadly and terrible, quite slow.

For a time he said nothing ; then he looked up at the clock and spoke. "If you don't mind my saying so, you'd better go now. This is an all-night restaurant. I don't sleep much in the night. Can't. Of late years I have always begun to get drunk at midnight. . . . You remember what Dr. Johnson said—about man being happy only when he's drunk ? There's a good deal of truth in it. . . . Good night. . . . Going back to England ? "

" Yes ; next month, I hope."

" Ah ! if you go near Bath. . . . No ! never mind. I am apt to forget at times. Leave me, please. Good night."

As I went out of the door of the cabaret I took a last look at him. He was sitting heaped up on his seat, and his expression was a foresight of what one might expect on the face of a dying man who believes that he has failed in everything on earth and that the hereafter will fail him.

Then I heard him call out to the *garçon* : " *Une absinthe, s'il vous plaît. Vite ! Je suis fatigué.*"

A DOG'S LIFE

TOLD TO IT

MARGOT—before you divide your affection between your master and those fine little pups that will be, I want to give you a sketch of your life, of our life together. For you understand your friends in proportion as they are fond of you and you are fond of them.

(Gently, please! Down! You are as tall as myself when you stand upright, and nearly as heavy, and of all dogs you Great Danes are the most cat-like in your movements; but I do not want your height and weight and activity used against me. So down, then! Down!)

Your life has been an almost unbroken web. Could the strands of human existence be so accurately traced. . . . Ben Jonson's words apply to you:

> In small proportions we just beauties see,
> And in short measures life may perfect be.

You have a well-grown shrub of life where your master and his fellow-men have trees with torn-off branches.

You date (for me) from a couple of years before you came here ; a year and five months before you were even born.   There was a dog show in Devonshire with a brindle Great Dane, like you, in it—not a prize-winner, only a V.H.C. Being very lonely, I watched with envious eyes how it jumped upon its keeper, placed its fore-paws on his shoulder, fondled him, licked his face, and whimpered with delight.   And I thought to myself, " Some day I will have a dog like that."

Heaven knows what happened between then and the day you were exchanged for gold !   I dare not call the whole of it to mind.   For one thing, I loved an invalid pointer called Bloom. Months I was occupied in nursing her back to health, coaxing her to eat ; and then they carted her away in a big box.   I've seen her since—in that huge glass barn at Sydenham—deafened with yapping and hemmed in by people who talked of show condition and patent nostrums, sales and values and judges' mistakes, points and prizes and champions.   I called her in the old way, " Bloom, beauty ! "   But she had forgotten.   She did not know me.   I was become to her only a desirable acquaintance, some one she would have taken to. Ashamed to let the kennelman see tears in my eyes, I turned away.   She might have recollected if I had stayed long enough.   More than you I loved her, Margot ; she was my only stay in great trouble ; but we were not together long.

You grew in your master's mind before you started growing.   A day came when he bought

the *Exchange and Mart* ; studied points, breeders,
strains and pedigrees ; and took the train for
London. He wanted a Great Dane, like the
one at the show—dog or bitch—brindle pre-
ferably—well-bred but not necessarily a prize-
winner—not unusually tall, but upstanding and
limber—strong enough to tramp the country—
affectionate and kindly with children. You are
all that. Two guineas was to have been the price
of you.

At several markets and menageries they told
me they had no Great Dane in stock, but could
get one to order. But how could one *order* a
dog, like a book or a suit of clothes ? There
might be implied obligations to purchase a brute.
So I tramped on through parts of London I had
never seen, and never shall see again, probably.
At last I came across a real Great Dane—your
father, Margot—in a stuffy little back shop somewhere just north of Whitechapel.

Had they Great Danes for sale ?

They produced two small steely-blue puddings
of pups.

" No ? " they asked when I refused the pups.
" Too young ? You want one old enough to
walk twenty miles a day ? "

They took me through a dismal North London
square, where empty tins and pickle pots grew
instead of grass on the central plot, through a
dingy house where a woman held a baby to her
bare breast with one hand and washed dirty
clothes with the other ; and we entered a high
iron cage inside of which eight huge dogs, barking

and growling, made one feel like Daniel in the lions' den.

"No?" they asked again. "You think these are too old? Too expensive, you say? D'you really mean to train a Dane puppy yourself?"

They opened a ramshackle little wooden kennel. A three-quarter-grown pup rushed out, sniffed at me, sprang on me, and had my best clothes dirtied all over in an instant. It was you, Margot, your own self! They tried to drag out your shy litter sister, but there was no need. You were mine—mine from that moment. I didn't choose you; you chose me.

But you were too expensive.

Next day I was back again in your kennel, and could have sworn you recognised me, so thickly did you plaster my clothes with filth. "But it's too much money," said I.

"You can't have a pedigree Dane for less," returned the breeder. "Her father, Lord Copenhagen, won two hundred prizes."

"That's very nice, of course. . . ."

"She's got the best blood in England in her."

"And about food?"

"Look, she's not delicate!" You were thrown a green-mouldy crust, Margot, which you gobbled up at once.

"I see she's not. But what's that lump on her haunch?"

"Oh, there? That's only a kennel bruise. A little warm water bathing. . . ."

"I'll give pounds instead of guineas."

"Can't do it. Her food has cost me that."

(Green-mouldy crusts, Margot!) " Look at her pedigree—sire, Lord Copenhagen—dam, Tricksey Jane ! "

" Very well, have it guineas, then."

It's my opinion you saw into my mind, Margot, and were begging me to take you away. I would have risen to ten guineas.

You were delivered with a collar at Paddington Station. Do you remember that we took a second-class ticket because porters and such-like are kindlier to second-class passengers ; how the inspector said you might travel in the carriage if those already there had no objection ; how I poked my head in at the window, asking, " Do you object to a puppy here ? "—how they said, " We love dogs ! " and how, when the door was opened, you, Margot, three-quarters of a yard high, young and frolicsome, jumped in upon them ? They did love dogs. You made them dirty, and nevertheless they praised you. Your master was like a woman with a naughty, pretty child. They asked your name.

> " I have no name ;
> I am but seven months old."
> What shall I call thee ?

There was once, Margot, an artist's model, a *petite* delicate pale Alsacienne, who used to frequent a certain café in the Latin Quarter. She knew how to dress her own particular type of beauty, so that we called her the Pre-Raphaelite Girl, and other pretty names. She used to make your master treat her to glasses of light French beer—" *Un bock pour moi, mon cher!* "—and cigarettes. She wanted to go on the stage, the real stage. She did sometimes perform in *cafés chantants*. One evening she sang a whole part from *Carmen* into my left ear. " *Belle, mon cher, n'est-ce pas?* " she said.

" *Tu es belle?* "

" *Non! Ma voix, cochon!* "

I had heard it very well, although the piano and fiddles were playing Wagner, billiard balls were clicking, white-aproned waiters were shouting, and a couple of hundred voices were going twenty to the dozen. It was the last I saw of her, her costume *à l'art nouveau*. Perhaps she was not highly respectable. I don't know. I never did. She is a *fleur du mal*, crystallised in my memory, and still a little fragrant. Her name was Margot. And so is yours.

Neither of you was made to run in traces. When you arrived, Margot, the first thing you did, after knocking down a child or two, was to bite your new leather lead into five moist chawed-up pieces.

Lucky that our landlady was at the seaside when you came home! You tore up one mat, demolished a slipper, bit my new sea-going rug into holes (that was put down to keep you off the cold stones between the kitchen and the scullery doors), and you took a flying leap upon the breakfast table. Strange to say, you only smashed a plate, a jug, the jam-jar and the lid of the best tea-pot. Your master feared he wouldn't be able to keep you; but he did, although you sent him

to bed every night trembling with fatigue, and
then had him out of it again to stop your
howling.

'Tis to be hoped you do not remember the so-
called kennel bruise, which grew into a cyst; and
the operation on it.   At the first attempt you
slipped off the tape twitch, put on to keep your
jaws close; you heaved up the four of us who
were holding you down; you bit wildly at your
master for the first and last time, when he had
you by the scruff of your neck whilst the veter-
inary surgeon's men stood around, prepared to
scatter in case you ran amuck.   You returned to
the surgery in an iron muzzle two sizes too small
for you, and the cyst. . . .   Never mind.   The
lance went in with a jerk.   Yet afterwards, without twitch or muzzle, you used to lie on the
ground, stretched out and groaning, while I
probed your wound with tincture on the stump of
a feather.   Other diseases you have had—eczema,
canker, parasites outside and in, and a touch of
bronchitis—but we have cured them all.   I think
you like a pill; castor oil is certainly to your taste.
You would hardly win a championship or a big prize.
You are not quite tall enough (though children
often take you for a lion broken loose); you have
too much loose skin about your neck, which makes
you look like a lady in a fluffy dressing-gown;
and your head is too snipey; but you are fatter,
glossier, in better muscular condition, more pleasing
to the eye, than half the flabby, splay-footed,
kennel-kept prize-winners at shows.   And your
face is partly human.   A poet says :—

> There is no laughter in the natural world
>   Of beast or fish or bird, though no sad doubt
> Of their futurity to them unfurled
>   Has dared to check the mirth-compelling shout.
> . . . . Who had dared foretell
> That only man, by some sad mockery,
> Should learn to laugh who learns that he must die.

But I've seen you laugh, Margot. I recollect your face when that whippet ran squeaking away from your ponderous civilities ; when the silly young woman screamed, " I can't abear dogs ! " —when, on those lovely mornings, the sun lit up Salisbury Plain and we rushed out of the house together. I know just where the wrinkles come when you laugh. A fig for the poet's philosophising ! Smile again.

We went a walking tour through the good West Country. It was then that we learnt the jog-trot of our life together. Everywhere they said, " Shouldn't like to meet he in the dead o' night, Mister." In stableyards they stood round watching while I washed your feet and groomed you with a borrowed dandy-brush. " Jest like a bloomin' hoss," they said. You opened the conversation at the inns where your master had his bread and cheese and beer, and you your pint of milk. Because you looked ferocious, they fed and patted you the more when they found you gentle. A man at Falkland wanted to thread worsted through the flaps of your ears, which was, he declared, an infallible cure for canker. I wonder what *you* would have been doing the while. At Wells they put you on a bed of damp peat-moss in a mouldy tower, and in revenge you

x

kept half the little town awake by howling all
night like two wild beast shows encamped together.　They were glad to be rid of us there !
And next day you were so tired for want of sleep
that you ran into every open cottage door and sat
down among the frightened inhabitants, as if you
had expected an Oriental hospitality.　Without a
cry you were hauled up by your tail as you were
slipping down into the crypt of Glastonbury Abbey
—without a yap, O game and well-bred Margot !
At Knowle you were dog-tired, and because the
landlady said with many sniffs that she couldn't
have dogs in *her* house, we mounted a load of
empty soda-water bottles, so proceeding into
Bridgewater, to a hotel recommended by the carter
because the proprietors kept dogs—*dogs* being
at that time an enormously fat pug that supped
nightly on chocolate creams.　While I was having
a bath you escaped from the hotel skittle-alley into
Bridgewater town, to find me.　Half-clothed, a
delight to the small boys of the place, helter-
skelter, I was after you.　" Have you seen a large
brindle boarhound this way ? " I asked people.
After they had put me on the tracks of an old
red setter, a yellow Airedale terrier and a black
retriever, we found one another in the market-
place, and for joy you almost knocked me down.

The flies on the Quantocks, where you made
your ears bleed with shaking them ; inhospitable
Crowcombe, where the rooks cawed so solemnly
in the twilight, and you begged a cottager to take
us in ; our weary tramp on to Stogumber ; the
kind butcher at Minehead who boiled a whole

sheep's head for you ; peaceful moonlit Brendon
in Exmoor, and the small boy who loved you at
sight ; the thrashing you had for eating garbage
in the Lyn valley ; that thundery afternoon on
the North Devon moors when the air was full
of flying ants and we were both dead-beat ; the
two wasps that stung you in the coffee-room at
Clovelly so that you dashed wildly over the
crockery and cold joints ; the spry, profane little
maid near Hartland who called your master a
" beastly devil" because he gave you the strap
for stealing a pound of fresh butter ; the games
you had with the little maid, head-over-heels,
somersault, roly-poly, batter pat, jump, flop !
Do you remember, Margot ? You have loved
little children ever since. How many of them
have you kissed off their feet ? Not every mother
says (like the one in Sheep Street) when you
peep into her perambulator, or tip over her child :
" Lard, look 'ee, Missis, if 'er an't a-been an'
kissed 'en ! "

  We made a pilgrimage to Morwenstow, to
Parson Hawker's church. In pious memory of
the good old poet who used to take his cats
to church, I took you with me, too ; and you
showed your piety by jumping the altar rails.

  Keeping you is not all meaty bones. Sometimes it is mere dry dog biscuit. Accidentally you
knocked your master down and sprained his arm ;
which led to one illness after another, ending up
with a week's bad temper and the worst thrashing
you ever had. A House that Margot built, that
fell about her faithful hide ! Would that one

never had to beat you. Yet I think you prefer hot anger to cold justice. Uncalculating love, a fit of muddy fury boiling up from the atavistic depths of one, a struggle, curses, and quick repentance. . . . You understand such people ; you have a fellow-feeling with them, and love them better than those cool, prudent, proper, respectable citizens, swaddled in civilisation, who seldom act without good reason and never repent nor abase themselves. You dogs keep one in touch with one's own primeval nature. You are the companions of joy and sorrow, not of a stagnant temperateness in all things. But I do wish you would not cry out under the strap. It stirs too much the brute in one. You, when you love us, may not comprehend our language fully, but you feel our feelings, communicated in some wordless way, like music among ourselves, or telepathically. Let those who wish write books on comparative psychology ; whether animals reason or not ; whether their actions are the result of instinct, of inherited compound reflex action, or of intelligence. There are bonds between us beyond reasoning. No man learns much of men except he love them. So if they love you, they will learn, and

The rest may reason and welcome ; 'tis we dog-lovers know.

When you become old ; when you chaw your last bone, prod my cheek for the last time with your cool nose, and wag the final wag of that heavy bruising tail. . . . Don't let us think about it.

Such ideas may be gross sentimentality, but the event will be very, very real.

> I saw a dead man's finer part
> Shining within each faithful heart
> Of those bereft.   Then said I : "This must be
> His immortality."

Yes, and a dog's too.   You don't know Byron's *Vision of Judgment*, where King George slips into heaven whilst Satan and the Archangel are wrangling for possession of his soul.   But I fancy that when the recording Angel presents his piebald account of me, he will say : that I loved dogs and cats and all animals, and they loved me ; and I shouldn't wonder if I don't get in ; and at the Celestial Gate to welcome me, there will be you, Margot, and Bloom and Peter, and with you, in waiting, Teager, alias Gyp, and Charlie and Doctor and Nell and Ginger and Jumbo and Jack and Jill and Nip, and perhaps Toby ; and Tabby and Whity and Tibbie and Jim and Ma and Pa and Baby, and that other Baby who was nineteen when I was, but never twenty ; and Jacob and Wild Cat and Tinker and Minnie and Manxie and Fluff and Bully and Fuzz, and ferrets and rabbits and birds—a Noah's Ark of them— all at the Celestial Gate to welcome me, because in varying degrees I loved them and they loved me.   You, Margot, you shall pilot me in.   For I am to you your Almighty and your slave. . . .

It's only a fantastical vision, I know ; yet the seer wrote : "*Everything possible to be believed is an image of truth.*"

P.S.—Margot ate the pups.

A STEAM-BURST AFLOAT

She is a small steel-built ship, with a high-sounding name, and a tonnage well under two thousand. Year in and year out, fair weather or foul, she hastens on her voyages, carrying Welsh coal to the Mediterranean ports, and lading with general cargoes for England; working overtime in harbour, and on Sundays, too; hustled by owners, hustled by agents; always at sea, or on the point of sailing. Eight and a half knots or less, according to weather and the coal, is her speed. She is never clean all over, because she hurries so much, and is so often smothered in sticky Welsh coal-dust that her mixed crew—Spaniards, Greeks, and Welshmen—cannot cleanse her for'ard before she is dirty aft, nor paint her aft, before her iron deck is once more rusty for'ard. Her officers get dirty with her. They wear no uniforms.

A collier, some might call her; a tramp, others; yet there are men aboard her acquainted with ships and shipping scandals, who say that in some respects at any rate her sea-going qualities are better than those of many well-known steamers; that her engines depreciate less, and run sweeter, than the engines of such cargo vessels usually do.

Deep down below decks, near the centre of gravity of the ship, are the engines that drive her. They also are not large. They weigh about forty-five tons.

Look down into the engine-room when the ship is under way—down two flights of iron steps, through two floors of iron grating. You can see the engineer on watch pacing up and down before his engines. He watches them tenderly and keenly, as wild animals at the Zoo watch succulent children. Now and then he feels the coolness of the bearings. He jerks up his head and listens to some chance noise, heard through the rattle and thump of the machinery. Every half-hour he pours oil into the swiftly oscillating oil-boxes with a movement of upraised arm, wrist, and shoulder that is singularly true and graceful. Damp, hot air and the smell of oil rise through the skylights. Machinery clanks below. Those black, metallic, slippery places familiar in nightmares. . . . The engine-room is like them.

Do you see that steam-joint there, above and behind the reversing wheel, to the right of the small high-pressure cylinder ?

We were in Leghorn Harbour, on the point of sailing, of course, and except for the racket aboard ship the place was very calm. The light of an opal sunset was dying away on the red walls of a tattered old house by the southern quay. The short Italian twilight was rapidly gathering in. Gangs were working overtime at all four hatches. It was impossible to go anywhere on the ship beyond reach of their sing-song volubility and the rattle of the four steam winches. We could hear them plainly in the otherwise quiet, expectant engine-room.

The chief engineer was on watch—a slight, muscular man, whose everything superfluous, including half his hair, had been sweated off him. In clean trousers and shirt, arms and chest bare, he was puffing cigarettes and marching up and down in front of his engines, exactly as he does when they are working, but even more sharply and with still keener eyes upon them. In the hot corner stood the donkey-engine man, gnawing his sweat - rag—that same strong, dark, impassive Greek, worthy of ancient days, who separated— and held separate with a finger and thumb on the throat of each—two seamen who had been fighting with knives. For some unaccountable reason there was that night a feeling of anxiety, not to say nervousness, in the engine-room. Each knew it, and smiled at the others because they knew it too. The best of marine engines will play tricks at starting, especially after minor repairs.

" Yes," remarked the Chief, reaching down the coffee-pot lamp to light another cigarette, "you wouldn't think there was steam the other side of that bulkhead at 180 lbs. pressure to the square inch."

One after another the winches on deck were becoming silent. The gangs were going over the ship's side, as dirty and as voluble as ever. Through the skylights we could hear the Old

Man's voice, "Finished, stevedore? Now then
—*passa in terra omne*—quick!"

"Steam," remarked the Chief again, "is a fine
thing when you've got it under your thumb. . . ."

The telegraph from the bridge rang out while
the finger circled the dial from *Full speed ahead*
to *Full speed astern*, and came to a stop at *Stand
by*. Donkey-man answered. The Chief placed
himself near the reversing wheel and valves. He
gave the wheel a turn, started the small reversing
engine. Slowly, very slowly, the links above
tumbled ahead and astern, and the eccentrics
shifted. Six masses of forged steel, the cranks,
rocked in their pits, half a turn towards us, half a
turn away. Fifteen tons of metal swayed backwards and forwards, up and down. . . .

Do you know how a cat sways just before she
springs? It was like that; like some monstrous
beast of prey whose limbs and claws were pistons,
crossheads, rods, and cranks.

"All clear for'ard? All clear aft? Cast off."

Half-speed ahead rang the telegraph.

Cocks are turned, valves opened. Steam rushes
from boiler to cylinders with a hollow gurgling
hiss. The cranks make half a turn, a whole turn.
She is under way.

There is a sudden loud report, followed by
a long, savage, deafening hiss. Almost instantly
the engine-room is filled with a stinking fog of
hot oily steam, driving upwards through the
gratings, but thickening, nevertheless.

It was the high-pressure steam-joint.

Lighted on the one side by a hundred candle-power burner and on the other by the smoky coffee-pot lamp, the Chief and Donkey stayed by the reversing wheel. Their faces were still turned towards the cocks and valves, but their eyes had shifted to the steam-joint overhead. Muscles taut and swollen—magnified, as it were, by the brilliant light and the deep, hard-cut shadows—they were like a group by some painter of heroes, like tormented forms peering in at the Gate of Hell.

It was only for a moment. One's first thought was to race up the iron steps to the open air; one's second, to face it out, as the engineers had to face it out; one's third, to realise that the steam would be more scalding above than below.

At last—so it seems, though the time is short enough—the valves are shut. The engine-room takes the telegraph in hand. *Stop* goes up to the bridge. *Half-speed ahead* rings down. *Stop* goes up once more.

"They must wait," says the Chief mournfully. "Call my second, Donkey, and tell the Old Man we can't go."

The engine-room was in command of the ship.

For half-an-hour three men, seated or crouched on a grating, lighted by the coffee-pot lamp, hammered, wrenched, screwed, damaged themselves and swore. In less than an hour the little steamer was hurrying off, over the silent moonlit sea, to Genoa.

All night, steam hissed and blew. All night, one or other of the three men watched the steam-joint alone down in the engine-room, and sweated in the damp hotness and became stupid with the hissing ; for the little steamer must never stop in her haste until the day when she is wrecked, or scrapped, or dry-docked for scamped repairs.

" Us have see'd it aforetime, an't us ? "

" Aye ! an' will again ! "

" If thee's live long enough. . . ."

" Just thee wait ! "

" 'Twon't make no difference in a hundred years' time."

" When we'm all underground."

" Thee casn't live but once."

" 'Tis a long time you'm dead ! "

Where fishermen gather together and talk, the aged philosophy of the beach reels itself off as slick as antiphonal singing in church, or the choruses of a Greek play. What generations have lived by will stand repetition.

But modernity was sighted in the offing. " 'Tisn't no good, I tell thee ! " the younger men were saying. " Thee's got to keep up with the times, nowadays, if thee's want to live."

" Times ! What's the times ? You'm in the times, bain't 'ee ? When they there ol' men was living, that was their times. An' now 'tis ours."

" Aye, but when you tries to act like they ol' men what you chatters about, then you'm behind *your* times."

" G'out ! Hold thee row ! "

The older well-tried philosophy, forgetting that in the end it was bound to win, spluttered and choked and swore, and then sulked, like an old fisherman who knows from long experience how to do things "fitty," but won't lend a hand, and hinders those who will.

Meanwhile, modernity approached close in-shore—in the guise, on this occasion, of a motor-boat. It was not merely the question of a motor-boat which was thrashed out ; not simply the probabilities of a business experiment : two systems, two ways of life, two moods, the back-ward-looking and the forward-looking, came into conflict with a clash of argument.

"Motor-boats ! They stinking things. . . ."

"Motor-boats is coming right enough. You see. They'm buzzing an' snorting round all they harbour places like blue-bottles round ol' Twister's crab-bait. They'm coming."

"That an't got nort to do wi' us. They won't come here, where us only got a lee shore, an' the beach to haul everything up-over, an' no shelter to run to nearer than Exmouth or Beer. You won't never see 'em on a beach like ours. You'd never be able to haul 'em out the water."

"You could haul up your sailing-boat wi' a couple or three bags o' ballast in her, cousn't ! "

"Course I could, if I had to."

"Well, that's about the weight of a little motor-engine. Where's the difference in hauling up ? They said motor-cars was never coming into Devonshire, didn' 'em, 'cause o' the hills ? But they'm here wi' their rattle an' their smeech."

"I reckon they bain't right, they motors. They blows 'ee up—I've a-see'd it on the paper, where they have. 'Tis like ol' Benjie says, God gave oars an' sails for to get a boat along with. He didn' hae nort to do wi' motors. They'm an invention, like, what man's made."

"God didn't make thy oars an' sails, n'eet pay for 'em nuther, did 'Er ! "

"Sure He didn't ! "

"An' motor-boats is coming, I tell thee ; us'll hae to hae 'em sooner or later, an' if us don't hae 'em pretty soon us'll be lef' behind."

"Why can't us jog along, like us always have a-done ? "

"Jog-along ! . . . . Aye, jog along backwards. That's what jogging along means. You got to be up-to-date, I tell 'ee, if you wants to be upsides wi' people an' earn your living nowadays."

"Give 'em rope ! You gie 'em rope ! Us have a-see'd they up-to-date people 'fore now. An' where be 'em ? Gone ! Dead ! In the 'sylum ! Brought low ! Us have a-picked up a living for twenty years on this here beach wi' fishing an' the little boats. . . ."

"An' thee wousn't like to see somebody what's got capital take thy living from thee, an' not hae nort to eat."

"Us could do summut else, couldn' us, or go short—like us have had to aforetime. I have, if thee hasn't, an' will again very likely. S'pose they motor-boats was to be all the go. . . . What's a poor fellow to do that can't afford one ? I don't want to take no advantage o' anybody

else. *Live an' let live* is my motto, only they
won't let 'ee do it."

" 'Tisn't no need to take away anybody's
living, if us had a little motor-boat for to take
people to Beer, an' Lyme, an' Exmouth, an'
Torquay—where rowing an' sailing boats don't
lay themselves out to go,—an' for fishing, an'
p'raps to tow out a drifter or two when you'd hae
to row out against one o' they there short
southerly chops.   Thee a'tn't so fond o' digging
away at the oars—a't ?—for all thee's say God
made 'em ! "

" But who's going to work a motor-boat ?
Us can't be out in a motor-boat an' out to sea in
the sailing boats too."

" Steve, here, 's said he'll work 'en, an't 'er ! "

" Be 'em going to make it any better for the
likes o' us, they motor-boats—that's what I wants
to know ? "

" I don't say they will.   But be 'em going
to make it any worse for the likes o' us if us
don't hae one—that's the point ?   Thee wousn't
never make thic fortune o' thine if thee doesn't
try."

" An' thee wousn't never make a fortune by
working hard.   *I* an't never see'd it done.   'Tis
artfulness an' luck does it. . . ."

Through summer into autumn the argument
continued.   Like a Hindoo prayer-wheel it
turned itself round and round—on the sea-wall
and down by the boats, at sea in fair weather and
under the lee side of the drifter in foul, after
bedtime at night and at dawn over an early cup

o' tay, at meals and even in bed. There was
no end to the discussion : there had never,
definitely, been any beginning. The knowledge
and ignorance, the lives themselves, of three men
were flung into it to keep it alive. That's how
'tis with men of small capital : small undertakings
absorb them. The finish was hardly in sight
when I went up-country to London with a roving
commission to look at and find out about marine
motor-engines—not to buy. For we had come
to no decision. We had merely worked ourselves
up so that a decision was bound, sooner or later,
to be forced upon us.

My qualifications were these : first, that I had
been pretty well trained in handling scientific
apparatus and boats on a lee shore ; second, that
in the early days of motor-cars I had spent some
hours grovelling underneath broken-down engines
in sweet sylvan spots ; third and best, that I had
to carry the job through.

Experts—men of 400 horse-power and thirty
knots — looked over my head. Each recommended a different engine (all too expensive), and
a moderate number of revolutions a minute.
Finally, on the off-chance, mainly because I had
a few hours to spare, I took the slowest of slow
trains to Erith, and lost myself on the over-built
marsh thereabout. And in a black wooden shed
—guarded by a hammering and a clanking and a
rattle of explosions from the exhausts of internal
combustion engines—I found an old engineer
who came out blinking, and handled his bits of
engines as if he loved them. We tried his

motor-boat upon the swirling muddy river. She
had life in her on the water. He advised us
frankly, if we could not afford an engine powerful enough for our work, to wait until we could.
That was our own feeling. I knew where we
should buy our engine—if we did.

The argument, Old Times *versus* New, re-
freshed itself.

In a month's time, however, two of us were
in the hill-bound harbour of Dartmouth, looking
with all our eyes at the motor-boats moored up
on the Kingswear side. Among a number of
squat sheds built beside a muddy creek we found
the boatbuilder, whom also we had lighted upon
more or less by chance. Treating us as if we
had been yacht-owners instead of small fishermen,
he ushered us into a cramped little room, which
was decorated with yachts' photographs, painted
wooden models, sheer and body plans, makers'
catalogues, and samples of cordage and fittings.
The boatbuilder, a small man of terrier-like
aspect—a man subtly different from, altogether
jumpier than, the solid slow-moving builders of
sailing and rowing boats whom we had known,—
placed chairs for us, sat down at his table, drew
a piece of paper towards him, sharpened his
pencil, and looked at us shrewdly : it was as if
we had gone to the doctor's to give birth to a
project.

"Well ?" inquired the boatbuilder.

"Well !" we replied, filling up each other's
gaps. "We'm thinking of getting a little motor-

Y

boat for our beach—'bout sixteen or seventeen foot long, and double-ended, so's the waves shan't flop aboard over a square starn when she's being shoved off and beached. She'll have to be light, if she's to heave about easy and haul up over the sea-wall in rough weather ; and she'll have to be strong enough to stand the knocking about our boats get when we run ashore on a big sea. Then she'll have to be flat-bottomed so's not to list over on the beach, and shallow in draught so as to float away quick in shoving off; and same time she ought to have enough hold in the water to be able to sail to win'ard a bit if she breaks down at sea. If she isn't beamy enough to stand a seaway she wouldn't be safe in our water ; and if she hasn't got some speed in her we might so well stick to our rowing and sailing boats. The propeller will have to be well up, out of the way of the shingle, else 'twould want six men to lift her about, if we couldn't shove her at the greasy ways ; but 'twouldn't do for it to rise out of the water and race in the short choppy seas that we get with a southerly breeze. That'd racket the engine to pieces, wouldn't it ? Besides, we want her for fishing and towing, though she'll have to help earn her living at passenger work. . . ."

All of which—as any one acquainted with boats will understand—were contradictory demands.

The boatbuilder looked at us meditatively.

"Your sort of harbour motor-boats wouldn't be any good to us," we added. "We want speed and lightness, and strength and seaworthiness, and protection all round for the propeller—else we might just so well not have a motor-boat at all. If you can build us a boat like that you've pretty well solved the question of motor - boats for beaches and lee shores."

The boatbuilder continued looking at us, like a man on the edge of a muddy brook, wondering whether he can jump it. At last: " Did you have a pleasant journey down ? " he asked.

" No, we didn't ! " we replied. " We took nearly five hours by the best train of the day coming thirty miles or so as the crow flies. We walked three miles over the cliffs to catch the Exmouth train at Otterton, crossed the Exe by the ferry, waited at Starcross for the Newton Abbot express, changed and waited again, got into the Kingswear through carriage, and crossed the harbour by that steam houseboat thing that plies between Kingswear and Dartmouth ; and when we were within half an hour of our journey's end we saw our own cliffs across the bay. That's how 'tis : when you'm aiming at speed, you've got to go all the slower. If you can't build us a motor-boat to get to Dartmouth quicker than that. . . ."

" What you want," said the boatbuilder, " is a butterfly boat."

We didn't know what a butterfly boat was ; we are not sure now ; but we were probably right in supposing it to be a boat which goes over the waves instead of cutting through them.

" Did you say you've got an engine coming down ? " the boatbuilder inquired.

" We've arranged to have one sent down from Erith."

"You've fixed it up ? "

"Yes."

"Ah ! " he exclaimed. "What a pity ! If you'd only had an 'Antelope' engine ! I could have got you an 'Antelope' that would have suited your purpose exactly. What did you say was the horse-power of yours ? "

"Single cylinder, four to five horse-power."

"*If* you get it out of her. You *would* out of an 'Antelope.' An eight horse-power twin cylinder 'Antelope'. . ."

"Would be too heavy and much too expensive for us ! "

We spent the greater part of two days working out the details of the boat and of the installation, and learning to hate "Antelopes" and all their cylinders. It was settled that we were to have an experimental beach motor-boat, built on our own lines, without a contract speed, without even contract behaviour. Thus a still greater responsibility and anxiety was cast upon us, and with it we returned home again, hoping against hope that an "Antelope" was not, after all, the one engine we wanted for the work. We were launched, so to speak, in a squally wind, through which we had to sail aboard a boat we didn't know. The seas of the old argument rose up around us higher than ever. Invoices and bills began coming in. Those were the wettings we had.

A winter's gales blew at us, driving the boats time after time to the top of the sea-wall. " 'Tis a good job us an't got thic motor-boat up eet,"

was the word while we were hauling and straining
at the cut-ropes, and boats were a-tilt on the edge
of the wall.

Then we went down to inspect our boat.

In one of the shadowy ramshackle sheds she
stood up high upon her stocks, enormously long
and empty to the eye. Bright copper nails glinted
on the soft brown of her smooth unvarnished elm
planks. Men hammered and chipped at her with
a sure aim. But—and it hit itself into us with a
glance—she was like a box, like a tub, like a
barrel cut off three parts of the way up. She was
wall-sided. She had no sheer. Owing to a difference in local boatbuilding terms, she had been
given in freeboard what we had meant to order in
total inside depth.

" That's why I wanted you to look at her
before we put the thwarts in," said the boatbuilder, rightly interpreting our faces.

" She'll have to be altered. She'll have to be
cut down."

" I shouldn't advise you to have her cut down ;
it's expensive, and you'll find a high freeboard all
the better for your open-sea work."

" I shan't go to sea in a wall-sided boat," I
snapped ; meaning really that I refused to try and
settle the great argument with a boat whose lines
offended my eye, even if I had to pay for the
building of a new one, or go without a motor-boat
at all.

" Perhaps," said the boatbuilder, "we might
push out the topstrake three or four inches.
That would give her more beam, and more sheer

too, and take off the wall-sidedness—make a lot of difference. I'll do that then."

For consolation we were shown our engine lying dismembered on the floor of a loft, and we were bidden to admire an "Antelope" that was lying alongside. Fortunately we were far too ignorant of engines to appreciate what experts call the refinements of detail in the "Antelope's" construction—her forced lubrication and magneto ignition. The engine, at all events, had not joined the conspiracy to post-date our satisfaction. More and more we looked towards the critical moment when our boat should be afloat. "For the Lord's sake, hold thee row!" occurred more frequently in the great argument.

The launching had to be witnessed. Our boat, all ready, painted white on the topstrakes and red underneath, was trigged up on some timbers in an outside shed. Now she looked handsome enough with her bluff easy-riding bows, her broad middle bearing, and the fine lines to her rounded stern. Her wall-sidedness had disappeared. The novel arrangement by which the keel was carried round outside the propeller, to protect it, had an air of lightness and strength. She was built "fitty"—that we saw in a glance—if she floated and ran "fitty."

We climbed inside, gave the engine her first meal of petrol and lubricating oil, and coupled up the ignition. "I hope this engine is going to start up all right," said the boatbuilder switching on. "I haven't tried to run her before.

I thought you had better be present when I did."

He gave the fly-wheel a turn. Nothing happened. " 'Antelopes' always start up all right," he remarked. Another turn. . . . Nothing ! And another. . . . Nothing still ! One more turn. . . . There was a banging and a rattle, as if the engine were breathing in explosions. The boat shook like a live thing. The bottom-boards, which were not yet screwed down, rose up around us like leaves in a storm, and jigged on end. I switched off quickly.

And one of the men said in my ear : " I've seen 'em fight these engines for a week before they got 'em to go."

" Was that an ' Antelope ' ? " I asked.

But he didn't seem to hear.

Half-a-dozen men were called ; rolling timbers brought. We shoved and hauled the boat down to the edge of the creek. Then, suddenly, we heard a small sharp crack. We looked at each other, at the engine. The elbow-joint between the engine and the exhaust had come into two pieces, as cast piping will do when it is jerked. " I thought so ! " exclaimed the boatbuilder. " I've never known an ' Antelope ' do that ! "

There was nothing for it but to telegraph for a new elbow-joint, and to wait yet a little longer for, as we almost thought, the non-realisation of our hopes.

The incoming tide floated the boat off. She looked well enough on the water, but we saw with a feeling of disappointment and hopeless

perplexity that her propeller was half out of it.
The boatbuilder himself was nonplussed for the
moment : it was his own work at fault, not a
strange engineer's.

"You'll have to weight her down by the
stern," he said. "You never can tell exactly how
a boat is going to float when you're building to a
new design. Her propeller will suck her down a
bit, and two or three people in her. . . ."

"But what speed d'you think we shall get ?"
I asked.

"I shouldn't like to say—not with that engine.
If you'd had an 'Antelope'. . . ."

"D'you think we shall get six miles an hour ?"

"You'll get five all right, I think. We'll run
her and see, when the new elbow-joint comes
down."

We did see. But first of all we saw that the
boatbuilder was smiling up his sleeve. "I've tried
her," he said, "up the river. She goes like a
witch ! You stay here and watch."

He went aboard ; started up the engine ; cast
off moorings ; and perched himself by the tiller on
the little after-deck.

The popping of the exhaust made one almost
continuous note ; the water churned up by the
propeller thumped under the stern of the boat.
Then, as she gathered way, the stern squatted
down in the water and the bow rose up, the engine
slowed down while the propeller took grip, and off
she sped across the river. The boatbuilder's
miscalculation was evidently to our advantage,
for in shoving off a beach the boat would float

away all the quicker on account of her shallow
draught astern, and at full speed her propeller was
sufficiently immersed.   When he returned to the
creek we asked him : " What speed d'you reckon
you were going at ? "

" She'll go a mile an hour faster," he replied,
" when the engine has run a bit."

" That's better than you expected, then ? "

He rubbed his hands.   "Goes like a witch,"
he repeated, " for her engine and horse-power."

Then we were well pleased with the engine ;
and when we judged that everybody at home
would be drinking a glass of beer, we telephoned
through to the "Cable and Anchor" : "Goes
like a witch !—What ?—Yes !   Goes like the
devil !   No end of a pace !—All right ?—Aye ! "

It was our first morsel of triumph—the first
real point scored in the great argument.

The next point was to get the boat home in
one successful run without a breakdown.   That,
we knew, though we hardly dared say so, was the
critical run, the most smashing retort possible,
the most anxious part of the whole undertaking.
Upon that depended the reputation of our boat ;
the reputation, for some time, of motors in general
upon our beach, and in a sense our own reputa-
tions, whether we were "mazed articles" or men
of enterprise.   It was a voyage of do or die.
And neither of us knew anything to speak of,
either about marine motors or about any other
kind of engine.

Tom had gone down to the ordering of the
boat.   Bob, the other partner, had gone to the

inspection and launch, because he is hard to please
and critical. It was Tom's turn to help bring the
boat home.

But the weather for a week or two was shuffling,
and the course from Dartmouth—round Berry
Head, across Torbay, and past the sandbanks and
shoals outside Exmouth—is such that any breeze
is bound to raise a head-sea somewhere. When
we did arrive in Dartmouth during the early
afternoon of the first reasonably fine day, they
said with some concern : " You're never going to
try and get to Sidmouth to-night ! It's thirty-
five or forty miles, isn't it ? "

" That don't matter, do it," retorted Tom, " so
long as it don't come on to blow ? Anyhow,
we'm going to make a start."

" You'll find it a long way in that little boat of
yours. . . ."

Which encouraged us the more ; for as lee-
shoremen, users of small open boats, we do not
think very highly of the harbour men, who, in
our view, having a soft job and fine big craft to
go to sea in, become soft themselves. And at the
same time we are a little envious of their ships
and their shelter—their " something under their
feet," and their " somewhere to run to, in out the
way o'it."

We hastened to the boatbuilding creek with
our provisions—two bottles of beer, a bottle of
cold tea, and a packet of bloater-paste sandwiches
—together with a sackful of odd gear and an
incongruous can of petrol. The boat was
afloat. Just as we were getting ready to go

aboard, a man ran up breathlessly to the boat-builder.

"Will you send a launch up the river at once to Mr. Sloper? His motor's broken down in Duncannon Reach and the tide's falling. He'll be stuck there if he doesn't get off quick."

"Has Mr. Sloper got an 'Antelope'?" I asked.

There was no reply. The most interesting questions are seldom answered.

"I'll come aboard with you and start her up," said the boatbuilder.

"If us can't start her going here, by ourselves," remarked Tom, "what be us going to do if her stops snorting half-way across Torbay, like thic motor-boat up the river?"

"But you're not going to try and make Sid-mouth to-day?"

"Iss, we be. Why for not! Fine weather, ain't it? Might come on to blow t'morrow."

"D'you know the coast?"

"Not this side of Torquay. But 'twon't be dark 'fore us gets into waters us do know—not if her goes all right."

"Ah, well," concluded the boatbuilder, "you've got a seaworthy little boat under you, though she is only seventeen-foot-six. Pity you couldn't have had one a little bigger, for your open-sea work, with a twin-cylinder 'Antelope'!"

He oiled up, turned on the petrol, and after two or three attempts he set the engine going, looking, while he handled it, like a yacht's skipper reduced to the command of a tramp steamer.

Then he gave us some hints as to the course out of harbour, and went ashore, saying, "I only hope your engine will get you up there all right."

Glad to have it in our own hands at last, gladder still to feel our own boat under us, gladdest of all to hear no more of "Antelopes," we swung out into mid-river with the reversible propeller three-quarter-way advanced. I touched the lever to advance it fully. There was a visible spark. I shook my finger as if a wasp were on the end of it (with very hot legs) and hugged a wrist that felt as if it had within it a collection of tingling cramps. Tom's eyes questioned me— the whole use and feasibility of motor-boats was included in that questioning—but I was so savage and disappointed that I could only say :

"Put back ! Put her back ! Us can't get up to Sidmouth like this ! "

The boatbuilder ran down to the water's edge. "What's the matter ? " he called out.

" Why, the electricity is leaking all over the place ! "

" I've never known an ' Antelope ' do that ! " he exclaimed.

" Oh, damn your ' Antelopes ' ! " was on the tip of my tongue ; but I didn't say it, which without doubt was very virtuous.

We rearranged the insulated wires and once more got under way, with the propeller fully advanced this time ; for we meant to get some-where before we touched the engine again. Leaving the *Hindostan* and the old *Britannia* astern of us, we passed the town pontoon at a quarter past four, and steered for the deep narrows between Dartmouth and Kingswear Castles. At last we were well under way. The valves of the engine were tapping regularly, the explosions of the exhaust astern were already dinning themselves into our heads. If we put in anywhere, it was not to be at Dartmouth. Better some little beach in a cove near Berry Head.

Beyond the two castles, standing opposite each other among the trees on either bank, the open sea begins, and at once the names of places seem to change their character. Up-river they have mostly a smiling sound—Dittisham, Greenway, Stoke Gabriel ;—but outside, the wildness and grimness of the sea runs like a ground-bass through them. We passed between the Western Blackstone and Inner Froward Point ; passed by the Castle Ledge buoy and submerged Bear's Rail ; and made for the narrow passage inside the Mew Stone.

Looked at from the heights above, especially in sunshine, the estuary of the Dart—with its thick green foliage, its ferns in every soily crevice and its lichen-covered cliffs descending sheer to the water—has a brilliant loveliness. Down below, in the deep shadow, among the swirling currents, the high cliffs seemed to frown, and the Mew Stone appeared hard, harsh, immense ; so that it was as if we were strangers, passing through some dim inferno, hardly knowing what threatened us ; and tales of furious tide-rips there, and of sudden waves swamping boats that were

never again seen or heard of, troubled the back
of one's mind. All that was human and familiar
was Tom's voice; "Her goes, don' 'er? Her
do go!" And by contrast, the engine also, weakly
tapping and popping and asking oil, was more
than a little human.

Keeping a sharp look-out for lobster-pot corks
and lines, which might have fouled our propeller,
we steered a mile or so off-shore, past Scabba-
combe Head and Crabrock Point. We call our
own coast ironbound, and so it is; but the cliffs
down there—partly, no doubt, on account of their
strangeness—appeared far blacker, steeper, and
more forbidding. "Poor things!" one could
imagine Benjie saying. "Poor things, what gets
drove ashore here! 'Tis all up wi' 'em! All
up!"

But fog, drifting in with a breath of south-east
wind, was already beginning to soften the jaggedness of the rocks, and even to hide the land.

"What time do 'ee make it?" asked Tom,
after we had passed Sharkham Point. "Only an
hour we've been? Then we must have travelled,
mustn't us? This here looks like Torbay right
'nuff."

It did look like Torbay in the vast and vague
fog. But it was only Mudstone Bay, a place
wonderfully like Torbay in miniature, even to
its outstanding rocks at the northern end. We
had not been doing nine or ten miles an hour,
as for a moment we hoped. Before long we
were rounding close under an unmistakable
Berry Head.

In Torbay itself we could see nothing, except a ghost-like Brixham.   Fog filled all the inside of the bay.

" 'Tisn't no good going in to Brixham," said Tom, " and 'tisn't no use trying to crawl round the bay in this here fog.   There's a lot of shipping hereabout.   Best thing us can do is to make straight for t'other side, out the way o'it, so soon as us can.   Got thy compass on 'ee ?   Do 'ee think her'll work wi' all this 'lectricity sculling round about the boat ?   I reckon if us steers due north us'll pick up land somewhere. . . ."

" Unless the engine breaks down in the middle of the bay !   What then ? "

" Her won't hae to break down ; an' that's all about it ! "

I oiled her up with care, but otherwise forbore to touch her ; and we steered along by compass. Soon we had lost the Berry—had lost everything. The loneliness of mid-ocean, from the deck of a ship, is not so great as the loneliness of a bay in a small open boat, in fog.   Paignton, we knew, lay somewhere four miles abeam of us ; Torquay as many miles to the nor'west.   The light south-easterly wind raised a scuffle on the water, proving the steadiness of our boat ; but it did not blow away the grey mist.   A Brixham trawler steered alongside to look at our impudent little craft. We waved our arms and splashed on.   There was nothing else to be done.

Presently Tom stood up in the boat and pointed over the bows.   " Lookse !   We'm right.   That's the loom of Torbay Rock.   That's it !   Now

us'll soon be out of this here shipping that us
can't see."

In the fog, which was at no time so thick to
seaward as nearer land, there stood up a dark
detached shadow, that could only have been the
Oar Stone.   Steering straight for it, we finished
up our bloater-paste sandwiches and second bottle
of beer.   It no longer mattered to keep up our
stock of provisions.   We were entering home
waters.   Torquay was left behind without a
glimpse of its harbour and terraced hills.   There
is something uncanny in passing near a great town
—in feeling its presence close by—with never a
sight or a sound of it.   Babbacombe was more
visible ; and six miles or so farther on, Teignmouth lay like a white stripe, like a comber
suddenly solidified, along its narrow spit of sand.
Over the hills behind, the fog was gathering
together into purple clouds and turning into
rain.

Once or twice, between the Oar Stone and
Teignmouth, the exhaust had given a sharp pop,
instead of its regular explosion.   Off Teignmouth
there were several such pops at shorter intervals.

. " What's that ? " asked Tom.

" I don't know."

" Can 'ee put it right if there's ort wrong ? "

" Hanged if I know ! "

Close to the Parson and Clerk Rock, between
Teignmouth and Dawlish, the motor gave a final
pop, turned two or three times, slowed down,
stopped.   It was as if the little engine, having
run for three hours continuously, had become

tired, and had fallen asleep. The sudden silence, broken only by the lapping of the wavelets against the boat's sides, was exquisitely restful—just for a moment. Then we

> Look'd at each other with a wild surmise—
> Silent :

and, leaving the tiller, Tom swore. " What's to do now ? " he asked. " Her's brought us twenty-one miles, I reckon, an' we'm fourteen miles from home ; an' that's far enough for to row, if her refuses to snort. P'raps we'm out of petrol. . . ."

" P'raps the sparking plug's sooted up. . . ."

Taking out the plug, I sparked it in the open air to burn off the soot, replaced it, and gave the fly-wheel a turn. She was off again with a terrifying racket till the propeller was advanced. That was it—the sparking plug. (I had been using an excess of lubricating oil, because the engine was new, and, as I found out afterwards, had been giving it too much petrol and too little air.)

We stood in for Dawlish to buy some more petrol. We also bought more beer. If we did have to row, we too should want some fuel. Our new-grown trust in the engine was shaken.

It was dusk when we left Dawlish, and made as good a course as possible for Straight Point, the other side of Exmouth. Unable to see very far ; unable, in the misty fading light, to judge distances accurately, we doubted whether we should clear the Pole Sand, and stood farther out to sea. The tide was ebbing ; and there are

z

banks outside Exmouth which only a seagull, standing in the water instead of swimming, will reveal.

"Us ought to be able to sight the fairway buoy," remarked Tom anxiously, and almost at once we did sight it. And then we heard its bell.

By day the estuary of the Exe is a wide waste of flat sand and flat shoal water. That evening, in the drizzling mist, yellowed by the sunset filtering through it, the place was an endless expanse of desolation. In the haphazard tolling of the bell-buoy all human misery seemed to be concentrated and contained; all the agony of all the wrecks that ever were, all the tragedy of all the lives that ever were lost, all the loneliness of all that sorrowed for them.

"For God's sake, let's get away from this!" I burst out, forgetting that we should get away just as fast as the engine carried us, and no faster.

"Aye!" replied Tom, whose nerves usually are like a rock that the sea dashes against. "Can't say I likes this here. Thic blasted bell. . . . Casn't make thy engine snort faster, an' git away out o'it? Gives a fellow the melancholies, like."

As if to mock us, there began a hollow booming in the fore-part of the boat. It was the partially empty petrol-tank, vibrating with the engine. I jammed it with a spanner and a piece of cotton-waste.

And then the engine gave a couple of gasps, and stopped.

With the intolerable tolling of the bell-buoy clanging in our ears, I cleaned the sparking plug

again, and again we got under way. The cliffs of
Straight Point, with its ledges and rock-bound
shore, were like a harbour to us. Over the dreary
sandbanks of the Exe the bell was still tolling ; is
tolling now ; but we had a sense of escape from
it, and already felt ourselves as good as home.

Once or twice more the engine stopped. It
was not its fault : I was driving it badly. Darkness prevented me from tinkering about with it ;
but I found that by putting the propeller at
neutral and letting it race for a few seconds the
sparking plug would clear itself.

Off Sidmouth we burnt flares, using the newspaper that had wrapped our bloater-paste sandwiches. Then we circled round, steered at full
speed for the beach, switched off the engine a boat's
length or so away, and ran ashore high upon the
shingle. Plenty of hands were there to haul us up.

It was ten o'clock. Reckoning three-quarters
of an hour for stoppages, the brave little engine
had brought us thirty-six miles in five working
hours. The boat was home—home successfully.

Not that the great argument came to an end
therewith. The building and home-coming of
the motor-boat were only two steps in the great
argument, which still continues, and will. Cheated
of breakdowns, which didn't occur, and bound
to admit seaworthiness, the disciples of the Old
Times complained loudly of the noise from the
exhaust. Therefore, being otherwise well pleased,
we brazened it out, and called the boat the *Puffin*.
And then we stopped the noise.

A THIRD-CLASS JOURNEY

THE Mediterranean or nowhere—that was our alternative. Most years we go to France for a bit of a holiday between the mackerel and herring seasons. But one early morning towards the end of the summer before last, when we were rowing for want of wind on a white-calm sea in a drizzling damping rain, and the mackerel were not on the feed, I happened to follow up a grumble of my skipper's with the remark : "Let's make a dash for the Mediterranean this year, Jim, where there's sunshine and flowers in the autumn. What's say? Shall us hae a shot?"

Jim whistled for a breeze before replying cautiously : "I reckon 'tis a place a chap ought to see, once in a lifetime, anyhow. But us bain't going to have no holiday this year. What's the good of going over to France wi' nort in your pocket to spend? A mump-headed turn-out that! When us gets ashore," he went on savagely, kicking the hollow fish-box, "they'll offer us three bob a hunderd for these here dozen or two of fish, and not a penny more; and any one of 'em is worth a penny or tuppence for to eat! That won't pay no railway fares, not even so far as Boulogne for to see thic perty li'l maid to the café, an' ol' skipper What's-his-name, what us went herring drifting 'long with in the *Marie-Marthe*. . . ."

Nevertheless the plan took root and grew. Sunlight, warmth, bright colour, the journey across a country from sea to sea, a sight of strange craft, a desire, after so bad a summer, to get far away out o'it for a while. . . . 'Twas the Mediterranean or nowhere!

We looked out in railway guides the nearest, quickest, cheapest point to make for.   Once started, we should spend as much as usual, whether we could afford it or not.   We knew that.   But the season had been a bad one, and we *felt* poor. Otherwise we would never have travelled to Marseilles by the slow third-class French trains. And had we gone by the cheapest way of all, from Newhaven to Dieppe, we should have been aboard the *Brighton* when she collided with the *Preussen*, the great German five-masted ship that drove ashore under Dover cliffs during the next day's gale.

We wanted, however, to pass through Boulogne in order to see our French fishing friends and " thic perty li'l maid " ; to hear what catches they had made ; to taste again the good food of our small inn ; and to have a drink or two at *Le Bon Pêcheur*, where men from sea stump through the door in their long sea-boots and crowd round the tables, arguing fish and laughing, till the room is brown with their barked jumpers and all of a buzz with their chackle.   Jim, I think, would rather meet an old acquaintance than travel the world over without seeing a face he knows.

There had been all night a calm and a thick fog in the Channel. The first of that fortnight's gales began only a quarter of an hour before the boat left Folkestone. Already, by the time we got outside, the smaller fishing boats were running for harbour. Midway across Channel, though a sea had not yet risen, the wind was lifting scud off the tops of the waves, and the sailing vessels in sight had shortened sail. At Boulogne it was blowing a full gale from the quarter most dreaded there, the sou'west.

We owed an honour done us to the gale. In *Le Bon Pêcheur*, after a great shaking of hands, we ordered *café-cognac* for tea, and sat down. Suddenly a tall fisherman jumped up on the other side of the room, brandishing his rope-worn paw. It was one of our *Marie-Marthe* shipmates. "Ah! 'tis the Englishmen!" he shouted, as if we had been the only Englishmen in the world. "Come over here to our table. My wife, this is ; and my brother-in-law, that. Have you had good fishing? We have not. Bad weather—fogs and great winds. You remember your trip with us in the *Marie-Marthe*?"

Then he turned to Jim. "And your children? Are they yet delivered over to the fishing?"

Jim mistook his meaning. He waved his hand gallantly towards Berthe, the maid of the café. "I've a-come over once more," he said, "for to see her perty li'l eyes."

"*Qu'est qu'il a dit?* What's he say?" asked Berthe.

"He says that he's come back to see your pretty eyes."

"*Oh, là, là, là, là, là! Et sa femme?*

"She told me to tell you that she's coming over another year to black those pretty eyes!"

"What have 'ee told her?"

"Told her thy wife is coming over another year for to hae a scrap with her."

Up hopped Jim, and chased her for a kiss.

When the laughter had died down, we inquired after the skipper of the *Marie-Marthe*.

"You have not seen him? He was here only half an hour ago. He is ashore to-night—the weather looks too bad. Will you come to his house? We will show you the way up there."

Knowing what a compliment it is to be invited into a Frenchman's house, we made haste to accept; and in the wake of two or three fishermen we clattered up the steep streets of the fishing quarter. While we waited outside a dark hole of a doorway, one of them went inside to make sure that the skipper would receive us.

In a tiny oblong kitchen, much like a ship's galley, except that its edges and corners were bound in polished brass, instead of white metal, the skipper was sitting at table with his family. They had just cleared away a very early dinner. His wife was there, and either his, or her, mother; his small son who goes to sea in the *Marie-Marthe*, a grown-up son who is mate in another fishing boat, and a paler slighter son in Government employ. They had coffee before them, and taking his ease in a blue flannel blouse, tied at the neck with tasselled cords, the good skipper (his ship is an exceptionally happy one) looked

solider than ever in every respect. White wine
was uncorked for us, and we drank all sorts of
healths. Then the mother ground fresh coffee ;
the wife brought out some dainty blue china
cups : and while we drank afresh, the womenfolk,
with a fine enthusiasm, helped the sons to tie
their bow-ties and otherwise decorate themselves
for a Sunday evening dance.

A long conversation in French, about Yar-
mouth, where the skipper had once been landed
ill, was too dull for Jim. We said "Good-bye,"
and hurried back towards *Le Bon Pêcheur* for an
absinthe to counteract so much coffee and give
us once again an appetite for dinner.

The gale was blowing harder than ever, in
fierce gusts but without much rain. We couldn't
but turn aside to see if anything was happening
out to sea, and against the wind squalls we forced
our way along the jetty. Down on the one side
of us, the water was heaving darkly in the harbour
channel. On the other side, and behind us, the
white-topped broken waves seemed to be rushing
bodily, in a howling confusion, upon the shallow
sandy shore that lies in front of the Casino and
the sea-side end of the town. A steamer hooted
outside. In a flash, all the electric lamps along
the two jetties on either side of the harbour
channel, lighted themselves up, first with a blinking, then with a bright steady glare. "What's
that for ?" said Jim. "'Tis pretty near so light
as day here. Blow'd if 'tisn't a fine thing, that !"

The Folkestone steamer was overdue by an
hour, and even while we were speaking, the high

brilliantly lighted ship rode stern first up the harbour channel to her quay, as if she were being slowly drawn along a roadway of dark, cold, troubled water. She was moored up : the electric lights flicked out ; and everything around, both the harbour and the wild sea, became doubly dark. Boulogne, having thrown out feelers to welcome the ship, seemed to have contracted and shrunk within herself, away from the fury of the storm.

"They don't light this here up for fishing boats to go in and out, do 'em ?" Jim asked.

"Not likely ! Fishing boats wouldn't pay for it," I explained.

"Oh !" he said. "No doubt they lights it up for they there passengers in fur coats, for to make it safe for 'em. 'Tis the same thing here as 'tis at home. The likes o'us can go to sea, fair weather or foul, catching their dinners for 'em while they'm snug. . . . *Our* lives don't matter. We only does the work, and when we drowns there's other fools for to take our places. Why, us breeds 'em ourselves, don' us? You see— an' you *will* see if you lives long enough—they wouldn't light up this here, and keep it lighted of a dirty night, not for to save a shipload of fishermen from drowning."

It sounded like mere grumbling on his part, but within ten days his words were terribly fulfilled.

Alone in *Le Bon Pêcheur* we found the round-bodied, rounder-faced, jolly old boat-owner, in whose lugger we had refused to go herring

drifting because we had wanted to see how they
fish in a modern steam drifter. After the greet-
ings were over he turned solemnly to Berthe,
while a tear of laughter trickled from his eye :
" It's serious. I said so. I said so last year.
Without doubt Monsieur is going to marry you,
Ma'm'selle Berthe ! "

" But Monsieur has a wife and children in
England—*beaucoup des enfants !* " she retorted.

With all possible speed, I translated.

" Aye ! Tell her I'd marry her t'morrow,"
said Jim, " if I was only single. I likes thic
happy laugh o' hers, thee's know."

" What's that ? " asked the old boy in his
turn.

" He regrets he isn't single. He's got a wife
and enough children for half-a-dozen French
families."

The old boy cast up his hands.

" *Mais ça n' fait rien !* " he exclaimed. " That
doesn't matter ! " Then, spreading himself over
the table, and laying his finger along his bunchy
nose, he said confidentially : " Listen to me.
Look at me, I say. I, me, I who speak to you—
I have a wife in every port from Dunkirk to
Brest. My wife at Dunkirk, she had no children.
Calais is too near Boulogne. One does not make
attachments on one's doorstep. Here, in Boulogne,
I have a son, a fine fellow. If you will come to
this café to-morrow morning I will present him to
you. He is twenty-five, no more, and already is
skipper of a lugger. His boat catches more fish
and arrives in port quicker than any. *Il est bon*

pêcheur. He will be skipper of a steam drifter when he is thirty, and an owner, like the owner of the *Marie-Marthe*, before he is forty. He is my only child at Boulogne, but at Dieppe I have two sons. They are in an engineering works and touch good wages. I am going there to see them very soon. But my wife at Dieppe. . . . Some women are inclined to be a little jealous, is it not so, Monsieur Jim? I go to Dieppe no more for fishing. I am getting old—*homme sérieux, vous savez*—a staid man. But I go sometimes to see my Dieppe family, in my Boulogne son's boat, you understand, when he is fishing on the Dieppe grounds and the wind is fair for a quick return. Then at Le Havre I have a daughter. Her mother is dead, but she has good friends. Ah, her mother. . . . *Quelle femme charmante!* When she was alive she could refuse me nothing. But alas! she is dead, and I weep for her. I would have gone to her. I would have remained with her always. I would have become a fisherman of Le Havre. But my wife at Boulogne, you see, she brought me the money with which to buy my boat. I could not have taken my boat with me to Le Havre, and without my boat I was nothing. As for my wife at Brest. . . . I have not seen her for twenty years. Perhaps she also is dead. We had no children so far as I know. But I have done my duty to my country. . . ."

He leaned farther over to give Jim a dig in the chest. "And you too, *mon gars!*"

"What a pity," he went on, turning to me,

"what a pity your sheep (*i.e.* ship, meaning shipmate) he no shpeak français. Tell him. If he will marry in Boulogne, there is Ma'm'selle Berthe who awaits him with open arms."

Mademoiselle Berthe shied a dishclout at his head. He rose up, holding out his glass to click with ours. "Tell him," he repeated, bowing towards her, "I drink to the ladies. *Vivent les femmes!*

Jim caught his meaning. He, too, rose up. "Hear, hear!" he cried, bowing also to Mademoiselle Berthe. "Here's to 'em! There's nort like 'em, an' I dearly loves 'em! Don' I, my dear?"

Eyes were kindling. The *patronne* of the café ceased smiling. It was time to go.

Our inn had changed hands. Although the food was no less good and plentiful, the arrangements and the company were rather different. A large front room, opening on the street, with tables, a stove, a small billiard board and a little zinc bar in one corner, still formed the public café. Behind that was a narrower room, unlighted by any window, and separated from the café only by a high wooden partition with a door. In spite of the long tables laid down each side, it was little more than a passage leading to the small square room in which we had formerly had our meals; which room led in turn, through more clattering doors, to Madame's kitchen. Altogether, a jug of hot coffee on its way from the kitchen to the café had to be carried through four doors, each one of which opened with a rattle and closed with

a bang.   The little dining-room was occupied by
a couple very much in love.   At least, when I
burst in there to hang up our hats and coats, they
were kissing each other most tenderly over their
coffee-cups.   Indefinably we were given to understand that the privacy of the small dining-room
was to be respected.   *L'amour*, in France, is treated
with such easy-going kindness.

Madame la patronne stayed in her dark little
kitchen all day long.   There her friends and her
market-women called upon her.   The guests in
the hinder café were attended to by a short, stout
Flemish widow of immense activity, full of laughter
and jokes.   As for the *patron*, a man with bulging
bespectacled eyes and a neckcloth instead of a
collar—he strutted about from room to room,
singing snatches of song in a powerful baritone
voice, and saying from time to time : " One
must laugh, laugh always, as much as possible.
Laugh, laugh ! "   And then he would take another
nip at the little zinc bar, from one of the bottles
of spirits labelled *de fantaisie*, that is to say,
adulterated or imitation.   But except at the very
height of his jokes it was noticeable that he made
the others look sad.   " He's off his head ! " the
bright little widow would hiss, glancing at him
behind his back with a quick hatred and un-
disguised contempt.   She was a close friend of
his wife's.   " Monsieur," she said to me one day,
and there was a bitterness underlying her jest,
" Monsieur, I see you are *homme sérieux*. . . .
Will you marry me and take me back to England
with you.   I am very weary here."

"But, Madame," I replied as bluntly, "I am a young man—not serious enough, perhaps."

"You have reason," she said. "I must stay with madame. Perhaps she will have need. . . ."

A knife - handle tapped on the table impatiently. "Yes, yes, Monsieur. At once! I come. What is it that it is that you want?" With which she started again her bustle and her jokes.

The *patron* was right. It was necessary to laugh, to laugh always, as much as possible. In his own person there was tragedy in the house, and a dog-like faithfulness on watch over his wife.

There was, moreover, something curious in his appearance. He reminded us of somebody, but we could not make out of whom, until next morning he asked us to write up and sign the customary police papers. "The police," he said, "will want it, and it is as well to satisfy them." At the mention of the word "police" we knew at once whom he resembled. He was Crippen the murderer's double. We didn't like him the better for it; we couldn't; and afterwards we had cause, as well, to remember those police papers. They were the first and last we were called upon to sign during the whole of our holiday. Thenceforward the police watched over us themselves.

On the evening of our arrival, we all sat down together for dinner at one of the long tables. In bad French and worse English we joked and laughed and teased one another. By themselves, in shadow, right at the end of the other long table, sat an old man and an old woman, plainly from the country, who took no part in our merriment. They were dressed in black : they were the kind of people who would dress in black. Hard-working frugality showed itself even in their manner of handling their food. The old man— a peasant farmer to the life—was clean-shaven. His face was simple and sorrowful, but not without traces of a certain cunning about the eyes. His wife's face, framed in a close-fitting velvet bonnet, was also simple ; and at the same time shrewd ; as if she were simple in herself and in her aims, but shrewd and wide awake in her dealings with other people. Sitting very close together, they ate their dinner silently. Then, with a scrap of paper and a pencil, they seemed to be making an account. They had little need for words. Probably they had done the same thing so many many times that each understood what the other was thinking. The wife jotted down the items. The husband nodded. Taking the papers, he appeared to be reckoning up the total, and his wife agreed. They chatted a moment ; put away the paper carefully ; sat for a while again in silence ; got up together ; said " Good-night " very quietly ; and together went to bed. They had held one's eye, and they haunted one's mind, as a statue does when, in its stillness and silence, it succeeds in expressing a whole life lived.

Next day we hardly saw them. It was blowing a whole gale from the westward. Weather-beaten fishing boats from the more distant fishing grounds were hurrying in for refuge. The women folk awaited them at the end of the jetty. A swell

running up the harbour, and the flooded River
Liane rushing downwards, jammed the craft
together in a violently swaying pack. Furious
disputes arose along the quayside, wherever a
small helpless wooden-built fishing boat was in
danger of being crushed between the high iron
sides of the larger craft, which also were helpless
to prevent their own slow steady ruthless squeez-
ing together. Men climbed about like monkeys ;
spat curses at each other ; shook their fists in one
another's faces ; and then, when the crack came—
something or other parted or smashed — they
suddenly became quiet, and with tears in their
eyes they clambered down to examine the damaged
little boat.

At dinner in the evening, the old couple were
present again, sitting close together at the end of
their long table. Very small they looked, and
broken. Their hands trembled when they hacked
small chunks from the long loaves of bread.
They went to bed early, at half-past eight, and it
was the old wife who ushered her husband out of
the door, as if he had been an invalid child.

By morning the gale had blown itself out.
The fishing fleet in all haste was putting to sea.
A small poor-looking fishing boat got blown upon
the flat rocks under the head of the jetty, and
with a few miserable bumps the breaking water
drove her firmly aground. Her two men worked
frantically to get her off, while the crews of the
outgoing steam-boats crowded to the sides and
laughed at them. No tug could get near, and
besides, it was only a wretched little fisherman-

owned craft ; such a craft as modern conditions have doomed to disappear. One of her men fell overboard, and when a line was thrown to her he swam for it. A score of us hauled her off, around the pier-head. They hoisted sail to go up harbour again. "Blow'd if they bain't going home !" exclaimed Jim contemptuously. "I've a-see'd men scores o' times go to sea like thic chap there. 'Tisn't no good to a man, us knows, for to lie all night in wet clothes, but when the weather's fine an' the fish is there to be catched. . . ."

We had not noticed the old peasant farmer and his wife on the pier. They were standing together in the lee of the lighthouse, looking out to sea, not with the intent gaze of seafaring folk, but with empty eyes. Leaving her husband, the old wife came across and spoke. It was bad weather for fishermen, she said. I remarked that they had been having poor catches, and hoped the weather was not spoiling her visit to Boulogne. "But isn't it too cold for you," I asked her, "here on the end of the jetty ? We have our oilskins, and yet we are chilled to the bone."

As if a tap had been turned on, she began talking. It was most like the chirping of a bird. She had only two or three large teeth, through which her voice whistled, and her tongue seemed swollen in her mouth so that she could not form her words properly. In addition to which, her dialect was very clipped. Several times I caught the word *ben* instead of *bien*, and I tried in vain to recall the Northern French dialect of some

2 A

of Maupassant's stories. She seemed to be saying that she had a son who was a fisherman; that it was a life full of danger; that fishermen are often lost at sea; that she had wanted to come and watch the fishing boats out and in. "*Pauv'* *pêcheurs!* Poor fishermen!" she repeated several times. "*Moi, j'suis mère, moi aussi.*"

"I am a fisherman's mother," I thought she meant; therefore I made the best of the weather, and wished him good luck.

With a curious little gesture of despair, almost of impatience, as if to say, "It's no good! You are quite useless! It's all over!" she returned to her husband, and with short shaky steps they walked back the length of the jetty into the town.

On our return to the inn, I asked the *patronne*: "Who were the old couple who sat alone? Have they a son, a fisherman?"

"*Mais non!* But no!" she replied. "Oh, it is sad! Their son is dead. They could not afford to take his body home, into the country, and they came up to bury him yesterday, and now, this morning, they are gone back again. He was their only child, chauffeur in an automobile. He met with a fatal accident just outside Boulogne. *Il s'est tué, leur fils.*"

He was killed, their son. . . . In a flash I understood what the old lady had been trying to tell me. She had come down to see the fishing boats and to be for a while among the fisher folk, because death is always lurking about a fishing port, and every week or so some man in his strength is drowned, wrecked sometimes, but oftener washed overboard. And she, too, she was a mother who had lost her son. She had come to us for sympathy, and we had not understood. We had wished her son good luck.

Boulogne is homelike to us. Paris wants plenty of money or plenty of time, and we had not much of either. It was but a junction, so to speak, between the Northern Railway and the Paris-Lyons-Mediterranée. Our train called itself a *rapide*. It was timed to do the journey to Marseilles in fourteen or fifteen hours.

We found an empty carriage, hired pillows for the night, spread ourselves about the seats, and told the usual lies. But railway lies are useless except where there are English people to believe them. Gradually our third-class horse-box filled up. A plump and haughty German young woman took the other end of Jim's longer seat. A young man travelling to Tarascon sat down in the centre. A very jaunty French girl bounced into the carriage, and flung some small baggage with a hat-box on the other end of my shorter seat. Her dress was smart, but a little worn, as if it had been turned. Her face, though heavy in the bone, was fresh and lively. She spoke in a deep contralto voice that was rich and at the same time hard, even devil-may-care, in tone. After examining us all with a perfectly frank bold gaze, she decided to make friends with the young man of Tarascon. She smiled at him, winked towards the German young woman, and remarked carelessly that there were always a lot of foreigners in the Mediterranean trains. They both smiled. A good-fellowship was established between them. She offered him a cigarette from her case, and lighted one herself. Both the match and the cigarette she knew how to handle. She was all there.

The German young woman, who hitherto had made no objection either to cigars or cigarettes, immediately began to sniff. She lowered the window. "Smoke stifles me," she said. For a time she held her head out of the window. Then, very quickly, she drew back. Her face was red and screwed up. A big smut had blown into her eye. She rocked herself with pain. She rubbed her eyelids with hands that were all of a shake. She burst into broken exclamations. She was nearly hysterical.

Thereupon, the French girl said very sweetly : " *Permettez-moi, Mademoiselle !* "

Like a trained nurse, she took command of the German young woman, placed her in the best light, and extracted the smut in several pieces, which she duly exhibited to the unaffected eye. Very neatly she did it. With the aid of the smut she conquered. The German young woman no longer shrank from her company with righteous sniffs. She allowed herself to be laid on the seat, and forthwith fell asleep. We smiled all round.

Through the long black night the train jogged on. Storms rattled against the windows. After passing Lyons (where the German young woman got out) we could hear from time to time the sound of a great torrent, the Rhone in flood. Faces in the carriage had long since lost their freshness. Even in sleep they were curiously lined. Dawn stole like a ghost into the Rhone valley. It showed up gradually the rocks, the dark olives, and the bare little almond trees. It made us all look ghastly. The sensation of a new day failed to make headway against the sensation of a stale unfinished night. We had still many hours to go.

At Avignon the young man changed for Tarascon. No one else got in. "I thought," said Jim, "that thic fellow belonged to Miss Ah-wee, there!" (Having caught the words *Ah, oui!* in French conversation, *Ah-wee* became his general nickname for French people.) "If I'd ha' know'd they wasn't no connexion, blow'd if I wouldn't ha' tried to entertain her better than *he* did." In sign of which, he took her his pillow, put it under her head, and tucked her skirts warmly around her. She smiled gratefully.

When she awoke, she asked us to look out her trains in our time-table. She was travelling to a town in the interior of Algeria, but knew neither the trains nor the steamers—only the route, and not all of that. "Do you know of a hotel at Marseilles?" she asked.

We were recommended to two hotels, I told her.

"I shall have to find a room, a cheap room," she said, "in order to wash and tidy myself— whether I go on by the next boat, or not." She

held out a pair of very dirty hands. We were all
of us grimed with railway smoke and smuts.

"What be you two talking 'bout ?" demanded
Jim.

"Wants a hotel to wash in before her goes
on."

"Well, ask her to come 'long wi' us to the
place we'm going to. Her'll come right 'nuff.
You see !"

"How can us take her to a strange hotel—
unless we say her's the wife of one o'us ?"

"Tell 'em her's my ol' woman, then. Her
isn't half a bad little client."

"Thee casn't even talk French to her."

"Tell 'em her's thine, then."

"Then how 'bout thee ? S'pose her decides
to stay a few days 'long wi' us, 'stead of going
straight on to Africa ?"

"I only wish I could talk the lingo ; I'd ask
her to myself."

"Hast got the coin on thee for to entertain
her ?"

"No. *I* an't."

"Me nuther. . . ."

There we were : admirable young lady, good
company, plucky, travelling alone, third-class, into
Algeria, without any precise information as to
trains and boats, and apparently in no great hurry
to get there ! What if she found us such nice
fellows—*très aimables, très très gentils !*—that she
decided to stay with us for a few days ? We
hadn't enough money for three. We had no
return tickets even.

If we ran short of money, we could of course write home for more, and wait its arrival. (It was fortunate we didn't : we should never have received it.) But suppose, in addition, a telegram came from home, that the herrings were in the bay. Before we started we had heard rumours of great bodies of herrings not far to the westward. Jim would want to fly from Mademoiselle Ah-wee to the herrings. And he would be obliged to wait. Then how he would fret, cuss, worry, complain, reckon up imaginary losses, and blame—not Mademoiselle Ah-wee, nor circumstances, nor luck, still less himself—but me, the unhappy proposer of the holiday ! We should have painted the Mediterranean a deeper blue with Devonian cuss-words. No more holidays together ! It was necessary to be firm. "What's told her ?" he asked.

"Told her we shall probably put up at a hotel in the town, but she'll find the Hôtel Suisse better for her, because it's on the tram-line to the harbour."

"Thee hastn't !" exclaimed Jim. "Well, I reckon thee a't a mump-head !"

A mump-head I felt, and had to feel more so. At the Station, Mademoiselle Ah-wee attached herself to us. There was nothing for it but to take her bag and see her to the Hôtel Suisse. An ungallant firmness appeared to be more than ever necessary.

Refusing the services of cabs, touts, and outporters, we made for the Hôtel Suisse—and lost our way. Peeping at the plan, we went ahead again, and again we came to a standstill. We put down Mademoiselle Ah-wee's bag, and under a tree near an ice-cream stall we examined the plan carefully. It landed us in a network of small steep streets. Finally, a kindly loiterer showed us the Hôtel Suisse close at hand. With hardly a " Good-bye ! " (to say *au revoir* seemed mockery) Mademoiselle Ah-wee disappeared within its narrow doorway. There was something almost deathlike in her going. She had been a bright travelling companion throughout the long weary night, and we knew we should never see her any more. We faced Marseilles afresh.

And promptly we lost ourselves again. A tout picked us up, and we were glad for him to take us to our hotel in the Place d'Aix. We rang the bell. Part-way up the stairs there was an inner door. Some one came down and peered through the glass at the top of it. " A couple of sailors ! " she shouted up contemptuously.

We rang again. The *patronne* herself came down. " We haven't any rooms . . ." she was beginning to say.

" But Monsieur is recommended," the tout interrupted.

" By M. Fletcher, the painter, of Paris, who was here last year," I hastened to add.

" You have come from Paris ? "

" Certainly. We have travelled all night, and are much too tired to go fooling round Marseilles for rooms."

" M. Fletcher. . . . Monsieur Flechaire. . . . Yes, yes ! I remember," said the *patronne* with a very quick change of tone. "This way, gentle-men."

We cheerfully paid the whole franc that the tout demanded, and followed the *patronne* to a large cool stone-floored room. Window-shutters darkened it. Dirty as we were, we could hardly keep ourselves from lying down at once, for the night still overshadowed us like a morning fog not yet lifted. It was still, as it were, yesterday. But after we had washed and had changed into clean clothes, we opened one of the shutters and looked out. A morning sun was shining in the untidy square and upon the tattered houses. The Arc de Triomphe, in the centre, cast a very black shadow. An incessant hum of tongues, like a buzz of busy insects, seemed to be welling up through a pool of lazy quietness. The sunshine was tinged with colour. . . .

We were in the South. We felt we were. Instead of lying down to sleep, we both said at once : "Let's get along out and see w'er there's any lunch to be had. Us can sleep this evening. 'Tis a fine day."

All in a moment, last night had become morning, and yesterday had changed into to-day. Though not from sleep, we were nevertheless awakened. The southern sunlight did it.

London and Paris are busy in a large way. Marseilles on a smaller scale is busier still—more multifariously alive. Not simply a few great nations, but all the tribes of the Mediterranean seem to have gathered together there, each in its own dress, with its own speech and habits. Beneath the heavy awnings of the cafés sit officers of the army and navy, soldiers of the African regiments in their semi-oriental uniforms, Turks wearing the fez, and Arabs in soiled white robes, with their *burnous* wrapped around them. The rapaciousness of the East has come that far west, in order to pursue a ceaseless grasping traffic in small goods for small money. The shops over-flow upon the broad pavements. Touts swoop down on the passers-by. Small boys, with dirty little boxes slung over their shoulders by knotted bits of string, run about everywhere and bother one to have one's boots cleaned. Hawkers hold nick-nacks under one's nose, or more furtively press upon one their smuggled goods and obscenities. Buying and selling, touting and bargaining, spread the whole breadth of the leafy streets. Business in Marseilles has no reticences. The Old Harbour—densely packed with sailing vessels, yachts, hulks, ships refitting, lateen-sailed fishing boats, motor craft, small steamers, pleasure boats and ferries—pushes its way lengthwise into the heart of the city. Over the far end of the harbour, a tall transporter bridge, gawky in outline, but not ungraceful in the slender strength of its steel wires and lattice-work, seems to be a barrier, a narrow gateway between the seething city and the wide sea. Notre Dame de la Garde uprears itself high on a bare rocky hill to the south of the Old Harbour. Along the coast, away from the hubbub of

Marseilles, the purple and blue mountains stand out tranquilly.

There seemed to be some sort of agreement among the touts and hawkers. We refused their wares ; we rejected their services ; we declined to answer them in English. Therefore they tried us with snippings from a dozen European languages. A half-bred negro, dressed like a welsher on a racecourse, who offered in good English slang to guide us to any Venusberg in Marseilles, became exceedingly angry on my answering in French : " *Non ! J'ai dit ' Non,' et ç'en est assez !* " But although he cursed us up the Cannebière in still more fluent English, he was the last of his tribe to pester us. Word must have gone round that we were bad eggs, no cop. They let us alone with a suddenness that was almost alarming ; for it made us feel that we were surrounded by a secret organisation for fleecing the likes of us.

But the small boys with the boot-brush boxes —there was no escaping from them, either inside the cafés or out. We called at the post office for our letters, and I left Jim on the high flight of steps that leads up to it. There were no letters for us (which was strange), and when I got outside again, Jim was still in the centre of the steps, hemmed about by a troop of boot-boys, and even girls, most of whom were on their knees around him, hopping up and down like grasshoppers, plucking at his trousers, dabbing at his boots, imploring him to have a beautiful polish, and generally making sport of him.

"Git 'long !'" he was saying, while he lifted first one foot, and then the other, away from their busy brushes. "Confound the kids ! What do 'em want, so many of 'em ? What be 'em saying ? Git out o'it, ye little hellers !'"

The faster he swore at them in Devon dialect the more they laughed at him and cheeked him in French. "*Monsieur !   Oh, m'sieur !   Beau cirage !* A lovely shine ! A magnificent shine ! Look, M'sieur, how your boots are filthy ! *Deux sous*—un penny ! A cigarette, then !'"

And after I had driven them off, they still followed us down the street, crying shrilly : "*Une cigarette !   Una cigarette !   Penny, m'sieur ! Anglish ?   Eh ?*'"

But they are good little kids, the Marseillais boot-boys. A *sou* a boot is their charge. For three *sous* and a cigarette they will work most merrily and polish one's boots to perfection.

Let into the corners of most of the side-streets are fish-stalls where woollen-bonneted old women sell small fish of all shapes and colours ; such grotesque small fish as no one would eat in England, and even chunks of cuttle-fish and squid. On some of the stalls there was a large red-fleshed fish, sold in slices, and a few rather weary-looking mackerel, but most of it was hardly bigger than fry. Were sticklebacks caught at Marseilles doubtless they, too, would all meet their end in a frying-pan.

According to Baedeker, "the great speciality of Marseilles is the *bouillabaisse*, of which the

praises have been sung by Thackeray. This con-
sists of a kind of 'chowder' or thick soup, made
of fish boiled in oil and white wine and flavoured
with saffron, orange-juice, onions, garlic, bay,
parsley and cloves."   It appeared comprehensive
enough, though after seeing on the fish-stalls so
much of what we call offal, we were rather inclined
to doubt Thackeray. However, just as we were
entering the Rue Thubaneau, the street of cheap
restaurants, a handbill was shoved into Jim's hand.
At the Restaurant de l'Europe et des Deux
Amériques, they provide (so we read) meals *à
prix fixe ou à la carte*, and *bouillabaisse* is served
every day at any hour.   The Restaurant de
l'Europe et des Deux Amériques consisted of one
long narrow room down each side of which was a
single row of crowded tables.   From her desk at
the upper end, hedged in by piled-up dishes under
an electric light, the *patronne* surveyed the company
like a sleek goddess of gluttony. One waiter,
small to deformity, scuttled up and down between
the tables, balancing an astonishing number of
dishes upon his hands and against his chest.   By
crying with immense energy : "At once, M'sieur !
This minute !   Yes, yes, it's ordered !" he made
the service seem fast, and kept the customers
quiet.   Those who entered he welcomed with
a cheery "*Bon jour, m'sieur 'dame !*" and those
who went, making room for more, he sped with
a still louder and cheerier "*Merci !   Au revoir !
Merci bien !*"   He missed one half the orders,
but the coming and going of guests he never
missed.

When we asked for *déjeuner* at 2 fr. 25, one
of the fixed prices, he shook his head violently.
"But look here," we said, showing him the yellow
handbill whereon the *déjeuner à* 2 *fr.* 25 was
advertised in detail — 1 plate of soup or fish,
1 plate of meat, 2 vegetables, the salad of the
day, cheese, pastry or fruit, wine, and bread at
discretion. . . .

"Oh, that!" he replied loftily, putting the
handbill aside and handing us the priced bill of
fare. "You must not take any notice of that.
It is only for outside, not for inside. There are
no *prix fixes* inside; there is only this card, and
it has the veritable prices on it. What do you
desire? *Bouillabaisse? Bien, m'sieur!*

"*Bouilla-baisse—DEUX!*" he shouted.

"*Bouillabaisse, deux!*" the goddess of gluttony
echoed.

It seemed that *bouillabaisse* was a dish of some
ceremony.

When at last it came, the smell of it caused us
to smell at it. So far as we could tell, it was
made up of a morsel of salt cod boiled in water,
a sodden sippet of stale bread, half an onion, three
slices of cold potato and a flavour of garlic. The
whole was flooded with gravy which appeared to
have come from an ordinary meat stew with some
vinegar and fish-water added. Maybe we didn't
eat enough of it to find the other flavours.
"*Bouillabaisse, deux! Voilà, messieurs!*" the
waiter had sing-songed triumphantly when he
clapped the plates down in front of us. "*Merci
bien, messieurs! Vous commandez . . .*" he sing-

songed just as triumphantly when we called him to take the stuff away.

Probably it did for some one else.

At the head of Old Harbour, where the Cannebière opens out upon the quays, half-a-dozen motor boats, as smartly kept as a yacht, are moored up for hire. "I wonder," said Jim with a professional interest, "how much an hour they lets 'em out for here. Casn't ask one o'em?"

We spoke to a boatman who smiled all over his face, and who might have passed for an English fisherman but for the tilt of his moustache and a certain glint in the eye. Five francs an hour, he told us, was the charge. Ours at home is five shillings.

"Shall us go and be frights [freights, *i.e.* boat hirers]," I asked Jim, "and see what 'tis like outside?"

"'Tis a lot of money, isn't it?" he answered, in almost the same words as our own frights use to us at home.

Unconsciously I rapped out our stock explanation : "Yes ; but see where you can go to in the time."

Meanwhile, the boatman eyed us just as on our own beach we eye the frights who don't know their own minds.

"Come on, if thee't coming," said Jim hurriedly. "Else he there 'll be cussing like we cusses 'em sometimes, when they keeps us waiting an' out of another job. *I* don't mind being a gen'leman for once."

But we did mind. We found it decidedly dull
to be frights. We felt strange, having nothing to
do in a small boat—we who ashore can do nothing
at all very nicely for hours together. We missed
responsibility, missed being in command : we did
not even know the right course. Very soon we
began examining the motor—a sprawling but
stout engine of local make—and our knowledge
of frighting caused the boatman to look at us
suspiciously, till we told him that we, too, had
a motor boat and used her for frighting in the
summer. At once the trade freemasonry, which
overlaps differences of nationality, altered his whole
bearing towards us, and he took us to see some
fishing.

Near the Île d'If—one of three rocky islands
which have the form and colouring of mountains
—is a submerged reef, marked at each end by
a white tower, and lengthwise along the top of
the reef lay a fine great steel cargo steamer. So
close was she to the outer tower that her bow,
apparently, had knocked the top off it. Partly
raised out of the water and canted over to port,
she lay like some huge animal, protesting dumbly
by its attitude against cruel treatment. It was a
clear starlight night, the boatman said, when she
went on the reef ; how, he could not or would
not explain. A tram conductor told us the rest
of the yarn afterwards in a curiously matter-of-
fact, cynical tone. " She got out of harbour safely
enough," he said, " and steered for the open sea.
A beautiful night, beautiful weather. But, you
see, *le capitano*, he was drunk, *ivre mort*, and

most of the crew as well. And then, well then, she ran aground. *C'est tout!*"

That, indeed, was all, and enough. But the great black hull lying there, so shapely and so helpless—it was as if she had been murdered.

A flotilla of fishing boats was paddling about near the inner tower, and on the base of it a net which the boatman called a *gangu* (*gangui* seems to be the correct name) was being hauled in by twenty or thirty fishermen. Jim was scandalised. "No wonder," he said, "they there French fishermen don't average so much each as us do! Look what a lot o'em 'tis for to share it up amongst, when they do catch ort. 'Tis only like one of our seines, thic net, an' us can haul ours in wi' eight men, or six—aye, wi' four, if 'tis four of the likes o' ourselves, an' we'm pushed to it! A pair of arms don't go for much hereabout, looks so."

The *gangu*, in fact, is lighter than our ground-seines which we shoot in a semicircle round a shoal of fish, and then draw ashore by hauling on both ends. Like a seine, it is corked along the head-rope and leaded along the foot, but the wings of it, instead of being made of ordinary mesh, consist only of parallel threads, like fiddle-strings, held together every six inches or so by cross threads from top to bottom. Consequently the wings of the *gangu* contain very little substance of net, and as they are hauled out of the water they go up together like a loosely-laid rope. The bunt, or centre of the net—the last to be hauled in—is made of small-scale mesh, and it contains a pocket, like the cod of a trawl, into which the fish go back.

Had we been using the net our way, we should have stood or knelt in one place, hauling hand over hand, gripping, puffing, and swearing. The Marseillais fishermen made easier work of it. Each carried in his hand a short lanyard with a small flat cork on the end of it. Advancing to the front he would twirl the lanyard bolas-fashion round the roped-up net, jam the cork behind the standing part, and then, hanging on to the lanyard, would walk back to the rear. There he would unbend his lanyard and amble up to the front again. So they all did, over and over, till the net was in; forming, on either side of the tower, a circular procession of men, very graceful and light-footed in their rough grass shoes, their faded print shirts, and their bright-coloured scarfs and sashes.

When the bunt came home they lifted it out of the water with the greatest care. There was scarcely a bushel of fish-fry in it, and nothing larger. "Why, 'tisn't a drink apiece for 'em," Jim was saying, when we saw a fish jump, and suddenly the sea was all alive with them, boiling and splashing on every side of us, so thick that they turned the water from blue to green. "Lookse, lookse!" cried Jim, as he yells it out on our own beach. "Lookse, there's fish! What sort is it at all? An't none o'em got another net for to shoot?—Lookse! There they be again! An' they chaps there got to stand looking at 'em!—Aye," he went on, sitting down in the boat, "can see that fishing here is the same thing as 'tis at home. You shoots your net for a maund-full, and then, 'fore you've got time to boat it again, the fish plays up in thousands.— I wish I know'd w'er Dick an' they have a-catched any herrings at home. 'Tis funny us an't had no letter. . . ."

It was more than funny. We knew that letters must have been sent, yet not a single one was delivered to us either at the Poste Restante or our hotel. And we badly wanted to know what the herrings were doing, for if the herrings are missed, when they do come, it is a winter's work as good as lost. We read in the newspapers, moreover, that the Boulogne herring drifters had been caught in a great storm. Several boats were lost and many men drowned. That decided us. Because Boulogne is homely to us, we wanted to be there, too, in its time of mourning. The lists of the drowned told us nothing : we did not know our friends' surnames. They had been so jolly and so full of life. . . .

Perhaps, also, we should find letters in Paris. What if our own boats had been caught out in the same storm ? The floods in the valley of the Seine were still rising. Paris might soon become impassable.

Therefore, in the evening, we went up to the station and took our third-class tickets, and found a carriage empty enough to sleep in. Daylight, next morning, revealed a desolation of flood. On the left-hand side of the railway, the snug little towns and villages, perched safely on the hillside around their churches, were just waking up. On the other side, stretching away to the far hills, was a lifeless expanse of muddy water, above which, in some places, only the roofs of the houses showed. In Paris itself, horses up to their bellies in water were hurriedly taking builders' materials away from the riverside quays.

No letters were waiting for us, and among the packets from Paris not delivered to us at Marseilles there had been, we found, a couple of letters and a small parcel. Neither the French nor English post had reached us. We wondered more than ever.

At Étaples, the next stop before Boulogne, two railway men with their baskets and coffee-cans got into the carriage. At once they began talking about the storm and wrecks. "The English steamer," said one of them, "smashed into the fishing boat and then steamed away for England, leaving them to drown."

"But," we objected, "it's difficult to understand that, because English ships have a reputation for standing-by in case of accident and English seamen are proud of it. How was it the steamer didn't stand-by?"

He did not answer the question, but went on talking in a hasty broken voice. Saying, "I'll explain it to you," he explained nothing. He was too full of it—too much possessed by the grief of a town hard hit. Inquiries were useless. Reasoning was beside the point. "Oh, it was shameful!"

he kept on saying, "twenty or more men drowned, who were alive, and now are dead." One knows it is the instinct of people in the first violence of their grief to blame somebody, whether justly or not, and we listened in silence, trusting that there was an explanation and that English seamanship had not disgraced itself on the shores of France.

Soon enough, in the quietened town, we learnt the whole pitiful tale. Out of Boulogne and its neighbouring villages, thirty-seven men were lost. They mostly had wives and children.

The previous Thursday had been the first fine day after a succession of gales. So fine it was, and calm, that seven custom-house men went whiting fishing, four in one small boat and three in another. The four were all drowned, and the other three, driven ashore at Wimereux, only saved themselves by clinging to the rocks half the night.

On such a fine day, when the weather appeared to have settled, hopes were high among the fishing folk that at last the herring season was going to begin. For herrings mean food to eat and coal to burn through the winter ; money to spend or save, and employment about the quays. Life in a fishing port quickens its pace when the herrings come along. Most of the drifters put to sea, one after another down the long narrow harbour channel and out between the jetties. Most of them were still at sea, away to the westward, when, about ten in the evening, a sudden violent storm, with hail and thunder in it, came up from the sou'west. The sea made rapidly.

Among the craft farthest from port was the *Suffren*, one of the largest sailing drifters, carrying twenty-one men and three boys. When the first of the squall struck her she was about to shoot her nets a second time : already she had seventeen thousand mackerel and four hundred measures of herrings aboard. So threatening was the weather, so fast did a heavy sea make, that she harded up for home, and about half-past three in the night she was hauling her wind in order to round the western jetty close to it, and thus enter the harbour channel well to windward. Another minute and she would have been inside.

At that moment the *Malta*, a small cargo steamer, one of a line that stops for no weather, was going out of harbour, bound in ballast for Goole. It was pitch dark, the air thick with a mist of spray.

The *Malta* held on her course. The *Suffren* was bound to hold on hers. She could not steer to the right, for in that case she would have run upon the jetty. Nor could she steer to the left without of a certainty running into the *Malta*. Her starboard light was invisible to the steamer.

"Luff! Luff!" yelled the fishermen as one man, but their cries were lost in the turmoil of the storm. In order to meet the seas bow-on, in that tricky harbour entrance, the *Malta* had to do rather the reverse. She crashed into the port quarter of the *Suffren*.

The *Suffren's* mainmast came down on her deck, killing two fishermen and the donkey-engine man. The water rushed into the hole, washing overboard the ship's punt together with a fourth man who happened to be in her.   Without steerage-way, though kept afloat by her empty barrels and net buoys, the *Suffren* drove along before the wind and sea and tide.   But for her buoyancy, she would have sunk there and then, and each fishing boat, as it ran home for safety, would have added itself to one awful pile of wreckage in the harbour mouth.   Grazing the end of the eastern jetty, she lurched along to the sands opposite the Casino. There she bumped and stuck—at a distance out, for the water on that side is shallow.   Great breaking waves foamed over the deck where the remainder of the crew had taken what refuge they could.   Except when flashes of lightning lit up the leaping white combers, the wreck was no more than a shapeless blot on the thick darkness.

The *Malta*, unable to stand-by among the shoals and cross-currents, unable to hang about outside in such a sea, unable to do anything, steamed off for England.

Then, between two peals of thunder, the life-boat gun was fired.   Lifeboat's men, pilots, fisher-men ashore, all ran down to the lifeboat-house on the eastern jetty.   Fifteen men were wanted to man the boat.   Thirty volunteered.   The *Providence* was launched down her slip-way, under-neath the deck of the jetty, into the harbour channel, and the steam pilot-boat towed her out-side.   The crew rowed frantically to reach the *Suffren*.   Just as they were coming alongside, a huge wave carried away the starboard oars. Spare oars were put out, and then a still greater

wave wrenched out of their hands every oar in the
boat. She drifted helplessly, and being lighter
than the *Suffren,* she ran aground a little to the
east of her and farther in. All the crew got
ashore through the surf.

The *Providence* could not be refloated where
she was, and still the cries of those aboard the
Suffren were coming down the wind. Willing
hands rushed up town to the offices of the Société
Humaine, and hauled out a second smaller lifeboat,
the *Farmer.* They dragged her on her carriage to
the slip-way on the lee side of the jetty, and there
they were stopped. In order to prevent the cart-
ing away of sand, the town authorities had planted
stout wooden posts across the road up from the
shore. Help could not be obtained ; for two
hours that night they called up the telephone exchange without reply. The lifeboat crew flung
themselves on the posts. Unable to loosen them
in the ground, they broke them off. A way was
made. The *Farmer* was launched. The same
crew to a man went off in her.

For three-quarters of an hour they fought to
get near the *Suffren,* while broken seas ran through
them from stem to stern. Meanwhile, the rocket
apparatus was tried, but against so much wind the
rockets failed to carry.

At last the second coxswain was able to make
a jump for the *Suffren.* The *Farmer* was brought
alongside. But although the coxswain warned
them, although their own skipper begged them
on his knees to keep their heads, the crew of the
Suffren had been so exhausted by cold, so over-

strung by waiting, so mazed by the infernal black confusion of wind and water, that they leapt pell-mell into the lifeboat. Only the skipper, the coxswain and one fisherman remained on board the wreck.

The *Farmer* cast off to go home. Overweighted, caught in an eddy, lurched high by a tremendous wave, she turned turtle completely. One of her crew, an apprentice pilot whose father and brother had met their death in trying to save life, was bashed head foremost against the wreck. Later on, the sea washed up his corpse on the beach. All the rest were thrown into the water, from which they were dragged by those ashore, some struggling blindly in the darkness, some unconscious, some dying, and several already dead.

The *Farmer*, which had righted herself, was caught near the end of the eastern jetty. Another crew put off in her, and succeeded in bringing home the last three men from the wreck.

All night and far on into the next day the doctors and their assistants worked at the Société Humaine, reviving the living, trying to drag back the dying from death, and laying out the dead. Fathers became conscious only to hear of the death of their sons, sons to be told their fathers were gone. Women refused to be told that their men and boys were dead.

That night, eight fishing boats out of Boulogne were lost, and most of their crews with them. The storm continued.

On the evening of our arrival we could just

glimpse the *Suffren*, a dark patch in the surf, as they had glimpsed her who tried to save her crew. The harbour was crammed with craft of all kinds in a broken-spirited disorder. Our café, *Le Bon Pêcheur*, was empty and sad. Outside, it blew in gusts and rained.

Next day the wind had veered, and at low tide we went down on the shore. The *Suffren* had been broken up by the sea—broken so violently that even the stout piece of oak which formed her stem was split straight up the middle, as if by a sledge-hammer and wedges. In one spot on the sand lay her deck ; in another place one of her sides, turned upside down, like a whaleback ; farther on was her other side, still fast to the keel ; and in yet another place her mast with some of its tackle tangled around it. Nets, buoys, spars and cordage were strewn far and wide, partially buried up in the sand. A very thin horse, harnessed to a long chain, was tearing the warp out of what had been the *Suffren's* hold, and every time it strained at the chain the mass of sand and coal heaved horribly and cracked, as if dead bodies were forcing their way up through. Hastily the work was being done ; for the *Suffren* had been sold to the ship-breakers, who were trying to save what they could before she sank altogether into the sand.

" I wonder," said Jim, bending down to look beneath the wreckage, " I wonder if there's other o' they fishing chaps still in under there."

But we did not look very hard. We might have seen a limb, a hand, or a head sticking out, sodden and discoloured, or ragged by the sand-crabs.   It was sad enough to see the ship herself, lying in little black jagged scrap-heaps upon the wide flat sands, with the lines of her dismembered hull not totally broken up beyond recognition.

A little farther still, they were trying to haul the stranded lifeboat over the sand, in order to launch her and take her into harbour ; and being harbour men, unused to beaching boats, were making very bad work of it.   We, who are used to beaches, could have told them how better to do it.   But we thought, perhaps, that they wanted to spin the job out, and we did not wish to spoil it for them.   No doubt they needed the money badly enough.   So we held our tongues.

Inside the harbour the fleet was putting to sea.   Once more the quays were animated.   Very noticeable were some lumbering coffin-shaped boats with bluff bows, high sterns, enormously tall mainmasts, and notches cut in the stern-posts for steps.   They belonged to St. Valery-sur-somme, where they have to be launched through the surf on flat sands, and the crews climb up the stern-post at the moment of floating off.   On the night of the great storm they had run to Boulogne for shelter.   Now they were going home, and hoping to make a catch on the way.   Their hulls were clumsily patched, their gear was old, and their crews were ragged and dirty.   A quarrel was in progress which made the bystanders roar with laughter.   One of the crew, a young man whose red face belonged to what is called the criminal type, had come from a *cabaret* crying-drunk, and the skipper, a stunted old man who resembled an unshaven smoked monkey, was trying for safety's sake to send him below. Persuasion had no effect. Kindness he flung off. They bawled at each other in an outlandish dialect. They ran about the narrow deck, raising their fists to heaven. They hit out—and missed ! The younger man all but fell overboard. With quick regret the grubby old skipper threw his arms round the younger man's neck and pressed on his face a flabby kiss ; then held him at arm's length and gazed at him proudly.

Perhaps it was the old man's son, or his grandson. In any case they had been at sea together, and now were going again. Their great barked lugsail was hoisted and a rope was thrown to a steam drifter which had offered to tow them out of harbour. But in shifting from the quayside the steam drifter collided with the little boat from St. Valery and smashed her gunwale. The skipper wrung his hands : the young man raved more furiously than ever. He pulled off his jumper and jersey. Three of his mates, hanging on to him at once, could scarcely prevent him from going aboard the steamer to avenge the little boat. The steamer's men cast off the tow-rope with gestures of tolerant contempt, and the men of St. Valery, followed by the jeers of the onlookers, had to work their way slowly out of harbour with their long oars.

Notwithstanding which, they did go to sea. All the boats went to sea : drifters, trawlers, longliners and hand-liners. On the night of the wrecks every resource had failed, except human courage and endurance. And now again, while the *Suffren* was sinking into the sands, the love of life, the need of food to eat, was driving men out to that same sea which had been so deadly.

Driving men to sea, one says, but perhaps should rather be said that the sea with its chances was drawing them ; for they were going out of harbour as fast as the tugs could take them, cheerily and full of hopes for a catch. Greater, it seemed, than the heroism of the storm was the common daily courage of all those fishermen in merely earning their livelihood. As Jim remarked : " 'Tis a won'erful thing, after a night like thic there, that anybody has the heart for to do it."

Their energy infected us. We wanted more than ever to know what was doing in our own bay, and by the next mail boat we hurried back to England. There were no herrings ; our herring-harvest was not to come for a couple of months. But we did find that several letters and post-cards had been sent us from various places to the right addresses in France. Such a series of losses in the post, coupled with the fact that after the first occasion in Boulogne we were never asked to fill up police-papers at any hotel, and that more than once we nearly ran into men extraordinarily like French detectives, can only point to one conclusion, namely, that the French police wanted to know our business and took charge of our correspondence. Spectacles are almost unknown

among English seamen : it may be that mine led
the police to believe I was a German who spoke
English suspiciously well. At all events, we trust
they had an enjoyable time shadowing us ; and if
by any chance they should ever read this, then
they'll know what our business was—a fishermen's
holiday.

THE END

Printed by R. & R. CLARK, LIMITED, *Edinburgh*